THE GOLDEN GIRL

GOLDEN BOOK TWO

Copyright © 2025 by Stephanie Rose

The story, names, characters, and incidents portrayed in this production are fictitious. No identification with actual persons (living or deceased), places, buildings, and products is intended or should be inferred.

Book Cover by Stephanie Rose
Chapter headers by Stephanie Rose
Edits by Ashley Warren

TRIGGERS

Please be advised, before moving forward, that THE GOLDEN GIRL discusses and sees certain topics that may or may not make readers uncomfortable.

Abusive relationship (mentioned) - Alcohol - Anxiety - Attempted murder (mentioned) - Bullying - Car accident; in this case, it's carriage accident (mentioned, accident itself not seen on the page) - Cheating - Child abuse (mentioned - mental/emotional) – Death (mentioned) - Depression (implied) - Emesis (mentioned) - Emotional abuse - Misogyny (historical theme) - Murder (mentioned) - Poisoning (attempted & mentioned) – Pregnancy & difficulty conceiving (discussed) - Prostitution (historical theme) - PTSD - Religion - Sexism (historical theme) - Violence (mentioned) - War (mentioned)

STEPHANIE ROSE

To all the brave
ones who stand
up to their
bullies despite
the odds.

6

A QUICK RECAP

Marguerite, a baby whose father and entourage were slaughtered in an apparent attack in a forest, is found in the aftermath carriage wreck by King Edouard of Totresia. He and his wife, Queen Clémentine, decide to raise her in their household, despite having no clue of her origins. They take her in, not as their own child, but as a duchess privy to all the advantages of such a station. She's to be Edouard's ward when she's older.

Marguerite quickly becomes close to their son, Crown Prince Antoine, who is the same age as her. She also develops bonds with their next son, Sébastien, as well as Jules, the third son. But when the final child, Cordelia, is born, a disconnect happens for Queen Clémentine. Once warm and kind to Marguerite, she becomes cold, stern, some might even say evil. No one notices but Marguerite; or if they do, they don't come to her aid and leave her to fend for herself.

Over the years, Marguerite and Antoine's proximity grows. They're inseparable, and King Edouard decides that Marguerite will be his son's advisor when he comes of age, and when he inherits the crown. This news displeases Clémentine, who seems to want nothing more than to get rid of Marguerite.

Clémentine's bitterness worsens over time. She claims to have uncovered certain of Edouard's secrets—some of which involve Marguerite, and possibly her unknown identity. Though Clémentine swears to keep these secrets to herself, she holds them over Edouard's head, using them to obtain whatever she wants from him. And she uses them against Marguerite, to make her stay at Torrinni Castle as miserable as possible.

Nothing stops the progression of Marguerite and Antoine's friendship, however. No matter how many times Clémentine tries to separate them—either within the castle itself, ensuring their paths never cross, or sending Marguerite off on pilgrimages to distract her—their course has been set from the start. Marguerite and Antoine confess their love for one another at their first Masquerade ball, at the age of sixteen, and they're so convinced no one can get in their way, they don't sense Clémentine brewing up plots in the background. They're unofficially engaged and the announcement brings joy across the land.

One of Clémentine's plots is to persuade King Edouard to hold a Season for Antoine when he turns eighteen. A tradition, he claims, but it's mostly urged on by Clémentine. While the king promises Antoine can still choose Marguerite in the end, Clémentine has other ideas.

Edouard falls deathly ill the night before the Masquerade, where Antoine is supposed to announce his betrothed. Since the king is unable to preside over the events as usual, Clémentine takes over. Through manipulation and scheming, she gets what she wants: Antoine is so distraught by his father's sickness that he lets his mother's threats get the best of him, and he chooses Adelaide as his wife—the daughter of a French military man.

Edouard dies, and without getting to say goodbye, Marguerite runs away from the castle. She's too hurt, too offended by what Antoine did and can't stick around to watch him marry someone else.

But Clémentine doesn't *want* her gone anymore—she has

other plans for Marguerite. The queen—now dowager—captures Marguerite and locks her up in the basement of the Totresian Royal Academy for Noble Girls, where she intends to keep her until she can secure certain alliances Marguerite ruined by running away.

One of those alliances is a marriage between Marguerite and a mystery noble of Clémentine's choosing.

At the academy, Marguerite is depressed, dreading her new life as a secret prisoner. Her only friend is Johanna, the handmaiden Clémentine left with her. Johanna is *supposed* to be spying on Marguerite, but she grows fond of the former duchess and instead helps her survive her imprisonment.

Secrets and lies and plots continue to unfold over the next few years. Antoine marries Adelaide. Prince Sébastien goes off on a tour of the surrounding countries, forfeiting his place in line for the throne. Prince Jules frolics in taverns and drinks. And Princess Cordelia becomes the perfect little daughter Clémentine always wanted. Or so, she lets the dowager think.

While wandering around the academy—permitted by its headmaster, Lord Knowles—Marguerite and Johanna discover more schemes brewing, and find out that there's a mysterious journal in the hands of one of the students, Céleste. A journal that apparently details *everything* about Marguerite's life with the royals. The problem? Clémentine erased Marguerite from history; she no longer features in any of the history books. It's as if she never existed. No one can know this *journal* exists, either.

When Clémentine's threats to marry Marguerite off feel closer to happening, Marguerite gets the urge to run away again. But she has nowhere to go, and no choice but to obey.

Johanna and Lord Knowles eavesdrop on a private conversation between two nobles who work for the dowager—nobles who aren't *pleased* with the dowager. Next the headmaster and handmaiden know, there are two letters that arrive for Marguerite—one from the dowager, and one from an unknown source. And the dowager plans to show up the next day to speak with Marguerite privately.

They speculate over what's going to happen, but ultimately, we'll never know until Marguerite opens those letters…

Part One

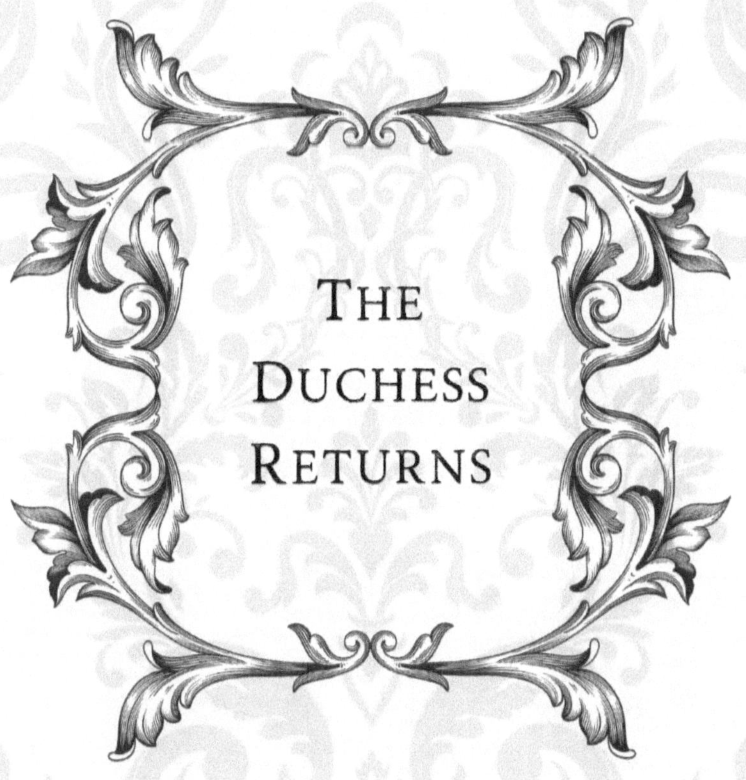

The Duchess Returns

It was a disaster.

Marguerite snickered at the two letters she'd received in an unexpected early morning delivery from her ever-loyal handmaiden Johanna.

As soft light from a flickering candle illuminated her dry hands, she glared at the parchments. At the precise, sharp, well-chosen remarks on the first, and the second, with its dramatically elongated calligraphy and its fake friendly tone.

A lock of golden hair fell over Marguerite's eyes as she stared at the two requests. The day's date decorated their headers, though she assumed their authors had written them the day before, if not weeks ago.

After all, it took time to plant such rotted seeds.

The night before, she'd paced in her bedroom—her *cage*—and debated leaving due to her bad hunch about the men Johanna and Lord Knowles overheard during the graduation ceremony.

Now she regretted not acting on that hunch, not fighting tooth-and-nail to get out of the academy while she still had the chance.

The eerie sensations swelling in her gut had given her the warning, but she hadn't listened. It was too late—the girls had graduated, and the courier who'd delivered these messages had returned to the castle.

The senders would be aware Marguerite had received their notes.

She placed one hand on each letter as memories haunted her. Memories she wished to forget, but that always caught up to her, no matter how hard she tried to erase them.

Torrinni Castle. The velvety walls of the corridors she used to run down. The delicious scents wafting up from the kitchens, beckoning her to steal pastries and leftover bread from dinner. The ballroom, where the dancing and the flirting took place; where she'd once listened to heavenly tunes while sneaking a peek from the balcony.

They were ruined memories. Terrifying moments put to the torch by the women who'd written the two letters resting beneath her palms.

She closed her eyes, inhaled, exhaled. "These aren't requests; they're *orders*." Her voice shook, and her wrists and forearms ached from how she clenched her fists. "If I deny them…"

She picked up the first report, and her back stiffened at the sight of the royal insignia at the bottom.

December the first, 1797
Marguerite,

I write to inform you that, as discussed, you will soon be married off to someone powerful and no longer my concern. However, there's been a slight change to the plan: I have need of you for other purposes before I ship you off. You'll prove yourself useful to me yet, and this delay is necessary.

Sébastien has returned from his travels, and though he's no longer second in line to the throne, he and Jules have expressed their desire to find brides by the end of this year. Our king has prepared the court for eligible ladies, and for such a grand occasion, Lord Knowles has agreed to send the academy's recent graduates as well.

You're to accompany these graduates as their chaperone. You may bring MY handmaiden, Johanna, along with whatever dresses you may have kept from the shipments I sent you. If you behave whilst at court, I may bequeath you additional dresses to properly fill the role of a noble chaperone.

DQT

Marguerite grunted. *DQT?* She presumed this was Clémentine's signature now—Dowager Queen of Totresia.

She replaced the note on the nightstand and shrugged her fingers through her hair. The comments bubbled in her mind and made her recoil, more so when she heard them out loud, in Clémentine's voice.

Clémentine.

She bit the insides of her cheeks. Her harsh feelings would never leave. She'd stuffed them down for three years, but they'd started a long while ago. Clémentine's shadow still crept in and clouded every pure aspect of her life.

"She summons me to the place I *ran* from?" Marguerite snarled. "The place she turned against me, made me nonexistent to?

To… What? Taunt me? The nerve."

If only that were the only piece of correspondence she'd received that morning.

She glanced at the next note, her insides burning up at the precise handwriting.

December the first, 1797

My dearest Marguerite,

Three years of praying and it turns out you were alive, living at the academy! I'm relieved. I hope you're well. I've missed you, ma chérie!

I confronted the dowager immediately upon my discovery, and while I don't condone her secrecy, I must express my deepest regrets at your rebellion towards the Totresian court. I understand why you ran, but others will judge you for hiding for so long.

The dowager also told me she is bringing you back to court, and I heartily support this! Return and redeem your name, my friend, and I can clue you in on all the scandals you've missed while you were gone. Perhaps we can pick up our friendship where it left off.

The nobles have mostly moved on from what happened all those years ago. I'm sure you'll find that the focus has shifted. And of course, you'll receive all the comforts you deserve.

Warm regards,
Queen Adelaide

"Pick up our friendship where it left off?" Marguerite was

about to spit on the paper, but held in her irritation; she had to control her temper, more so if she was returning to the source of its flare-up. "What friendship? She stabbed me in the back, that black-hearted bitch—"

She tossed the note aside before she tore it to shreds.

Conflict raged in her head, her heart. She wasn't sure which letter provoked the most anguish within her. That of the woman who raised her but never cared for her well-being, or her archenemy, the contender-turned-queen who'd stolen all she'd ever loved.

What a pair they made. Did they work together, conspiring to make Marguerite miserable, to drive her into insanity? Or were they enemies, working towards different goals that happened to involve Marguerite being at court?

Marguerite had little choice. Clémentine was her jailer, and had been for three years. If Clémentine *wanted* her at court, she'd be forced to go.

And much as she loathed the notion of returning to the place that haunted her nightmares, such a trip could provide answers Marguerite had long sought.

Who was she? Where did she come from? Why did Clémentine claim she was the daughter of an enemy, and that Edouard had conspired to have her father murdered, and to keep her as his ward?

Who was that enemy, if they were real?

And who was this mysterious betrothed Clémentine worked so hard to find for her?

Why would the dowager want to bring back the woman she spent so long trying to erase the existence of?

"There is always an ulterior motive with her," Marguerite said to herself, crumbling the letters in both hands, wishing she had a fireplace to toss them into.

The candlelight created shadows that danced across her face, swirling around her, shrouding her in confusion.

"Torrinni Castle: I'll see you soon, whether or not I like it."

***

Semi-comfortable amidst a mess of journals and wads of half-written letters spread all over her bed, Marguerite sighed.

A few hours had passed since receiving the unwanted correspondence from Torrinni, and she'd dove into her past to find answers for her present.

How could she evade Clémentine and somehow *not* go to court?

Someone rapped their knuckles on the dungeon door, a habit some guards had taken upon accidentally finding her bathing when doing their hourly checks on her.

She shot to her feet, papers flying to the floor. "Yes?"

When the door slid open to reveal Lord Knowles, headmaster of the Totresian Royal Academy for Noble Girls, she relaxed and released a breath. She'd been anticipating the worst since those letters—like castle soldiers coming to take her in fetters, to toss her into a carriage and sneak her into Torrinni to preserve Clémentine's ruse.

It was a lie she'd spent three years convincing the entire court of, a ruse Marguerite wanted to believe was true—that she'd never existed.

"What is it?" she asked, one hand pressing to her chest.

He loitered silently in the door-frame, the white curls of his wig falling over his paling cheeks. She'd asked Lord Knowles about the outdated wig more than once, but he claimed his old traditions ran deep.

He was on edge; he wasn't one to stay quiet unless he was worried or afraid. He was stiff. Too stiff. "Your Grace—"

"Please, my lord," she gritted her teeth, "don't call me that. I'm not a duchess anymore."

"Yes, well, we have a visitor who may have come to say otherwise." He glanced side to side nervously.

Lord Knowles was *never* nervous.

"Who?" she asked.

From the way he shifted with uncertainty, she didn't want to know the answer.

Before he could muster a response, a woman in a yellow and white servant garb brushed inside the cell, shoving past him.

"Miss!" Marguerite's personal maid panted as if she'd run up and down several flights of stairs. Her gray eyes widened in fear. "*She* is here! I should have told you, but I didn't think, I hoped that she—"

Marguerite scrunched her eyebrows. "Johanna, calm down."

The servant girl hunched over to catch her breath. A bead of sweat formed above her brow and her face was paler than usual. "You were right, last night. It was true, the dowager—"

"What?" Marguerite tilted her head, trying to keep her tone under control, though it begged to squeak through the room like a blaring trumpet.

A lady never raises her voice.

"She's here." Johanna gulped. "*Her.* The dowager queen."

"Wh—Why?" Marguerite fell onto her bed.

Sending a message hadn't sufficed. The woman had showed up in person in case Marguerite gave anyone trouble about leaving the academy.

The haphazard scrolls and journals across her mattress and over the floor, the books littering her dresser, the lingering smell of the coffee Johanna had managed to smuggle to her—those wouldn't please the dowager.

Marguerite's legs wobbled as her gaze flitted to Lord Knowles. "Is that…is she…?"

"She speaks true, Your Grace." He put his hands behind his back, inclining forward. "The dowager awaits you." He cleared his throat. "To meet in my office."

Marguerite's shoulders drooped. "Oh, thank the Heavens, not in here."

Naturally, the dowager wouldn't want to visit Marguerite in her prison cell. She'd done so only once, and her cruel words and accusations still echoed in Marguerite's head.

"How long has she been waiting?"

Johanna shrugged, and Lord Knowles tried not to gape at a pair of stockings protruding from a half-opened drawer in the dresser. Marguerite hurried to close it, but his cheeks turned scarlet.

"A few minutes," he said. "I figured you may need a moment to compose yourself. Then we must bring you up via the service stairs, and she will meet you."

Marguerite stared at her maid of three years. "Has she been given refreshment yet?" Johanna shook her head, and Marguerite groaned. "She'll need something. Go to the kitchens and fix her some lavender tea. Hurry."

The young woman acquiesced, curtsied, and scurried out.

No matter how many times Marguerite reminded her not to curtsy, the young woman couldn't help herself.

Marguerite peeked at her mirror and sneered. Clémentine wouldn't approve of her appearance; she'd wanted her to take care of herself, to comport herself as a noble at all times, despite being locked up under the academy for three years.

But her golden curls were too loose, her lips too chapped, her emerald eyes too bloodshot. She'd barely slept after the events of the graduation, and in her haze she'd put on a standard dress that Clémentine would most definitely think too simple.

Changing into something more Clémentine-appropriate would take too much time. The longer Marguerite waited for this confrontation, the more the dowager would lash out at her.

She swirled to Lord Knowles, grasping the edges of her demure brown dress. "This is the best she'll get for showing up unannounced. I might as well get this over with."

"Then let's go," he said, offering his arm.

As Marguerite and Lord Knowles rushed down the hall, through the servant's quarters, and up the kitchen stairs, she recalled the nicknames she'd given the former queen over the years.

Clémentine the snake. Clémentine the crazy queen. Clémentine the sorceress.

She adjusted her posture as Lord Knowles led her to the service stairs up to the second floor.

Clémentine the evil queen. Clémentine the traitor.

This wouldn't be a pleasant meeting—not that any meeting with the dowager ever was. But if Clémentine visited in person, matters were dire. She wouldn't travel for nothing. Something must have happened for her to seek a tête-a-tête with Marguerite.

It'd been years since their last direct encounter, when the woman graced the halls of the academy with her decadent wardrobe choices and her stone-cold presence. When she'd revealed to Marguerite that her blood was that of an enemy, and that she was lucky to be alive.

Why would the foul woman drag herself there today?

At the top of the service steps, Marguerite readied herself for the wave of insults that would be disguised as nitpicking. She was used to them, but it had been so long; she'd hoped to never have to deal with them again.

She imagined Clémentine fussing in the parlor, being told she had to wait—the notion of *Her Grace* being upset pleased Marguerite.

Inside the office, Lord Knowles gestured at her to sit on the sofa. He offered an apologetic smile as he disappeared to go fetch the dowager.

Marguerite slouched in her seat, tapping her feet. All manners of scenarios passed through her, each more morbid than the last.

When the door burst open, she sat up straight; old habits died hard.

How she wished she could avoid this meeting.

"**M**arguerite."

Dowager Queen Clémentine of Totresia loomed in the doorway, her aubergine skirts fanned out like waves of poison, a deadly flower ready to devour her enemies. She loved having that kind of power over everyone; especially over Marguerite.

"Your Grace," said Marguerite, rising at once, color draining from her face. Another sight Clémentine enjoyed.

She set her lacy gloved hands onto her hips. "I thought you were expecting me. I notified Lord Knowles of my intention to visit."

Marguerite curtsied, her smile evidently forced.

Clémentine knew she'd been warned only moments before— she'd seen the strain in Lord Knowles' expression, and heard the handmaiden Johanna running off to warn her.

"I beg your pardon, Your Grace." Marguerite motioned at the

flower-patterned chair opposite the couch, and flinched.

Of course she should have known not to imply where Clémentine should sit.

Clémentine gazed over Marguerite's figure, nostrils flaring. This muddy brown dress was what she'd chosen to wear to welcome a member of the royal family?

"You may beg all you'd like, if that's your wish."

Though well into her late thirties, Dowager Clémentine still inspired the same fear as she had at seventeen, after marrying Edouard—the queen who always had her way, and hardly lifted a finger to get it. One scowl, one snap and constituents, ladies, even men would bend over backwards to obey her.

She jutted her chin at the sofa. "I'd prefer something with a more comfortable cushion. My trip here was most unpleasant."

"My apologies, Your Grace." Marguerite switched spots with her, the coffee table remaining between them.

Johanna brought in a silver platter with porcelain cups, a steaming kettle, and biscuits and macarons. Clémentine nodded in approval—a rarity—as Johanna poured the boiling water into their mugs.

Johanna excused herself once finished.

Clémentine picked up her cup, holding in a grimace at the rigid cushions beneath and behind her. "I suppose I shouldn't make you wait to explain my visit." She glared into the scalding liquid, her pinned mahogany curls coating with steam. She kept her cards well hidden, even to Marguerite, who thought she knew her better than most.

Marguerite opened her mouth, then closed it, opting instead for a curt nod.

"As I said in my note, this is an important moment for Totresia. Jules and Sébastien are to choose wives. Some ladies are already at the castle, along with a few foreign girls. We're missing our precious academy candidates, who find themselves without a chaperone, this year. Which is why I volunteered you. You'll have a brand new identity, and anyone who thinks they recognize you, well… they won't say a word."

Marguerite sipped her drink, her nose twitching ever so subtly. She'd always hated tea, and watching her forced to drink it made Clémentine almost giddy.

"Yes, and Queen Adelaide seems quite thrilled about my return," said Marguerite. "She sent me a letter to tell me how disappointed she was that I've been alive all this time. Did she never know I was here all along?"

"She didn't need to." Sighing, and elongating the sound as much as she could for effect, Clémentine shifted in her seat. "She's supposed to oversee the academy, and therefore *should* have known you were here, but after what happened with you… she was too new at court to handle it. It was best to keep her in the dark."

"Yet she found out." Marguerite flinched again; she knew better than to take tones.

But the bitterness in Clémentine was directed toward Adelaide, for once. "Indeed." She envisioned the red-haired wife of her eldest son and tried not to frown, to not betray her true feelings about her. "She's the queen. She has her resources, I suppose."

"I'm surprised you allowed her to write that letter." Marguerite took another gulp, her jaw taut.

Clémentine fidgeted. She loathed being reminded how Queen

Adelaide had nearly bested her. The letter was never supposed to go out, yet the red-headed monster of a daughter-in-law had prevailed.

"I was aware of it, yes, and as it coincided with my needs, I permitted it," Clémentine lied. "She and I have a few arrangements."

Marguerite let out a light cough, and Clémentine wondered if she'd nearly choked on her beverage.

Clémentine and Adelaide, working together? It shouldn't have surprised Marguerite; after all, the two had conspired to get Adelaide on the throne. Marguerite was mostly aware of that. Clémentine's part, at least.

But it was well known that Clémentine and Adelaide despised one another. Adelaide complained about Clémentine constantly, and Clémentine never masked her lack of affection for her, either.

Marguerite put down her teacup and straightened out her skirts. "So I'll be coming back to court, then."

"It wasn't a suggestion. Nor a request. It was an order." Clémentine pursed her lips, refraining from smirking as Marguerite showed her weakness—her fear of Torrinni Court, of the ghosts she'd left behind, the man she'd never been allowed to love publicly. "It's not my wish to see you return, but it's what you will do. Of all people to ever come back, you're my last choice. Our castle is four hours away, and I never visit you, with reason."

"I didn't mean to offend, Your Grace," said the young woman, plucking her teacup from the table.

"Ah, if you only knew." Clémentine brought her own cup to her lips to avoid growling.

Marguerite clenched the cup as if releasing it meant giving

away her soul.

"What would offend me most is if you argued, which I'm sure you're about to. Your life is in my hands, Marguerite. It always has been. Refusing to abide by my order," Clémentine hissed the words through her teeth, "may see your treatment worsened."

Another cough from Marguerite; this one harder to muffle, harder to act like she hadn't been about to spit out her drink.

She *couldn't* refuse, and she knew it. If she did, Clémentine would still drag her back to the castle by any means possible. She had special marriage arrangements for Marguerite, after all— Marguerite would be far too curious about those.

"Understood, Your Grace. I don't have much, but I will pack my things and be ready to leave when you need me to."

"Soon, unfortunately." Clémentine closed her eyes as she savored her drink. "Far too soon."

"**I** should have poisoned her beverage." Clémentine's departing sneer floated in Marguerite's mind for what felt like hours. She glowered at her dresser, hands on her hips. "Johanna!"

The maid arrived at the door as if by magic. "Miss?"

"Do you have any more of that coffee hidden somewhere?" She needed something to rid her palate from the sourness imprinted on her tongue—the tea *and* Clémentine's snark.

Once Johanna hurried out, Marguerite returned to the parchment she'd been staring at for so long that her eyes hurt.

It was the schedule of events for the prince's season—which the dowager would be supervising—as well as requirements for each lady: a *trousseau* comprised of a white dress for the presentation, as large a wardrobe as possible, riding gear, heavy cloaks, and money for other expenses. The academy would fund part of their stay, but the rest the parents would have to provide.

These recent graduates would face constant scrutiny, expected to be nothing short of perfect for the princes. At least Marguerite wouldn't have to endure all that again.

She perused the activities—tea parties, dinners, balls, promenades.

Her stomach clenched when she saw the event on December thirty-first.

The Masquerade Ball.

The party of the year in Totresia—it brought back recollections of Marguerite's golden-threaded gown, her matching mask, the music. The delectable smell of roast and pies still haunted her, as did the sounds of the bubbly champagne and rising laughter, and her footsteps echoing as she ran away from it all.

"I won't attend it."

The dowager had chosen the finest students the academy could provide. Five eighteen-year-old debutantes to handle— Marguerite was allowed to bring Johanna, but she'd need more help.

An idea sparked to life in her mind; one she'd surely be reprimanded for, but the dowager was no longer around to decline it.

When Johanna returned, Marguerite transmitted her idea to her, so she'd notify Lord Knowles.

"I'd like to bring someone else with us. A sort of… assistant, perhaps?"

"An assistant." Johanna scratched her chin.

"A junior student. From here." Marguerite sucked in her lips, then blew them out with a heavy breath. "It'd be a wonderful learning experience, no?"

"A junior student from here." Johanna narrowed her gaze. "To bring with us to court so you may continue to watch her, because she carries vital information about you, and her brother is already at court to spy for their father?"

Marguerite rubbed her hands conspiratorially. "Johanna, I fear you know me too well."

***

Marguerite stood in the far corner of the office near Lord Knowles' desk. Five graduates gawked at her, having just found out she was to be their chaperone for a special event.

Her, an unknown woman they had no clue had been locked up in the basement of their academy for three years.

Lord Knowles brought in the final guest to the impromptu meeting—Céleste Richel. The young junior student Marguerite had begged him to let her take with her.

He waved at the shy girl as she lingered in the threshold. "Miss Richel, please, come in." He sat, his eyes narrowed on her.

The girl was immediately scrutinized by the other guests of the room—most of whom she wasn't friendly with, according to Johanna.

Harriet Thatcher's strawberry curls were tied back, her grassy-green gaze confused, though not unkind. Esther Bristol, clad in bright, macaron-pink layers, blinked. Cristina Condello, stiff-backed and scowling, held up the middle seat. But they weren't who Marguerite was most worried about.

On Cristina's other side was Charlotte Geitz and her perfect blonde tresses, her perfect porcelain skin, her perfect snarl disguised as a smile. And Julia Espinar, hues of blue cloaking her svelte figure, her cruel eyes the color of a summer sky.

They both narrowed in Céleste's direction.

"We don't have all day." Lord Knowles' voice peppered with impatience.

Céleste sealed the door and leaned against it. Surely she wondered why she was asked to convene with five seniors and a mystery woman in the middle of the afternoon, the day after graduation.

Lord Knowles addressed the graduates. "You're here today because I have selected all five of you to be presented to the King and Queen of Totresia in a week and a half. You will take part in Prince Sébastien and Prince Jules' seasons. Congratulations."

A few gasps came from the girls; Céleste's jaw dropped.

Lord Knowles' gaze whipped to her. "You, Céleste, are to accompany our chaperone, Lady Marjorie," he motioned at Marguerite, using her agreed-upon alias, "as her assistant."

"Me?" Céleste stiffened.

"Yes, you." Lord Knowles turned to the five graduates; all silent, staring. "Working with Lady Marjorie."

Céleste's gaze couldn't seem to focus.

"*She's* a chaperone?" Esther scoffed, fixated on Marguerite. "She's too young."

"She was helping last night," whispered Charlotte, snickering. "I remember her."

Marguerite refrained from reminding Charlotte that she, too, was memorable, and not for any good reason.

Lord Knowles raised his eyebrows. "She's not too young, Esther."

He was far too calm considering the circumstances, or so Marguerite thought. How was he not more worried about the girls? Being summoned to the castle, having thousands of questions, tossed into the lion's den with no hope for survival—that was what going to Torrinni Court felt like.

"Don't be wary—this is marvelous news." Lord Knowles tapped his fingertips to a steady rhythm, but Marguerite caught a slight tremble in his wrist. "A royal presentation is a matter of celebration! It shocks me to not see you all jumping up and down."

Harriet clapped a hand over her mouth. "Jumping?"

Esther gasped, pinched back into reality. "Oh, of course! What an honor!" She beamed. "The biggest!"

Lord Knowles pulled his lips into a tight smile.

Cristina Condello, dressed in luxurious silks with a neckline too low for Marguerite's taste, inclined her head of chestnut curls. "It's an absolute praise that you would consider me. It will please Father, too. He expected I would meet better suitors at court."

Charlotte scoffed, but Lord Knowles ignored her, saying, "Speaking of suitors: Prince Jules and Prince Sébastien have expressed the wish to find wives, and fast, so that they might continue on with the royal legacy."

Legacy. Marguerite's throat constricted. In her mind formed the image of a red-headed seductress curling her crimson skirts around a pair of muscular legs, the fabric pushed up to a broad chest, strong shoulders, a sturdy chin—

She muffled her internal thoughts; she couldn't show an ounce of discomfort in front of these girls.

Charlotte Geitz perked up. "The princes are prospects my father will accept." She, more than anyone else present, was an ambitious lady, with two older sisters married to foreign royalty, according to Johanna's reports. Charlotte was top of the senior class and never hesitated to remind everyone about it.

Céleste snorted in a most unladylike fashion. From what Johanna had related to Marguerite, the junior hated Charlotte, who bullied her—and Harriet—at every occasion she got.

Julia, her raven-colored strands loosening down her temples, tapped Charlotte's arm. "One for you, one for me?" She let out a girlish squeak.

"Julia," said Lord Knowles, snapping to get her attention.

The girl whipped toward him as if about to scold her own headmaster for interrupting. She quickly realized her mistake and looked into her lap. "Apologies, my lord."

"I doubt the Viscount of Malaros would appreciate you deciding such things before having met the princes," he said.

Johanna said the viscount often stopped by the academy, leaving notes of instructions for Julia. He'd reprimand her if he heard of her behaviors, more so if he discovered Charlotte egging her on.

"Your fathers will be notified soon. I spoke with their emissaries this morning, and I don't expect any opposition." He glanced at Céleste, who'd shrunk against the wall. "I've sent word to your father in Valeville, and your brother at the castle. They wouldn't decline the opportunity for you to visit court before you go there in a more official manner."

The Marquess of Valeville was tricky. Marguerite met him many years ago. He'd since then lost his wife, sent his son off to the military academy and then to court, and shipped his daughter here.

Céleste turned out to be a quiet maiden hidden in a book, with a habit of disobedience. Marguerite had charged Johanna with watching her—and now, at Marguerite's behest, she'd be coming to Torrinni Court.

"And they'll contribute?" Harriet's meek tone drew Marguerite's attention. "My father included?"

The Vidame of Limesdale didn't have a history of paying debts—of paying *anything*, from what Marguerite understood.

Lord Knowles grimaced. "Whatever your families can't commit, the academy will cover. You'll bring the belongings you have here, and your fathers will send the rest to the castle."

Harriet's fingers twitched, but she nodded.

"Your families have expectations. Ours aren't so high. There are many valuable noblemen at court who would delight in having you as wives. Julia's brother, Mr. Axel Espinar, and Céleste's brother, Mr. Emeric Richel, are both eligible bachelors."

Charlotte lifted her nose, and Julia smirked.

Lord Knowles stood and marched to the other side of his desk. "You'll head to your rooms and put on your graduation gowns. A seamstress will join you and adjust them for the royal presentation ceremony. Since they're already the traditional white color, it shouldn't take long to alter them to Torrinni's standards. Lady Marjorie will come check on you."

Marguerite nearly burst out saying, *"Oh, will I, now?"* but remembered her place. She was the chaperone, the lesser noble, not the disappeared duchess who had more authority than Lord Knowles could ever aspire to.

Cristina crossed her arms, and Esther's cheeks flashed to the same magenta shade as her dress.

"We depart in a week, so practice your manners and work on your charms. The Totresian royal court is nothing like the academy."

One by one, the ladies curtsied and left. Harriet and Céleste lingered, the former shaking like a leaf in a storm.

"Father is at court, too," she said, shuffling in her chair. "He told me last night. He seeks a bride… these girls—"

"I know." Lord Knowles guided Harriet into the hallway. "Lady Marjorie will be briefed and do her best to keep him from our graduates, but you must do as he asks, whatever that may be. No matter how grueling it may seem. He's unpleasant, but he's your father."

Marguerite's heart pinched to witness Harriet so distraught, so afraid of her own kin. Trifling with the Vidame of Limesdale was dangerous, she knew from rumors and from experience.

Lord Knowles returned to find Céleste shriveled near the wall, eyes shifting to a light, feathery gray. He forced her into the seat vacated by Cristina, and waved at Marguerite to sit beside her.

"Lady Marjorie," he said, going back to his seat, gaze on Céleste, "will be your guide for this trip to court. This isn't a punishment, you understand that?"

Céleste acquiesced.

"You're to assist her as a proper lady-in-waiting would. Monitor the girls and report to her should they fuss too much or spread too many rumors. Especially Charlotte."

"I… I…" Céleste's mouth opened and closed, like a fish out of water.

"Miss Richel, are you all right?"

A few uneasy noises crept through the girl's lips, but she

composed herself enough to speak, so softly Marguerite strained to hear her. "I'm sorry, my lord, but I don't understand. I'm a junior. Not a decent one. The issue last month, the book…"

"It's in the past." Lord Knowles' quill glided over a document placed before him. "Yes, you're a junior—meaning, you've not yet formed a mountain of bad habits and you'll be more impressionable to the wonders of court."

Marguerite didn't add how she hoped Céleste would help her as she navigated the treacherous halls of the place she used to call home, seeking secrets—new and old.

"But why me? There are other juniors this year, and my father…"

Lord Knowles set his quill down. "He'll approve. In fact, he'd agree with me that it's a suitable occasion to teach you, get you away from your books and in front of people." Céleste gawked, making Lord Knowles laugh. "All right, not *too* many people. But there must be more to you than daydreams of myths and fairy tales."

"I've been asked to chaperone," Marguerite said, keeping her chin down. "And I'll need assistance. I thought we worked well together last night, getting the girls ready."

Céleste perked up and twisted in her seat, eyes on Marguerite. "*That's* where I know you from! You were the handmaiden who helped Esther! But you're… a *lady?*"

Lord Knowles tapped on the desk. "Céleste, you know better than all of us how much of a handful five seniors can be. Those five in particular."

"Indeed." Céleste hiccupped. "Oh! I mean, no, they're not a handful. They're fine. I mean—whatever you say, Lord Knowles."

He steepled his fingers. "I won't force you. Should you not wish to do this, should you be reluctant—"

Céleste leapt up, but lost her balance and fell back into the chair. "No!" Her cheeks turned a vivid scarlet shade. "No, my lord, I'm not reluctant. You took me by surprise, but I'm most honored and wouldn't dare refuse such an offer."

"Very well. Hurry on to prepare your things, then. You won't need a white dress, but pack everything you have here. Our court values variety in clothing."

Marguerite tried not to snort, remembering her own royal season—the bickering over colors and patterns and fabrics, the scandals caused.

She almost snorted again when she imagined Céleste going through the same ordeal.

"No more daydreaming in excess, Miss Richel, understood? Lady Marjorie *will* report to me on a weekly basis, and I'm sure she won't hesitate to denounce bad behavior."

Céleste scrunched her nose as she got up. "I won't disappoint you, Lord Knowles." She curtsied, then swirled to Marguerite. "Nor you, my lady." She proceeded to the door, but before her hand reached the knob, she flipped around, grinning. "Thank you."

Lord Knowles gave Marguerite a nod of dismissal, so she walked up to Céleste. "We'll be very busy, so I expect you won't have time for the bad behavior he speaks of." She opened the door. "When we're alone, you may call me Marjorie, all right?"

Céleste was four years younger than her, but perhaps they'd become friends. Perhaps Marguerite would have someone to trust, other than Johanna. A new ally at court, one with a powerful family that might help her against whatever atrocities Clémentine was planning.

And potentially get out of that sordid marriage agreement.

"Marjorie. It's a beautiful name." Céleste clasped the edge of her dress and curtsied once more. "I'll be the best assistant you ever had. A veritable lady-in-waiting."

Marguerite watched her skip down the hallway. She wouldn't tell her she'd never had a lady-in-waiting because Clémentine had refused it. She wouldn't mention she had no idea what she was doing, that the life she'd grown used to was spinning out of control and she needed a tether to reality.

She squeezed her eyes shut and prayed Céleste might be that tether.

Céleste looked out the window of the downstairs parlor. Four carriages were parked outside in the pebbled courtyard; the drivers paced nearby.

In the window's reflection, she caught a glimmer of the silver chain hanging around her neck—the one her mother had gifted her what felt like an eternity ago.

Lady Richel would have been ecstatic to see her at the academy, becoming a proper lady of Totresia. Wherever she was now—up in Heaven, most likely—Céleste prayed she gazed down at her with pride.

Céleste had had a few bumps in the road, a few mistakes she'd made to warrant attention from the headmaster, but she still excelled in her studies. She wooed her professors, perfected her manners, and earned praise.

And now, she was headed to Torrinni Court.

At the prospect of escaping the royal academy, her excitement threatened to surface in the form of a squeal. She knew better—proper etiquette prevented her from making that terrible faux pas in public. Instead, she squeezed the velvet curtain as an enormous smile spread across her face.

After a week of strenuous fittings, ladies screeching commands at maids, and constant deliveries, the moment had come to embark on the ride to the capital. To get lost in its famed picturesque, cobbled streets, to admire its surrounding lush green hills.

Céleste had tried three times to secure her two overflowing trunks, pulled everything out and rearranged three more times, and failed. After a fourth attempt, and much huffing, she'd succeeded.

Footsteps echoed in the entryway to her left. The main doors swung open, followed by Lord Knowles' booming voice, announcing the carriages were ready.

Last month, a professor had caught her reading her favorite non-fiction novel in class—*The Golden Girl*. A forbidden book, Lord Knowles had warned her; a dangerous one, claimed the mysterious handmaiden Johanna. Lord Knowles had scolded her for having it in class.

She wished she hadn't already packed it. How she yearned to browse its pages, following the Duchess of Torrinni on her adventures in the castle, wooing Crown Prince Antoine, incurring the wrath of Queen Clémentine. Prince Sébastien and his books; Prince Jules and his adventures; Princess Cordelia and her etiquette lessons.

While the royal personages were real, the Duchess of Torrinni was a myth. She'd never existed; royal texts and lineages never mentioned her.

Céleste's overly imaginative mind couldn't help but wonder—had she truly existed, causing too big of a scandal at court to be kept alive? Where else would her story come from, if not from some spark of truth?

She fastened her cloak, pulled her traveling mittens up, and straightened her posture in time for Lord Knowles to peep into the parlor and motion her towards him.

Albeit stern, Lord Knowles was a gentleman, always kind to her when she respected her manners. "Your ride awaits, Miss Richel. You'll voyage with Lady Marjorie and Johanna. We received word from your father earlier this morning—your imminent departure thrills him."

"Many thanks, my lord."

As she moved into the lobby, Charlotte and Julia shoved by her, bundled in their matching white travel cloaks. They sneered at her as they passed, several overworked servants hastening behind them with trunks.

Charlotte and Julia had more than once mentioned Céleste's over-the-top reading habits to Lord Knowles. Other girls in her grade whispered about how shy she acted when in fact she was more outspoken and opinionated than most.

Journeying to the castle with these bullies seemed daunting, but Céleste wouldn't be alone.

Cristina scampered out next, not a glance spared in Céleste's direction. Esther hurried towards the middle carriage that she'd share with Harriet, who waited outside, rubbing her gloved hands together.

After a quick inhale, Céleste whisked out. A rush of wind bit her cheeks. It was cold this winter, more so than any other at the academy, and she wondered if Torrinni would be warmer.

A few paces down the stone stairs, she stopped to watch the courtyard—ladies climbing into vehicles as chests and bags were piled into baggage carriages. Maids and butlers ensured all belongings were secure and the horses geared to go.

Céleste captured the moment to memory. She wouldn't see the school again for a while, and despite the torment she'd endured there from some of the girls, she'd also had grand days within the canary-colored walls of the academy.

Someone cleared their throat behind her.

She pivoted to Lady Marjorie, clad in a deep azure travel cloak that concealed a cream dress. A small hat was nestled over her golden curls, shading her jade eyes.

"Don't block the way, Miss Richel." She took Céleste's arm and led her to the bottom of the steps. "The sooner we leave, the more time we'll have to settle in." She glided over the pebbles as if she'd done so a million times.

They approached their carriage, its doors stamped with a Totresian crown and olive branch, and a feather slicing through the middle, representing a quill for knowledge. Faded blue curtain flaps over the windows parted to show the regal interior.

Lady Marjorie entered first, helped by her handmaiden, Johanna, who then aided Céleste and hopped in herself as a footman closed the door.

A fresh linen scent permeated the compact space, sifting into Céleste's nose. The velvety cushions were worn-down, and the floor had many scratches, but it was cozy enough for a short trip to the capital.

She sat opposite Lady Marjorie and Johanna, who kept their

backs to the driver. The horses took off, and she peeked out a window, turning for one last glance at the school in all its late morning splendor. The three-story building, its silver-coated roofs glistening in the sun, became smaller and smaller.

Céleste already missed her room. What sort of accommodations would she have at the castle? As a lady-in-waiting to a noble chaperone, she prayed for a decent-sized bed, an adequate fireplace, someplace to sit and read. Well, if she'd even have *time* for reading.

An hour went by, then another, and another. The carriage fell into partial darkness as they traversed a forest that sheltered them from sunlight. Branches whipped in the wind and unidentified noises emanated from either side of the road.

She'd never been to court, let alone to Torrinni itself. The sudden anxiety of such a change sent disturbing images to fizzle through her brain. She envisioned tall ladies in bright-hued gowns, sporting jewelry the likes of which she'd never compete with. They'd share eloquent speeches and snippets of gossip she wouldn't understand. They'd giggle coquettishly behind their gloved hands as she walked by in her mother's old dresses.

Lady Marjorie let out steady breaths, eyes closed but not sleeping. Johanna focused on the landscape from her mistress' open window.

To ease her mind, Céleste thought of her lessons. Torrinni City spread out for miles; as one of the largest towns in the country, it was its own province as well as the capital of Totresia. Books described the castle as pleasurable to the eyes, though less impressive than most European structures.

"Miss Richel, your brother is at court, yes?" asked Johanna, her tone polite, but not stiff or unpleasant.

"Yes, he arrived last year. Father wanted him to find a wife, but…" She sensed herself flushing with warmth; it'd be best not to admit he was also spying in their father's name. "He's been unsuccessful."

Telling Johanna that her brother was an absolute rake would also be inappropriate. She sealed her lips and continued to look outside.

***

Céleste's eyes shot open as the carriage sprung up, sending her lurching forward. The lantern inside the vehicle had been lit.

Had she fallen asleep? Had the ride taken longer than expected?

Johanna caught her before she planted into her lap. "Careful, Miss!"

Céleste blinked, recentering her vision, regaining her bearings.

Lady Marjorie's features were mostly obscured by the rim of her hat. Voice low and throaty, she said, "We're almost there."

Anticipation rose in Céleste's chest. She lifted the window flap to glimpse outside. The sky had turned a deep blue, streaking with orange and pink, decorated with tiny white specks.

She pushed her head out, gushing as she spotted the illuminated city walls up ahead. "Torrinni!"

The imposing stone fortifications were yards away. Buildings towered in the distance behind them; houses and businesses near glimmering lights that showered the streets in a golden glow.

"Incredible," she gushed.

Someone inside tugged at the hem of her dress, but she ignored it—she wasn't done looking.

To the far right, beyond the fortified wall, she saw the top of an observation tower—the one she recalled from drawings of the Torrinni Castle. "Truly incredible!"

At the gates, the horses stopped, and her heart swelled. Torrinni—they were finally arriving. The tugging on her skirts became more insistent, so she returned inside the carriage. "It's magnificent!"

Lady Marjorie scowled at her. "Yes, and you will see it up close, but don't hang out the window like an uneducated child. You should know better!"

Céleste bit her lip and glanced anywhere but at Lady Marjorie. She'd never heard her speak much until a week ago, when she'd officially met her. A woman of impressive beauty, she'd been mostly a mystery since they were introduced.

Lady Marjorie rubbed the back of her neck, puffing a few breaths from her mouth. "My apologies. My nerves are a tad rattled, I'm afraid. Torrinni isn't my favorite place to be."

Céleste squinted at her. She'd been to Torrinni before?

Lady Marjorie shrugged half-heartedly. "You may continue to look outside, but please, no hanging, understood?"

Smirking, Céleste slipped past the window flap.

As they rolled within the city limits, every inch of her begged to jump out and explore the cobblestone streets drenched in moonlight. To touch the symmetrical torches lining the two, three, four-story buildings. To peer through the windows with bold-colored curtains, listen to the laughter and conversation wafting out, filling the avenue with life.

She read signs posted above shops and inhaled the frosty air. A few villagers walked near the carriages—they waved, and Céleste waved back, bursting with excitement.

She noticed a bakery, a blacksmith, a forge, an armory. A boutique with displays of hats and scarves and headpieces; another with rolls of lavish fabrics and shoes with heels so high she wouldn't dream of trying to walk in them.

Deeper into the town, grocers were closing for the evening. Goldsmiths towered at their thresholds, ogling passers-by with greed. She noticed taverns with battered doors from which loud cheers escaped into the street.

Torrinni was all she'd ever dreamed of, and more. It was bigger than her native city of Valeville, with more diverging streets and curious onlookers; more ruckus and merriment, and a slight scent of spilled liquor.

"All right, that's enough," said Lady Marjorie, yanking Céleste back in.

She'd been hanging out again, without realizing it. "I'm sorry, my lady."

The chaperone frowned. "Sit and act poised, please." Her tone chilled like a wintry stream. "You mustn't make us appear as foreigners before we arrive at the castle. The royals will expect proper ladies, yourself included."

Readjusting her position, Céleste tried to conceal her disappointment. Lady Marjorie had seemed like she might be a friend during this adventure; here, she resembled a stern professor or worrisome mother.

"Of course, my lady."

Lady Marjorie's posture relaxed as she fingered a golden pendant dangling from her neck. "Again, I ask you to forgive me. I'm stressed."

Johanna slid a strand of her black curls behind her ear. "Torrinni Court is a tough place to fit in."

Céleste had never met such an articulate servant girl. The way she easily conversed with Lady Marjorie implied they were close and knew each other well.

"Whilst we're there, you must behave yourself." Impatience fizzled into the chaperone's tone again, but she shook her head and winced. "Let's change the subject. Have you heard of the Torrinni Palace? North of the town, near the Royal Guard Academy?"

Céleste's brows knitted together. "A palace? I know of the Military Academy, since my brother attended it. And the Royal Academy for Young Men, he mentioned that, too. But a palace?" Her lashes fluttered as she gaped between Marguerite and Johanna. "Whose is it? A summer home?"

"It belonged to," Lady Marjorie cleared her throat, "the Duchess of Torrinni."

Céleste gasped so fast she had no time to block the sound from her mouth. "*The* Duchess of Torrinni? She's… real?"

All the mentions of the noblewoman from Céleste's book flashed before her eyes—followed by Lord Knowles' adamant claims that such a woman had never existed.

Lady Marjorie showed no sign of surprise at Céleste's question. "I assume the palace belongs to the dowager, now, though she resides at court." Lady Marjorie lidded her eyes and her shoulders tilted forward. She pushed her hat backward, revealing her forehead glistening with perspiration.

"Duchess of Torrinni?" Céleste repeated, still in shock from the ease with which Lady Marjorie had mentioned the mysterious woman. "Did you know her? Was she a friend of yours? Someone who attended our academy?"

Lady Marjorie's eyes washed with tears as she raised the carriage flap on her side of the vehicle. "Something like that." Her arm trembled as she held up the fabric.

An ominous sting of cold unleashed within the confined space.

Why did she bring the duchess up if she didn't want to speak of her?

Johanna said nothing, watching her hands in her lap.

The Duchess of Torrinni—the nonexistent woman from Céleste's favorite book, *The Golden Girl?* It couldn't be. She wasn't made-up by the author? Not a rumor, a piece of gossip for bored girls to spread for a good laugh?

Céleste wished she'd known before leaving the academy. She might have rubbed the knowledge in Lord Knowles' face, if anything to get the last word.

She didn't know Lady Marjorie well, but why would she mention this duchess if she wasn't a true figure of Torrinni Court? Why would she lie?

Céleste had stashed the book between cloaks and heavy dresses in her luggage, to not get in trouble like she had a month ago. It wasn't acceptable reading for Torrinni Court, but to investigate this, and interrogate folk who may have known the duchess, she'd have to dig it out.

Lady Marjorie removed a kerchief from her coat pocket and dabbed at her eyes. Johanna sat in grave silence, but kept an eye on her mistress, as if expecting something more dramatic to happen.

Had this duchess been closer to Lady Marjorie than she'd implied? Did coming to Torrinni rouse sour memories of time passed between them?

Céleste didn't want to overstep. She wouldn't dare guess what this woman was going through. She wanted to offer encouraging words, but what did one say to someone who grieved and didn't want to talk about it? Céleste had hated when others tried to comfort her after her mother's death. She'd loathed their sympathies and fake apologies and pitiful smiles. She wouldn't wish Lady Marjorie to endure the same.

"I'm fine. Caught a chill. Torrinni is glacial this year," said Lady Marjorie at last. Her hat tumbled over her forehead again as she sniffled. "Once we arrive and rest, I'll be in tip-top shape."

Céleste's legs were restless.

A castle where the duchess from her book might have grown up, earned her title, played with the princess. Where she might have thwarted the dowager's cruelty, might have spent time with the former king. Where she might have been engaged to the current king, and had her heart shattered to pieces on the night of the Masquerade.

Despite the sadness that last thought caused, Céleste grinned. She loved books of adventures and mysteries—and her trip had transformed into one such novel.

5.

Marguerite

The gentle trotting through town did nothing to soothe Marguerite's aching heart. Instead, the journey made her nauseous.

Rambling about the Duchess of Torrinni—in front of Céleste, no less—almost gave away the memories of her youth, those that flared up her temper and made her raise her voice.

She wasn't sure why she'd done it. She and Johanna had discussed keeping the truth to themselves until the time was right. They'd planned to warn Céleste that not only the Duchess of Torrinni was real, but she was Marguerite.

Marguerite had ruined half of that plan by speaking up too soon.

Staring out the window, she was jolted by a slight kick on her thigh. Céleste was yet again hanging out the other side.

She bit her tongue as the coach stopped and the driver spoke to the castle gate guard.

The serene hue of the lantern kept her calm, its flames dancing over the carriage's interior walls. She lowered her hat as the vehicle continued to the castle. She leaned out the window, rotating to face the building—candelabras brightened the end of the lengthy driveway, lining the path to the grand doors.

The pebbles beneath the wheels prompted the freight to wobble back and forth; Céleste grumbled about it as she came back inside.

Marguerite was used to the discomfort, but held in her malaise as best as she could.

Candlelight poured into the vehicle as they navigated towards the courtyard. In her teenage days, Marguerite hadn't often seen the driveway at night, rarely allowed to wander out after supper. If she did venture out, she stuck to the gardens in the rear, accompanied by a guard.

She gazed at the castle's four stories of enchanting windows, hypnotizing arches, fairytale balconies. The ghosts of her past slid over the weathered pale-yellow facade, moaning her name from the tiled rooftops, beckoning her to the observation tower.

Her world broke apart, seam by seam, as images she'd wished to keep concealed forever resurfaced. Her eyes welled with tears for the second time since they'd departed. But she willed them away, because she wasn't alone in the carriage; Johanna knew why she struggled, but Céleste didn't.

Marguerite shifted left to right, her spine stiff as a board as she dropped the window flap. "Remember your manners when you enter the castle, Céleste. Even if the halls appear empty, someone is always watching."

Céleste's smile was full of verve and curiosity. "Of course! I wish to honor the academy, not embarrass it," she said, with an excitement Marguerite couldn't share.

The coach turned; their arrival was imminent, and each breath Marguerite took signaled the dread to come.

What had Clémentine told the court about her? Would they recognize her, or pretend she'd never been real, as they'd been bribed to? The dowager hadn't given her any further instruction aside from to show up, and use an alias until otherwise stated.

The royals thought she was dead. The courtiers had been sworn into believing that she'd never existed in the first place.

She tightened her cloak, pulled up her gloves, and exhaled.

Johanna's hand brushed her leg. She'd promised she would be with Marguerite every step of the way, as much as possible for a servant girl in a royal household.

The carriage halted and a weight dropped from the front. *Oohs* and *ahhs* echoed all around as the graduates alighted.

Marguerite's door opened, and a blinding glow illuminated the agonizing path she wished she wasn't forced to take.

The chauffeur had deposited them at the foot of the primary doors, which were wide open, a hint of the yellow vestibule peeking out.

The staff had rolled out the carpet used for big occasions; it started at the carriage and torches followed it all the way to the top of the small flight of steps leading to the doorway. Servants and guards stood at the ready, some already fetching luggage.

The boulder-like surface of the building appeared golden. In contrast to the smooth gate walls, these were old, harsh, but barren of moss or ivy, as impeccable as before her departure. White stone pillars encased the giant oak doors, and the sophisticated arch above sparkled in the moonlight.

Johanna touched her arm. "My lady, we should get off," she whispered.

The chauffeur helped Marguerite down the steps, and a butler rushed up to greet her. At once, she dropped her chin, ensuring her hat veiled her face.

"Lady Marjorie, chaperone of the Totresian Royal Academy for Noble Girls, welcome to Torrinni Castle," said the man, gesturing her down the carpet. Céleste and Johanna shuffled up behind her.

"Many thanks." Marguerite motioned at the five contenders. "Girls, come along!"

The butler offered his arm, and Marguerite took it, heart thumping in her chest, throat turning to sandpaper.

As they ambled forward, she glimpsed the pointed top of the Winter Garden's glass roof. Lights beneath it shimmered like a pool of sparkling water. How she wished she could hide in there, surrounded by trees and plants, far from the whispers that would occur in her presence.

"I'm afraid the royals are all otherwise occupied, else they would have welcomed you themselves," said the butler.

Marguerite pried her focus from the roofs to check on the graduates. They'd fixed their skirts and shut their mouths, but there was no mistaking the wonder in their gazes.

"That's unfortunate, but we'll manage," she replied.

In truth, such news elated her. Not having Clémentine there to begin her judging process—deciding ahead of time which contender she'd allow to marry her sons—eased a handful of her worries.

After one last whiff of fresh air, she prepared to pass under the threshold. And as if to stop her from entering, a familiar pine scent wafted into her nostrils.

She pictured the nearby Torrinni forest: the narrow but thick woods were where she'd spent her childhood exploring, playing in. Trees she'd climbed, roots she'd jumped over, caverns she'd hidden in for some alone time with—

She urged herself into the foyer and caught her breath before she took the two steps down into the entryway.

Céleste jammed into her back. "Heavens."

Muffled gasps came from the contenders as they scooched in on either side of Marguerite, Johanna, and Céleste. They marveled at the yellow rug that expanded from the door, stopping at the bottom of the stairs, revealing a grand room with a bejeweled ceiling. A marvelous, gold chandelier hung from it, hundreds of tiny candles swaying in the breeze, sending flecks of light onto the polished wooden floors.

Marguerite couldn't move. Her vision blurred, her stomach lurched—

Johanna nudged her farther into the hall.

Marguerite scanned the yellow and white walls, the royal family paintings, the oak doors, the sturdy curving white marble stairs to the left—and all the hallways leading to places she wished to forget.

Straight ahead was the Long Corridor, to the right was the King's Corridor. And all she could think of were the main doors behind her and how she might slip out to run away.

She gulped, clutching the edge of her dress—and froze as a majestic figure emerged from the King's Corridor.

Clad in a voluminous gray dress, the figure—a young woman—addressed two ladies beside her. She halted mid-sentence at the sight of visitors.

A flowing mane of dark chestnut hair fell down her back, and a fluffy flower was tucked near her ear. Her chocolate gaze moved from lady to lady, but widened, then narrowed, as it found Marguerite.

Hat or no hat, this person knew her.

At once, and despite the distance separating them, Marguerite dropped into a curtsy. "Your Highness."

The butler bowed, then coughed into his hand. "Ladies of the Totresian Royal Academy, I present to you Princess Cordelia of Totresia."

Céleste, Johanna, and the others sank into graceful curtsies, uttering polite salutations.

Marguerite kept her chin down.

"My brother's debutantes?" Princess Cordelia moved forward, every bit as refined as her mother had raised her. "Welcome, ladies."

She waved everyone up, but Marguerite didn't dare move. She sensed Cordelia's glare over the top of her hat. She suppressed a shiver and muttered a prayer, begging the girl not to divulge her true identity.

Thankfully, the princess kept mum. The hem of her skirts swooshed over the polished floors as she paused a foot away from Marguerite.

"You're the chaperone?" Her tone was identical to Dowager Clémentine's, raw and crackling like a bonfire.

Unable to ignore a direct question, Marguerite glanced up.

"Indeed, Highness. It's a pleasure to meet you."

Cordelia stared at her, one eyebrow cocked, recognition passing through her icy expression. Something else shone in her eyes: emotion tinged with rage. Perhaps she fought the urge to blurt out the truth, or she hid excitement. Marguerite wasn't sure she'd ever find out.

"Pleasure." Cordelia drew towards the stairs. "If you will excuse me, I have other matters to attend to." She bustled upward without another word, her ladies at her heels.

The butler motioned for Marguerite and the girls to follow the princess. "Your rooms are on the second floor, my lady. Names are on the doors. Other contenders arrived weeks ago, but we reserved the best for our seniors of the royal academy." He softened his voice. "The dowager has asked that no one explore the grounds tonight. Preparations are underway for tomorrow's presentation, and she wishes for all contenders to confine to their rooms. For refreshments, send for a servant."

Marguerite's legs shook beneath her gown. "We appreciate the hospitality and will comply with Her Grace's requests."

The man scampered down the King's Corridor, and Marguerite ushered everyone up the carpeted staircase.

The girls studied the paintings, portraits, potted plants, and sculptures along the way. But halfway up, Marguerite paused at the sound of a piano, a royal tune she'd never forget. Fast-paced, low notes peppered with high spurts—*The dowager's song.*

Was she purposely playing with the music room door open?

Marguerite wouldn't let the evil rhythm draw her off course. She hastened up the stairs, where Céleste waited for her on the last step.

"Everyone already found their rooms," she cringed, "and I can't find mine. This place is quite… large."

Dread settled into Marguerite's stomach as she strained to hide her distress. "Then we must go on a hunt to locate it."

6.
Marguerite

On the second-floor landing, the yellow color scheme from below switched to turquoise. Detailed portraits and landscapes hung from every wall, entrapped by white marble pillars and glowing chandeliers. The polished wood-paneled floor was, in places, coated in thick red carpeting.

Céleste paused, in awe, but Marguerite had no time to waste, swishing past her.

"Do you know the princess?" the girl asked, voice lowered.

Caught off-guard, Marguerite gulped. "No." She brushed herself off. "What would make you think such a thing?"

Céleste shrugged. "Her behavior towards you was odd."

Breaking the conversation before it got too far, Marguerite flitted across the vast area, stopping before two doors with parchments affixed to them.

She studied the first. "Harriet's," then the door on the left, "and this isn't one of ours."

Céleste motioned to a hallway on the left, containing more grand doors with inscriptions. "Charlotte and Julia meandered down there."

"I presume there are more chambers that way." Marguerite set her hands on her hips, picturing the entire second-floor layout. "Did you see where Cristina went?"

Céleste pointed to another oak door with a note, to the left of the stairs they'd come up. "In there."

An upward staircase began at the foot of that door. Marguerite glanced at it warily and shivered. "Don't go up there, ever." Céleste opened her mouth, surely to ask where the stairs led, but Marguerite tutted. "It's by invitation only." She gestured at the hall to the right of Harriet's door. "Let's go that way."

Céleste drifted closer to the forbidden stairs, staring at the golden-threaded carpeting covering each step. "Where does it lead?"

Marguerite tugged her sleeve. "It's for royals and higher nobility, or their representatives." She grimaced as she led Céleste away. "Come, our rooms will be this way."

"How did you—" Céleste planted her feet, barring Marguerite from pulling her any further. "Did you say *higher nobility?* So, my family's apartments are up there? That means I *can* go—"

Marguerite yanked her down the corridor. "Under other circumstances, yes. But you're not with your family—you're with me, as my lady-in-waiting. Not the daughter of a marquess."

Céleste scrunched her nose, but quit her bickering.

Marguerite followed the wall as it curved to the right. A new corridor opened, and to their left they found a door labeled *Esther*

Bristol. She motioned Céleste past it.

In this new area, turquoise shifted to pastel pinks. Red carpeting covered the entire floor, and the corridor was smaller. Rich portraits rested next to golden chandeliers and beautiful designs carved into the pillars and walls.

The lengthy hall concluded in a square space with a few doors, and two sets of rickety wooden stairs; one downward, and one up.

Marguerite stopped at a door not far before the shabby staircases. A bunched up parchment was hooked near the doorknob.

M. - Totresian Royal Academy chaperone.

"They didn't even bother to write out my name," she muttered.

"Those are service stairs, aren't they?" Céleste sneered at the aforementioned stairs. "Why would your room be so close to them? Why not closer to the other girls?"

Marguerite rushed past the service stairways, her instinct drawing her to another landmark she'd nearly forgotten.

Céleste ran to catch up. "Wait!"

Marguerite didn't slow down the narrow path lining the indoor balcony. Only halfway past it she halted, gaping at the ballroom below.

This was her spot, with Antoine—where they hid to watch the Masquerade, every year until they were old enough to attend it.

A large chandelier—like the one in the entryway—swayed from the ceiling above, drooping past the railing and overlooking polished wooden floors so bright they almost appeared orange.

Marguerite pulled Céleste from the lustrous white-wood fencing, where she'd begun to lean. "There are more rooms that way," she pointed to the right, "and yes, we've won chambers close to the service stairs. But we won't complain. I'm a lesser noble, and lucky enough to not have to sleep in the basement with the servants." She tugged at Céleste's sleeve.

Céleste dragged her feet. "Something's not right," she said.

Marguerite agreed—but she didn't have time to address the girl's concerns yet.

Despite its unpleasant location, Marguerite's chamber was splendid. The walls were a deep basil, and the large canopy bed, centered against the wall across from the door, had a pastel rose bedspread. A laundered scent permeated the air. Candles in gold sconces brightened the suite, accompanying a roaring fire to the left of the door. A comfortable sitting space of two couches and a chaise sat beside a moderate-sized vanity, an ornate closet, and a divider. On the left side of the bed, a thick emerald curtain concealed a small window.

Céleste spun on her heels. "I take back what I said about being near the service stairs. This is lovely."

Marguerite plopped onto the bed. "Better than I'd have expected."

There was a door at the right end of the room; Céleste thrust it open. Another chamber waited behind it, matching Marguerite's, though narrower.

"Is this mine?" the girl whispered, teetering at the edge of the room.

Marguerite saw enough from where she sat. The bed was less extravagant, pushed up against the far-left wall, near the warmth of a burning hearth. A worn-down oak armoire rested by the facade near the adjoining door. She knew the general set-up of such rooms, meant for young women assisting noble daughters.

"It's a lady-in-waiting suite," she said, as Céleste rushed back into the main room. "It's not much, but hopefully it suits you."

Céleste shook with excitement. "It's perfect." Her shoulders sank once she saw her mistress' frown. "My lady, are you unwell? Your face is quite pale."

Marguerite inhaled, then shook her head. "Tired, that's all."

"Have you caught another chill? Should I fetch Johanna?"

Marguerite patted a spot on the bed beside her. "I must be frank with you."

Céleste hesitated, but sat. "Did I do something wrong?"

Marguerite nearly said she had, but it wouldn't be the truth. "No. It's me. I'm acquainted with the Totresian court, with this castle. I've been here before, and it pains me to return, because I dislike it."

Céleste clapped a hand over her mouth. "Why didn't you say so? Here I am, pressing you, acting as a child—"

"I wanted none of the students to know." Marguerite smiled through her pain. "But if you're to be my lady, *you* should. I'm no stranger to these halls, these rooms, and I'm not happy to be here."

Flickers of various emotions swarmed Céleste's face; as if she weren't sure how to feel, nor how to express those feelings. "If you attended Torrinni Court... you know the royals? You said you didn't know the princess."

"I couldn't speak of it out there." Lady Marjorie adjusted her skirts, keeping her trembling hands busy. "Yes, I've met the royals, but they don't know me well, nor would they care to."

The corners of Céleste's mouth turned up. "The Duchess of Torrinni lived here with them, yes?"

Marguerite's brows snapped together; instant regret pooled

inside her. Céleste would come to all sorts of conclusions if she allowed this important information to slip out so soon.

"It's not for me to confirm."

Céleste sprung from the bed and hopped from foot to foot. "She's *real,* you told me that in the carriage. Do you deny she dwelled at court? And all the other stories told about her?"

Marguerite whipped her chin up, glowering. "Stories?" She rose from the bed. "You refer to your little journal?"

"My," Céleste gulped, "journal?"

Marguerite pinched her lips, swaying away from the bed. "Lord Knowles informed me of your reading habits, and this tattered book you carry around with you, that your professors caught you peeking at in class—"

"I *wasn't* peeking at it in class!"

"—and it's a journal, Céleste. A collection of thoughts from someone who overheard rumors and wrote their own fairytales about what they interpreted."

Céleste's eyebrows drew together. "But you said the Duchess of Torrinni was real."

"I did." She groaned and removed her hat, throwing it onto the mattress. "But I didn't say she lived here with the royals, or that she was once betrothed to the—" She sucked in a breath, then released it slowly, leveling with her nerves. She'd done this to herself by being too forthcoming earlier; the consequences were a demanding, curious lady-in-waiting. "She was real, yes, but that's where the truth ends.

Céleste drew her lower lip between her teeth. "Lady Marjorie, I—"

"No." Marguerite waved her off. "You were told to behave,

and spreading word of this journal of yours is *not* good behavior, Céleste. Do I know the royals personally? No, but I *do* know they'll scrutinize our every move whilst we're here. You must remember your place. Set aside your daydreams for the rest of our stay. No more talk of that silly book." Before Céleste could muster a reply, Marguerite slid into the hallway. "Do you understand?"

Céleste said nothing.

"You won't ignore me and venture into your dreamworld, Miss Richel!" Marguerite poked her head back inside the room. "You spoke of honoring the school in the carriage, do you remember?"

"I'm sorry, my lady." Céleste lowered her chin, poorly hiding the flush creeping up her cheeks. "I remember, and I will keep my promises."

Though she remained silent as they waited for Johanna to arrive with their trunks, Marguerite sensed Céleste wouldn't drop this topic easily.

The last time Marguerite had set foot in Torrinni Castle, she wore a golden-threaded gown, shoes meant for a queen, and a bodice so tight she couldn't breathe. Now, in her looser fitting corset, her traveling gloves, her hair woven in a plain bun, she was title-less. Unimportant and boring.

And she preferred it that way.

Céleste had retired to her quarters to freshen up, and judging by the confusion swimming in her eyes and her sagging shoulders, Marguerite knew the girl was upset.

She shouldn't have been so harsh. Céleste was new to all this. She needed guidance, not reprimands.

Marguerite edged up to the ajar door. Céleste sat on the bed as royal servants put her clothes in drawers and the armoire.

"Miss Richel." Marguerite slid across the doorway. "I want to take you on a quick tour."

Céleste frowned, though a flicker of mischief ignited in her gaze. "But what of the dowager's orders? Are we not to stay in our chambers?"

Marguerite was nervous and fearful of being at court, but that didn't mean Céleste needed to be, too. It was her first time there—perhaps her only time. She deserved to experience it through the eyes of someone knowledgeable. Someone like Marguerite. Before all the festivities and the excitement, before the gossip started spreading.

To hell with the woman's requests; Marguerite knew the dowager's routine. Surely it hadn't changed.

"Fret not about that. Besides, we're not contenders, are we? We can bend the rules."

Céleste stood, and though she kept a straight face, Marguerite saw the quirk in her lips, her slightly raised brow.

They snuck into the corridor, then downstairs. At the bottom of the steps, they took a left towards the Long Corridor Marguerite had so dreaded seeing earlier. Chandeliers cast faint lights on the chestnut walls, and a clock chimed seven times. Everyone would be preparing for supper.

If she and Céleste steered clear of the dining room, they wouldn't bump into anyone.

At the end of the aisle lined with painted landscapes, Marguerite veered left into an elegant hallway with floor-to-ceiling windows on its right side—the West Wing. They bypassed a narrow turn on the left—the Visitor's Corridor—but Céleste missed it, her gaze glued to the glass panes, beyond which lay rows of hedges and pebbled pathways, lit up by candelabras.

"The royal gardens. Beautiful in daylight, intriguing at night."

Once they reached the edge of the hall, they found the reading room, which Marguerite introduced as a common meeting spot.

To the left of the reading room was the royal library—shelves of books in English, French, Italian, German, Latin, ancient Greek. Pictures, paintings, famous journals, mysteries—it was all there. Bookcases bordered the walls, and vast tables with cozy chairs sat to the right. An elaborate royal portrait in the rear hung over a large hearth.

Céleste gawked, but Marguerite didn't give her time to linger. She led her back the way they'd come from, whooshing by a great archway to their right, slowing to peer in—the royal art gallery.

Moving on, the lofty windows came to a halt as the wall curved inward. Céleste's pace lessened as she noticed the door positioned after the curve. It was open—*unusual*—and Céleste glanced in, but Marguerite tugged her aside.

"No, we can't."

Céleste grew rigid. "What's in there?"

Marguerite gritted her teeth. "It's the Queen's Music Room. Not a place one wanders into."

Céleste didn't argue. She swished after Marguerite down the Long Corridor, and they stopped by the clock.

Marguerite jutted at the glass door nearest them. "Go on, enter."

Céleste passed the threshold and froze once inside. "Oh my Lord."

Marguerite closed the door behind her and rested against it as starlight sprinkled over her face. "The Winter Garden."

The pebbled ground and the high, sparkling glass ceiling filled Marguerite with a rare sense of peace. The highest point towered above, gleaming stars shining through. For a moment, all the tension in her muscles dissipated. As if they were outside, and not in an indoor garden of exotic florals and vibrant colors.

Céleste twirled in the middle of a large, pebbled circle surrounded by greenery, where four cobbled paths joined before leading to the four entrances. "This is heaven!"

Marguerite's hands grazed shrubs and brushed over red roses. Benches littered the corners, hid behind bushes, and perched before tree-trunks.

She grimaced at recollections of the princes trying to climb everything in sight, while Céleste sniffed at the multi-colored tulips dotting the vivid green thickets.

Marguerite motioned at the door to the left. "That way will take you to the Queen's Corridor." She directed her pointer finger to the right. "Over there, the King's Corridor." She thrust her thumb behind her. "The Long Corridor, where we came from," and nudged at the pathway ahead, "and the East Wing."

Marguerite couldn't forget that, though *this* area pleased her heart, everywhere else didn't.

She snatched Céleste's hand. "On to the East Wing."

They swung by more fragrant tulips and bubbly daisies. Another glass door waited, and she pushed it, taking one final gulp of the soothing Winter Garden before ushering Céleste out.

The East Wing's color scheme mimicked that of the entrance hall, but this corridor was brighter, its carpets plusher. Portraits were bigger, and guards patrolled at every corner.

A guard perked up as he saw them; his features almost warmed when he noticed Marguerite. Thankfully, he said nothing. He stood in front of a place she dreaded, but that Céleste would find exquisite. It was essential to their tour.

"I must warn you." Marguerite gaped at the grand doors. "Our next stop will be brief." She maneuvered Céleste to the copper and gold door-frame. "I'll explain a few things, and then we'll leave."

With a quick shake of her head, she dismissed the visions of her past.

The oversized oak doors towered before them, so tall they rivaled those of the main castle entrance. Glowing brass chandeliers encircled them. A few muffled yells came from the other side.

Her blood became ice as it raced through her veins. She nodded at the guard protecting the entrance. Usually there would be two, but festivities weren't slated to start yet. "May we go in?"

He inclined his head. "Make it quick."

Blinding light rushed out as the doors creaked open. Céleste covered her eyes, but Marguerite pulled her past the massive door-frame.

"This is, as you may have guessed, the ballroom."

The burnt orange floor glistened as the chandelier's flames sent shadows dancing over the surface. Torches stuck to the sparkling white pillars lining the burgundy-splashed walls. Not much had changed, aside from the flooring—it used to be white marble.

"They want it over there!" A man in uniform brisked by without seeing them. He hastened to the far-left corner where the buffet tables sat, their dazzling white tablecloths being pressed by maids in charcoal dresses.

"This way," said Marguerite, taking Céleste to the right, where no staff-members loitered.

This section of the ballroom was a perfect viewpoint to observe the entire area. Moonlight poured in through the towering windows showcasing the darkened patio. The silver curtains swayed in gentle motions, like misty ghosts reaching out for an eternal embrace.

To the right of the windows, propped atop a green and gold dais, were the thrones.

Marguerite lost her wits as all the workers seemed to whiz about in slow-motion, their voices morphing, their bodies specter-like, their faces covered in masks. *Ghosts*. Reminders.

No matter the beauty of the place, the thrill of the events it would soon host, all she felt was reluctance. All she saw were the spirits of her last night in Torrinni.

She clenched her fists, transfixed. Her racing pulse, her rising body temperature, her throbbing temples—

She flipped to Céleste and opened her mouth, but no sound came out.

"Yes?" The young lady was quick to reply, voice soft as she gawked all around, unable to focus on one thing at once.

"Everything happens here. Grand dinners, coronations, noble blessings, normal court proceedings, tomorrow's presentation, and the year-end Masquerade Ball." Shivers ran down Marguerite's spine.

Céleste lit up like a bonfire. "*The* Masquerade?"

"That will be later—" Marguerite's speech was cut off when a door creaked open to the far-right.

She stilled; staff-members never used that door. It was a secret side entrance from the King's Corridor, an exit for royals needing to disappear from the ballroom.

One royal in particular always used it for his escapes.

On instinct, and before she saw anyone coming through said exit, Marguerite stepped in front of Céleste.

"Keep quiet." She spun the girl to face away, towards the wall. "Try to blend in, stay calm."

"Blend in *with a wall?*" Céleste stiffened as Marguerite lined up beside her. "Who's coming? Are we in trouble?"

Fear skittered up Marguerite's arms in waves of goosebumps. "I don't know."

Footsteps came, two sets of boots pounding on the floorboards.

The ladies kept their backs to them. Marguerite prayed to turn invisible.

The footsteps progressed, and one of the individuals spoke. "We had no alternative, Séb! Otherwise he would have trapped us there to sign us up for his war to conquer Europe and the southern continent."

Marguerite had no trouble recognizing the voice; too familiar, too evoking of moments in this very room.

More chills spiraled down her spine as the men crept close, close, *closer*.

"His offers towards us? Years of refusals, but he insists? Years! Why does he think we would change Father's request? *Don't sell Totresia to Napoléon.* He thinks to sway us with his peace treaty? Ridiculous."

From the corner of her eye, she spotted the two figures passing to her left, not noticing she and Céleste gaping in the other direction. They walked by, their steps veering towards the royal dais.

Was the coast clear yet? Could she and Céleste run out without being seen?

Unable to stop herself, Marguerite swiveled slightly to peek at them. Even from afar, she'd never mistake them. Their measured strides, their towering heights, their strong postures. And of course—the ruby-encrusted, golden crowns atop their curls.

Her heart fluttered.

"You act like you know Napoléon," said the second man, his pitch also recognizable. He shook out his long black mane as he set his hands on his hips and glimpsed the thrones. "All looks well?"

The two men whipped around in tandem, and at once their gazes rested on Marguerite and Céleste standing in the distance.

Marguerite had no chance to react, to flip back around; it was too late.

She spun Céleste around and yanked her into a curtsy with her. Marguerite tucked her chin, fighting the feelings bubbling up inside her.

Céleste didn't resist, but squirmed. "My lady—"

"Hush! Keep low!"

The men's boots clicked as they wandered over.

"We scared these poor ladies, Antoine," said the second voice, airy with a hint of sarcasm.

Marguerite dipped her chin further as her heartbeat thrummed in her ears. Her breaths were so labored, they made her dizzy.

She recalled Sébastien from years ago, a dark-haired boy with chocolate eyes full of warmth. If they were warm now, she had no idea, and refused to check.

Céleste trembled beside her. She now knew who'd stumbled upon them, having heard the familiar royal names.

"It surprises me that any showed up, Séb. Some for you, no less! Mister, *I prefer reading a book over dancing*! Shocking," said King Antoine.

Marguerite's jaw clenched. Without her hat or a hooded cloak, she was exposed.

"Our apologies, ladies. Please, rise," he said; deep, commanding. Every inch the king he was always meant to become.

Marguerite winced as she took her time straightening from her curtsy. She kept her head down, but noticed Céleste shooting up at once. *She* didn't hesitate to glance at the two arrivals.

Marguerite only dared a tiny peek at the darker-haired man. He stepped in Céleste's direction, his face flooding with color and a soupçon of a smirk playing over his lips.

"You don't look familiar. Your name?"

Sébastien had been such a shy teenager, but perhaps he'd matured into a self-assured, flirtatious prince. Perhaps he *wanted* to find a suitable wife. In his adolescence, all he cared about was reading and going on adventures in the forest. Here, at eighteen, he seemed to have become a grown man. A prince.

He lingered before Céleste, whose cheeks were ashen. "I-I'm Céleste Richel, daughter of the Marquess of Valeville." She lowered into another clumsy curtsy. Antoine, she'd figured out, but Sébastien was still unknown to her. "But... who are you?"

Marguerite had no choice—she had to interfere, to save Céleste's reputation.

Jeopardizing her anonymity, she jerked her head up. "Céleste," she said, drawing Sébastien's attention. His muddy brown eyes fixed on her, widening as he opened his mouth to speak. "This is His Highness, Prince Sébastien."

The prince's hand flew to his chest, and though he didn't immediately squeak in shock, he couldn't quit staring at Marguerite. "Indeed."

Her insides were about to spill out, but Marguerite gestured at Antoine. In awe—or shock, she couldn't tell—he squinted at her, lips parting, not a sound coming out.

"And as you may have guessed, this is His Majesty," she said. "King Antoine."

When she met his hazel-lit gaze, his cheeks flushed. "You…"

Those eyes were still as captivating as in their youth. Still able to draw Marguerite in and swallow her whole, drag her into a spiral of emotions she'd refused to confront for years.

Sébastien nudged him, clearly catching on to the situation. "Hush, Brother, you've scared them enough already."

Sébastien had unknowingly saved her hide.

Marguerite turned to Céleste. There was no point delaying the inevitable; the two men would want explanations.

"Hurry to the Winter Garden and wait for me. I'll meet you there soon." She shoved the girl towards the ballroom exit. "I must speak with the king and the prince about the presentation."

Céleste backed off as commanded, though her features were pinched with confusion. "Is that allowed without a chaperone?"

"I *am* a chaperone." Marguerite's brows flicked upward. "Now go!"

Céleste let out a weakened whimper and buzzed off.

Marguerite shifted to the men in time to catch Sébastien following the girl's silhouette as she scampered out, a twinkle of interest lingering in his gaze.

Once the doors closed, he dropped his act and gave

Marguerite a proper once-over. "You… you're…"

She wanted to say something witty, but Antoine took her breath away before she could formulate coherent words. She saw parts of the old him—the fun-loving prince who wanted nothing more than to make his father proud. The dashing young man who'd made her heart flutter with all sorts of feelings she couldn't identify.

She willed her heart to settle down now, before those feelings resurfaced tenfold. He'd *hurt* her. She couldn't fall victim to the subtle but serious ways her body woke up when he was near.

"Yes," she said, her entire body trembling. "I'm here."

"I was going to say," Sébastien's voice choked, "*alive.*"

Marguerite heard him, but her focus wouldn't leave Antoine's face. She could try her damndest to pretend he no longer had an effect on her, but she'd be lying. He was more handsome than she remembered. His hair was darker, splashed with light strands. Tall, rugged, elegantly dressed—a copy of his father, grown-up and responsible.

A King.

She cowered, her legs aching from how they shook. And they shook harder as years of words Antoine hadn't had an opportunity to say unveiled all over his face, darkening his expression.

His ash-brown brows furrowed, and he crossed his arms over his broad chest. His gaze linked with hers once more, but no warmth emanated from him. Only questions she wasn't sure how to answer.

"Marguerite? What are you doing here?"

Céleste backed into the East Wing, leaving the ballroom door ajar—unsure if it was proper to leave Marguerite alone with the two royals. Two men.

She squinted at the door-frame, recalling the king and the prince's familiarity with Lady Marjorie.

Lady Marjorie claimed she didn't *know* the royals, though she'd been to the Totresian royal court before today. So why did the king and his younger brother look at her as if having seen her many times? It was obvious recognition that Céleste had caught in their gazes.

They *knew* her, didn't they?

Abandoning her lady made her uneasy, but disobeying would get Céleste in trouble. The more trouble she caused, the bigger the chances she'd be sent home—before finding out if the duchess in her book was nothing but a wild story invented by a jealous court-dweller.

Céleste's thirst for adventure made her want to pursue this mystery, like a quest. She knew it deep in her bones. The duchess had lived here. She'd dined, danced with the royals, shared the same roof as them.

She meandered into the Winter Garden. Inside, she embraced the silence and the flowery scents and closed her eyes. Serenity soothed the wild thoughts crashing through her.

Her nose led her a few paces forward to sniff at a rosebush. The petals were a bright, vibrant red, dripping with fragrance and life. Winter beauties—the most exquisite roses Céleste had ever seen. Surrounding the bush were daisies, turned golden from the torchlight cast on them.

She was about to lean down to smell them when a far-right door squeaked open.

She jumped backwards, her heart skipping a beat. The castle overflowed with wandering royals, as she'd learned an instant before in the ballroom. She needed to be careful.

Two women entered, extravagance evident with every step they took. One had fiery scarlet tresses and wore a majestic dress of the same shade. A glittering, golden crown rested on her head, nestled between flowers and fluffy feathers. She spoke to the second person who followed her in.

"So she came, Your Grace?" The gorgeous woman pursed her lips in a fake smile. Céleste could detect the insincerity from where she stood.

The second lady, just as radiant but with a much stiffer posture, wore a sapphire dress with demure sleeves and a high collar.

She entered and stood near the red-headed lady, but leaned

away, nostrils wrinkling. "She had no choice, so yes." Her dark chocolate curls were wound up into a tight bun, blue feathers protruding from it. No crown—yet there was something regal about how she carried herself.

Céleste raised to her full height, pretending to be absorbed in the flower bush, hoping to blend in with the scenery. She backed too far into the shrubs and nearly lost her balance trying to extract herself.

The crowned woman peered in Céleste's direction. She was hard to ignore. Her presence lit up the Winter Garden, exuding confidence and command.

"We have company." Her voice was pleasant, like the higher notes of a harp, with the tiniest hints of a French accent—Céleste had overheard French many a time at the academy and identified it with ease.

She sank into a trembling curtsy, raising her chin enough to see the crimson-coiffed lady sweeping closer, the brunette on her heels.

With a silent curse, Céleste tucked her jaw to her neck.

They paused near her, and the scarlet-dressed lady spoke again, soft like a peach. "And who might you be?"

Céleste swallowed. "Céleste Richel, daughter of the Marquess of Valeville, Your Graces." She hiccuped, then gasped. "Your Majesties! I meant Your Majesties!"

A shameful howling in her skull put her on the verge of tears.

If news of such mistakes traveled to her father, he'd disown her. Issuing erroneous addresses towards royals? Awful.

"Rise, child," said the other lady, her tone so raspy it sent chills down Céleste's spine.

Céleste was hesitant to lift her chin fully—but as soon as she steadied on her feet, a hand reached out and did so for her.

The second woman's fingertips pressed hard into Céleste's skin. Her face showed discreet signs of age—a few subtle lines near her mouth and over her forehead—and her cold, mahogany eyes glared at every inch of Céleste's complexion, seeking every imperfection. She clenched Céleste so tight, her teeth ached.

"Richel, you said?" Her warm, liquor-tinted breath splashed over Céleste's cheeks, turning them uncomfortably hot.

When the woman released her, Céleste's spit caught in her throat as she struggled to stop the lower part of her face from plummeting. "Yes, Your… Majesty?"

The red-headed lady was unfazed by her companion's harsher demeanor. Her unnaturally bright blue eyes sparkled in the torchlight, in rhythm with the intricate rubies on her crown. "Who are you here with, Miss Richel? You're not unaccompanied, correct?" The accent surfaced again—tangy like a ripe fruit.

Céleste's tongue tied in her mouth. "I'm with my chaperone, Lady Marjorie. She's attending business elsewhere and asked me to wait for her here."

Something told her *not* to reveal Lady Marjorie's location, lest it bring on more complications.

The red-head grinned eerily; the brunette's eyebrows furrowed. "Marjorie? Interesting. And she told you to wait here?" said the latter.

"She, uh… yes, she did." Céleste's knees buckled, but she forced herself upright.

"Marjorie?" A pinch of irritation infused the brunette's timbre as she sent a cryptic side-glance to the red-head.

Céleste shifted her weight from foot to foot. The mention of her chaperone seemed to spark a silent debate between them. For the second instance that evening, she wondered if her mistress was more popular than she'd claimed.

"Where are our manners?" The red-haired woman thrust her chest out. "I'm Queen Adelaide, and it's a pleasure to make your acquaintance, Miss Richel. Next time, please address only *me* as Majesty. I understand your confusion, since the former queen is with me."

The former queen in question—the dowager—flinched.

Céleste set a hand over her breastbone. "Of course, Your Majesty, Your Grace. My sincerest apologies. It's a pleasure to meet you as well."

"You're new at court; your chaperone isn't. She should have asked you to wait in the hallway, or closer to wherever she's having her business. You attend her, do you not?" The queen's accent thickened as her tone soured, despite her never faltering grin.

Unease settled in Céleste's gut. "Yes, Majesty. Again, I beg that you forgive me."

The queen forced a wider smile and brushed Céleste's cheek, her fingers less abrasive than the dowager's frigid touch. "This is a warning. You're not in trouble and I don't mean to frighten you." She dropped her head in a polite nod. "Enjoy the rest of your evening."

With a shiver, Céleste dipped into another curtsy. "Thank you, Majesty. I wish you the same."

The queen crept to the door to the right, muttering in French under her breath, a trail of vanilla musk in her wake.

The dowager, not so keen to follow, approached Céleste. "I

recommend you not to meander about the castle, Miss Richel. I'm sure my staff warned you about that when you arrived. You're lucky to not be one of my son's contenders." A mix of fire and ice swirled in her eyes when she pulled away. "I would remove you from court at once, were I queen. An underage girl parading the halls unaccompanied before the presentation ceremony? Please," she sneered, "remind your *chaperone* of this." She trudged out without another word.

Once the door closed, Céleste deflated. Tremors took over her, almost knocking her to her knees.

If she'd jeopardized her stay at the castle, or put Lady Marjorie in serious trouble, she'd never forgive herself.

She dashed to the door she'd come through, and buzzed into the East Wing, panting. Dizzy.

Dowager Clémentine.

The name alone quieted an entire room when uttered. Rumors spoke of her cruelty and sternness. Céleste's father's advisors whispered of her controlling nature.

She'd come to the academy on the day after graduation, or so the reports said. No one knew what for, but the girls spoke of her haunting presence for weeks. Céleste had listened, and taken note—*do not infuriate the dowager.*

She fanned herself, exhaling in quick breaths. After a few minutes, she wobbled towards the ballroom doors, intent on getting her chaperone out.

One step, two steps, three—and she smashed into someone arriving from her right.

They both stumbled, fighting against gravity.

The other individual—a man, by the sound of his informal

grunt and string of unpleasant curses—chuckled as he straightened up.

"Oh, dear," he said, "*that* will teach me to think I know my castle's corridors better than anyone."

Céleste regained her balance, blew out her cheeks, and faced him. He had lively brown eyes, this tall, muscular man, and a white linen shirt tucked into dark trousers. His frock coat, covering part of the shirt, had buttons slipping through the wrong holes. He held a tricorn hat in one hand and brushed his fingers through his short, dark-colored hair.

He grinned; no, he *smirked.* Céleste's heart skipped a few beats as she came to terms with how dashingly handsome he was.

"I'm not upset to bump into someone like you," he said, wiggling his eyebrows.

Céleste gulped, her curiosity fading at once—he was a flirt, like those in her scandalous books. "I'm sorry, my lord, I didn't see you."

"No, *my* apologies, Miss." He tugged on the hem of his coat, trying and failing to adjust it. "Though I daresay, you should be more careful when running from door to door like that."

She took in his appearance—expensive threads, the kind of rich fabrics only wealthy folk wore, and polished shoes. He had to be noble. "Yes, you're right."

She couldn't stop staring at him, certain she'd seen him before, and yet she would have remembered someone as good-looking as him.

His physique was familiar; high cheekbones, broad shoulders, the style of his hair similar to—

"Oh!" She dropped into a delayed curtsy.

My castle, he'd said, when they bumped into one another.

A wave of heat crept down her neck. This man who stood before her, grinning from cheek to cheek, could only be Prince Jules. The resemblance between him and the king and the other prince was uncanny, explaining why she felt she knew him.

"I called you *my lord*?" Her legs shook from the constant dips to the ground; she feared she'd never get used to them. "You're not a lord. Your *Highness*, forgive me, I'm so sorry."

She sensed his hand extend towards her. "Fret not, Miss." His fingertips were warm between hers as he pulled her up. "It's as much my fault as yours. And you are?"

Captivated by his almond gaze, Céleste fumbled. "Oh, uh, Céleste Richel, daughter of—"

"Richel? Emeric's sister?" He lit up. "I should have recognized those feathery gray and blue eyes, identical to his!"

Every section of her body overheated. "Oh… erm…"

The prince laughed. "He said his sibling would arrive at court soon, but didn't mention when. Nor how lovely she was."

Céleste couldn't move, her hand still trapped in his. "M-my brother spoke of me?"

"Oh, that he did." His charm was infectious, showing his ease with wooing women—quite the flirt, indeed. He appeared nothing like the imposing king, or the mysterious Prince Sébastien. Nor did he come off as sharp as his mother, the dowager queen. "It's delightful to meet you, Miss Richel, but I must ask: why are you roaming the halls of my home unaccompanied?"

Something twitched in Céleste's belly. "I'm waiting for Lady Marjorie, my chaperone. She's in the ballroom, and told me to—"

"Marjorie?" Prince Jules' pupils rounded, glistening with

intrigue. He raised a hand to halt her from saying anything else. "I don't know Marjorie."

"Our chaperone from the Totresian Royal Academy for Noble Girls. Asked here by the dowager, from what I understand—"

"*Asked* here? By the dowager?" He pointed to the ballroom door. "She's in there? With whom?"

Céleste hesitated. "With your... with your brothers, Highness."

Before she could utter another word, the prince zoomed past the guards and into the ballroom.

Céleste's jaw dropped. Did everyone in this godforsaken castle know Lady Marjorie? Or was there something else she'd yet to find out?

She crossed her arms and paced up and down the East Wing.

He stood with his arms tucked tightly to his sides—*tightly,* because if he let them loose, he'd pull her into a bone-crushing hug and never let go.

Marguerite. *His* Marguerite. The one he'd been told was dead, the one whose name had been erased from court by his mother… was here. Alive. Breathing.

Beautiful. The same wisps of golden blond hair framing her rosy cheeks; that same sparkle in her turquoise eyes. The same comely figure, the same delicate perfection to her every movement. Graceful like a flower, poised like the princess she should have been.

Like the woman he should have married.

"I'm sorry," she said, shaking her head. "I had no means to let you know I was coming. Nor could I refuse, she…"

"She?" Antoine's voice croaked as it came out, as if he hadn't used it in centuries. As if he no longer knew how to, especially when talking to her.

Sébastien grunted—Antoine had almost forgotten he was there, so wrapped up in Marguerite's presence. "Mother, I presume? She has something to do with all this?"

Marguerite shuddered, shaking her head again, faster this time. "I can't… I'm not…"

As Sébastien lurched forward to grab a hold of her before she fainted, the ballroom doors blasted open, letting in Jules. His eyes were wild—and his coat wasn't fastened properly, as usual—as he stormed over, gawking at Marguerite.

"I *knew* you were this so-called Marjorie!" He didn't wait for approval and drew Marguerite into his arms.

Marguerite bristled slightly, but didn't shove him away. Her eyes coated with tears as Jules squeezed her.

"Leave her alone," said Antoine, gripping Jules' arm to tug him away. "This must be traumatizing for her."

"For *her?*" Jules scoffed. "We were told she was *dead!*"

"And she's not," said Sébastien, ever the calm, composed sibling, stepping between Antoine and Jules before either had a chance to argue. "And I guarantee it has to do with—"

"Perhaps," Antoine interjected, eyes narrowing between his two brothers, "we should save such conversations for more private venues? There are far too many people wandering about who would easily spread rumors."

Sébastien nodded, Jules groaned.

Antoine felt his arm lifting, his hand reaching for Marguerite, to touch her, assure himself that she was real. He was about to lean in close, as if drawn to her by magic—but he stopped himself. The last time he'd seen her, she'd run from him, from his betrayal, from his callousness. She had ran from everything; this was likely the last place she wanted to be.

"I…" She swallowed and lowered her chin, unable to maintain Antoine's gaze. "I must go. Céleste… out there…"

"Oh," Jules chuckled, "she's fine. Pacing back and forth but she won't go anywhere. What an adorable little—"

"No!" snapped Antoine and Marguerite at the same time, glowering at the younger, looser-lipped prince.

Never would Antoine allow Jules to defile such an innocent young lady.

Sébastien, more demure in his flirtations, smirked briefly before refocusing on Marguerite. "You should go. Head back upstairs before Mother finds you."

"Indeed," said Marguerite, a heavy breath escaping her lips; thin, soft lips that Antoine remembered with far too much detail, considering how long it'd been since he'd last tasted them.

How he longed to taste them again. But it'd never happen; she'd never *let* it happen, and he had no right to hope for it.

"Please," he said, taking a chance—he took her hand in his and squeezed it.

He sensed her reluctance at once, but she didn't tug away. She peered at their joined hands as if trying to decide how she felt. She was cold to the touch, yet the contact sent heat swarming to all his extremities.

"Meet me at our spot, later."

"O-our…spot?" Marguerite's eyebrows furrowed. Still, she didn't pull from his grip. "Later?"

"Please." He hated the desperation in his tone, but knew he wouldn't get another chance to meet with her. With how busy court was, he'd be swamped with work and queries that would have to take precedence.

His brothers would hound him with questions, and they'd track down their mother to interrogate her—clearly, she was responsible for this.

But before all that, he needed to see *her*—alone.

After one acquiesce, Marguerite bit her lower lip, curtsied, and scurried out of the room.

The ghost of her touch remained on Antoine's skin.

"She's returned," said Sébastien, clapping Antoine's back. "She's… here."

Antoine couldn't move, though he cringed at the sting caused by his brother's hand.

"Yes, and pleased as I am to see her, what does that mean?" Jules crossed his arms, staring at the ballroom doors as they shut behind the former duchess.

"Would that I knew," whispered Antoine, touching his lips, once more recalling the final kiss they'd exchanged, days before the famed Masquerade that took her away from him. The kiss he hadn't known would be their last.

And that kiss made him wonder—if she was alive, what did that mean?

She'd returned, and he had no clue if it was for the better, or for worse.

Once outside of the ballroom, Marguerite released a heavy breath. Seeing Sébastien and Jules was a whirlwind; confronting Antoine nearly caused her to collapse.

He'd grown into such a majestic man, and her heart throbbed achingly in her chest—to resist the pull to him had been excruciating.

But she had to. There was no way she'd be able to forgive him for what he did, no matter if her body was drawn to his. No matter that something deep within her still wanted to be with him.

And now she had to meet with him later, by the gardener's cottage—*their spot.* And pretend like she wasn't still affected by him?

A clock chimed, and she counted eight rings—past time for the dowager's after-dinner stroll.

Before she could leave room for more panic, a whirl of cream frills and dark blond hair plowed into her.

"I've done something *very* wrong!" Céleste's voice was low, but Marguerite heard the worry laced in it.

What could be worse than bumping into an ex-fiancé who thought you were dead?

"What happened?"

Céleste's breaths were deep, strained. She splayed a palm over her chest. "I met the queen. The *queens*, in fact, since the dowager was with her—"

"You *what?*" Marguerite tugged Céleste away from the ballroom. "I told you to wait in the Winter Garden!"

"I did!" Céleste winced. "I traveled straight there! But they visited by surprise. I was discreet, and I curtsied, but I fear I may have displeased them, since I was unaccompanied. They were *not* happy."

Marguerite's heart raced as she pulled the girl down the King's Corridor, which led to the main entrance—to the stairs.

She'd thought seeing Antoine would be the worst part of her stay, but she'd forgotten about the queens. She let out a low groan, angry with herself for not thinking ahead. Of course they'd scour the castle, seeking disobedient ladies.

"I also startled Prince Jules!"

Marguerite peered left and right, biting her tongue. "The princes are the least of our concerns." She shook herself, willing the ice slithering down her spine to cease tormenting her. She didn't have time for this; they had to get upstairs. "Quickly!"

"But—"

"No, not here. If the queens saw you and weren't happy, then you must return to your room." Again Céleste's lips pried apart, but

Marguerite shoved her farther up. "No questions. Do as I say!"

Céleste grumbled as she climbed. Marguerite ascended after her, keeping a watchful eye in front but glancing backwards to be sure no one followed.

After arriving at the top of the stairs, they dashed forward, rounding the corridor by Esther's door, and almost slammed into a lady in swirling heaps of light blue skirts.

"Oh, pardon us, Miss." Marguerite squinted at her, and when honing in on her pointed nose, her airs of disdain, she recognized her.

Marguerite had never officially met her, yet she'd seen portraits of her; small paintings Johanna had *borrowed* from Lord Knowles when he was reviewing applications for the academy.

This was Frances Allard, daughter of the Marquess of Mara— a high-placed noble and royal advisor rumored to have had a rift with Edouard in the past.

Johanna had told Marguerite of the marquess and his nose-in-the-air daughter. She'd stumbled upon a meeting between them and Lord Knowles during one of her attempts to speak with the headmaster regarding Marguerite's freedom.

Frances wrinkled her nose as she passed them. "Good evening." She flipped a strand of dark hair from her face and resumed her trek—in a hurry.

When the young woman was out of earshot, Céleste cleared her throat. "Is she a contender?"

"I'd assume so," Marguerite said flatly.

"Should we have warned her the queens are out and about?"

Marguerite stifled a chuckle. "Not her. I happen to know her father disrespected our academy in the past. She doesn't deserve our help."

Johanna had recounted the meeting—she'd eavesdropped at the door, the sly thing. The marquess, unimpressed by the building and the grounds, had removed Frances from the academy and taken her elsewhere for the rest of her upper-level education.

Marguerite urged Céleste towards her own bedroom. "I suggest you retire for the night. Request supper to your room if you wish, but stay in it. No more wandering."

Céleste slumped. "All right. Good evening, Lady Marjorie."

Marguerite watched as she walked to her door, sighed, and wrapped her fingers around the handle. Once the latch *clicked* behind her, Marguerite twirled and raced back to the main stairs.

Antoine wouldn't wait long. But what would he say? What *was* there to say after all this time?

Once she reached the carpeted steps, she steadied herself, one hand on the banister, the other flexing and relaxing at her side.

The discussion to come was years in the waiting, and she wasn't ready for it.

11.
Céleste

Céleste waited for her adrenaline to decrease before she collapsed onto her bed. She was tempted to sneak back out, to spy on the royals at her own pace—but the encounter with the queens *and* the younger prince had spiked her nerves enough as it was.

How she yearned to figure out why Lady Marjorie was so distraught. How she wondered why Lady Marjorie's presence at court stirred up the royals—the princes, the queens, *the king.* She seemed so strangely linked to the mystery Céleste craved to solve—since the woman *knew the royals.* If she knew the royals, then surely she knew more about the duchess.

Since their arrival, Lady Marjorie's awkward attitude nudged Céleste towards disobedience. Like she'd fallen into an action-packed book, unable to flip the pages ahead to determine what would happen, unless she overstepped boundaries and peeked past walls and doors she wasn't allowed to.

She had to find out more about the *Golden Girl* from her book: the Duchess of Torrinni. Lady Marjorie knew her. The royals obviously knew her. It all began here, in this Totresian royal court.

She pried her armoire open, analyzing all the dresses within. They were proper enough, but some still had the wider hoops of earlier times. Most European women had regressed to smaller, higher-waisted dresses, though Totresia lingered a little behind in fashion; she lingered even farther behind, re-using her mother's old attire. Not out of lack of funds—her father was plenty wealthy—but because she refused to part from the beautiful fabrics her mother once wore.

It was her only way to keep the woman's memory alive within her. She'd been only fourteen when Lady Richel had died, leaving her with a bitter brother and a father who refused to show emotion, even after losing his wife.

A chill spiraled down her spine as she envisioned herself in the ballroom. What a sight she'd be in her outdated gowns, improperly addressing those around her, warranting glares from those seated atop the dais.

She closed the closet, pressing her hands to it as she took deep breaths. What she needed was counsel—a reassuring ear.

Perhaps Lady Marjorie wasn't in bed yet. She'd given Céleste a tour, but hadn't gone over any other basics of Torrinni court. Céleste wouldn't sleep if she didn't get some information to avoid future mistakes.

She knocked on the adjoining door once, twice, to no avail. "My lady?" She twisted the latch, pushed—and was met with nothing.

Lady Marjorie wasn't in her room.

"Odd. Did she not go in right after I did?" Céleste said to herself, returning to her room just as someone knocked on her door. "Where could she be?"

She tiptoed over, unsure who'd visit her at this hour. Perhaps one of the contenders, searching for their chaperone?

With a wince, she opened her door—and started.

A tall man, frills protruding from the sleeves of his fluffed-up coat, gawked down at her. "Céleste!" he said, his voice one she'd known all her life.

A voice that should have brought comfort, a smile, excitement. Yet at the sight of him, she sensed herself shriveling, and she didn't know why—her brother normally never intimidated her like this.

"Céleste?" He tipped forward, eyeing her as if she'd grown two heads. "Are you all right?" His playful grimace—one he always used when they were teasing one another—pulled her out of whatever eerie feelings she'd been experiencing.

"Emeric!" she said, her voice a touch too bubbly. "What are you doing, disturbing a lady at such an indecent hour?"

He'd tied his dark-blond hair behind his neck, and his matching ensemble of olive-green showed him as a striking courtier with flair; the image he'd told her he wanted to give of himself while at court. "If only you *were* a lady!"

She jumped into his arms. "Emeric!"

He rubbed her back. "Sister dearest, I'm overjoyed to see you." He held her at arm's length, inspecting her from head-to-toe, and scowled. "But have you not learned it's unladylike to hop into a man's arms?"

"Not when that man is my brother!" She tapped his shoulder.

"What are you doing here? Shouldn't you be in some Torrinni tavern frolicking with your latest conquest?"

His cheeks flared a deep shade of magenta. "Watch your language! And no, because I was craving a spot of evening tea—you know, like in the old days? You used to join me, and we would exchange gossip about Father's advisors. But this time," he grinned, "we can gossip about other things."

"I don't think I'm supposed to have guests…" She thought of her chaperone—her *missing* chaperone—and chewed the insides of her cheeks.

"Nonsense." Without awaiting her answer, he barreled into her room. "I'm your brother."

Her stomach bubbled with anticipation as he summoned a servant girl, who appeared slightly squeamish about bringing him and Céleste drinks.

He extracted a few coins from his pocket, dropping them into her palm. "Do bring us the best tea blend, with a few snacks. I insist."

The girl scampered off, leaving Céleste to wonder if she admired her brother's audacity, or worried about it.

Holding his lantern, Antoine shuffled his feet in front of the gardener's cottage.

Would she show? He hadn't issued a formal invitation, but surely she wouldn't dare refuse him, *the king*.

Or would she? They hadn't seen each other in three years. She'd departed in tears, her heart torn to pieces. Who knew who this new version of his beloved Marguerite was?

If she chose to show, she'd encounter no obstacles on her way. Clémentine would be in the solar, Adelaide with the dowager or yelling at servants in the ballroom. Sébastien would be lounging in the library, and Jules had snuck out to town.

A whiff of ice nipped at his cheeks as he got onto his tip-toes, peering down the pathway leading to the castle. It was slippery at night—he worried she may have forgotten that. Or that she'd be questioned by the guards, who'd wonder why a young woman of her caliber attempted to walk in the moonlit gardens—

He heard her before he saw her. Her footsteps echoed in tandem with the royal pond's fountain. Her shadow flitted over the ghosts of tulip bushes and wildflowers.

It was her. It had to be.

He perked up, standing in front of the darkened, worn-out facade of the gardener's cottage, trees swaying in the breeze overhead.

She appeared at the beginning of the path towards the cottage, her head lowered.

Antoine's lungs compressed inside his chest. He couldn't move, for fear of scaring her. He wasn't sure if she'd seen him. A part of him didn't *want* her to see him, so he could continue looking at her so candidly.

A vision he'd only thought possible in his dreams.

She looked up suddenly, breath catching as she spotted him. "Our spot," she said, taking a stride backwards as Antoine approached.

"Maggie?" His voice came out deep, but quaking.

She said nothing, hoisting her lantern up, as if double-checking that he was, indeed, the king.

He lifted his own light, tipping his head back slightly so she'd see his eyes beneath his tricorn hat. His ruddy mahogany travel cloak flapped in the gentle wind, the only movement keeping him alert.

She came. He'd seen her earlier, yet the fluttering in his ribcage returned as if he hadn't gazed at her in years.

"Maggie. It *is* you." He lessened the distance between them.

She dropped into a curtsy. "Your Majesty." Her tone was icy, foreign to him. Her cheeks were red, and not from the low temperature, he could tell.

He studied her: the perfection of her lips, the glittering eyes, the proud posture she often didn't realize she had. "No need to be so formal."

She readjusted herself, rolling her golden flower pendant between gloved fingers. "It doesn't change the truth, Antoine."

He shuddered at his name uttered in her gracious voice.

"Please, explain this to me," he said, stepping forward again. "Where have you been? We thought you were… wait, let me rephrase that. How have you been? Why are you here? What's going on?"

Her grimace deepened with his every word. Did she loathe him that much? Had three years not given her enough time to consider forgiving him?

He recalled Sébastien's words, earlier, when they left the ballroom. *"But would you forgive her if she had chosen another man over you, no matter the circumstances?"*

Antoine's answer was a firm yes, but seeing her now, imagining her with another man made him think otherwise.

All the color melted from her cheeks. "The court summoned me; I told you this earlier. There's nothing to add. I'm a chaperone for Jules' and Sébastien's contenders."

She was cold. A statue of beauty, thorns outlining every inch of her.

No, she hadn't forgiven him, and never would. And sadly, he couldn't blame her. How could he ever hold this against her? *He* was to blame.

He released a low groan. "Yes, you said that—but why? Who summoned you? Why was I, *the king*, unaware of it?"

Her eyebrows furrowed. "Didn't you sign an agreement for a batch of ladies to present themselves to your brothers?" He nodded, though not without an eye-roll. "Didn't that document state that a chaperone, Lady Marjorie, was coming with?"

Again he nodded—but this time he frowned. "Well, I didn't know *you* were Lady Marjorie, but yes, I approved it."

"It's a code name the academy's headmaster came up with to protect my identity, and communicated it to the court." She released her pendant and straightened up. "So there, that explains my being here. Any other questions?"

"Why must you—" He huffed. She'd been mildly polite back in the ballroom, mostly shocked to see him. But this woman was fierce, unforgiving.

Not the Maggie he was used to.

They used to confide in one another. She'd pretend to not be affected by his mother's cruelty, and he'd pretend his father's reign didn't intimidate him. But that was then; in happier days where they were too young to understand the troubles around them. Now, they were adults. He was a king, and she was far more wounded by him than she wanted to show.

And more beautiful than she'd ever been. How was that possible?

"The Totresian Royal Academy for Noble Girls? You've been there? For how long? You didn't answer that."

"Roughly three years. In January. After…" She scooched backwards.

"Three years. You've been so close for that long and I had no idea?" He shook his head. "Who is behind this nonsense? Tell me, so I can arrest them. Smuggling and sheltering a noble of your standing…"

"I'm not a high-placed noble anymore." She tapped her foot to the ground. "And you know who did it. Don't act like you're oblivious of who controls everything in this kingdom."

His huff of defiance was so pronounced, it surprised even him. "How dare you—"

"It's true!" Frosty fog floated out of her mouth as her breaths turned harsh. "*She* did this. She locked me up. Kept me alive to torment me. Then brought me here to torment me *more.*"

He slipped his hands into his pockets. Another minute and he'd reach for her, draw her close.

He shouldn't have done this, shouldn't have put her on the spot. They weren't ready for this kind of proximity, and yet he hadn't been able to resist being alone with her, once more.

Potentially for the last time, if Marguerite had her way.

"Then I'm appalled at her, at what you imply she did. But she said you were dead. We had no reason to think she was lying. She *erased* you."

"I ran away." She placed a hand over her stomach. "I dishonored her. This was my punishment. But I'm here now, alive, somewhat well. No need to worry about me."

She pivoted, prepared to leave, but Antoine caved and snatched her hand, stopping her.

The leather of their gloves collided, and the gesture sent a jolt of warmth racing to his heart.

She turned her blurry gaze to him as he snuck his fingers between hers. She didn't pull away, but her arm shook as if about to.

"Maggie, I…" Mountains of words piled up inside, but he had

no idea where to start, how to beseech her for forgiveness.

She attempted to yank away. "Antoine—"

"I'm sorry. For my choices. For *her* behavior, for all these years. Truly sorry. She had no right. I'm the king, for God's sake, though I wasn't when this started, but she continues to defy me. I will find a way to fix this. I will."

Marguerite's strength took him by surprise—she retracted her hand, seething. "And now you'll tell me you can't control her?"

His lips parted, but no sound escaped. Could he lie to her? After all these years, and finally seeing her alive, as he'd always prayed?

She cracked her knuckles. "I had access to all sorts of rumors at the academy, despite being a prisoner."

"Rumors?" His voice crackled. "*Prisoner?*"

"How she acted as if she were still queen, abusing her power, using spies for who knows what. You let that slide?" His arm twitched, about to touch her again, but Marguerite slanted away before he could. "Yes, you're the king, yet your mother acts as the supreme ruler of this country." He attempted to speak, but she wouldn't have it. "No. Your apologies mean nothing. Too little, too late. You permitted the dowager to manipulate you. And in any case," she scoffed, "you chose *her*, remember? How am I supposed to forgive that? How am I supposed to forgive you?"

He sensed a vein throbbing under his jaw as he put his mouth back in place. "I had no choice, Maggie. I know you're aware of this, somewhere in that beautifully intricate mind of yours."

He dared another step forward, but she curtsied to once more escape him. "My name is Marguerite." The sound of her rage bit him, poisoned him like a deadly snake. "In public, it's *Marjorie.*"

She flashed one last look at him, as if ending the chapter, closing the book that was their love.

He jolted forward, worried she was about to walk out of his life—again. And if he didn't catch her, didn't block her route, they'd never speak again. "Maggie, please—"

"This has been inappropriate enough, so if you'll please excuse me, Majesty, I will retire to my room."

Without waiting for his approval, she whisked around and hurried the way she'd come.

He remained rooted to the spot, gawking at her disappearing form. All the anger, the confusion pent up for almost three years surfaced at last as he swiveled—and punched his fist into the weak facade of the gardener's cottage.

13.
Céleste

Emeric's order of tea and biscuits arrived promptly. It was past nine o'clock, but that didn't seem to bother him in the slightest.

"You didn't eat dinner, I assume?" he said, as Céleste dug into the pastries like a starving scavenger.

She sat on her bed, facing the fire, the flames mighty and warming, the popping sounds soothing. A golden teapot rested on the nightstand, atop a gold-encrusted tray glimmering in the firelight.

The ticking of the clock mirrored Céleste's steady heartbeats.

"Travel suits you." Emeric served her, then himself. The scorching liquid deposited into the porcelain mugs, filling to the rim. "You look refreshed as ever."

"And you, all grown up! Respected by royal staff and handing out money to obtain tea and biscuits after hours—you fit in with ease." She took her drink and blew the steam away.

Emeric laughed. "Yes, well, that's the way of things. For the role Father assigned me, I must play the game. Everything works with money and word-of-mouth at court." He sat beside her and sipped, not waiting for the liquid to cool down, eyes turning a radiant blue behind the steam. "Last I saw you, you hid in the academy library. Tell me—how many books did you bring with you?"

"A few." She giggled at the recollection of Emeric finding romantic titles in the library during a visit in her Sophomore year. "Nothing too improper."

"Such ladylike manners! Might you *be* a lady, now?"

She squinted at him. "I may have grown into my future role."

"You have! Your behavior—aside from the hug—has been prim and proper. I'm proud!" He set his teacup down on the nightstand and clasped his hands. "So, confess: how are the ladies you came here with?"

She set a hand over her heart. "How indecent!"

"What? Isn't it a valid question? Have I overstepped?"

She sniffed at the citrus and jasmine scent emanating from her cup. When she took a swig, the flavor exploded on her tongue, filling her with delight. "No, you haven't. But do you wish to spend our evening discussing *them?*"

Emeric clapped his thigh. "Don't make me beg! We'll chat about other things, I promise, but I need to know—are any of the girls from the royal academy worth my time? Would Father approve of them?"

A crooked smile slid across her face as she put down her cup. "You should wait to meet them for yourself."

Esther's over-the-top attitude. Harriet's mistrust of

everything. Cristina's less than appropriate necklines. Charlotte's snotty reputation. Julia's clingy nature. Did Emeric expect genuine prospects? Was he done frolicking about with women of no meaning, those he thought Céleste and Marquess Richel knew nothing about?

He joined his hands below his chin. "Tell me! The noblewomen already here disappointed me. Boring, prudish pests who fawned over the princes. Tell me if the ones you accompanied are interesting! Able to hold a semi-intelligent conversation? Dare I say, pretty?"

Céleste fought a snort, settling for a polite laugh to cover it up. "My, my, you're so shallow!"

"Help me!" He resembled the teenager she once ran through the orchards and cherry-tree backyard with, impatient and uncaring for etiquette. "The ladies-in-waiting only lust after the princes, too. The foreigners have accents I can't understand. I'm tolerant, but if I'm to joke and my beloved doesn't understand, what's the point? Tell me not to abandon hope! Tell me at least one Totresian lady will appease me!"

"They're from well-known, well-reputed families. Well-bred, well-mannered. As for pretty," she bunched her lips, pretending to think it through, "I suppose they're decent enough. A redhead, one with dark auburn curls, one brunette, one with raven hair, one blonde—"

The corners of Emeric's mouth upturned. "Pretty, then? Not," he feigned choking, "*hideous*?"

Céleste had to admit—the five academy graduates were beautiful. She envied their effortless poise and ease with face-paint and hairstyles and knowledge of fashion.

When she didn't respond, Emeric whimpered like an abandoned puppy begging for attention. "How about this: would you accept any of them as your sister?"

Céleste actually choked on another macaron. "Emeric! Please! Not while I'm eating!" She forced down the rest of her bite and brushed crumbs from her lap. "I'm not interested in speaking of them. They're graduates, eager to marry, to be the fancy ladies their teachers taught them to become. So yes, they're beautiful. They're here to find husbands. They're prettily powdered, with too many layers of rouge. But they're also here for the princes. Not for you."

"So serious tonight," he said, seizing a biscuit, taking a bite. "But the princes only get two. If my math is correct, that leaves me seven? Nine contenders in total."

Céleste's jaw fell open. "You haven't changed, have you?" A grin drew across his lips, and she tapped his shoulder. "Still playing with hearts? This is important!"

His smile faltered as he got to his feet and stepped away from the bed. "Since when are you so motherly? Have you started enjoying books written for adults?"

Céleste scrunched her nose. "My books have taught me more than you will ever know, brother dearest."

The energy in the room had shifted—no longer fun, but soon to turn disappointing.

She knew better than to have important conversations with Emeric. His stubbornness was relentless, and his temper was monstrous. She hadn't witnessed it in years, not since their mother's death, but she recognized the signs.

"So *you* have not changed, either. Still daydreaming your way through your studies."

She huffed. "My daydreaming never interfered with my studies."

"So you intend to honor Father after your graduation? To put away your fairytales and focus on learning to be a wife?"

The comment burned through her. Emeric was old-fashioned, despite his frivolous ways. He wanted an intelligent lady to chat with and marry, but refused for his sister to have more modern morals.

"These fairytales you refer to are *mysteries*. They're a distraction after my classes. Many students enjoy similar pastimes." Her voice lost its intensity. "Not all men frown upon women opening a novel from time to time."

He retrieved his mug and chugged from it. "*From time to time* being the key. Real novels don't bother me in the slightest. What crazy adventures have your mysteries put you on now? Any daydreams you concocted involving anyone or anything at court? Should I warn the staff to beware of the girl who reads as she walks?"

She placed her hands in her lap. Since she'd found her favorite book, she'd kept it hidden from everyone. Only Lord Knowles and Johanna knew of it, and as of recently, Lady Marjorie. She'd promised herself to never reveal it to Emeric.

But he'd lived at court for over a year; he spied for their father, mingled among nobles, which meant he may be able to locate the answers she needed to figure out if the duchess was real. No matter how uncomfortable it made her to ask.

"If you must know, the story I'm reading has pushed me to solve a legitimate mystery."

"Ah, and what mystery would that be?" He finished his beverage. "Figuring out which pattern the ladies will knit tomorrow? Who will wear the prettiest dress at the ball?"

"Must you be so condescending?" She reached for her teacup. "I'm investigating the identity of a duchess from my favorite book, *The Golden Girl*."

He cocked his head. "*The Golden Girl?* What an odd title."

"It's a non-fiction book, about," she said slowly, "the Duchess of Torrinni."

"The Duchess of…" He smacked his palm to his forehead. "Oh, Heavens, you don't mean the rumored woman who was supposedly engaged to our good King Antoine?"

Céleste focused on the platter of macarons. "The very same."

"You mean to tell me there's a book about this rumor?" Emeric's nose turned up. "And you claim it's a real mystery you aim to solve?"

Céleste nodded, but regretted it when Emeric's up-turned nose became a snarl.

"Nonsense. Those are myths and made-up stories of a child. A few nobles spoke of this rumor—but that's all it is. A preposterous one, at that. To imply King Antoine loved someone else before he married Queen Adelaide? You disappoint me, Céleste. I mocked you in brotherly tenderness, but this is different. I thought you read better books. Less romanticized and childish." He stomped towards the front of her room.

"The duchess is real, and I'll prove it!" She got up and stamped her foot as she set her fists on her hips. "And I'm sorry to disappoint you, but I'm a woman! Women read romanticized books! That, and I knit patterns and try on dresses for balls, yes!

Fruitless actions in your eyes, but they're the foundation of ours, as ladies of Totresia."

Emeric's neck snapped towards her. "Not *you*. We hoped for you to act as a decent, well-raised lady, but this? Father expects much more, including balls and knitting. He wants to see a mature woman; not a back-talking, novel-reading girl. I'd started the groundwork, seeking a suitable husband for you here, but with that attitude? That dreadful book clouding your vision? You will stay unwed and bring shame to us."

"You know nothing about it!" She detested fighting with him, and had avoided it for years, but it seemed inevitable.

"No one will ever take you seriously. It's not proper reading material. And the rumor is *false*."

She strained not to scream at him as her cheeks heated, anger boiling below the surface. "You sound like *them*."

He kept his distance, his eyes a charcoal fury, like thick smoke from a bonfire. "Like whom? Your headmaster? He endorses such stupid stories? Allows them at the academy? A real man would have confiscated such a novel if he had found it."

"Since when do you say such crude things about noblemen?"

After Mother's death, he'd become bitter, it was true. But it had never been this bad.

His jaw clenched and he stuffed his fists behind his back. "Since I realized men like him are the reason we have such slim pickings at this court. And now, my sister will do nothing to aid me. Upon seeing you this evening, I thought… well, it matters not, because I was wrong." He sneered. "The way you implied all I deserved were scraps of the women the princes chose? That was rude. You must be more supportive of me." He leveled his tone, yet

Céleste heard the lingering shame in it and saw the disgust as it washed over his expression.

She wished she could put something between them, an obstacle to ensure he wouldn't march over and hit her for speaking up. "I have grown up, and I do support you. Was it not you who jested about having seven girls to yourself?"

"I *jested*. *You* were serious! Thank the Heavens you have another year to learn before becoming a lady of the court."

His cruelty had reached levels she hadn't pictured in her nightmares. Their mother would have reminded him of his place, and she doubted her father would let such behaviors slide.

Her brows knitted together. "I'm the top of my junior class. I earned high marks from all my professors. My headmaster sent me here so I'd learn the ways of the court because he expects me to succeed!" She sensed herself start to growl. "I *will* uncover this mystery, whether or not you believe it."

Emeric massaged the bridge of his nose. "Enough, please—"

"No. You need to hear it." She wouldn't let him leave the room before getting the last word. "Father *will* be proud of me, because my reading habits won't affect my performance. They never have, and never will. I will graduate, and return to court and marry the most decent noble alive, and you will regret your words!"

Emeric pressed his fingertips to his temples, using his free hand to open the door. "I've had enough for one night. Good evening, sister."

The door slammed behind him, and Céleste shuddered. "Good evening to *you,* too."

Had he turned drearier since he'd moved to court? Had the

men he frequented warped him into being demeaning and disrespectful while demanding the respect of others, women in particular?

A part of her regretted her implosions. But the duchess was real, and he wouldn't stop her from proving it. His spiteful comments wouldn't deter her from investigating.

14.
Marguerite

Marguerite ran faster than she ever had, faster even than the night she'd escaped from Torrinni Castle.

She still felt his fingers squeezing between hers; the warmth of his gloves against her frozen ones. Still sensed her heart racing out of control, urging her to do something stupid like fall into his arms, seek his comforting embrace—

No, that was out of the question. He was the reason she needed comfort in the first place.

She had to ignore her body's requests, and learn fast. Surely that wasn't the last time she'd end up alone with him. Surely he'd want to communicate with her again, and she needed to be stronger than that.

She rounded the corner in time to see someone slipping out of Céleste's room. Even through eyes blurred with tears, she had no doubt; from the tall stature, the suited silhouette, to the chock-full of dark blond hair atop his head, it was a man.

She opened her mouth to call him out, but she was too far—she'd have to yell across the hallway, and that was ill-viewed for a lady, no matter what time it was.

Furthermore, she was out in the hallways when she wasn't supposed to be.

She waited for him to disappear up the service steps—a nobleman, then, if he was headed to the royal floor—and hurried to Céleste's door, prying it open and slipping into her room.

"Lady Marjorie?" Céleste gasped, jumping up from her bed.

"Who was that?" Marguerite set her fists to her hips, narrowing her gaze on the girl. "A man exiting your chambers? And after-hours, of all things?"

"Your eyes," said the girl, slowly approaching Marguerite, head cocked in confusion. "They're bloodshot. Are you all right?"

Marguerite shimmied backwards. "Answer my question!"

"That was my brother." Céleste sniffled; she, too, had been crying. She mentioned Marguerite's eyes, but her own were red and watery as well.

"Oh." Marguerite's arms fell to her sides as relief flushed over her. "I… didn't recognize him from afar."

Céleste's eyebrows lurched up. "You know my brother?"

"No." Marguerite peered over at the adjoining room to her suite. "I've seen him before, when he visited you at the academy."

"Where were you?" Céleste folded her arms over her chest, inspecting Marguerite from head-to-toe.

The accusatory tone of her words took Marguerite aback. "None of your business. I'm back, and no more nightly visits, even from family members, please." Céleste's mouth opened for a smart retort, but Marguerite wouldn't have it. "Good night. I will see you in the morning."

In her chambers, Marguerite disrobed, not bothering to remove the paint from her face nor comb the tangles in her hair. The meeting with Antoine took far more energy and emotion than she'd expected, and exhaustion wrapped around her limbs, numbing them.

She stared at the roaring fire, praying for a soothing sleep.

But the restful slumber she yearned for never came. Instead, it was turbulent.

Being in the Torrinni Castle brought back every memory, from pleasant to awful. Marguerite experienced them all in her dreams. Dark stares from atop bright thrones; fiery hair twirling in dizzying motions; dangerous scowls concealed by flowery masks; hooves beating on wet cobblestones.

She forced herself into a seated position. A slither of light escaped through the side of her curtain-covered window.

The clock above her fireplace chimed six times, worsening her headache. Like drums hammering, rattling her nerves, screeching—

There were no drums. Someone was knocking on the door.

She grumbled as she threw off her covers. "At six o'clock?"

She slipped a robe over her night chemise and tiptoed to the door.

A page boy stood on the other side. "A summons for you, my lady." He handed her a note and ran off.

Marguerite closed her door as she squinted at the royal crest on the paper. The familiar handwriting accompanying it made her muscles turn rigid.

My dearest Marguerite,

Would you join me for a spot of tea before breakfast? Eight o'clock sharp in my solar.

Queen A.

She dropped the note as her knuckles tightened.

The adjoining door burst open, and Céleste tumbled through, a peach-colored dress half-draping over her undergarments.

"What was that?" She yawned, clumsily bouncing into the area.

If Marguerite hadn't been so preoccupied, she would have laughed. Céleste's tresses were a tangled mess, her eyes puffy, her clothes wrinkled like she'd slept in them.

Marguerite picked up the message and set it on her vanity table. "A summons. Nothing that should concern you."

She hesitated to ring the bell by her door and wake Johanna. She didn't want to attend this meeting, to confront the *other woman*. But Adelaide would seek her out, no matter what.

She pinched the bridge of her nose.

Céleste combed her fingers through her knotted strands and scratched her cheek. "Should I not," she yawned again, "go with you?"

"No." If Marguerite said too much, the girl wouldn't let her leave; if she said nothing, the girl might follow her to spy. "The queen wants to meet with me to discuss the presentation ceremony and my role in it as a chaperone."

Céleste's brows tugged up. "Didn't you discuss that with the king and the princes yesterday?"

Marguerite flinched. "I did, but the queen has a right to inquire, as well." She fixed her face into a frown. "You mustn't pry. It's unladylike."

Céleste backed off, wringing her hands.

As the girl's foot passed the threshold back into her suite, Marguerite relaxed her tense muscles. "I apologize for my harshness. Enjoy your day, but make yourself scarce. Spend more time with your brother." She trudged to the string linking to Johanna's room. "Avoid run-ins with royals."

Céleste slunk behind her door.

Alone again, Marguerite sat at her vanity.

She didn't want to see Queen Adelaide, inevitable as that was.

***

Clad in a cream and pale-green gown, Marguerite set off with cautious strides. She should have nestled a hat or a bonnet atop her half-pinned curls, in case she bumped into anyone—but last she heard bonnets were forbidden at court, by none other than the woman she was about to meet with.

Each step broke her spirit. The everlasting image from three years ago refused to leave her thoughts—Adelaide curtsying before Antoine, parting her lips in a brilliant grin as he beckoned her to join him.

That same woman, now queen, was about to taunt her more.

Adelaide was an ally in the past, but that was no longer the case. The red-headed devil had seized the man Marguerite had loved. Staying poised and polite in her presence would be difficult.

For her own sanity—and to avoid upsetting the dowager—

Marguerite had to try.

She trod down the Long Corridor as the clock chimed eight times, each ring mirroring her thumping heartbeat.

When she stopped in front of the solar's familiar oak door, she swallowed, and closed her eyes as the nearest guard knocked for her.

The door opened at once, and a man in the traditional light burgundy Totresian butler's uniform gaped at the guard, then at her. "Yes?"

"The queen invited me." She clutched a corner of her dress. "For tea."

The man turned to a woman perched on an immense sofa in the middle of the room. Marguerite peered in the same direction, and a sharp pain spread in her chest.

The woman's majestic white petticoat, decorated with bold scarlet roses, covered the red-tinted cushions.

Raising her sparkling crystal gaze in their direction, the queen waved, her crimson curls pooling like waves of satin over her shoulders. "Let her in, Marcus. She's my guest." She smiled as the man ushered Marguerite inside. "Don't mind him—he's overprotective."

Marguerite paused, tempted to return to her suite.

"Please, sit with me," said Adelaide, patting the only space on the settee that wasn't drowning under her skirts.

Reluctance swelled in Marguerite's belly. She ignored the thundering in her scalp as she noticed the touches of vermilion and gold that accentuated every inch of the grand room. Clémentine once kept it dreary and stuffy, but Adelaide had applied exuberance and vibrancy.

Light poured in through the floor-to-ceiling windows across from the door, blinding Marguerite as she moved.

A hint of vanilla wafted from the two steaming cups on the table in front of Adelaide's couch. Several chaises spread out around her, each of different materials and patterns, but all red. The hearth glowing in the far-right fizzled.

She curtsied before the queen, glimpsing the game tables and seats on the other side of the sofa, the bunches of yarn and patchwork, the books and empty cups, a glass of what might have been wine.

Where were all the ladies? Didn't they attend their queen at all hours of the night and day?

"Majesty." Memories rushed in so fast Marguerite came close to tipping forward. "What an honor for you to—"

"Oh, stop that, Maggie." The queen flicked her wrist. "This isn't a formal meeting, for God's sake! Now come sit with me!"

Shocked to hear her nickname—the second instance in less than twenty-four hours—Marguerite straightened up.

In their teenage days at court, Adelaide had been full of spunk and adventure. She'd loved lavish balls and sumptuous dinners, and spent her time bad-mouthing Clémentine.

This woman wasn't the same, despite her unchanged French accent and her still perfect features. She wasn't reputed as an informal queen; the gossip in the academy corridors didn't match this behavior.

As soon as Marguerite's bottom reached the sofa, Adelaide's lacy gloved hands touched hers.

"I must apologize for everything. I've felt terrible about your predicament. Appalled. You deserve to be at court. You lived here your entire life, you—" Her lower lip trembled, and she let out a strained breath. "I'm sorry."

Marguerite was unsure how to tell this woman she'd never forgive her—though she wasn't the only person to blame. "Majesty—"

"Adelaide, please." The queen picked a teacup from the table. "I want you to know, they ambushed me. I never confessed this to anyone—I had no option but to accept the union, because of my father. It seems he and the dowager... well, anyway, I've not the slightest notion why Antoine chose me, and not you."

Adelaide's father and the dowager, working together?

Marguerite reached for the other teacup, chewing the insides of her cheeks, wondering why the queen sought to unsettle her mere seconds into their conversation.

After flipping her curls with a dramatic sigh, the queen glued her watery gaze to Marguerite. "You were his promised one. And yet... Oh, Maggie." Her free hand pinched around Marguerite's arm. "Please, forgive me!"

Marguerite sipped her beverage to cover her frustration, to give herself a moment to mull over a response.

The queen retracted her hand, shame soaking her face in shades of violet. "Oh, dear. I'm sorry." She curled and uncurled her fingers and settled them in her lap. "I should have found you sooner. I knew you weren't dead."

Marguerite took another sip, imagining herself dashing out of the solar, escaping this melodrama and whatever its significance might be.

"I'm happy you're well and alive. Almost three years you were in that academy? I can't believe the dowager didn't see fit to inform me until recently. It's mine, after all, isn't it?" Adelaide's voice squeaked, higher-pitched than usual.

Marguerite swigged down yet another sip, the taste turning bitter on her tongue. "You mourned me?"

The queen stiffened as she lifted her cup to her mouth. "Of course! You were a valuable friend. I wanted to further investigate your disappearance, but," she glowered into her tea, "I had less authority than I expected."

Marguerite's mind raced with questions. She held in every single one, though she'd yearned to ask them for years. All the anger, the fear, the disappointment—she'd have to cling to it a little longer, until the right moment.

It was too soon. She didn't know enough about the dowager's true motives, or what Adelaide knew of them.

Adelaide lowered her cup to the table with such force a few drops spilled over the rim. "Will you forgive me? Might we be friends, like before?"

Marguerite clutched her teacup close to her heart, allowing the warmth to break some of the ice inside her. "I have to think about this, Maj—Adelaide. This is all so… overwhelming. Court is quite different compared to my days."

"It is, but if you accept my friendship, it won't be so bad, I promise." Adelaide flinched. "You're correct, though. This castle is uncomfortable, no?"

Her sudden hush piqued Marguerite's interest. Why would the queen need to lower her voice in her own solar?

"What do you mean?" Marguerite surveyed the queen's face, wondering if she'd be able to glimpse below her powdered layers and decipher whose games she played.

Her own? Clémentine's? A third party? Or was she, by some miracle, on Marguerite's side?

Adelaide's expression became sour. "Clémentine. She makes this place dreadful to live in. I confess it—we were right to abhor her. She's cold, and doesn't trust Antoine to rule on his own. After three years, it's baffling, no?"

Marguerite's mouth opened to answer, but she froze. Adelaide's words echoed her own from the night before, when speaking with Antoine. She never expected she and the queen would agree on anything.

Confirming that out loud would start a rumor that would reach Clémentine's ears in seconds.

Yet to disagree would upset Adelaide.

Marguerite retrieved her teacup and admired the flaring flames in the fireplace.

"Do you remember the good days?" Adelaide's chipper tone interrupted Marguerite's soothing vision of climbing out of the solar via the chimney. "When we would trick her so you could avoid her wrath and sneak off with Antoine? The castle was entertaining, back then. But now? Oh, how I miss that." Her chin dipped down.

Holding in a bark of laughter—could Queen Adelaide have genuine remorse?—Marguerite almost dropped her teacup. "I miss those days, too."

Taking another vanilla-flavored gulp, she peeked at the portrait above the hearth—Adelaide in all her resplendent beauty, seated on her throne. Antoine stood behind her, his eyes frosty as his mother's, while the queen's were like bright sapphires in the sun.

"Oh, Maggie!" With a wail, the queen threw her arms around her. "I'm sorry, but I *missed* you! I'm so alone here! Antoine doesn't love me, Clémentine despises me, the princes snarl when they walk past me. The princess only meets with me out of pity."

Marguerite suffocated in Adelaide's fragrant embrace. She thought of a silent prayer, something to save her from Adelaide's gracious yet ever tightening and unwelcome hug.

She patted the queen's arm, a groan bubbling in her throat. "There, there."

A rapping noise on the solar door forced Adelaide off her. The queen jolted up from the sofa, fixed her skirts, touched under her eyes, and glared at her attendant.

"Well? Marcus! Open it!" Her French accent surfaced in her irritation. "And fetch me a handkerchief!"

He hurried to the door, and Marguerite, still seated, craned her neck to witness the arrival.

In the doorway was Princess Cordelia, garbed in auburn layers with her hair swept up in a tight bun. She was the spitting image of her mother, but younger, slightly more serene.

Until her ice-coated gaze landed on Marguerite.

"I'm here to take you to breakfast, Majesty," said Cordelia, lowering into a curtsy. Her ladies-in-waiting giggled behind her.

Adelaide waited for Marcus to deliver the handkerchief, and as she dabbed at the corners of her eyes, she swiveled to Marguerite. "I must take my leave. We must resume this conversation soon, though. You're welcome to finish your tea, but I warn you—after breakfast the ladies will be in here and your tranquility," she mimicked an explosion with her hands, "*poof.*"

Marguerite received the hint, and curtsied first to the queen, who rushed out; then to Cordelia, whose cruel glare sent frozen chills down her legs.

"Highness—"

"Good day, *Marguerite*," said the princess, lifting her nose to the air as she swept around, Marcus at her heels.

Once the door closed behind them, Marguerite sank into the sofa, caught between laughter and sobs.

Why would Queen Adelaide summon Lady Marjorie so early to speak of presentation details? Why would Lady Marjorie's opinion matter? She was a chaperone. Noble, perhaps, but not essential to the organization.

Or… was she?

After falling asleep again, Céleste woke and fixed her tangled chaos of curls and rubbed away the imprints of her pillow indented on her cheeks.

Once she'd slipped into her comfortable shoes, she peeked out into the hallway.

It was past eight o'clock—she'd heard the chimes from Marjorie's suite when fastening her shoes. The castle's occupants would awaken soon, and she couldn't afford to cross any more royals.

Where would the chaperone and the queen meet?

She made a dash for the main stairs, hoping to sneak towards the music room. Perhaps they'd be close by.

She pretended to know where she was going as she glided down the hall. Curiosity ate her on the inside; she couldn't sit still and wait.

Her sour encounter with Emeric came to mind. The nerve—how could he speak like that to her? How could he be so demeaning?

Recoiling at the memory of his resentful speech, she swayed across the hall and descended the stairs with caution.

On the ground floor, servants rushed about. A butler carried a heavy tray down the King's Corridor to the right. Guards flanked the main doors.

She looked left and right before hurrying down the Long Corridor.

She didn't forget where the queen's social rooms were located—near the crossing of the Queen's Corridor and the West Wing. As she arrived, her gaze found the music room door and another not far from it.

She tiptoed closer and read: ***Queen's Solar***.

"Oh, they might be in there," she whispered under her breath.

A hunch warned her she'd best not knock to request access—it wouldn't please the queen to find her dawdling about when not permitted to.

A flash of sunlight drew her to the music room instead, the door of which was partly open. At the threshold her intrigue tugged her towards the source of the light.

She took one breath of encouragement and swished through the narrow door's opening.

Within the room were burnt-orange walls, polished floors, lofty sofas, ornate coffee-tables, intricate-patterned chairs—and instruments *everywhere*.

One instrument in the middle captured her attention most: a grand piano. Blood rushed to her cheeks. She itched to approach it, admire its beauty up close, but her feet were stuck, as if to warn her not to indulge in her cravings.

She'd been unlucky thus far when venturing into places she didn't belong… but the temptation was too much for her to bear. She knew answers were *there*, in front of her, for the taking. Was it possible such answers were in *this* room?

"So be it," she said, ambling over to the grand piano.

Its golden lid glittered, drenched in gentle sunbeams from the floor-to-ceiling windows. The piano's legs were also gold, and the strings below the lid were a silvery white.

Céleste yearned to touch it, but it was so precious, she feared it would shatter under her clumsy fingertips. She floated her hand above it, as if absorbing its energy.

She braced to sit on the bench when a creak in the hallway caused her to realize she'd left the door ajar. She pressed her hands over her mouth to muffle her breathing and lowered behind the piano.

A few instants passed, and she lifted her chin to view the doorway. In the corridor, clicking heels and rustling skirts whooshed by, an icy voice accompanying them. She couldn't decipher the words, but she recognized the sharp tone as that of the dowager queen.

She slowly returned to her crouch. Any movement could give her away; at the academy, she'd never showed much stealth while eavesdropping. But by some stroke of luck, the dowager's voice faded down the end of the hall.

Céleste released a deep sigh of relief. Adrenaline pumped through her so fast it rendered her dizzy, blurred her vision.

That was close, she thought. She tiptoed to a sofa and paused, listening for any more passers-by. Once she decided it was safe, she fell onto the cushions. "I need to be more careful," she whispered as she sighted the portraits on the walls.

Men with instruments, women holding music sheets. One of the women looked like the dowager, her dark hair and glacial facial expression familiar, captured on the canvas. She perched at a golden piano, her back arched, fingers grazing the keys.

Céleste wondered if she played, or only posed for the painter.

Her gaze switched to a portrait on the wall across from her, its grandeur impossible to miss. A redheaded woman lounged on a lavish chair, a shining tiara atop her head. A man with chestnut hair, sporting a similar crown, stood behind her. His hazel eyes were flat—but the redhead's blue ones were luminous and glowing.

The king and queen clearly had quite opposite reactions to being painted.

Céleste homed in on the vivid colors in the painting. So palpable, as if the king and queen were there, watching her. The queen's mouth curved upwards, while the king's was a thin, straight line. He was handsome, but coldness pooled from his demeanor.

Did he ever smile? He'd come off as so imposing, the night before, broad and unyielding. A dashing man, but with such a chilly attitude, it rendered him too frightful to look at. The way he'd watched Marjorie, with a mix of unease and fascination…

As she settled deeper into the cushions, Céleste thought of the princes. Both were as tall as the king, had similar features, identical builds. Jules, the youngest, had a sassy and charming air about him, his mane short like the king's but more obscure. He had an athletic frame, and a permanent glow framed his boyish face.

Sébastien's locks were the darkest and longest. His timbre—though she only heard it briefly—was uplifting, melodious. Those enigmatic chocolate eyes were hard to pry away from. He'd worn somber colors, but carried himself with elegance, flaunting his powerful arms.

All three brothers had a near terrifying resemblance to the dowager and yet, there was something softer about them. Smoother, kinder. Even, to some extent, the king—

The music room door swung open.

The hairs on Céleste's arms pricked up. She turned in slow-motion to determine who'd caught her, beads of perspiration forming on her forehead.

"Funny finding you here," said Lady Marjorie, standing in the doorway. A storm brewed in her eyes. "Of all the places I thought to find you, what are you doing *in here*?"

Céleste had been quiet, or so she'd thought. "And how did you—"

"Answer me."

Sliding off the couch and wiping her clammy hands on her dress, Céleste fought to keep her balance. "The door was open, and the piano…"

"I told you yesterday that you're not to be in here without invitation, open door or not." Lady Marjorie's nose wrinkled.

Céleste chewed on her lower lip. "I've been foolish." An

unladylike grunt escaped from her chaperone's clenched jaw. "I'm sorry, but I can't help my curiosity. You left, I was confined, my limbs were stiff—" She gulped, but her throat was so dry she grimaced.

Lady Marjorie shook her head. "Your curious nature will be the end of us. Come on, then. We will hurry upstairs and have lunch while I help you review your etiquette lessons. I hope you've learned something I can use to explain to you the direness of your actions. Had anyone else caught you," her free hand bunched into a fist, "it might have been our last day in the castle. You and I, sent home following the girls' presentation? Is that what you want?"

Céleste's chin sank as she followed her chaperone out. "No, it isn't, but—"

"No buts." Lady Marjorie tugged her from the music room. Her skin drained of all its color. "I'd hoped to consider you as a friend, eventually. An equal. But you continue to disobey. Lord Knowles never warned me you were the type to be so rebellious."

Pain spread up Céleste's forearms from Marguerite's tightening grip. "My nosiness has worsened since we arrived, I confess. My wish to immerse myself in court life, meet the nobles and ask them questions—the thrill has taken over me." She bit her tongue to omit mentioning what those questions would be. Lady Marjorie's anger would worsen.

At the bottom of the stairs, the woman lessened her grasp. A ripple of sympathy breezed over her expression. "You'll immerse yourself soon enough." She motioned for Céleste to climb. "After the girls' ceremonies, they'll be allowed out of their rooms, which means so will we. You must be patient. It's in poor taste to meander about as you have, against royal orders. Yes, I did it, too, but I know my way around. I won't get caught."

They reached the second floor, where Céleste's shoulders drooped. "I've forgotten myself."

"Then remember. You must be the portrait of perfection tonight, to not embarrass the girls in front of the royals and Totresia's upper-class citizens. Understood?"

Céleste hadn't realized how far they'd walked—they'd arrived before Lady Marjorie's bedroom. "Yes, I'll be on my best behavior, I swear it. But…"

She needed answers, transparency to better assist her chaperone. She needed a compromise.

She'd behave—if Lady Marjorie explained her knowledge and strange behavior.

Lady Marjorie's gaze narrowed. "But what?"

"Something has upset you, and you've been secretive. I wish to understand why." The chaperone scoffed, but Céleste refused to relent. "I can't help you if you keep me out of everything! You said you wanted us to be friends, no?" She chewed on her lip, uncertain how she could save herself from the woman's temper that was sure to flare at any moment.

It didn't.

She studied Céleste in silence, then unleashed an exasperated huff. "Fine. But only in due time. We have other matters to focus on first, such as getting the girls through the ceremony. *Then* I will be more candid with you. Does that appease you?"

Céleste deflated, smiling. "It does."

Lady Marjorie opened her door. "I won't tolerate any more creeping into unauthorized rooms. If this happens again, I will be forced to inform Lord Knowles."

Céleste would be the embodiment of perfection if it prevented her chaperone from speaking with her headmaster, who would undeniably speak to her father, who would surely cut her out of the family tree for such behavior.

To find out more about the Duchess of Torrinni, she had to befriend anyone who might have known her.

Lady Marjorie was one such person.

"I will behave, my lady, I promise."

16.
Marguerite

For the presentation, Marguerite chose a mustard-colored gown with floral patterns on the bodice and long, ruffled sleeves. Johanna had sculpted her hair into a perfect, round bun, with a few white roses tucked near her ear.

Céleste emerged a while later, garbed in pale blue. Together, they fetched the graduates.

Harriet, Esther, and Julia opted for moderately luxurious dresses; safe choices. Cristina wore a high neckline with an open back, which made Marguerite wince, but that detail aside, it was demure enough. Charlotte's gown carried the most extravagance, with a bow at the bottom of her spine, a matching bow in her curls, and a plunging decolletage. She'd dabbed a vibrant shade of red onto her lips and smirked as Marguerite sneered at her excessive choice.

Downstairs, they weaved through throngs of servants and

butlers, lesser nobles and revered guests—all curious to peek at the contenders before they were announced.

Marguerite brought her crew down the Long Corridor, going around the Winter Garden to avoid the bigger crowds in the King's Corridor.

"Remember," she said, addressing them as she marched, "walk with poise, don't flinch, and curtsy low for the king and queen."

When they reached the East Wing, more attendees were entering the ballroom. She saw a flock of men in modest suits. Some wore hats, others combed their hair from their faces, a few sported sashes littered in badges of honor.

The fathers—the escorts.

Céleste wished the graduates luck, and Marguerite ushered them towards their families.

Colorful dresses, sparkling jewels, frilly lace collars and hems—all of it intimidated Marguerite. Her own dress was far more simple, something she'd be mocked for if anyone knew who she was.

But being incognito was important, tonight of all nights, for the man she was betrothed to might be in the ballroom, anonymous at Clémentine's behest. This was Marguerite's best night to investigate; before all the major festivities began.

Soft music escaped from the ballroom, and her heart fluttered as the doors opened.

"Are you all right, my lady?" Céleste squeezed her elbow. "You seem sick."

Marguerite blinked away the fog from her eyes. "Crowds make me uneasy."

At the top of the queue of contenders, one man had turned around, his hand clasping Harriet's wrist as he snarled.

His thick, bushy brown brows and his graying mustache were visible even from afar. He spoke loudly, though incoherently, and seemed undisturbed by the commotion he caused.

If ever Marguerite had disliked a man, it was this one. His deceptively soft eyes full of contempt, his sly smile always concealing secrets—a monster in disguise as a gentleman.

"Beware of him," she said, nudging Céleste.

"Who?" The girl gazed towards the crowd of gentlemen.

"The one holding Harriet." Marguerite yanked her backwards as the girl got on her tip-toes to see better. "Don't make it obvious. He's the Vidame of Limesdale, Eugene Thatcher. Harriet's father. If you see him near any of the girls, except for Harriet, tell me at once. He's dangerous."

Céleste's brows laced together. "I've heard of him. I will be on the look-out, I promise."

A shiver ran down Marguerite's spine as Eugene mouthed something in Harriet's ear. It didn't please her that Harriet was there, accessible to his plots—but she'd had no say in the matter. According to Johanna, Harriet was often his puppet, much as she loathed being used for his sordid purposes.

From within the ballroom, the herald thrummed his staff.

"We must enter. Quickly!" Marguerite hauled Céleste forward as the line moved.

Hordes of people were already packed inside. Most were locals, or citizens of Serese County, where the academy was located. A few hailed from farther parts of the land; some Marguerite recognized. They'd immediately recognize her.

She kept her chin tucked as she and Céleste rushed towards the front of the crowd for a better view; which meant standing much closer to the royals than she'd wanted. But if she stood out in the open, someone would point her out—and she wasn't ready to explain herself to Céleste yet.

Before the thrones, she curtsied, and Céleste did the same. But as she straightened up, Marguerite couldn't tear her gaze from the dais.

Standing in front of his royal seat was Antoine, decked in regal burgundy, his attention locked onto her figure.

How handsome he was, more so than last time she saw him, and that was only half a day ago.

Yet how stern, almost sad he appeared. And how hard it was not to look at him because… *damn her,* Marguerite knew all those former feelings were still inside somewhere, deep in her gut, weighed down by all the mistakes he'd made.

She simply couldn't fully loathe him. She couldn't bring herself to abhor the sight of him as she'd coached herself to for years.

She froze when his eyes met hers. So light, yet so dark, plagued with all the worries of a king striving to keep his kingdom afloat.

And haunted by the errors of his youth.

She prayed he'd carry on with his duties as if she weren't there, and stop looking at her like no one else was there. Because like the night before, his majestic presence made her legs quiver beneath her skirts.

Biting her lip, she pivoted to the carpeted pathway the girls would walk down with their fathers. She had a perfect view on the doors, next to which the herald tapped the floor thrice with his golden staff; a final warning to settle down. The sound plunged the room into a deep silence, and everyone watched the contenders at the threshold, arm in arm with their escorts.

The herald unrolled a parchment. "The Totresian Royal Court welcomes nine noble ladies seeking official presentation."

Overcome with an odd compulsion, Marguerite side-glanced at the dais. She noticed Antoine, in the same spot, finally focused. Adelaide, beside him, wore crimson from head to toe, her loose scarlet strands falling over her daring low-cut bodice. She slid her arm under his and batted her lashes, pride oozing from her posture.

Clémentine sidled up on the king's other side, her hair pulling at the edges of her eyes so much that she appeared more menacing than usual.

What a sight—Antoine, encircled by the vipers who manipulated him.

"Announcing the Vidame of Limesdale," a few groans broke out, "and his daughter, Miss Harriet Thatcher!"

They received glares as they passed. Eugene remained stoic, but Harriet's shoulders were losing a battle with gravity. Marguerite flashed her a smile of encouragement, but when Eugene spotted her, and his lips twitched into a snarl, she recoiled.

Had he recognized her? Or did he simply wish to incur everyone's wrath while at court?

Before the podium, Harriet dipped into a low curtsy. Adelaide's nostrils flared.

"Harriet Thatcher of Limesdale?" She sent a glance in Clémentine's direction, and the dowager gave a curt nod. "Welcome to court, Miss Thatcher."

A rush of emotions washed over Marguerite as she ogled the royal woman's intricate crown of garnets. But she lingered too long, and Adelaide caught her staring.

The queen tilted her head in acknowledgement, a trace of greed polluting her otherwise perfect face.

"The Count of Rosford, and his daughter, Miss Esther Bristol!"

A wide smile plastered over the bubbly young lady's pink-hued lips. No one booed her; her father was well-loved. She curtsied, and Adelaide accepted her without hesitation.

Discreet until that moment, the two princes, clad in matching navy ensembles, appeared in the corner of Marguerite's vision. They peered at Esther with varying degrees of interest. Sébastien was somber, almost bored. Jules' expression carried a spark of curiosity and mischief.

"The Marquess of Trecuse, and his daughter, Miss Cristina Condello!"

Another flawless walk and curtsy, another nod from Adelaide.

Frances and her father came next, followed by three contenders Marguerite didn't know.

Never one to shy from a bit of scandal, Clémentine stepped in to dismiss the third girl, claiming her attire was far too inappropriate for the royal court. As the guards accompanied the poor thing out, the attendees muttered about the dowager using authority over the queen.

Yet no one had ever stopped her from abusing that authority, had they?

"The Count of Belnau, and his daughter, Miss Charlotte Geitz!"

The blonde glided down the path like a princess, her chin raised high. Not a lock of hair out of place, not a hint of worry coloring her cheeks. Her curtsy was the embodiment of perfection, and she garnered interest from many men in the crowd.

Clémentine sneered at her, but Adelaide coughed into her hand and leaned forward. "I'm pleased to welcome you to court, Miss Geitz."

Charlotte was valuable. Her family was respectable. The Count of Belnau contributed to Totresian society and charities more than most, and was among the few who always sat at the king's council table. He had with Edouard, as his father had before him, with Edouard's father.

Everyone focused on Charlotte, who sauntered off with a lightness to her step.

Marguerite fixed on Clémentine, instead. Something was wrong.

Clémentine snickered at Adelaide, then at Charlotte, even as the last contender, Julia, made her way down the carpet.

Why did Clémentine dislike one of the most eligible ladies in the room?

Marguerite refocused her energy on the Viscount of Malaros, Julia's father. As an important figure in Totresian trade with southern Europe, he'd give his daughter an advantage at court. Her older brother, a close friend of the princes, lived in the castle and would also do wonders for her reputation.

Once the queen accepted Julia, she declared the ceremonial parts of the event over, warranting a moment of respite.

As royals waited for refreshments, Marguerite let her guard down and scanned the platform, remembering the days when she was allowed to perch up there.

In her reverie, she met Antoine's gaze once more. His hand twitched at his side, looking ready to reach down and haul her up, as he had so many years ago.

He wouldn't dare now, yet the memory was vivid as ever.

She *almost* missed being up there with him.

Marguerite's cheeks were overheating, so she lowered her head to concentrate on the hem of her dress. Her heart thrashed in her rib-cage, and an acidic taste shot up her throat, settling in her mouth.

Why would he look at her in the open, not seeming to care who noticed?

She whirled to her right, eager to rush to the buffet for a drink—but she smacked into Céleste, whose eyebrows arched as she crossed her arms.

"What's going on?" The girl's eyes narrowed between Marguerite and the king. None of her usual chipperness flooded her tone.

Marguerite fumbled for excuses. "I… uh… I wished to thank the queen for accepting all our girls, but she appears occupied. Shall we fetch drinks and celebrate?"

Céleste didn't budge. "Are you sure that's all?"

A burning sensation woke in Marguerite's stomach. Had Céleste detected Antoine's ogling? Or hers? Had their exchange piqued the girl's curiosity?

Marguerite's nostrils widened at the scent of pastries and rich finger foods. "I'm sure I don't know what you're talking about."

Céleste planted her feet. "You thought I'd be too overwhelmed to notice?"

The room *was* overwhelming. A sea of noblemen in their finest frock coats, ladies in large hooped dresses; clashing colors, vibrant patterns, silks and velvets and shimmers. For anyone unused to a royal ball, it'd be a lot to take in.

Then there was the ravishing queen, and her dashing but uninterested king. The dowager and her scowls, the princes and their expectations.

"Notice what?" A chill skidded down Marguerite's back.

"You." Céleste pinched her lips, approaching as she lowered her voice. "The king. That look between you, like a look between—"

"Please, Céleste, don't be absurd."

Marguerite hurried through the guests, desperate for a spot of wine. A cup. Two. Perhaps three, to drown her worries and find some stroke of genius to continue to conceal her identity a while longer.

17.
Céleste

"Why would she lie?" Céleste whispered to herself, watching her chaperone dodge attendees in her way, keeping her chin low as she made straight for the buffet line.

It was a direct question—and hadn't Marjorie promised to be more upfront with Céleste?

Céleste had *caught* them. The king was distracted, not a care for his beautiful wife. He'd only cared for Lady Marjorie.

Was it possible Lady Marjorie hadn't noticed? Surely no one would ignore a king when they ogled you like that.

When Céleste looked toward at the platform again, the king was gone. The dowager sat in her chaise, scrutinizing the crowd as her ladies fanned about. The queen hid behind the thrones to adjust her décolleté. Prince Jules was in deep conversation with someone Céleste didn't know. And Prince Sébastien, standing at the other extremity—

"Oh," she said aloud, taken aback.

Prince Sébastien was looking at *her*.

Her heartbeat accelerated.

Yes, *her*. With one brow cocked in interest, his chin lifted, his hands tucked behind his back. He'd pulled his black hair into a ponytail, but one strand dangled down the side of his face.

Not once did his gaze falter, even when Céleste returned it. He observed her with ease, as if he'd been doing so for a while, waiting for her to sense it.

He devoured her.

She gulped, wondering if she had a splotch of dirt on her bodice. Or if her lip-stain had smeared. Or if her skirts had bunched up too high. Why else would he be staring at her?

Her corset pressed hard into her chest, suffocating her as she tried to catch her breath.

Never had a man looked at her that way. Never had a man looked at her *at all*.

As a flush crept down her neck in warm waves, the prince raised both brows, the edges of his mouth turning up. He grinned, a gentle hint of redness on his cheeks.

When the herald slammed his staff onto the floor three times, Céleste disconnected from the staring contest. She straightened up as King Antoine resurfaced atop the platform.

His commanding voice hypnotized the room. "Noble Totresians, please hurry and help yourself to refreshments. I will give a speech in a few moments, to complete this evening's events."

The already daunting line at the buffet grew as men and women brushed past Céleste. Whirls of fabrics whipped at her skin, intoxicating perfumes slithered up her nostrils. Noises distorted, lights flickered overhead, and the pastry scent that once woke her hunger made her nauseous. The music playing in the background lulled her into an eerie daze.

Dizziness overcame her fast. Her vision blurred as she swayed on the spot, struggling to keep her balance. The orchestra's tunes drew out, deafening.

She clapped her hands over her ears and prayed for the stampede of nobles to disappear.

Through blurry eyes, she surveyed the windows, thirsty for fresh air. But her heartbeat took off again at the sudden sight of Prince Sébastien speaking with his brothers—and blocking the patio doors.

She wished for someone to bring her water, a fan, a bed. It was all too much—the crowd, the king watching Marguerite, the prince watching *her*.

The prince spun her way and spotted her, despite the hordes of people around her. He offered her a brief nod.

Her breaths quickened. He had no notion of how she shriveled on the inside, submerged by strangers, stunned by his unexpected attention. Yet… a part of her wanted that attention. It *was* thrilling. Like she was a character in one of her romance novels—

He abruptly returned to his discussion with his sibling, which prompted her to wake up.

She'd lost her mind, hadn't she? He wasn't acknowledging her. There had to be someone else behind her, some other lady he knew, draped in luxurious fineries and glittering with precious gems.

A lady of a presentable age.

Céleste was only a student, a teenager in a pretty dress.

Had she imagined it all?

Something was going on in the ballroom. Something involving the king, Lady Marjorie, and the prince. And something ominous about that vidame, according to Lady Marjorie. Céleste's father had advised her he was treacherous.

Something was off.

Goosebumps crawled up and down her arms.

The prince had eight contenders to contemplate, yet he'd spared *her* a lengthy glance. The king had a spouse—a gorgeous one, too—but undressed Lady Marjorie with his eyes instead.

Céleste saw Prince Sébastien again, holding a glass of sparkling wine. His grin, dripping with charm, brought a sudden weakness to her knees. As did his muscular arms, as she envisioned herself in their embrace—

As she pivoted away from the sight, fanning herself, she nearly jammed into Lady Marjorie.

She held two goblets of wine, and furrowed her brows. "What, pray tell, has happened to you?"

Céleste shook out her hands. "The… the crowd affected me a bit more than I expected."

A playful glow swirled in Lady Marjorie's eyes. "Affected by the crowd?" She focused on where Céleste's gaze had been moments before, and smirked. "Ah, yes, the *crowd*. Which noble has you so flustered?"

"No." Céleste's words caught in her throat. "*No*. The number of people in here, I'm not used to that. Like you, I'm… wary of crowds." She was certain her entire face had turned purple.

"It's all right to look." Marjorie gave Céleste one of the glasses. "You may not be of age, but—"

"No!" Céleste snatched the cup, then cringed. "I mean, *no*, I assure you, that wasn't my issue."

"Fine." Lady Marjorie clutched her goblet near her breastbone. "But get used to these crowds. There will be more social events to attend, and they have many guests."

Céleste gripped her cup so tight she might have shattered it. "Right. Of course."

She peeked into the scintillating liquid of her glass, licking her lips. The herald's staff interrupted before she was able to prod Lady Marjorie about what was going on in this place.

The king cleared his throat as his siblings perched on either side of him. "The nine—I'm sorry, eight—contenders we met this evening are, by my official say-so, eligible ladies of court. Though they're here for my two lucky brothers, they're available to all eligible bachelors. As is tradition for Totresian royals, the princes will announce their choice at the end of the Masquerade Ball, on the last night of December. That gives them only a few weeks to choose, but I know them. It won't be a problem."

A bout of laughter erupted as Prince Sébastien groaned, and Prince Jules wiggled his eyebrows.

"I have no doubt they'll find a suitable match in one of the ladies we encountered tonight, or among those already present at court. As is also tradition, we will hold an inaugural ball in two days' time. The princes—and other qualified nobles—may send formal invitations to request a proper introduction with the ladies of their choice, before the event. This isn't mandatory. They still have a chance for an introduction at the ball itself."

Prince Sébastien glanced at Céleste again, which made her cheeks flare up so much they hurt.

King Antoine lifted his glass. Others mimicked him, as did Céleste, after struggling to fix herself. "To a successful royal season, and to my brothers finding wives. To a happy and prosperous Totresia. Peace Above All!"

The guests echoed his words.

Céleste nearly spit up the liquid when she spotted the king squinting at Lady Marjorie.

The woman clenched her cup and maintained the king's gaze, seemingly unaware of Céleste watching her. She was moving— *swaying* slightly side-to-side, dreamily enjoying the king's attention.

No… it couldn't be. Was Céleste imagining this?

She guzzled down half her wine and abruptly slid in front of Marjorie. "Are you ill?"

Marjorie swallowed a few gulps in haste, as if choking in surprise. "What are you talking about?"

"Are you quite sure?" Céleste zeroed in on her expression, yearning to read the truth in it. "Because I sense—"

"There's nothing to sense." Marjorie waved a hand in dismissal, and veered around as she finished her beverage. "All is well, I told you."

Céleste bit the insides of her cheeks to refrain from causing a scandal, much as she craved to get answers immediately.

The wine's bubbles tickled down her insides and her stomach churned.

No, nothing was well.

With Céleste's incessant questions, and Antoine's gazes becoming less and less discreet, and with her will to keep her distance fading, Marguerite knew it was time to go. She rounded up the girls and brought them to the dais to bid goodnight to the queen—Antoine wasn't there, and Marguerite wouldn't look for him.

Some protested the early departure—mainly Charlotte—but they'd have plenty more opportunities to mingle with courtiers. Marguerite dragged them out of the ballroom and up the stairs, to the semi-safety of their chambers.

Semi—because Marguerite trusted no one in this place.

It was a relief to leave. Her own presentation ceremony had lasted hours; ladies stayed up late, drinking too much, overindulging in pastries, flirting. She'd spent the evening hidden on the patio with Antoine.

But this presentation, this year, was different. Too many

dangers lurked about—she recalled the vidame sneaking around, gawking at contenders—and Céleste was catching on to her ruse, no doubt.

As they traveled across the second-floor landing, Esther stopped, setting free a whimper that caught them all unawares.

Marguerite paused near her. "Is everything all right?"

Charlotte and Julia scowled, but before they could speak, Esther let out a low moan. "Lady Marjorie, please tell me, otherwise I won't sleep. What were those *formal invitations* the king mentioned?"

Harriet's questioning gaze rested on Marguerite. "I would also like to know."

Cristina muttered something about agreeing, and Charlotte and Julia nodded.

Marguerite watched the staircase, on alert for other guests making their way to their chambers. "It's a royal court tradition. Noblemen can meet a lady in a more private setting, with a chaperone, before she decks herself in fineries and is hard to recognize."

Harriet's hand shot skyward. "And if we don't receive one such invitation?" Her voice was low, weakened. Esther squeezed her arm.

"It means nothing." Marguerite's hands clenched briefly. "Each man at court is different. Don't let this deter you."

During Antoine's Season, he'd sent no invitations. The other men did the same and waited until the inaugural ball to introduce themselves. Marguerite recalled that all the ladies in that season found husbands—all but her.

"How would you know?" Julia's mousy tone broke

Marguerite's momentary relapse into recollections she wished to erase.

"I don't know for sure." Marguerite shifted her weight, her stays digging into her ribs. "The princes may invite you all, as a polite gesture. Or they might not communicate with you at all."

Jules was always a flirt, even as a youngster. Sébastien was more reserved. She imagined the younger prince would invite his favorites without hesitation; Sébastien would observe before narrowing his options.

"And what of their brothers?" Cristina pointed to Julia, then Céleste, who hid in Marguerite's shadow. "Should we consider them? They're not princes, but they *are* eligible nobles."

Julia tossed her raven curls. "Axel will do what he pleases. *If* you please him, he won't hesitate to say so. But if I were you, I wouldn't hold my breath."

As Charlotte applauded her friend's jape, Marguerite got between Julia and Cristina, desperate to avert a screaming fit in the hallways. "Julia, watch your tongue." She motioned for the girl to move and then pointed Cristina towards her chambers. "It's late, and you can debate on your own time, out of earshot."

Charlotte tried to question her again, but Marguerite ground her teeth, shaking her head. "Enough, Miss Geitz."

The blonde backed away, cursing under her breath, but Marguerite was too tired to care.

She beckoned Céleste to her side. "Some might have already picked out a favorite. Others might need to meet you in formal-wear. Be patient. They're of unique backgrounds; don't forget that. Now off to bed! I have no doubt this season will bring you happiness."

No one protested any further. They sulked over to their chambers, and Marguerite blew out her cheeks as she tugged Céleste out of the main landing.

Tension hung in the air between them. Their heavy silence was dotted with unresolved issues, unspoken words, unanswered questions.

It was only a matter of time before Céleste spoke up—and it happened once they passed Esther's door.

"Are you *quite* sure you don't know the king more than you claim?"

Marguerite grimaced. More lying, more deception. She loathed it, but had no choice. It wasn't the right time yet. Best if she figured out who her betrothed was and survived the next few events, first. Tonight, she'd barely made it.

"I told you—I've been here before. The king doesn't know me. We crossed paths at balls or in the corridors. Nothing more."

"He looked at you with such insistence. Did you think I wouldn't notice? He flustered you. Why did he stare like that?"

"You shouldn't—"

"And why did Prince Sébastien look at *me?* Of all the ladies in attendance?" Céleste's chest heaved up and down, her breaths strained. "Does he have any clue who I am? Does he care? *Why* would he care? I'm no one. I'm not a contender."

An uneasy feeling grew in Marguerite's belly. "Prince Sébastien looked at you?"

Céleste grunted. "And that damned vidame, he's eerie, no? Very odd man—"

"The vidame?" Marguerite froze.

Céleste snapped her fingers, her bright eyes turning gray as she blocked the passage to their rooms. "Are you listening? The king, the prince—what's happening? I've had enough confusion. This is absurd. Tell me the truth."

Marguerite's glower prompted the girl to clap her mouth shut. "You will beware of your tone, Céleste. Absurd? What's absurd is the nonsense you speak. The vidame aside, your imagination is creative."

Céleste's eyebrows jumped up. "Creative? You… you don't believe me?" She stomped her feet. "You must! I saw the king, I saw the prince, I saw the vidame—and I demand explanations! Why were the royals so interested in us?"

"The king might have been trying to remember me from days past." Marguerite tucked a stray curl behind her ears as Céleste's face flashed to a lava-like red. "And the prince? Well, have you considered your brother might have mentioned you, seeking a future husband for you? Who better to ask than a prince who has met all the eligible noblemen at court?"

Céleste's mouth fell open, and she lifted a finger, then lowered it as she squinted. "I thought so, but… well…"

Marguerite seized Céleste's hand. "See? Everything has an explanation. Except the vidame and his business, but that's another story."

Céleste's expression didn't shift in the slightest. "You're correct about that."

"Your inquiries will draw unwanted attention, and we don't want that." She patted the top of Céleste's hand and gave her a gentle nudge towards her bedroom. "Go on, get to sleep. Tomorrow we will discuss ways to control your curiosity, since you're here to learn."

Though she acquiesced, Céleste seemed to fight a cringe when Marguerite released her. "My apologies, Lady Marjorie. I will be better, I promise." With a polite curtsy, she slipped into her quarters.

Marguerite found Johanna waiting inside her own room.

"Oh, thank goodness you're here."

The servant girl helped her disrobe. "Tough night?"

Marguerite grumbled as Johanna ripped the corset from her sweating middle. "The girls passed Clémentine's test, but I fear Antoine had one of his own. And I failed." Her throat ached as she swallowed, wishing she'd had more alcohol.

"The king tested you?" Johanna undid the pins in Marguerite's hair, and the locks flowed below her shoulders. "Anything I can do? I can speak with other servants, if you wish."

"No, but I would appreciate a warm bath early in the morning. And coffee, please. I'm sure coffee beans are stashed in the kitchens."

After putting on her nightgown, Marguerite got into bed. The fire crackled, and Johanna extinguished the candle on the bedside table. "Are you certain you don't need to talk about—"

"No." Marguerite stretched out her legs, settling down under the blankets. "It's been an insufferable evening, and I'm beyond fatigued."

Without further prodding, Johanna bid her a good night and left.

Marguerite frowned at the hearth. Its flames morphed into a figure that haunted her—Antoine scrutinizing her every move, enamored as ever, as if they hadn't argued the night before. As if he hadn't chosen another woman over her.

He was persuasive. He'd almost gotten Marguerite to give in and forgive him, with a few fiery gazes and a body language so open, so inviting, she'd been tempted.

But no, she *wouldn't* cave.

Swell for him if he'd moved on, but she never would. Whatever games he was playing, she wanted no part of.

She'd come to court to figure out who Clémentine had promised her to, and devise a way to escape her fate.

She had no time for Antoine's antics… even if she couldn't stop thinking about the way he'd admired her in the ballroom.

Marjorie was lying, *again*.

Céleste thought of her excuses as she washed her face, unfastened her curls, and changed into her nightwear.

She pictured the woman's mildly flustered face as she hung her dress in her closet. And she was about to grumble about it, when she sighted all her gowns—their simple patterns and old-fashioned collars and sleeves, their outdated styles.

Would any of these suffice for the royal court?

She'd waited so long to have a reason to mingle with ladies and practice her manners. At the academy, all she wore most days were her plain school outfits—worn-down and itchy wools. But here, she'd at last wear proper attire, fancy velvets, dazzling bodices, heeled slippers.

That was, if her father sent her more dresses, or money to purchase new ones.

Only one gown in her armoire made her heart truly flutter. She touched it, caressing its intricate material, its exquisite ruffles, its delicate pearls.

This white gown she'd brought for the Masquerade. She pictured herself twirling in it, looking refined—then burst into a fit of laughter.

"Me? Dancing? Heavens, no."

Her gaze caught on something hidden on the floor of the closet, under the gowns.

The Golden Girl.

It called her, promising to fill her with theories and ideas and lull her to sleep, as it always did.

Releasing a large breath, she trailed her fingers over the intricate lettering on the faded cover.

She had to understand.

"*You* can explain the king's behavior. The prince's attitude. You hold their true story."

She set the candle on her nightstand and crept under the covers, clutching the book to her chest.

As the fire crackled, she opened *The Golden Girl* and fluttered through it, scanning for clues—like why the king would gaze upon lesser nobles as if knowing them. Or why the prince would gawk at a seventeen-year-old student assisting the chaperone.

She mouthed the sentences she nearly knew by heart, her eyes growing tired.

Céleste yawned, stopping on a passage talking about Prince Sébastien's yearning for adventure. She sensed her eyelids becoming heavy, and the novel slithered from her hands.

***

"Ahhhhhh!"

Céleste sat up so fast she might have broken her spine. Her heart ached from beating with such intensity, and perspiration coated her forehead.

She shielded her face as she wrenched her eyes open to a sliver of light escaping from the window to her right. Had she forgotten to close the curtains?

She inhaled, exhaled, and thrust a hand over her chest, waiting for her frantic heartbeats to settle.

What a dream that was—ladies in bright colors dancing around her, faces masked. A line of gentlemen kissing her hand, their faces masked, too. And at the end of said line, one man stood out. Eyes like chocolate, dark hair falling on either side of his face, dropping below his chiseled jaw.

Prince Sébastien, reaching his hand out, inviting her to dance.

She smiled at the recollection—he'd been so vivid in the dream, as if he'd been in her head, experiencing everything with her.

But why had she screamed?

As her vision began to clear, she nearly fell from the bed—a blurry blob of a person stood at the foot of her mattress.

Another yelp pried out of her mouth.

"Stop, *stop!*" The intruder lowered to the bed-spread and covered Céleste's mouth. "Be quiet!"

That voice—a feminine intonation laced with sternness, the same one that had scolded her last night.

"Marjorie?" Céleste rubbed her eyes and saw her chaperone's permanent frown.

The woman's turquoise and burgundy gown came into view as she removed her hand from Céleste's mouth. "Will you relax? You'll wake the entire castle."

Céleste unleashed a breath of relief. "You frightened me!"

"My apologies, but," Marjorie flinched, "you need to wake up." A few strands of golden hair glided over her shoulders.

Céleste couldn't stop shaking, still reeling from the surprise. "What time is it?" She peeked at the window. "Why are my curtains open?"

"A little after seven-thirty," said Marjorie. "Are you unwell? What was that yelp for?"

"A dream." Céleste stretched. "Too real for my taste." She threw the covers off. "It's hot in here!"

Marguerite handed her a robe. "Put this on. We…" She wrinkled her nose and looked at her shoes. "We have a problem."

After accepting the robe, Céleste got to her feet, wobbly from standing too fast. "What do you mean?" She shrugged on the silky fabric, her throat dry. "Some tea would be nice."

Marguerite's chin tipped up but the corners of her lips dragged downward. She held on to a parchment, but Céleste couldn't see what it said. "You should sit down."

"Oh, God." Céleste fell onto her sweaty sheets. "Did Father write?" Fear spiked her blood. "He won't send more dresses. No— he wants me home? Or the dowager has dismissed me. Or my brother denounced my unladylike attitude when I met with him the night we arrived—"

Marjorie's forehead wrinkled. "This is none of that. *This* news… I'm not sure how to interpret it."

Céleste gulped. "Then what is it? What did I do?"

Crunching the message in her grip, Marguerite glanced at the ceiling, exhaled slowly, then returned her focus to Céleste. "This," she waved the parchment, "is an invitation for an afternoon stroll. For you."

"A stroll?" Céleste glared at the note. "A stroll with whom?"

Marguerite's free hand clenched into a fist at her side. "It's a formal invitation from Prince Sébastien."

160

PART TWO

THE
GOLDEN
GIRL

162

Restless dreams had caused Marguerite to wake earlier than normal. Even a warm bath and a delicious brew of coffee hadn't aided her plight. And now, Céleste's shrill voice worsened her migraine.

"Would you read it again? Please. I still don't understand."

Her head already pounded from lack of sleep, and the girl's two consecutive screams had done nothing to help it.

She cleared her throat. *"Dearest Lady Marjorie, I ask your permission to meet your assistant chaperone, Miss Céleste Richel. I wish to take her on an afternoon stroll through the gardens."* She lowered the parchment. The words had imprinted onto her brain.

As Céleste stuffed her nose between her knees, Sébastien's voice filled Marguerite's ears. The way he'd ogled Céleste, their first night at the castle, when she'd exited the ballroom…

It was Marguerite's fault. She'd brought Céleste with her for selfish reasons, and now the girl had drawn royal attention.

Céleste winced. "But what does it mean? I'm not even an official lady."

Swallowing what she wanted to say—that Céleste was a target who'd soon feature in all gossip at court—Marguerite crumpled the note. "It's a royal invitation, so you have little choice."

"But *why*?"

Marguerite had no explanation. She no longer knew the boy she'd grown up with, the shy child who wanted to read and play sword-fighting in the orchards. He was a man now. An eighteen-year-old prince who'd placed his interest in Céleste.

"That's not for me to answer."

Céleste hobbled to her vanity. She dampened a cloth in the water bowl, then dabbed it over her brows. "*Can* I meet him? I'm not a contender. I attend the contender's chaperone! It makes no sense."

Marguerite chewed the insides of her cheeks. "It's confusing, but no Totresian law states you can't be courted. You're still eligible for courtship by noblemen or royalty. It's rare, and you're underage, but yes, you can meet him." She stroked her jaw, watching the girl hunch over. "But a measure so bold, close to a presentation ceremony, and during a royal Season, will make people talk. It's ill-viewed. Bad-timing."

Céleste glared at Marguerite in the mirror. "People already talk! He spent the evening staring at me, which must have drawn rumors. And now this?"

Marguerite's fingers tightened around the bunched-up message. She should have known, should have reacted sooner.

In the ballroom, the night they bumped into Antoine and Sébastien, the latter had watched Céleste leave, interest sparking all over his face. She should have said something before he made a move. Before this.

Jules was the rebellious one; it would have shocked her less if he'd invited Céleste. But Sébastien? Reserved, solemn, the docile prince?

Céleste was correct—it made no sense.

Marguerite walked up to stand behind Céleste's seat. "He knows better. This behavior is preposterous. Most unlike him." Her pupils enlarged. "I mean—he had a royal tutor, he understands how these things work. His attitude appalls me."

She prayed that Céleste, busy groaning as she tugged on her curls, hadn't caught the near slip of the truth.

"Why, *why*?" Céleste let out another groan. "Wait." She released her hair and gawked at Marguerite in the mirror. "Why did he send the note to *you*?"

Marguerite focused on fixing her lower-than-usual neckline. "I'm the chaperone, Céleste. You're not of age, remember? It's normal to request my permission."

Céleste moved the chair backwards, its legs scraping on the floors. She stood, one brow cocked at Marguerite's reflection. "There's more to this. You're hiding something." She jolted around. "I sense it even more since last night, with the king, the vidame, the prince. You know too much. You dodge questions with talent. I deserve legitimate facts, no? If I'm to be introduced to a prince, shouldn't I be warned of what I'm walking into?"

Marguerite pursed her lips. "Careful, Céleste—"

Céleste shoved the chair out of her way. "Careful of what? The truth?" She set her fists on her hips. "I must know. I *must*. This invitation is so sudden, and you seem to know all about it. It's not fair to throw me into the lion's den like this!"

Marguerite rolled her eyes. "It's not a lion's den. It's a meeting with a prince—"

"*Exactly*! A meeting with a prince!" Barefoot, in her cotton nightgown, her robe's sleeves dangling from her arms, her tresses tangled and wild, Céleste appeared as a mad inmate.

Marguerite laughed. She'd do anything to distract the girl away from the truth she was getting far too close to. "You're overreacting."

The girl stomped her feet. "It's not funny! How are you acquainted with the royals? Why are they so familiar with you?"

A mix of concern and rage tore through Marguerite. "You will mind your tone." Though her legs were weak as every memory of her life at the castle flashed before her, she held her ground. "I don't know the royals, I told you. They recognized me from before, that's all."

Céleste clenched her jaw. "Please, Marjorie. I can't be your friend if you're not honest with me. How am I to serve you with half-truths and cover-ups? It's too obvious that you lie and it wounds me."

The girl was simply too smart for her own good.

With a grunt, Marguerite marched to the bed. She kicked at the mattress and snickered at the wall. "This is… and if you… *ah!* You can't speak to me this way, Céleste, and eventually you'll understand why, but…" She sucked in a breath, and another, and one more before flipping to Céleste.

A slow smirk formed over Céleste's mouth—something akin to satisfaction, to triumph. "I'll understand eventually?" She shook her head slowly. "No, I understand *now*. I know what you're hiding, *my lady."*

The way she said *my lady,* almost in mockery, froze Marguerite in shock. She ran her trembling fingers through her hair. "What do you mean? I'm not hiding anything."

Céleste took one step forward, hands on her hips. She no longer resembled a mad inmate—she was a witty young woman who'd figured it all out. Something Marguerite had said had tipped the girl off.

She knew.

"You're *her,* aren't you?" Céleste let out a puff of laughter. "The duchess in my book. The one I've been trying to prove was real, the one you *confirmed* was real, but you wouldn't give me more information? It's *you.*"

"Céleste—"

"*No,* don't cut me off." The girl's eyes were determined, her words sharp like knives. "Your knowledge of the royals, your knowledge of this castle and all its intricacies and secret stairways, your flighty demeanor, all of it… *You* are the Duchess of Torrinni, aren't you?"

Much as Marguerite wanted to keep denying her, it was too late.

It was far too soon to divulge the truth, but if she didn't, she feared Céleste would knock on every noble's door until someone spat it out. Until she had the entire castle discussing Marguerite's true identity.

"Céleste…" Marguerite inhaled, exhaled, and her shoulders drooped. "Yes, fine. *Fine.* I *am* the duchess. I'm your *Golden Girl,* the one you've been searching for. My name isn't Marjorie, but Marguerite. And you will keep this information with your life, do you hear me? That's imperative."

Céleste swallowed and nodded. "I promise."

Céleste paced.

And paced.

And paced more.

She refused breakfast, declined tea, wouldn't sit down.

The clock ticked away, each hour bringing on new waves of panic, new questions.

When the clock's hands reached eleven, the chaperone—*the duchess!*—insisted Céleste had best get ready.

"Sébastien prefers simplicity," said Marjorie—*Marguerite!*—choosing a pastel orange gown from Céleste's wardrobe.

"He won't like you over-powdered," she added, then gestured at her vanity. "You'll need to put your hair up."

Céleste said nothing while the duchess helped her into her dress, then covered her skin in thin layers of face-paint, then brushed through her matted curls.

She frowned at her reflection once the duchess was finished with her—a basic girl in a pretty outfit, with no notion of what she was doing. Her cheeks flushed as she pulled up her collar, her breasts not quite filling the bodice.

The timing of the invitation puzzled her, coinciding with her dream about Prince Sébastien inviting her to dance. How had she dreamed of this before it had happened?

"This is… a lot to take in," she whispered, scratching her wrist where the gown's sleeves stopped.

"I know." Marguerite inspected her from head to toe. "I wish I knew the prince's intentions, but… well, you heard the king. He must hurry and decide."

Why would a prince—and such a handsome one, too—consider Céleste as a potential bride?

After grimacing a few more times at her reflection, she cleared her throat. "I think I'm ready."

Marguerite, who'd perched on her sofa, sipping on her third cup of coffee, deposited her mug onto the table. "Yes, you are. As I advised you thirty minutes ago." She sighed and got up, draping a heavy cloak over Céleste's shoulders, one matching her own. Johanna had mentioned it was fairly cold out that day.

Céleste huffed, which prompted the duchess to lift her eyebrows.

"Are you about to use that tone of yours to disagree with me?"

"No," Céleste swallowed, "but before we go, I must ask: why did you lie to me?

Marguerite wound the gold chain of her flower pendant around her finger. "When I found out you had that book, I wanted to confiscate it. But I prayed you would never guess *I* was the woman in the story, rumored to have done… too many things to describe right now. So yes, I fibbed, to persuade you away from the mystery that is my life."

"But how has no one at court recognized you?"

"Oh, they have, but they know better than to say anything. You see," she shifted her weight, "the dowager sought to erase me from history. She also bribed the aristocrats at court to forget I ever existed, and told her children that I was dead."

"*Dead?*" Céleste's hand flew to her chest. "How awful. How cruel."

"Yes, well," Marguerite puffed out a breath, releasing her necklace, "it's in the past. So far no one has completely figured out who I am, just that I look familiar. And until the dowager decides to announce me, which I'm certain is her plan, it must stay that way. Especially with the other girls. They enjoy gossip too much." She straightened up. "This isn't the moment to dwell on such details. We must leave."

Céleste's lungs filled with air too fast, and she coughed. "Why me?"

Marguerite took hold of Céleste's shoulders. "Not now. If we want to find out why Sébastien wants to meet you, you must keep your wits about you. You must be a lady."

Céleste hiccuped. "Yes." She dug her teeth into her lip and nodded, no matter how unconvinced she was on the inside. "Right. We can go."

Her heart was about to burst. Mocking laughter echoed in her ears, her father's scalding glare burned in her temples.

But Marguerite was correct. She had to remain calm.

The duchess took Céleste's hands in hers and squeezed.

"You're underage, but know this: a girl of your standing belongs at court. This might serve as a learning experience. When you return to school, you can share with others how you met a prince. You can go over what you did right, what you did wrong. So," she tipped Céleste's chin up, "keep your nose up, and never slouch, understood?"

"Understood." She faked a grin, if only to reassure Marguerite she would succeed in this introduction.

But more queries developed inside.

Why was Marguerite beckoned to the castle after three years of pretending to be dead? Why had she been at the academy in the first place, posing as a chaperone? Then the night before; the king's stares, the prince, the vidame…

Céleste let out an accidental whimper before they exited the room, and Marguerite halted at once, groaning. "What is it now?"

Céleste wrung her hands. "Is something afoot in this castle? Am I, are *we* part of some foul plot?"

Marguerite set a finger over her lips. "Watch your tongue when doors are open."

"But why are you here after all this time? *Was* it the dowager's doing? Or the king, changing his mind about you? Or someone worse, like the vidame? You mentioned him, said he was dangerous—"

"Céleste!" Marguerite took a deep breath and held it in as she sealed the door shut. The air she expelled came out slowly, laboriously. "I can't tell you much, because I don't *know* much."

"What *do* you know?" Céleste was about to scrape a hand through her hair before remembering she couldn't touch it; her hairstyle took far too long to put together. "I can't meet the prince, not like this, not without knowing—"

Marguerite patted at a drop of sweat forming on her forehead. "Yes, the dowager summoned me. The academy… that was my prison. It was where she kept me away to maintain her ruse. I didn't want to come here. She left me no choice." She flinched, as if about to add something else, but opting not to.

"And the vidame?"

"I have no inkling what the vidame plays at, but he's evil."

"And… the king?" Céleste recalled the passages in her book describing the Duchess of Torrinni's *flight from the ballroom*, and the scandal it had caused. "You ran from him."

Marguerite tapped her fingers impatiently on the door. "Is this an interrogation? You're going to be late—"

"Didn't you love him? The king?" Céleste's arms fell to her sides. "I mean… I apologize. That was…uncalled for."

"Of course I did." Marguerite rubbed her brow, as if wanting to ward off a headache. "But he chose someone else, and I wouldn't stand by and watch him love *her* instead."

Céleste couldn't help her curiosity. "And do you still love him?"

"You had *hours* to ask me about this, but you choose now?" Marguerite looked like a ripe tomato about to explode.

A knock on Marguerite's door, followed by excited whispering on the other side, interrupted her.

She shooed Céleste towards her quarters. "Wait in your room—no one can know where I'm about to take you."

***

The excited whispers were from Esther—she'd received an invitation from Emeric.

Céleste scoffed when Marguerite told her, as she led her downstairs. "Well, I suppose she *is* his type. Bubbly, too chipper, snippy—and pretty."

As they descended the grand stairs, Marguerite mentioned to Céleste how the other girls were jealous—except Harriet—and said cruel things to Esther. How it disappointed her to see such catty, childish ladies at court.

Servants busied about in the entryway as they arrived, and Marguerite tensed. She whipped Céleste around to face her, and pulled the girl's thick hood over her curls, tugging down until it concealed her eyes.

"Some of the staff like to start rumors, too."

"Does this," Céleste pointed at the hood, "not draw more attention?"

Marguerite adjusted her own cloak and hood. "Not if we hurry. The king is holding court, the queen is in the solar, and the dowager is either in the music room or in her chambers. We might bump into Jules, but he won't say anything."

Céleste's lips pressed flat. "You certainly know their routines well."

Marguerite caught her by the forearm. "Come."

As they cruised down the Long Corridor, the clock chimed; it was noon. Marguerite had mentioned Sébastien's punctuality, and how to him, afternoon meant *immediately* after twelve o'clock.

They made it to the glass garden doors, sun blaring through, blinding them.

"Ready?"

Céleste sighed heavily. "Does it change anything if I say no?"

Outside, a cool wind hit her cheeks as she took her first steps into the gardens. The pebbled path was lined with faded bushes, and a few stray winter flowers peppered the ground. The sound of rushing water came from ahead, at the end of a smaller pathway. She happily breathed in the scent of pine trees.

She noticed a dense forest towering to her left, but didn't have a chance to ask if it was *the* forest where the duchess and the crown prince used to play.

Marguerite walked faster, forcing Céleste to trip on her dress as she tried to keep up.

After what felt like a hundred paces, a larger path opened before them. Sitting to Céleste's left, by the forest, was a one-story, worn-down cottage with decaying ivy cascading down its sides. Shrubs and trees surrounded it, crashing against its stone walls. The wooden door and windows hung from their hinges, but the rustic aura gave it a certain charm.

"Is this the—"

"Gardener's cottage," said Marguerite, speeding up. "The prince will be waiting up ahead." Cupping a palm over her forehead, she peeked at the area she'd mentioned. "Ah, yes. There he is."

Céleste followed the duchess's gaze—a tall figure stood in front of a row of bushes several dozen feet away. More pebbled paths continued behind him, leading to undiscovered parts of the royal yard.

The figure strode forward, though not coming too close. His pitch black hair flew about in the breeze, like sheets of satin catching sunlight. His brown cloak flapped open, revealing a beige suit. He puffed his chest as he waved.

They approached, but Marguerite released Céleste before they got too close. "Wait here. I must speak with him first."

Céleste slid her hands into her cloak's pockets and shuffled her feet as Marguerite walked over to the dashing Prince Sébastien.

Marguerite's balanced steps radiated a confidence she wasn't sure she had as she approached Prince Sébastien. Though he, of all royals, was her truest and dearest friend, she couldn't help but set up walls around her heart.

If Antoine had harmed her—who was to say his brother wouldn't?

She gritted her teeth as she curtsied. He'd better not harm Céleste, either.

"Marguerite." His dark eyes sparkled, full of a warmth she hadn't realized she'd missed. "I assume it's safe to call you that out of earshot?"

Marguerite made a face as she straightened up. "She knows. It no longer matters what you call me."

Sébastien blinked rapidly, taken aback. "Does she? And you're all right with that?"

"I have no choice," said Marguerite, one fist tightening at her side. "If I didn't confess it to her, she would have asked the entire court for confirmation, and that would have been worse."

"Well, whatever your name is… how wonderful to have you back at court. No matter the reason. No matter what you did, what *he* did, this is your home. Where you belong."

Sandpaper lined her throat as she lowered her gaze to his boots. "How much did you rehearse that?"

A soft chuckle escaped his lips. "Oh, Maggie. I missed you."

"And I you," she said, reverting to a scowl, "but what are you doing?" She folded her arms to her chest, closing up. "Inviting Céleste Richel for a formal meeting? She's not one of your contenders. The academy didn't present her. What are your intentions?"

He combed a hand through his hair. "So inquisitive."

"Answer me. This is quite unlike you."

"I intend to meet her—that's what an introduction is." He looked over her shoulder and grinned.

Marguerite couldn't help the growl rumbling to life in her throat. "Don't be evasive!"

He lifted his arms and sighed. "She's haunted my mind since I saw her with you two days ago, in the ballroom."

"She's young." Marguerite's mouth curved downwards. "Vulnerable and naïve and clueless about how court works. You shouldn't have done this."

Since receiving his letter, Marguerite's insides had been knotted. It was her fault; she'd dragged Céleste to the castle for her selfish needs. Delightful and pretty as the young woman was, men at court would prey on her, desire her—

"I shouldn't have picked a lady who sparks my interest?" Sébastien's expression turned stony. "You sound like Mother."

"*You* sound like a capricious child! She's not yours to pick. She's seventeen. This ordeal scared her to death, poor thing. We…" She bit her lip. "*I* smell a plot brewing."

"A plot?" He pointed at himself. "With me? Never. I don't partake in such activities. Jules, perhaps, but I seek simpler things. No drama or theatrics. And Miss Richel," he smiled, "I have a feeling she's one such lady."

"Her? You're confusing me. Confusing us both."

A gust of wind whooshed into Marguerite, almost sending her toppling backwards. Sébastien clutched her hand, aiding her in keeping her balance.

"I don't mean to," he said. "She appears less stuffy, less frilly than the others. A dreamy air on her features at all times—"

"Have you been watching her?" Marguerite's jaw dropped.

Redness spread from his chin to his temples. "No! I just observed her at the presentation last night. I daresay, she made me dreamy, too."

"So she enticed you to break the rules? Are you calling her a sorceress?"

He patted the top of Marguerite's hand. "She bewitched me, so… maybe. I paid no regard to the official contenders. None swept my attention like she did. I'm intrigued." He let go of Marguerite, fussing with his flapping cloak. "I'm curious about her, and can't hide it. That's why I invited her. Not as part of some scheme."

Marguerite shifted her weight. "And your mother? What will she say when she finds out? Because she will."

He narrowed his gaze, upper lip curling as his cheeks lost all their color. "To hell with Mother. She lied to us all by stating you were dead. I care naught for her reactions. She's not the monarch's wife anymore."

His unusual irritation made Marguerite cringe. "She's your mother."

He bunched his fists and turned around. "She doesn't decide for me. I'm eighteen, a grown man. Antoine will support me, and his opinion is the only one that carries value at court."

Marguerite itched to warn Sébastien how sly the dowager was, how she'd do anything to control her son's lives and who they allowed in them. How she'd controlled *hers*.

"Are you sure? Céleste is a newcomer. Must you put her through such trials? I brought her here to learn; not to drown among envious, viperous contenders."

He kicked at a few pebbles. "From what I understand, she can fend for herself." Marguerite's eyebrows shot up. "Yes, rumors of the academy reach *me*, too. The whispers in my ear, about her, have been nothing but good."

"The whispers? Ah." She gave a slight head nod. "Mr. Richel Junior, I presume?"

"I beg you, let me meet her. I'm not playing games." He spun Marguerite towards Céleste, who waited in the distance, pretending not to stare in their direction. "I operate for myself. I wish to speak with Miss Richel."

Her heart was unsettled, but Marguerite had no alternative; it was too late now. "In that case…"

They both glimpsed Céleste, her chin down, her curls golden in the sunlight. Unsteady on her feet but a hint of natural poise in her posture, she acted like no one was there, like no one watched her.

Like a prince hadn't set his stubborn sights on her.

"She's a rare gem of a girl, I can tell. I'm dying to get to know her." The sincerity in his timbre prompted Marguerite to scan his face, to ensure he spoke the truth.

"Fine." She stepped aside. "But be careful, Highness. Don't give her false hope if Antoine can't abide by your requests, or if your mother interferes. Don't hurt her like *he* hurt me."

23.
Sébastien

Sébastien's breaths quickened as Marguerite hurried over to fetch Céleste.

This was it—this was the moment to emulate his siblings, for once: the proud king, the overconfident younger brother, the headstrong sister. Shoulders squared, standing tall, displaying all his God-given features—those he'd been told by other women were *seductive*.

This *wasn't* the moment to be his introverted self.

Céleste Richel had captured his attention, and he refused to fail at capturing hers.

While she and her chaperone exchanged a few words, he coughed into his hand, checking his breath. His legs jittered, and he did his best to plant his feet firmly to the ground as he waited.

How many women had he wooed without meaning to? Surely if he put effort into this, there'd be no question that Céleste would be as intrigued by him as he was by her.

Finally, they moved in his direction, and it charmed him to see he wasn't the only one nervous; Céleste's footsteps were slightly clumsy and uneven.

She and Marguerite sank into curtsies; *she* focused on the ground, cheeks flushed. Sébastien bit his tongue to stop his smile from spreading too wide.

Marguerite rose. "Your Highness, I present to you Miss Céleste Richel, daughter of the Marquess of Valeville."

Céleste wobbled up from her curtsy. "It's a pleasure to meet you, Highness."

Sébastien responded with a low bow, maintaining eye-contact. "Miss Richel."

"Céleste, this is Prince Sébastien." Marguerite clutched Céleste's upper arm, as if nervous to let her go. "I will leave you to acquaint yourselves. I won't be far, but I *will* be watching." She gave them some space, swerving towards the castle.

Céleste twisted the corners of her gown, peering about with widened eyes.

She *was* nervous, and rightly so. Had Sébastien jumped the gun, seeking to meet her so soon? She wasn't a contender, as Marguerite had so deftly reminded him. Surely she'd been shocked by his attention, and might need time to understand what was happening.

It was up to him to set the tone, calm the mood. Reassure her and not frighten her.

He'd been frightened—by the way his heart thumped with his first sight of her. By the weakness he'd felt upon recognizing her, based on her brother's description.

And by how much *more* she'd turned out to be. More

beautiful, more demure, and yet more enticing than any woman he'd ever met.

He took one of her hands; something jolted through him at the contact. His long, slender fingers curled around hers as he placed a kiss atop her knuckles. "*Enchanté.*"

Their gazes met, and though he was several inches taller than her, he felt like they were the same height, floating on the same cloud, experiencing the same pinch in their hearts.

Her hand trembled in his. "Likewise, Highness."

He kept his mouth on her glove for several seconds, unwilling to break the thrill thrumming through him. But she appeared unsteady, her fingertips shivering, so he freed her.

He motioned to the pathway leading away from the castle. "Would you care to walk? I abhor standing still."

"Certainly," she said, clasping her hands in front of her.

He wanted to steer her arm under his, but it was far too soon for that. She'd been stunned enough by their hands touching.

"How are you enjoying the castle so far, Miss Richel? I assume life at court differs from what you're used to."

He watched her jaw tightening. "It's fascinating, Highness. Our academy is grand, but nothing compared to this."

He wrinkled his nose. "Ah, the academy. Mother's pride and joy. How I wish to visit it and determine what the fuss is about. Our castle tutor educated me. A stuffy old man."

Céleste adjusted her coat. "There are a few of those at the academy, too."

He slowed his pace, smirking at such boldness. Most women would balk at the word *stuffy*. "You have a sense of humor! I appreciate that."

She looked askance. "I do? Normally my brother is the only one who laughs at anything I say."

Sébastien thought of Emeric and his stern stance on women's behavior in society. Had Céleste spent much time with him in recent years? Or did he reserve a different treatment for his little sister?

"And what's your favorite subject at the academy?" He halted their march and pivoted to face the castle.

Céleste did the same, her gaze fixed on the faded canary yellow walls of the four-story building. "I enjoy music lessons. Languages are interesting, too. I like art, but I'm not the most skilled artist." She glanced at him, warmth flaring across her skin. "I don't think I have a favorite subject, but I have a favorite place."

He tilted his head to the side as he surveyed her. "A favorite place? Which is it?"

"The library," she said, barely allowing him to finish speaking.

"The library?" He grinned. A bookish girl? How had the Heavens granted him the chance to chat with this young woman? "So you enjoy reading?"

Her demeanor relaxed a little—perhaps speaking of books would loosen them up, make it easier for them to get to know one another. "I do, Highness. Very much so."

"I apologize if this is too personal, as many women have scolded me for prying," he tapped his chin, "but do you have a favorite book?"

She frowned. "Well, I…" She stared off, as if lost in thought.

The prince flinched. "I'm sorry, have I stumbled on a tough topic? I don't wish to make you uncomfortable."

"No, Highness, *I'm* sorry." She returned her focus to him, but the color had faded from her cheeks. "My favorite book isn't one you would expect. Not... for a lady."

"Oh." He sensed the tips of his ears growing hot, imagining her curled up on a chair, licking her lips as she read the most scandalous novel. "Well, forget I asked, then."

She gasped, shuddering. "Oh, Heavens, no! Not *that* kind of novel, Highness! Never!"

He blew out a breath. "Thank goodness. Not that I'm in any place to judge your tastes, but I couldn't envision you reading raunchy tales. So then, what is it? I must know; now you've tempted me."

She lowered her chin. "It's called *The Golden Girl*."

He racked his brain for the title. "*The Golden Girl*, you say?" He'd read a lot in his youth, and more so while he traveled abroad, but not this book. "I've never heard of it."

"It's not a widely published novel. I believe there's only one copy." Her voice lowered and she tucked her arms to her sides. "Some may call it... non-fiction."

"Non-fiction?" He tilted his body closer to her, as if to whisper a secret. "A true story, then? Based on who?"

"Oh," Céleste fumbled with her hands, "it's based on... um... you. Your family. And the Duchess of Torrinni."

"Ah. So... a memoir, then?" He swallowed, his intrigue replaced by confusion. Someone had written about his family? Someone had written about *Maggie?* Who'd have access to such private information? "Who wrote it?"

Céleste sucked in her lips and rotated away from him. "It's... an anonymous author."

"Anonymous." Sébastien refrained from letting out all his worried thoughts. "Well, I thought I was well-read, but I'll admit, you've stumped me, Miss Richel."

"You're not… mad?" She blinked up at him, lashes batting like wings of a butterfly.

"Mad? No. Confused, perhaps. A bit afraid, also. Strange to know someone wrote about you but you don't know who they are, nor what they wrote."

"I never should have mentioned it," she whispered, chin drawing to her chest.

"If there's anything I appreciate, above all things, it's honesty." He gestured behind Céleste, at Marguerite. He recalled she'd said the young woman knew her true identity; had the book revealed it? "So you know who *she* is, then?"

"I do. And she knows I know." She swiveled in Marguerite's direction—she loomed in the distance, out of earshot. "She confessed."

Sébastien whistled. "The name *Marjorie* didn't suit her well, anyway. How did you get her to confess, Miss Richel?"

She took a deep breath, puffing up her cheeks before releasing it. "Please, Highness, call me Céleste. And I… well I… threw a bit of a fit, I suppose? I didn't give her much of a choice."

"Someone more stubborn than her? I find that shocking." His fingertips grazed hers, and he worried she may bristle, back away; she didn't.

Was she, like him, submerged by a desire to keep talking, to remain close? She was no longer visibly shaking, and the tension she'd harbored had dissipated.

"And you may call me Sébastien, by the way. In fact, I urge

you to, if we're away from the public, like this."

She opened her mouth, snapped it shut, squinted, then opened her mouth again. "It doesn't offend you that I would read such a book?"

He displayed a wide grin. "Your brother spoke true about you."

"My brother? He spoke to you about me?" She gripped her cloak tight to her body, angling away.

"He said you never held your tongue. Which fascinates me. *You* fascinate me, Céleste."

"M-me?" She pointed at herself. "You must have me confused with someone else."

"You're the one who caught my attention. If Marguerite allowed this encounter, she must believe me. She would never let you come near someone she didn't trust."

Céleste peered over at the duchess, who still had her back to them, her golden curls flowing freely in the wind. "I believe you. She's quite protective."

"She and I have always been close. After her departure, I became tired of court, of royals, of my mother's manipulations. So I renounced my claim as the next in line to the throne and traveled around Europe." He captured her hands in his, his thumb brushing over the top of her knuckles. "In all my excursions, I found no one who captivated me so easily, so quickly. I don't wish to frighten you, but I must get to know you."

His eyes bore through hers, so clear, soft like a dove's wings. Butterflies swarmed his insides.

She tugged one hand from his to fan herself, but didn't try to run off, didn't show fear at his abruptness. "And I you, High—

Sébastien. But it doesn't matter, does it? I'm not a contender."

"Don't worry about that." He released her and proceeded towards Marguerite. "The other ladies have my brother to fight over. One less prince shouldn't be an issue. He'll love the attention." The look of bewilderment on her face made him nearly chuckle. "Those women lack the wonder I detect in you."

She pressed a hand to her heart, and though she averted her gaze, Sébastien could have sworn he saw her beaming. "I'm sorry, Highness, this is… new to me."

"New? Ah." He nodded. "A man declaring his affections. Something one only dreams about, no?"

They ambled closer to Marguerite, and he sensed Céleste fidgeting beside him. "Highness, I can't help but worry—"

"*Sébastien*, I insist." He spun her to him, and tucked a stray string of her hair behind her ears; a daring gesture that only a brash prince like Jules might have attempted. But Sébastien didn't want to waste time. He wanted to make his intentions clear, and fast—he wanted to court Céleste before any other man at the castle got wind of how marvelous she was. "I have a feeling about you, Céleste Richel. One I have only read about in books." He brought her hand to his mouth for a quick kiss atop her knuckles.

She licked her lips, then stammered, "I-I sense it too."

He lingered another moment before letting her go. "Then I will see you again soon, Céleste." He bowed, then offered a brief nod at Marguerite before rushing off toward the castle.

Was her heart singing like his? Did she mean it when she said she sensed something, too?

"Only time will tell," he said as he entered the castle's warmth, smiling so wide that guards and servants looked at him as

if he'd lost his mind.
And he didn't care.

Marguerite struggled to get Céleste into the castle. Getting upstairs was the worst—every few steps, Céleste would stop, fan her face, and mutter, *"Why me?"* or *"He was so dreamy!"*

It took so long to haul her into her bedroom, Marguerite worried she'd be late to oversee the meeting between Esther and Emeric.

"What did he tell you to get you so flustered?"

Céleste plopped onto her bed with a sigh. "He said he had a *feeling* about me." Her cheeks flushed a deep crimson as she shoved her head into a pillow. "A *feeling*? About me? Why me?"

Marguerite exited the room and took a heavy breath. As a chaperone, she'd have many more meetings like this one to supervise.

Bracing herself for more flushing and gasping, she hastened to Esther's door, and knocked. "Round two."

***

Esther was jittery, but her introduction to Emeric went well. Once they'd had their walk around the gardens, he returned Esther with a wide, satisfied smile.

The entire time they were together, Marguerite thought of Céleste meeting Sébastien. She'd sensed the spark between them the moment their eyes met, an invisible link establishing between them, an attraction wrapping them in an isolated bubble.

Their encounter had woken butterflies in *her* stomach, too, reminding her of the night she and Antoine had first admitted their feelings.

The butterflies tickled inside her, reminding her of how Antoine had looked at her the night before. The longing, the aching sorrow he must have felt to see her there, after so long. Seeing him that way had reanimated physical feelings she hadn't had in a while. Physical feelings she hadn't been capable of in her years of being locked in a basement as his mother's prisoner.

The butterflies exploded, and pangs of pain replaced the gentle flapping of their wings. Hatred took nostalgia's place, and her heart tore apart all over again.

Would Sébastien dare betray Céleste as Antoine had betrayed her?

She wished she hadn't allowed them to meet. Sébastien was nothing like his brother, but who knew what had happened to him while he was abroad? Who knew if he hadn't become a heart-breaking scoundrel, or a flirtatious alcoholic like Jules?

What if Clémentine *did* pull his strings, using him as a puppet for her sick games?

Marguerite would have to pay for Céleste's agony if the prince led her on—she'd have to pick up the pieces of the girl's shattered heart.

Once upstairs, Marguerite patted Esther's arm; she'd been silent since they reentered the castle. "So that went well?"

Esther shrugged, her entire demeanor that of a depressed widow, not a young woman who'd just met a potential spouse. "It did." Her eyes were usually so full of life and vibrant with excitement; here, they were dulled.

"Why the long face?" Marguerite frowned. "Is something wrong? I was watching the two of you, everything seemed swell."

Esther released an exaggerated sigh. "Yes, everything was swell."

"Was he not to your liking? Not handsome enough? I find that rather hard to believe."

"He was much to my taste, my lady. Smart. Funny. Dashing. We discussed many things." Her voice was shaky. "But he's not a prince."

Marguerite scowled. "He's the son of a marquess, which is a higher station than yours. A splendid thing, no?"

"I know, but—"

Marguerite tugged the girl farther down the hall. "You won't sulk about not catching a prince's eye. Emeric Richel is a fine gentleman, and if he has set his sights on you, you should rejoice."

She knew little about Mr. Richel Junior, though she'd met his father and garnered his glares on more than one occasion.

"Won't that disappoint? I'm not here for him." Esther dragged her feet. "He's not royal, and I came for the princes."

"That's absurd." Marguerite ushered her the remaining paces towards her bedroom. "He's a high-placed match that will thrill your parents. If he continues to court you, consider yourself lucky."

Marguerite vaguely recalled the palatial Valeville manor, its lofty arches, its luxurious decorations, the cherry trees in the orchard. Esther would love it there.

But the memory of the birthday festivities held within the massive ballroom triggered an image of Marguerite and Antoine exploring the hallways and frightening servants as they ran from their chaperones.

"He *was* charming." A coy grin was etched across Esther's face.

They stopped at her door, and as Marguerite prepared to wish her a good day, said door blew open.

"There you are." Charlotte towered in the threshold in her pastel silks, mischief in her blueberry eyes. "How did it go?"

Esther pushed past her, into her quarters. "What are you doing in my room?"

Though evidently about to spit out one of her usual retorts, Charlotte sighted Marguerite and fixed her lips into a curt smile. "Oh, Lady Marjorie, good afternoon."

Marguerite peeked past her to see she wasn't alone; Cristina sat on the bed and Julia at the vanity. Harriet was there too, though hurrying up to Esther and wincing at her, clearly uninvolved in whatever this break-in entailed.

Marguerite narrowed her gaze on Charlotte. "I must also ask—what *are* you doing here?"

The blonde opened her mouth, then closed it as she scratched the bridge of her nose.

Julia swooped in. "We had to know about Esther's meeting with Mr. Richel! She's the first of us to receive an invitation."

Charlotte sneered. "I still can't believe it."

Cristina rushed up to Esther, invading her space. "How was he? How were you? Will he propose?"

"It's too soon for that," said Harriet with a dismissive wave.

Julia sneered. "Only princes propose! They're all that matters."

Charlotte shoved through them all and stood so close to Esther, their noses touched. "Mr. Richel Junior will do fine for someone like you. Leave the princes to more deserving ladies."

Marguerite slammed the door behind her, garnering everyone's attention. They eyed her, mouths agape at the abrupt gesture.

She had far more important things to do—such as identifying her supposed betrothed and investigating why Sébastien was so interested in Céleste—yet there she was, scolding five young women who couldn't pretend to be civil.

"Stirring up drama like this is unacceptable. Breaking into someone's private rooms? You should all be ashamed of yourselves!"

Charlotte flashed a bold glower at Marguerite. "I'm not stirring up drama. I speak the truth—some families have higher standards. My father expects me to marry a prince. Esther's," she bunched her lips, "doesn't."

Esther pouted. "How can you assume—"

"Leave her," said Harriet, yanking her friend away from the viperous contender. "She's not worth wasting your breath."

"You will *all* cease this behavior. Under this roof—the *royal* roof—you're to act like ladies, not whining children! What would the princes do if they heard you sputtering such nonsense, lurking in bedrooms that don't belong to you?" Marguerite took one stride towards them; all five took a stride back. "The queens would ban you at once!"

They hid their faces, hunched their shoulders. Charlotte didn't cower, but even she sported a certain degree of discomfort.

Marguerite loosened her tightened fists. "Whoever becomes interested in you, prince or noble, you will reply with tact and not judge one another. Though you covet the same men, you shouldn't act like enemies."

Harriet lifted a shaking arm. "My lady… might I add to that?" Marguerite acquiesced; Harriet was one of the more mature girls present. "My father, the vidame—*he* is the only one you shouldn't accept an invitation from."

"Agreed." Marguerite reached behind her for the door-latch. "I've heard enough for today. Return to your rooms, and no more surprises like this."

She retired to her own chambers, massaging her temples, praying for the thrumming in her head to stop.

When she entered, a delightful aroma drifted from her sitting area—*coffee*.

"Bless you, Johanna." A fresh cup rested on the tea-table, along with a plate of cured meats and cheeses, and a flaky croissant. The curtains hid the mid-afternoon sun, preventing her migraine from worsening. "She knows me too well."

The instant the mug nestled in her hands, its warmth radiating through her extremities, Marguerite almost forgot her misery. Almost rid herself of the disgust of the scandalous demeanors.

Almost buried all her fears of marrying a stranger and playing into Clémentine's schemes.

She sank into the sofa cushions and closed her eyes. She'd been summoned to see her own life slip between her fingers, but so far, all she'd done was get involved in everyone *else's* life.

When would she have time to figure out who Clémentine had betrothed her to? Or time to process her reanimating feelings for Antoine, and discern how to destroy them?

éleste shook out her curls after unfastening her pins. Her heart-beats had settled—somewhat—and the fog around her senses had dissipated—only a tad—and her body crumbled in exhaustion.

A royal prince had an interest in her. *Her.*

But she wasn't available for him to choose—why would he break tradition and go after her?

After some time ruminating, pacing, she rushed to the adjoining door, desperate to talk things over with someone who knew these feelings all too well. "Marguerite? Are you in there?"

"Come in, Céleste." Marguerite's voice was distant, tired.

Céleste found her resting on her bed, a damp cloth over her forehead. The room was grim, as if a storm brewed within.

Marguerite sat up and waved her over. Parts of her up-do had come undone, and deep frown lines dug into her forehead as she removed her cloth.

Céleste sniffed at the coffee scent in the air. "I don't mean to interrupt anything."

Despite her obvious distress, Marguerite patted the spot beside her. "You interrupt nothing. I had a difficult encounter with the girls, and it caused a migraine. Nothing new."

Céleste propped herself onto the mattress. "I'd like some… information on the prince."

Marguerite exhaled and reached for the mug on her nightstand. "Of course."

"I'm sure this is too much to ask, but," Céleste peered into her lap, "I must understand. Why—"

"'Why you', yes. You repeated that all afternoon." Marguerite swallowed a few swigs of her beverage. "But I fear I have no answer for you."

"But you know him, yes? Is he trustworthy?"

Marguerite peeked into her mug. "Sébastien is the most trustworthy royal I know." She whipped her neck up, eyes darkening as she zoned in on Céleste. "What else did he say?"

Lumps formed at the top of Céleste's throat. "He detected wonder in me."

Marguerite stroked her chin, clutching her cup with her other hand. "Wonder, hm? Sébastien doesn't normally play games, but I've yet to find out what he did while he was abroad. He may have changed."

"Did the king change? Is that why he didn't choose you in the end?" Céleste blinked, taken aback by her own words. "I mean… forgive my bluntness, but—"

A knock forced both ladies off the bed. Céleste fussed with her dress, and Marguerite deposited her cup on her nightstand before gliding to the door and wrenching it open.

A small voice replied, "A note for you, my lady."

"Thank you." Marguerite mumbled something else and latched the door. She opened the note, read, and for a few moments after, she held the message to her chest, eyes closed.

She swiveled to Céleste as if nothing had happened. "What were you saying?" She padded over to her sitting area.

"Is that from the prince?" Céleste squinted at Marguerite. "Or the queen? The dowager? *Ooh*, is it from the king?"

Marguerite crumpled the parchment and squeezed her hand shut, concealing the words forever. "It's nothing."

"But *is* it him?" Céleste took a few cautious strides in her direction. "The king? Marguerite, tell me."

"Enough." Marguerite tucked the squished paper into her décolleté and wandered to her vanity. "I must cut this discussion short for now." She sank into her chair, combed her hair, put fresh powder onto her face. "Go check on the girls, would you? They were bickering earlier, and I hope they ceased their awful behaviors."

"But I—"

"No!" Marguerite hastened to her floor-length mirror, before which she'd left her shoes. She slipped into them and took a deep breath. "I must attend some business, alone."

After a polite incline of her head, she took off.

Céleste waited, listening to the chaperone's fading footsteps—then darted to the door.

She poked out, looking left and right in search of Marguerite's golden mane, and nearly gasped when she caught her taking the service stairs downward.

Before she could formulate a proper plan, or come up with an excuse in case someone spotted her, Céleste hurried into the corridor, chasing after her chaperone, trying her hardest to not stomp.

At the banister, hearing Marguerite's footsteps below, she froze, imagining Marguerite's words. *"You're disobeying, Céleste, sneaking around..."*

It was unladylike, risky—but what if this important business was about Céleste, about the prince? What if he'd changed his mind and didn't have the nerve to tell her himself?

Her heart squeezed in her ribcage as she tried to keep her steps light. She grimaced at each creak of the wood beneath her shoes.

At the bottom, Marguerite continued down another set of stairs—to the basement. What was in the basement that required the chaperone's attention?

Céleste waited for Marguerite to be halfway down before she scurried behind her, praying to not bump into any royals.

These stairs curved to the right. When she reached the final few, she kneeled as low as possible behind the thick banister, watching Marguerite stop feet away from a slightly battered door.

Such a secluded spot meant the person Marguerite was about to meet with didn't want anyone to find them together.

Céleste backed a few steps up, crouching in the curving of the stairs. The landing only had a handful of rusted sconces, providing little illumination—which worked to her advantage.

Another door opened across from the staircase—a figure clad in a long black cloak emerged, a hat concealing their features.

When they looked up, revealing their defined cheekbones and glowing hazel eyes, Céleste held in a gasp.

The king's shoulders tensed. "Thank you for coming," he whispered to Marguerite, each word fluttering under Céleste's skin.

Antoine scanned Marguerite from head to toe, lingering on how perfectly her curls cascaded over her shoulders.

How many secrets did those curls hold? How many deceptions had she been involved in—likely not of her own volition?

For years, he'd seen her silently suffering from his mother's wrath, and he'd dismissed it. But now, the woman before him had reached a breaking point.

He couldn't sleep, couldn't concentrate until he knew why she'd been thrust into his life again after years of not existing. His mother's secrecy—and refusal to explain herself to him—had brought him to a boiling point.

Marguerite curtsied. "Good afternoon, Majesty."

He twitched at her formal address, and as he opened his mouth to reprimand her, he caught her staring at his lips—which made him stare at hers, recalling how soft they were. How close they'd been to his in those old days; how far they were now.

She remained in her curtsy, as if stuck, glossing over the same memories he was. Almost too quickly, she straightened up. "Might I ask why you summoned me here?

"Summoned, yes, perfect word choice." He leaned against the door, averting his gaze before more memories poured in. "Why did the dowager summon you to court? We don't need a chaperone for contenders. We have our own." He sensed his tone turning too similar to his mother's; cool like a winter breeze. "I'm glad you're alive, but I'm suspicious. You declined to be candid with me the other night, and it has troubled me since. Please, tell me."

"Perhaps you should ask *her*, Majesty. I'm at her mercy, after all."

"Call me Antoine," he hissed as he strode closer. "Don't act like we're strangers."

Marguerite's jaw clenched as she backed away. "I spent years dreaming of this moment, you know. But the truth is, *Antoine*, that's what we are. Strangers. You're the King of Totresia, and I'm no one."

He nearly reached out to seize her hand, but refrained, shrinking against the door once more. "Why did Mother make you come? And why did Ade write to you, too? What did she want with you?"

"*Ade,* hm?" Her nostrils flared. "Using her nickname, are you?"

"Maggie, please—"

"Answer my question first, if you would," she said, cheeks reddening. "What does Sébastien want with Céleste Richel?"

"Séb is interested in her?" He blinked. "What... how did you find out?"

"He invited her for a stroll this afternoon." She pressed her lips into a fine line. "You didn't know?"

Antoine snorted. "Don't assume he tells me everything."

"He has eight contenders to choose from, but he fancies *her*?" Her fists bunched, and he chuckled; she was always so fiercely beautiful when irritated. "Do you find this amusing?"

"No, your *reaction* is amusing. What's the problem? You brought her here to find a husband, did you not? Sébastien is a prince. I'd hardly call that a problem."

Her hands moved in jerky movements in front of her. "I brought her here to teach her. She's too young to find a husband. And don't you dare use us as an example."

Antoine *had* been about to mention their own young romance and how they hadn't been able to deny it. His shoulders drooped. "Fine. Well, I can't speak for Sébastien. He makes his own decisions, and I support them. I always have." He glanced at her for a moment, trying and failing to figure her out. "Now, tell me what *you* know so I might support *your* decisions."

Her gaze lingered on his suit as he fidgeted with his cloak, airing it out as warmth spread under his clothes. A flush rose to her cheeks as she shook her head, as if snapping out of whatever reverie she'd entered.

She still cared. She still lusted for him, perhaps still loved him, deep down. But it was clear she didn't want to give in, didn't want to fix things between them. Still, there was something more to her demeanor, and Antoine would stop at nothing to find out why she'd come home, if not to rekindle their love.

"Your support? Is that what those looks were the other night? Supporting my presence at court? And in public, too! What possessed you to do such a thing? What if someone caught us?" She flinched. "I guarantee someone did."

He lifted his hat and rubbed his forehead. "I wasn't aware how insistent my gaze was, I'm sorry. I can't help that I'm always drawn to you."

In truth, he'd been so captivated by her that he indeed hadn't realized what he was doing. He'd forgotten what it was like to see her in a ball gown, and simply couldn't look at *anyone* else. Especially not the woman at his arm; the one he'd married in Marguerite's place *to save her.*

She curled her lip. "Antoine—"

"Maggie, please. I have suspicions and I must understand how your presence fits in with them." He removed his hat, and his short waves tumbled out.

It was a lie. In fact he had absolutely no inkling why his mother would want Marguerite back at court.

She took a deep inhale. "Your mother imprisoned me, Antoine, I told you that. She'd arranged a marriage for me that night, at the Masquerade. Did you know? No, of course you didn't. When I ran away, I ruined the prospect. As it happens, whoever she bribed into marrying me has renewed their interest, or so she claims. That's why I'm here. To be married off to the man of her choice, as she'd always planned."

Heat developed in his chest. His gut churned, and all sorts of sordid images brewed in his mind—Maggie dancing with another man, holding hands with another man, *kissing* another man.

Marriage? How hadn't he been informed of that? Any such

arrangements between high-placed nobles were to be brought to his attention.

This was the first he'd heard of Marguerite being engaged.

He held in the growl that wanted to breach out.

"As for your wife," she snickered, "I have no clue what role she plays and why she wrote to me. Someone must have informed her of me being alive. Her letter arrived at the same time as your mother's."

His fingertips curled around the rim of his hat. "I… this is… and she wrote to tell you this? And Ade discovered you were alive?"

"Your mother would rather die than be in the same room as me, but she visited, too. A follow-up to make sure I received and understood her threats." She joined her hands, which Antoine noticed had started shaking. "I can't read Adelaide. She pretends like we're still friends, like nothing has changed."

"You were never friends," said Antoine, hardly able to keep the anger from his tone. "I don't know why she'd write to you. Why the timing would coincide with Mother's… demands."

Marguerite's eyes swelled with tears, but she sniffled them away before Antoine could offer a kerchief or dare to wipe them with his fingers. Such contact would reignite feelings he'd kept dormant for years, feelings she likely never wanted to experience again.

"They have some sort of agreement," she said. "They may work together. I wouldn't put it past them; they loathe one another, but the enemy of one's enemy is one's friend, so…"

It didn't make sense for his mother and his wife to plot together. Adelaide was, much to everyone's shock, not necessarily a bad person. She was vain, liked her luxuries, but Marguerite had never done anything to harm her, and for her to assist Clémentine with sordid marriage plans…

Antoine threw his hat to the ground. "Marriage arrangements." He huffed and tilted his head to glare at the ceiling. "Behind my back? I'm the king. She can't make such decisions without my consent." He bent over to retrieve his hat, then faced Marguerite. "Ade's behavior? No, it can't be that."

"You can say *no* all you want, but the fact remains—"

He raised a hand. "It pleases me that you're here, at home, but these circumstances puzzle me."

"They puzzle me too." She adjusted the collar of her dress, looking askance. "And this isn't home to me anymore."

He balked at her. "But you—"

"Why is your mother still here?" She took a small step closer, and her lightly floral scent swept over him, making it hard for him to not pull her close and absorb her completely. "It's been almost three years, but she's still at court. Commanding you, controlling everyone as if she were still Queen of Totresia. You should have sent her away, as most sons do with their mothers once the mourning phase is over."

No one else would dare such blunt words directed at a king. But for years, she'd prepared to be his advisor, on Edouard's orders. She'd prepared to raise her voice and throw reason at him when he acted like a fool.

He'd been a fool since she'd left Torrinni—he knew that better than anyone.

"You have quite insightful informants for a prisoner." His eyebrows pulled in. "Mother is treacherous, but she still mourns.

She *is* my mother, despite her cruelty. She has the kingdom's best interests at heart."

"Are you sure of that?" Marguerite scowled. "I learned the hard way that your mother cares only about herself and her family. The realm matters little to her."

She turned away, sniffling again, which drew him to her immediately. She'd surely rebuff him, or so he thought; to his surprise, she didn't bar him from touching her.

He wrapped his arms around her, pulling her to his chest. Something akin to relief bloomed within him; she hadn't rejected him. He was holding her, like he'd seen himself doing in his dreams for years. Dreams she still haunted to this day.

"Maggie."

For an instant, they were transported into the past. Out on the patio, on a cool winter's night, enlightened by soft candles. She wore her white dress, her flowery mask; he pressed his lips to hers and declared his love.

As he reminisced, she swayed in his embrace, relaxing somewhat. He fully expected her to faint, to sink into a mess of frills and petticoats and sobs.

She released an abrupt cough; the intensity seemed to shake her awake, and she tore from him. "No, I can't—" She curtsied. "I must go." Without another glance, she wrenched the kitchen doors open, slipping in. Disappearing.

He barely had a second to react, thinking to rush after her, before he noticed sudden movement, and a gentle whimper—

Someone was crouched in the curved staircase leading upstairs.

"Hello?" His heart raced. If there'd been an eavesdropper, he might have jeopardized Marguerite's position. Possibly his own.

The spy shot up and cursed under their breath; a light, female tone he didn't recognize.

He took a few tentative steps forward, praying it wasn't one of his mother's ladies-in-waiting. "Who's there?"

"My apologies, Your Majesty," said the woman—young, from the looks of her, as she made herself visible. She clutched the sides of her gown and dipped into a curtsy, holding her head low. "I beg your forgiveness."

He squinted at her, and gasped as she lifted her chin and made eye-contact—her gray and blue gaze, reminiscent of her brother's, jogged his memory. "Miss Richel?"

She chewed on her lip and shrank further into her curtsy. "I'm sorry, I'm *so* sorry—"

He came closer, unthreatened. She was Marguerite's ward; surely she wouldn't spread rumors of what she'd overheard.

But before he could verify, she bolted up the stairs, leaving him speechless—and slightly impressed at her spying skills.

27.
Céleste

Céleste dashed up the stairs.

Adrenaline spiked her blood with each step, but she didn't lose her footing. She didn't turn around until she'd arrived at the top, breathless.

The king hadn't followed, but for all she knew, he'd gone through a different door in search of guards to detain her.

She'd landed in a service hall. Three servant girls showed up from a doorway ahead of her, holding silver platters of dirty dishes.

Céleste brisked over to them, adjusting a few curls that had tumbled over her forehead. "Where am I?"

Two of them panicked and scurried off. The third one pointed at the door she'd come through. "That's the dining room, Miss. And that," she gestured at a door to Céleste's left, "is the Queen's Corridor." She hastened after her fellow servants before Céleste could thank her.

If she wanted to confuse the king, Céleste couldn't take the service staircase. She'd have to use the main steps or find an alternative means to escape.

She slipped into the hallway, inhaling several gulps of air as she sealed the door behind her.

Right away, she recognized one of the glass Winter Garden entrances. Before she could decide whether to enter, a distinct voice full of disdain echoed from the junction between the three corridors, straight ahead from her.

"Marguerite? What are you doing here?"

Céleste froze, at once recognizing the dowager's dreadful timbre.

Sucking in her breath, she flattened against the wall, desperate to blend in with the wallpaper. If the dowager saw her, she'd have two royals on her tail instead of one.

She was too far to hear whatever else they said, but by leaning forward half an inch, Céleste could visualize the scene.

Marguerite inclined her head. The dowager had her back to Céleste, curls pinned up tight and spine stiff as a board. The layers of her dress unfurled about her like tentacles.

The dowager made a sound that resembled a snort and a chortle rolled into one, then approached Marguerite, heels clicking on the floors like a ticking clock. She said something near Marguerite's ear, and Marguerite paled as she spun to obey the dowager's command. They disappeared down the hall, past the floor-to-ceiling windows overlooking the gardens.

Céleste exhaled, but she was far from relieved.

After their footsteps dissipated, she decided it was safe to move. She glided down the Queen's Corridor, then swerved left into the Long Corridor as the clock chimed five times. She hurried to the main stairs, and once on the second floor, she raced through the landing, picking up her pace past Esther's room.

Once in her quarters, she wiped a bead of sweat from her forehead and groaned. "No more spying!"

***

An hour later, Johanna stopped by. "Are you hungry?"

Céleste nodded, still slightly appalled at what she'd witnessed in the basement.

"And your chaperone?" Johanna fiddled with a patchy spot of her apron. "She's not in her room, and I've seen her little today. Is she all right?"

Céleste scrunched her nose. "I don't know. She took me to my meeting, then chaperoned another, then met with the king in secret, and then the dowager intercepted her—"

Johanna's gasp broke out so fast Céleste angled away from her in shock. "She met with the king? *And* the dowager?"

"Yes," said Céleste, placing a hand over her racing heart. "It's been a while since they marched down the West Wing. I'm a bit concerned."

"If she's meeting with the dowager, I'm concerned, too." Johanna bolted to the bedroom exit. "Don't leave your quarters— I'll return with your supper soon."

Johanna closed the door, and Céleste huffed and threw her pillow to the floor. Her legs were restless, and her feet were falling asleep—so she paced. Her hands squeezed and released at her sides, tension enveloping every inch of her body.

Then she thought of *him*—the mysterious prince who wanted

to get to know her better.

His beautiful eyes, loaded with emotion. The way he smiled, so carefree and poised at the same time. His luscious dark locks, his strong jawline. That swoon-worthy charm. And the best part: how he hadn't discouraged the type of novels she liked, unlike most men.

There were the butterflies again, coming to life in her abdomen. They fluttered faster as she heard his dreamy voice in her mind. Faster still as she realized King Antoine wouldn't stand in his brother's way should he wish to formally court Céleste.

Such thoughts were treacherous. What guarantee did she have that the prince *would* court her?

And if he did, would it put her in a vulnerable situation? Ogled by jealous men, rumors sparking from envious ladies? Would she end up like the *Golden Girl*, running away during the Masquerade Ball to be imprisoned in an academy?

Or would she be—she dared think it—*happy?* Lucky to find the perfect man?

"Me? An underage, not-yet-graduated and eavesdropping mess?" She visualized the five contenders mocking her, kicking her out of the castle in anger at the prince's affection for her.

She dreaded the days to come.

What seemed like hours later, Johanna deposited a tray of food on Céleste's bedside table.

"Thank you." Her stomach grumbled as she reached for a piece of cheese and nibbled on it.

"Is she back?" Johanna glanced at the adjoining door, extracting from her apron a bulging kerchief of elements Céleste couldn't identify. "I wanted to bring her something to snack on.

She'll need it."

"How thoughtful." Céleste stuffed another morsel into her mouth. "I haven't heard her return."

The handmaiden twirled her raven tresses around her index finger and gave the packaged goods to Céleste. "Would you give her this when she does? Please, tell her to ring for me, no matter what time." She bit her lower lip.

"You really worry for her." Céleste set the package in her lap.

Johanna backed away. "I know her, and the dowager. So yes, I do." She forced a smile. "But you need not. Our Lady Marjorie knows what she's doing."

Céleste snorted. "I know the truth, Johanna. She's Marguerite."

"Ah. She told you." Johanna opened the door, hardly concealing her grimace. "Then I worry for you, too."

28.
Clémentine

Her ladies and supplicants finally cleared out of the reading room, leaving her alone with the one guest she dreaded entertaining. The one who'd remained perched in a corner, peering into her lap, while Clémentine found solutions and offered advice to those who sought it.

But now, the reading room felt far smaller than it truly was. When filled with ladies and their frilly dresses, Clémentine could forget *she* was here.

No longer.

She stared at Marguerite, into those falsely innocent emerald eyes she'd been threatened by for eighteen years and wished she could erase from her mind.

"Sit," Clémentine said to Marguerite, gesturing at the chaise across from her. She spread out her icy blue dress and adjusted her position, preparing for the dreadful conversation to come.

Sure, she enjoyed torturing the former duchess, but she hadn't meant to find her running down the West Wing earlier that afternoon. She'd meant to rest in the reading room, entertain her usual visitors, have a few cups of tea. Now, not only had she stumbled upon her least favorite person in the castle, but their meeting had been postponed countless times for more important issues.

Marguerite sat, keeping her chin tucked to her chest.

"Nothing surprises me anymore." Clémentine picked up her gold encrusted teacup and sipped. "But sneaking around is improper."

Marguerite shuffled, glancing about the area, surely regretting not choosing a more comfortable chair.

"Marguerite." Clémentine snapped her fingers as the hearth's flames crackled. "I need your full attention when I speak."

The corners of Marguerite's lips twitched. "Apologies, Your Grace."

Clémentine's nostrils flared. "Since your arrival, your attitude has displeased me. You're lucky only I have caught it."

"Again, I apologize, but I don't understand what you refer to, Your Grace."

Clémentine stiffened. "Sneaking around. Didn't you hear me say that seconds ago?"

The former duchess flinched. "Sneaking around?"

"I expected rebellious behavior from the contenders. They're young. But you?" The dowager sneered. "You're representing our interests, in case you forgot. Your betrothed, should he see you comporting yourself this way…" She tutted. "I require more tact from you. I won't forgive you if you ruin this opportunity."

Marguerite reached for her teacup on the coffee-table. "What would happen if I did ruin this opportunity, Your Grace?"

"Watch your tongue, young lady. You don't want to know the consequences of such actions, so I doubt you'll attempt anything." She wrapped both hands around her teacup. "I still wonder why anyone would want to marry you. You're no longer part of our family, not a permanent resident at court, hardly a royal subject at all. A lesser-noble, a former prisoner."

Still a prisoner, by some accounts, Clémentine realized—but she wouldn't voice that. There was no need.

"You have no idea the efforts and payments required to renegotiate this marriage arrangement, Marguerite." Her tongue burned saying the name aloud. "If you make all my work be in vain, I won't forgive you."

After taking another sip, failing to conceal a frown, Marguerite set her cup down. "I'm sorry for implying otherwise. I would never ruin it, Your Grace."

Clémentine focused on the brilliant brassy rings decorating her fingers. "Swell."

It had taken so much money, so many back and forth letters with underlined words and pleas she'd hated to write—but finally, she'd reestablished the terms set three years ago.

These were terms that couldn't be broken. Too many things were at stake: her life, her children's lives, the prosperity of the country. It all depended on the one person Clémentine loathed above all else.

Marguerite's gaze wandered to the door. "Do you plan to discipline me, or are these only threats? Because I must—"

"Threats?" Clémentine glared; Marguerite gulped and lowered her chin. "Is that what you call this?" The dowager leaned closer. "I'm not threatening you. You're an adult. These are warnings. But I have no issue sending you back to the academy if things don't go my way. Or locking you up in Torrinni Prison. Is that more of a threat for you?"

"I…" The former duchess' lips pinched. "Yes. I understand."

"If you don't believe me, remember what happened last time you defied me." Clémentine lifted one leg over the other. "Remember your getaway attempt, how I intercepted it, and locked you in the academy for your insubordination. It took nearly three years to convince your betrothed to reconsider, and much groveling. I loathe groveling." She swirled the liquid in her cup. "Sneaking around is unbecoming, and your betrothed needs someone proper, or our accords are off. Know this, Marguerite: I have eyes and ears everywhere. People loyal to Edouard, loyal to me. Let that sink in."

"Yes, Your Grace." Marguerite inclined her head; obedient, sullen. The only way Clémentine could somewhat tolerate her.

"Threat or warning, I mean it. Your prison could be much worse than a luxurious basement in a school."

Her words were meant to destabilize, and to see Marguerite physically crumble signified she'd succeeded. She wanted Marguerite petrified, doing penance for the trouble she'd caused three years ago.

Though she'd spoken of forgiveness, Clémentine knew deep in her soul that she'd *never* forgive Marguerite, no matter what she did.

"I didn't want you here." Clémentine placed her mug on the table and stood up. "You don't belong here. You never have. All those years ago, my husband insisted, so we kept a roof over your head. But when you ran, that changed everything."

Marguerite shifted in her seat. "I know."

Clémentine paraded over to the window. "You're lucky your betrothed demanded to meet you here. That the queen caught wind of your existence and insisted on you being here. And since she's the queen… Well, that's one of the few aspects I can't control. Her power." She turned away. "Now go. I've had enough of you. If I catch you running about again, you know what to prepare for. Good day."

29.
Marguerite

Marguerite bolted out to the West Wing.

It felt like her childhood all over again—though back then, she never got caught. There'd always been someone to look out for her, in those days.

She'd been so distraught by the argument with Antoine, and the affection that had been a part of it, that she'd ventured to the wrong staircase. She knew better—in the late afternoon, Clémentine took a walk near the garden windows before resting in the reading room to meet with supplicants or ladies requesting counsel.

Once the door closed, Marguerite exhaled heavy puffs of air, willing the tension in her shoulders and hips to dissipate. Her heart rate slowed as she fanned herself. So much time spent sharing the same oxygen as Clémentine was intoxicating; possibly perilous to her health. More so having to watch her play at dowager queen, receiving her ladies and gossiping, pretending Marguerite wasn't there.

For hours.

Marguerite needed to lie down. So much information in one fell swoop made her head spin.

Was her betrothed in the castle at that very moment? Or in town, staying at an inn, waiting to be summoned? Or on the way, soon to arrive to sweep her away?

Why did Clémentine have to *grovel* to reinitiate this arrangement?

She scurried to the junction of the three hallways, passing the garden doors as they blasted open.

She toppled aside as two figures emerged from the dusk's darkness. Both sported long cloaks and hoods concealing their expressions, but were evidently courtiers having gone on an early evening stroll.

They hadn't seen her, too busy laughing.

Marguerite smacked a hand over her chest as she regained her balance, surprised by their abruptness.

The two meandered farther inside and shook out their grass and mud stained coats. One of them removed their hood, revealing their identity. Unmistakable, mischievous—

Marguerite gasped. "Prince Jules?" She hadn't meant to say it out loud, to draw his attention.

While the other individual backed away, the younger prince didn't budge, completely unfazed by Marguerite standing there, scowling.

His messy chestnut curls unfurled about his head as he chuckled. "Hello, there, milady."

Marguerite couldn't tell who the other person was; as a

precaution, she sank into a curtsy. "I apologize for disturbing your outing, Highness."

Jules waved at her. "Rise. No need for apologies." He sounded so mature, so proper, so unlike himself.

He unfastened his cloak to reveal his shirt untucked, several buttons undone at the top.

Marguerite crossed her arms, one brow arching in suspicion. Jules wasn't known for proper behavior, but to be so easily caught returning from a frolic outside? Suspicious.

She peeped at the second person, assuming it wasn't some random courtier. They wore a ruby coat, and a few strands of milk chocolate tresses cascaded from under the hood.

As they lifted their chin, tossing the hood back, Marguerite frowned. The mystery woman's radiant complexion was stuck in a grimace; the same grimace Marguerite had seen upstairs on the day of her arrival, after bumping into a fellow contender.

Frances, daughter of the Marquess of Mara.

"Highness?" Marguerite wasn't sure whether to laugh or scold Jules. He surely knew his mother would disapprove; was he taunting her, or acting on her orders?

Jules' cheeks flushed three distinct shades of red as he nudged the young woman. "Go on up. I will, uh," he smirked, "I'll see you later."

She whispered something in his ear, then hurried down the Long Corridor.

Once she'd disappeared, Jules looked left and right. "Maggie." Wood and grass scents wavered up her nostrils as he approached her. "I'm so happy *you* found me, and not someone else."

"You mean someone like your mother?" She wiped her hands on her skirts, her palms clammy. The situation with Antoine, the scolding from Clémentine, and now this—she was a bundle of nerves. "You do realize she's in the reading room, a few dozen feet away?"

Jules rolled his eyes. "No, not her. I meant one of the other contenders. If they saw me frolicking with one of them already…" He sighed. "Mother doesn't frighten me. Her opinions matter little."

Marguerite felt that there was more to *his* opinion, but out in the hallway was the wrong place to push for more information.

"Even if she's in a mood?" She brushed a few blades of grass from the prince's sleeves. "She's up to something, so you had best beware."

He peeked towards the reading room and winced, then he blew out his cheeks, splashing Marguerite's face with his liquor-whiffed breath. "She's always up to something. Nothing new." He groaned. "Forgive me—I must hurry before Antoine sees me. I promised not to fall into my bad habits, and this would qualify as *bad.*"

He scampered off, his cloak flapping behind him like a bat's wings in the night.

Marguerite resumed her trek to her quarters, wary of knocking into other wandering royals.

This place she once called home looked the same as before. The same corridors, the same polished sconces, the same servants completing their chores. The same polite greetings concealing insults, folk creeping under the royals' noses.

Yet something was different. The castle was shrouded in

deeper secrecy than usual, blanketed in conspiracies that might become dangerous. And somewhere in these halls loomed a person Marguerite didn't even know yet—

Her betrothed.

As she swayed through the entryway, she slowed to gape down the King's Corridor. Her gaze rested on the oak doors that led to Antoine's study. Was he in there, brooding over their meeting? Or trying to figure out what his mother's final plans were?

Or did he already know them?

30.
Céleste

Céleste opened her eyes to see her candles had burned out, but a soft glow flickered in the hearth. Her curtains were closed.

She shivered, wiping her forehead with the back of her hand; it was damp with sweat, and so was her nightgown.

She'd had a nightmare about her mother. The nightmares didn't happen often, but when they did, they were intense. Swirls of color and foreign objects and coughs of blood—she trembled at the memory.

She forced away the images, her chest rising and falling in heavy motions. Nausea bubbled in her belly, so she stood and approached the fire, rubbing her hands together. The chills scrambling down her back caused goosebumps to pop up on her arms.

Her usual tactic to get rid of the haunting flashes of her mother's death was to take a walk. She gaped at the adjoining door, unsure of the time or if Marguerite had returned. *No one said I couldn't take a nightly stroll...*

Yawning, she grabbed her thick night-robe and fastened it around herself. She slid into a pair of slippers and tiptoed to her door. It opened without a creak, and she snuck into the hallway.

She scanned the corridor; only a few sconces were lit.

She crept to the service stairs, her footfalls muffled by the carpets. At the top of the staircase, she peered down and saw nothing but engulfing darkness, prompting her to rethink her decision.

What did the castle look like when everyone was asleep? *Was* everyone asleep, or were others sneaking out, like her? How many more mysteries could she uncover while the lights were out?

Before she knew it, she'd placed a foot on the first step. Then the next. Each foot moving of its own volition, down, *down,* through halls and doorways—until she stood before one of the doors to the Winter Garden.

"Am I allowed in?" She wrapped her robe tighter around herself, noticing there was a guard on duty. "Oh, I didn't mean to say that out loud."

The guard shrugged. "I don't see why not."

She hadn't checked the time before leaving, and lights were sparse here. But she recalled the tranquility she'd found in the Winter Garden when Marguerite had brought her there—so she crept inside, and the guard latched the door behind her.

A pale glimmer coated the walls, turning them to a frosty blue. She tilted her head towards the glass ceiling. Stars bedecked the skies, big and brilliant, looking in; curious, like her.

From her left, the Long Corridor clock chimed. *Midnight.*

She again pulled her robe tighter around her, and rotated to her right. A whiff of florals and wood crept up her nostrils. This was the perfect location to stretch her legs and forget her horrid dream.

She tiptoed to the center of the garden, keeping her footsteps light as she marveled at all the trees, their leaves in various hues of green, their barks of rich mahoganies. Fluffy shrubs lined the walkway, dotted with tulips, roses, daisies.

Once she reached the beginning of the path that led to the King's Corridor entrance, she stilled, noticing movement ahead.

A tree with swaying branches loomed between her and an individual who paced on the grass, features concealed in darkness. Someone else was there, too, slumped on a bench, another tree towering behind them.

Why hadn't the guard warned her the area was already occupied?

On instinct, she wanted to hide, but she must have been too obvious, because the seated person straightened up and glanced in her direction.

"Who's there?" The words were feminine, sharp, like how the dowager would have pronounced them, the same coarseness in each syllable.

Céleste's lungs constricted so much she couldn't speak. As she panicked at the idea of the dowager finding her in the wrong place again, the pacing figure whirled around.

Her eyesight had blurred, but she visualized someone with long, obscure locks of messy hair and broad shoulders covered by a wool cloak.

They strode towards her, halting in a patch of grass as they sighted her. "Miss Richel?"

Moonlight spilled over the person, exposing their face. Céleste's lungs expanded, overflowing with air as she stumbled backward.

"Highness?" Heat swarmed from her jaw to her cheeks as Prince Sébastien whisked closer, squinting. "Oh dear, I'm sorry, I—"

She lost her balance, but he kept her from falling.

His proximity made her woozier.

"Easy now, it's all right," he said, his voice like a harmony as he scooped her into his arms and guided her to the bench he'd been pacing in front of.

The other mystery individual became visible, her sculpted eyebrows wrenching upward as Céleste approached with Sébastien.

"What's going on?" Princess Cordelia watched as he deposited Céleste on the stone seat. He sat beside her, and the princess got up and planted before him. "Séb? What is this?"

"*Who* is this," he rectified, his tone sharp towards his sister. "Would you give us a moment?" His arm brushed against Céleste's, making her shudder.

The princess narrowed her gaze. "Why do you need a moment?" Her satin robe covered her from collar to toe, and her deep chestnut curls cascaded over her shoulders like waves of silk. She was a copy of her mother, minus the cruelty that flowed from the latter in clouds of toxicity.

"It's *her*." Sébastien leaned forward and mouthed something else at the princess, but Céleste was too dizzy to figure out what.

"Oh." The princess deflated. "Oh, yes. I'll wait." She gestured at a spot across the way. "I'll be over there. But hurry." She traveled towards the door Céleste had come through.

Céleste's jaw slipped out of place as the prince lifted off the bench and kneeled before her. His unkempt tresses clung to his forehead and the sides of his neck, and his shawl was fuzzy with bits of wool coming undone. "Are you all right?"

Her heart skipped a beat. Two beats. Three—then she sucked in a weighted breath. "I apologize for intruding."

She dropped her chin, but he steered it up, his soft, bare fingers against her skin. "Nothing to apologize for. My sister and I apparently aren't the only ones enjoying a midnight stroll."

Struggling to maintain his gaze, she chewed on her lip. He was so mesmerizing, and finding him here, just as she sought comfort, felt too good to be true.

"Midnight stroll, yes, Highness. I had an unpleasant dream, and I…" She blinked. "Not that you should care about that, and I rarely take nightly walks, I promise."

"Sébastien." His thumb circled over her chin in gentle motions. It was beyond improper for a man to be so intimate with her, and yet she sensed herself easing up the longer he touched her. "There's nothing wrong with nightly walks. Cordelia and I try to have at least one per week."

Céleste's shoulders had been shaking, but the prince's dazzling smile reassured her she wasn't in trouble. Heat curled down her neck, from his touch, his proximity; that delightful face she'd seen in her dreams before they'd even officially met. "I… *Sébastien*, yes, my apologies."

He released her and slid onto the spot by her. "Bad dream, you said?" A pinch of fatigue coated his voice, making it raspy. "Do those happen often?"

Céleste nodded, unsure how much to reveal.

"I understand." He sighed. "I've had nightmares on and off since my father's death."

She gulped, examining his face for the same torment she experienced, the same fear from the revenants in her dreams. "Grief still haunts *you*, too?"

"Of course it does. He was my father." He flinched. "You mean to say grief causes *your* nightmares?"

Looking askance—the princess was in the distance, gazing their way—Céleste shifted in her seat. "Yes. My mother, a few years ago."

"Forgive me for being so forward." Sébastien took her hand in his and squeezed. She twisted to him, and their eyes connected. "We have more in common than I thought."

***

They chatted for what felt like hours. Explaining their terrifying dreams, confiding their woes, describing habits their deceased loved ones had that always made them smile.

The princess lingered at first, acting as a distant—but not quite legal—chaperone. Eventually she grew bored with waiting and quietly left.

Céleste and Sébastien shed a tear or two—at least, Céleste did—and when the sky began to brighten overhead, Sébastien stretched.

"It may be best if we return to our quarters." He extended a hand to help her up. "My sister has snuck off and we're unchaperoned. I'm sure Marguerite will be asking for you. And my mother will prowl the halls once she wakes. Which will be soon."

Tingling jolts shot up Céleste's arms, bringing her back down to earth. "Yes, you're right." She lowered into a curtsy, but he yanked her up and held her close enough for his warm breath to blow over her cheeks.

He stared at her for a moment, lost in thought, then pulled away to bring her knuckles to his lips.

Céleste's knees buckled as he said, his voice still raspy, "I'm sorry you had a nightmare. Such things shouldn't burden lovely ladies like you when they sleep."

She shuffled her feet. Somehow, while she was busy fawning over this man and confessing her woes, she'd forgotten she was in her nightwear—clearly not a lady. But this prince had called her one. This man, impressive and awe-inspiring, garbed in elegance, his words eloquent and never scornful, inspired peace in her.

"I'm sorry your father haunts you, High—*Sébastien*." She'd fought during their entire discussion to not address him so formally, but she couldn't help it. He was so radiant, so tall; she was but a tiny girl in luxurious night-silks.

His cheeks turned a faint shade of red. "I thought of you all day, after our meeting." He led her down the path to the Long Corridor exit. "Imagining you, beautiful in your grand ball-gown, aiding the contenders instead of displaying your beauty to all the suitors."

She'd imagined it, too, but she'd never pictured him in her projections until recently.

"I hope to steal you from your duties at the inauguration. I'll save you a dance." His grip on her hand tightened as they arrived at the door, and he spun her to him.

She balked. "Are you sure? They won't let you—your mother, your brother… I'm not a contender, I can't compete—"

He lifted her fingertips to his mouth and pressed his lips to them. "I don't care."

A horde of butterflies broke loose in her gut; more violent than when they'd met. She squirmed, unsure how to hide such a feeling, how to contain it within her without letting it spill out and drown him.

He finally released her, smirking. "I'm a prince, and will bend the rules as I please. I will dance with my contenders, but only *you* matter."

The butterflies banged about like a drum out of rhythm, booming to its own beat. "Only I… are you… really?"

Charmed by her reaction—or sickened by her obvious infatuation, she couldn't tell—he moved in the opposite direction, taking his leave. "You're the contender for my heart, Céleste."

He hastened through the door to the East Wing, and the wild winged creatures continued to flutter about in Céleste's abdomen; restless, awake. So out of control that she feared their every motion might lift her off the ground.

Marguerite yawned as a slither of illumination came from behind the closed curtains. She detected a gentle pitter-patter of rain, a sound that rustled all sorts of memories from the back of her mind.

She tossed the blankets off and tousled her tangled tresses. "Another day in paradise."

She stood, rubbing her arms for warmth. Her fire had gone out. The chamber was gloomy and gray, the pinks of the bedspread wilting like dead roses, the green walls covered in shadows.

She rang Johanna's bell as she checked the clock—seven-thirty.

Her eyes were scratchy as she drifted to the window to push her drapes aside. Raindrops splattered against the glass, and the garden below resembled a washed out watercolor painting. The dreary sky poured its tears onto the faded shrubs and drenched the grass.

How she wished to unleash *her* tears.

She'd had another round of nightmares—Clémentine and Adelaide colluding, conspiring, whispering in each other's ears and cackling.

Antoine was there, too, looming, his laughter crueler, more piercing. He repeated *I never loved you, I never loved you* while curling his arms around Adelaide's waist.

Marguerite gripped the curtain tight as she watched the storm outside, sensing thunder roaring inside her.

With each shivering breath she took, she recalled the other visitors in her dream. Cordelia, her stony stares, a majestic dress coiling about her like a snake. Jules yelling about how he'd kissed all the contenders and they were all his now.

The bedroom door opened, and Marguerite jumped from the window.

Johanna shuffled inside. "My lady?"

"Heavens," Marguerite placed a hand over her thumping heart, "don't frighten me like that!"

The handmaiden deposited a steaming mug of coffee on the nightstand. "I will knock next time." She straightened up, seeing Marguerite shriveling by the window. "Are you all right? More bad dreams?"

Marguerite gaped down at her numb toes. "They won't stop until I leave this place."

Johanna tugged her away from the rain-soaked glass. "Staring out there won't help." She shoved Marguerite behind the divider and hastened to the wardrobe.

"Yes, I must check on the girls, and they always have issues," grumbled Marguerite as she slipped out of her nightgown. "Was I that bad at their age? I hope not."

Once Marguerite had her undergarments on, Johanna tightened the corset and threw a dress over her head—black, with orange and pink floral patterns. The long sleeves were soft, momentarily easing the tension in her muscles.

"The coffee will awaken you, Miss. I made it stronger than usual." Johanna inspected every crease, ensuring the material fell from Marguerite's hips in flattering ways.

Marguerite pressed her fingertips to her pounding temples as Johanna left. "You're a spark of light in the darkness."

"I do what I can, Miss," said Johanna, flushing.

Marguerite took her mug and wandered to her sitting area.

When the clock hands showed nine o'clock, she set off to visit the girls, prepared for the bickering, the drama.

Esther rambled on and on about Emeric. If she'd been distraught the day before, it didn't show anymore.

Harriet wasn't so positive. She sulked, dreading a celebration during which she'd have to witness her father lurking, hungry to pounce on young ladies. Marguerite vowed to protect her from his shady deals.

Cristina had picked out a gown much too revealing for a courtier of her age and standing. Several eyebrow raises and pointed comments later, she changed to something demure. "Princes and noblemen will dislike a neckline that reaches the navel," Marguerite had said.

She steeled herself for the next stops; Charlotte would sneer and snicker, and Julia would be unpredictable and moody.

To her surprise—though in truth, nothing much shocked her anymore with those two—Julia was in Charlotte's room.

"Ladies?" Marguerite entered the area with a scowl. "What are you doing?"

Julia issued a polite smile, her cheeks reddening.

Charlotte gave no such courtesy, remaining near her wardrobe, perusing her collection of evening gowns. A few were spread out on her duvet, and more still formed a giant pile below the window.

"Reviewing our options," she said as she extracted a golden gown and held it out in front of her. She shook her head and threw it on the bed.

Julia snatched it up. "But gold is elegant, no?"

Charlotte ripped the dress from Julia's grasp. "It is, but this is an inauguration, Julia, not a holiday." She padded to the pile of unwanted clothes, dropping the golden outfit. "Do you disagree, Lady Marjorie?"

Julia gauged her chaperone's reaction, her blue eyes wide and inquisitive.

"Gold is a fine choice for any festivity, Miss Geitz." Marguerite smiled at Julia. "You can wear whatever pleases you, Miss Espinar, so long as it doesn't reveal more flesh than necessary."

One of Charlotte's eyelids twitched as she returned to the closet. "Not that it matters if we don't receive invitations."

Julia huffed. "But who will? Aside from Esther, of course— we all know she has, since she won't shut her mouth about it."

"Watch your tone." Marguerite glared at the girl, who sucked her lips in. "There's still plenty of time to meet with a bachelor before the ball. And if you receive nothing, I still expect you to act poised, like presentable ladies! No more pouting like children, understood?"

Julia's chin sank, but Charlotte's gaze never faltered, nor did Marguerite's warnings seem to faze her.

"As you wish." Her voice was flat, yet lightly tinged with bitterness.

Once out in the hall, Marguerite breathed at last. As she shuffled forward, desperate for another cup of coffee, a page boy intercepted her.

"Lady Marjorie?"

She tried not to grimace at the name. "Yes?"

He shoved a note into her hand and bowed. "For you."

"From whom?"

He bowed again and skidded off without answering.

Bracing for the worst, she unfolded the parchment.

Dearest Marguerite,

Please join me for a late breakfast in the dining room!

Queen A.

She bunched the note, her knuckles turning white from clenching her hands.

Another morning of enduring Adelaide's exaggerated apologies, saddened stares, fake sympathies? She groaned. The queen was the person in Torrinni whose motives were the hardest to uncover, and Marguerite had little energy to do so today.

But disobeying, feigning illness, running away—those weren't options anymore. If she acted like a child, especially after ordering the girls not to, she'd draw the attention of the dowager.

She preferred not to have another tête-a-tête with the woman who inspired so much hatred.

She stomped to the main stairs, heels digging into the hardwood floors.

Whose cards did Adelaide play? Her own? Someone else's? Did she work with Clémentine? Or did she serve a player not yet entered into the game?

Something told Marguerite that the queen might know more about the infamous betrothed, too. Perhaps this meeting, dreadful as it would be, might give her more information.

By the time she arrived at the bottom of the steps, her stomach was in knots. Her lungs squeezed as she stepped closer to the dining room.

32.
Céleste

Céleste had no idea what time it was when she woke, but the raindrops pattering against her window made her smile as she pried her eyelids apart. She loved the rain, almost to the point of forgetting everything she'd eavesdropped on the day before, and everything that had happened to her after that.

A breakfast tray rested on her nightstand—scents of baked goods and eggs and cheese filtered into her nostrils, widening her smile.

Jerking out of her mess of covers, she scurried to the glass pane and smudged her nose against it. Thick drops thumped on the roof, then trickled onto the garden pebbles like tiny diamonds. The window's icy surface sent a chill up her spine and covered her arms in goosebumps.

Goosebumps like those caused by—

Prince Sébastien.

Last night, the Winter Garden had wrapped them in a bubble far from the castle drama. Her cheeks swarmed with heat as she remembered his hands holding hers, the way he'd blushed when she'd complimented him.

Her eyes were full of stars as she returned to her blankets and picked up a biscuit from her breakfast tray. She sank her teeth in, and the dough, still warm from the kitchens, delighted her.

Halfway through the eggs and ham, she recalled Sébastien's intention of dancing with her.

At the inauguration.

Meaning in front of everyone.

She grimaced as she wiped her mouth.

If she accepted that dance, he'd expose her to the contenders and their fury, to his family and their judgment. From what she'd noticed about the dowager, Céleste didn't stand a chance at impressing any of them. She'd already created a bad name for herself as the girl who snuck about the corridors with the supposed-to-be-dead duchess.

She fished for a cheery outfit in her closet; something bright, to contrast the weather. She plucked out a pale beige number with golden accents, and froze, gaping at her other dresses.

The inaugural ball was that night, and she had nothing decent enough for a dance with a prince.

As she struggled to fasten her undergarments and gown and gathered her curls into a messy bun, she peeked at the adjoining door. *Marguerite will help, no?*

Once fully dressed, she shoved into Marguerite's suite to find it empty. The clock showed a little after eleven, and the bed was made.

Céleste draped a shawl over her shoulders. "I will hunt her down."

The instant she exited into the corridor, she smacked into Johanna, who was carrying a set of laundered sheets. The servant girl teetered backwards, and Céleste grabbed her arm to stop her from falling.

"Apologies, Miss Richel. I must get these into Lady Marjorie's room." She adjusted her pile of fabrics.

"Where is she? I must speak with her."

"I spotted her near the dining room earlier." Johanna clutched the sheets closer to her chest. "Best not to disturb her. You could check on the other girls. They may need help with their outfits for tonight." Johanna squeezed into Marguerite's room and sealed the door behind her.

Céleste dared a peek at the service stairs, one foot tapping to the ground. She could hasten down there, like the day before; press an ear to the service door to the dining room, or even disguise herself to get inside and overhear.

But she knew better.

She swerved towards the contender rooms instead.

A shrill squeak occurred up ahead, beyond Esther's room. Céleste tiptoed to the source.

When the scream happened again, she glued herself to the wall.

Had the squeal been one of elation, or of fear?

Instinct told her to stay put, to wait. But her feet led her into the main landing, empty but for a servant holding heaps of clothes.

Céleste spun on her heel, then stopped upon finding Harriet's door open. Several loud whispers came from inside the room.

Cautiously, she approached the threshold. It wasn't Harriet who spoke—it was Esther.

"…doubtful. Did she need to boast about it like that?"

Céleste knocked to signal her arrival. "Is everything all right?"

Harriet, closest to the door, bounced around, her strawberry curls swaying. "Céleste?"

Esther, who'd been pacing in the tiny space between the bed and vanity-dresser, tilted sideways. "What is it?"

"There was a loud squeal, so I thought…" Céleste joined her hands. "Are you all right?"

Harriet pivoted to Esther, who nodded. She then yanked Céleste inside and slammed the door behind her. "Surely you can keep your mouth shut."

Céleste pulled her shawl tighter around herself. "What's happening? Who screamed?"

Esther threw her hands to the air. "Not us. We received no royal invitations, so no squeals of joy from our chambers. Excluded? Me, the daughter of the Count of Rosford? And Harriet…" She lowered her arms halfway. "Well, you're beautiful, and it shouldn't matter who your father is—"

"Hush." Harriet leaned against the edge of her minuscule hearth. "I didn't expect anyone to wish to meet me, so this is no surprise. But you? You should have men lining up at your feet." Her eyes sparkled with tears, but they didn't fall.

Esther, garbed in the brightest pink silk Céleste had ever seen, huffed. "Thank you." She shook a few auburn curls from her reddening face. "No consideration? I hoped at least one of the princes would have some interest, but neither? How cruel."

Céleste scowled at her. "Is my brother not interested in you?"

A mix of a hiccup and a chuckle erupted from Harriet. "How adorable and innocent."

"Céleste, your brother is charming. Perfect, in fact. But the goal is to gain attention from a prince, no matter what Lady Marjorie says. Such an exclusion," Esther slammed a palm to her forehead and mimicked fainting, "it's an arrow to the heart!"

Harriet wrenched the wardrobe open. "It's absurd." She tossed a gown to the ground, and its hem brushed against Céleste's shoes.

These quarters were cramped like a broom closet. Guilt tightened in Céleste's chest. Her own room was bigger than this, and she wasn't even a contender.

"Charlotte and I have the same status!" Again, Esther's arms shot up. "Yet she attracts royal attention, and I don't? How? Why?"

Céleste shuffled her feet. "Charlotte received invitations from the princes?"

Harriet grunted. "Only from Prince Jules. She's not that loved, thank the Heavens."

Esther's bouffant skirts barely allowed her to sit at the vanity without being squished against its chipped wooden surface. "Thankfully, no one wanted to meet that mouse, Julia. That should cause discord between them. One can only hope."

Céleste bit her lip, refraining from adding her own comments about Miss Espinar.

Harriet's legs dangled from the bed as she sat. "Not that I dislike her, but Cristina—"

"You do dislike her!" Esther snorted. "Don't pretend!"

Harriet blew out a heavy breath. "Well… all right, fine, I do.

But at least her invitation makes sense. Prince Sébastien likes her type, rumor has it. Quiet, not sticking her nose in everyone's business like those other two."

Tremors rushed from Céleste's fingertips to her shoulders. "Cristina?" Her voice was so low neither of the girls caught what she said.

"He won't like her plunging necklines and color preferences, I bet. He wears dark shades," said Esther, dabbing loose powder under her eyes. "At least she was polite enough to tell us without screaming."

"Who screamed?" Céleste cleared her throat, ensuring they both heard her this time.

"Keep up, dear. Charlotte screamed. How else could she be certain that everyone found out about Prince Jules' invitation? But let her reap the consequences of her unladylike behavior." Harriet pulled out a dress, glanced at it, then threw it onto the bed.

Esther snatched up the discarded gown. "You *should* wear this one. You need to show off your figure. Let them see what they're missing."

"Me?" Harriet paled. "I could never. I'm not sure how it got into my closet. Only someone with real curves can pull off something like this."

Esther held the dress up to Harriet's body. "Nonsense! You can wear it. All the men will regret not seeking your attention!"

Swallowing became painful, and Céleste expected her sobs to break out at any moment. She had to leave—to not give the girls any inkling of what had upset her.

"I see you don't need help," she said, stepping backwards. "Good day, ladies."

She scrambled down the hall and into her quarters. After latching the door, she sank to the floor, propping herself against the wood.

Sébastien said he would dance with other contenders, not *meet* with them!

But it made sense, after all—he was one of the stars of this show. Handsome, pursued by official ladies who would do anything to win his affections. He had to consider them.

Prince Sébastien had made Céleste so weak in the knees that he'd clouded her judgment. She'd read enough novels with sorrowful endings to know how this would go: she wouldn't be able to dance with him that night.

Her heart pounded in her rib-cage. She'd been foolish to think for a single second that a prince would want to court her. His pretty words, batting eyelashes, hours of confessions—a trick. A game. A mockery; some cruel way to embarrass her.

A feeble voice in her brain tried to persuade her that perhaps he'd had no choice. To keep up appearances, he requested an encounter with one of the contenders, while he figured out how to express that in reality, he wanted Céleste.

Desperate for air, she crawled to her window and pushed it open. She stuck her head out, letting the rain pummel her scalp, soak her curls, drizzle down her face, and slither into her mouth.

What a sight she must have been. A disgraceful child in outdated clothing, drowning under the weight of manners and etiquette she hadn't yet learned. Nothing distinguished her from the more refined, more experienced girls, with their luscious locks of hair, perfect pouty lips, a sway to their step. Who never lacked for topics, who didn't wander the obscure corridors after nightmares of their deceased mothers.

She was a fool. An utter, unmistakable fool, to think she had an opportunity to twirl in the arms of a prince as dashing as Sébastien.

247

33.
Marguerite

Marguerite arrived at the dining room, where Adelaide and her horde of ladies-in-waiting gossiped. She almost turned tail and ran upstairs, but it was too late—the queen had spotted her and beckoned her over.

Her vivid curls were like blood gushing from a wound, her crown glittering under the chandeliers. She wore a low-cut, ruby and gold dress that nearly blended in with the cushions of her seat.

Before Marguerite could curtsy, the queen gestured at the nearest seat. "Sit, sit! Eat!"

Marguerite's already weak appetite died as she lowered between the queen and an over-perfumed girl garbed in heaps of silver silk. A plate of breakfast goods loomed on the table before her.

The queen dismissed her crew of gushing girls, allowing Marguerite a few seconds to breathe.

Adelaide summoned another cup of tea. "For you, too?" Marguerite cringed, but the queen took that as a yes.

She glared at the food to avoid spitting out what she thought about tea. "Thank you, Majesty."

"Adelaide." The queen set her lacy hand atop Marguerite's. "My ladies are gone, so we can be more candid."

Marguerite was unable to meet the woman's gaze, so she peered out at the soaked gardens beyond the windows. Being stuck in the rain would have been a better predicament than this.

"It reminds me of our days as ladies-in-waiting." The queen stuffed a bite of eggs past her crimson lips. "Do you remember?"

Marguerite issued a half-smirk—she remembered their times of bustling down cramped corridors to respond to the dowager's every beck and call. "I do. Hard to forget."

When her teacup arrived, Marguerite did all in her power not to gag. How she wished she'd been allowed to drink coffee, but doing so in front of Adelaide might spark a discussion she didn't want to have.

"I appreciate you joining me." The queen put her utensil down. "I only have those yapping prissies as company, most days. The princess abhors me, the dowager evades me, and my husband," she made a face, "is always in meetings. He never dines with me."

"What about the princes?" Marguerite knew the answer, but she had to keep the conversation afloat before Adelaide controlled it again, filling it with her fake apologies.

The queen guffawed. "They pretend I don't exist. I have no friends here."

Marguerite forced down a few gulps of the black liquid she detested. It burned her throat, but she swallowed and puckered her lips as if she enjoyed it. "I'm sorry."

She almost released the cup when Adelaide's fickle fingers wrapped around her hand. "*You're* my friend, yes? I've done nothing to deserve it, what with our history, but I hoped that now that you're home, you would grant me some redemption."

Marguerite choked. *Friend*? She dared say it out loud, dared imply it was possible?

She feigned a coughing fit to cover up her snort. "Hot—tea—" She lowered her cup and fanned herself as she pretended to suffocate. "Very hot."

Adelaide pulled away. "Are you all right? Should I call for help?" Butlers stood off to the left, the servants on the right. "If I snap, they come running."

Marguerite whipped a few stray curls from her dewy forehead. "No, I'm fine. Apologies, I drank that too fast."

The queen tapped a finger to her chin. "Odd, for a second I thought my question had caused that reaction."

Marguerite's cheeks heated. "No." She wrinkled her nose. "Though it puzzled me, I will admit."

"I understand." The queen snapped at her staff. "Ici, tout-de-suite!"

A butler hastened over and bowed. "More tea, Majesty?"

"No, bring my chair closer to the lady."

Without so much as a twitch, the man pulled her dining throne to Marguerite's side, shoving her so close their gowns smooshed into one.

Adelaide shooed him off, and once he was a few dozen feet away, she huddled in close to the table, motioning for Marguerite to do the same. "You're the only one I trust in this godforsaken place."

It took every ounce of Marguerite's willpower to not push the woman away. An overly sweet vanilla perfume tickled inside her nostrils, and she clenched every muscle in her body to hold still.

"Me? Why?"

Adelaide's lips tightened. "Because you're a woman. You understand the consequences of… well, of not being capable of… of not having…"

In their days as courtiers for Antoine, Adelaide never hesitated to speak her mind. Everyone knew her for her sharp tongue and outward opinions. To see her so hesitant prompted Marguerite to worry.

"What is it?"

"I fear for my position." Her bright blue eyes narrowed. "I can't tell anyone, not even the king, but…" She dropped her chin. "I think I can't conceive."

Marguerite's heart skipped a beat. "I don't believe I'm qualified to speak on this matter with you."

"Nearly three years. Three years! I should have given birth to an heir by now. I should have added to the Totresian legacy, I—" Adelaide clapped a palm over her mouth. "Do you understand the gravity of this?"

Marguerite fought her fidgeting legs. "Majesty, this is inappropriate."

"He used to come to my chambers at least every month, but he stopped. Four months since he has shared my bed. Four months! Is he sick of trying to impregnate me? Has the spark disappeared? I thought we—"

Marguerite pushed from the table—the scraping of her chair

on the hardwood floor was so loud it muted whatever Adelaide was saying.

She expected vice from Clémentine, but such blatant disrespect from Adelaide shocked her. Why would she utter such things in the presence of her husband's ex-fiancée? Why would she seek to render her so jealous, so angry?

Or was that her plan—to push Marguerite into speaking her mind and saying something she'd regret?

She straightened up, ignoring the pounding in her ears. "I must ask that you cease this discussion, Majesty. It makes me uneasy."

If she cared for Marguerite's complaints, Adelaide said nothing. "All his private meetings, more of them since Sébastien's return. Something's up." With a whimper, she fell deeper into her chair, rousing three servant girls to rush up and fan her face, offer her a goblet of water, and set a cushion behind her head.

The drama of it all irked Marguerite. Adelaide always drew attention and loved it, but this? It was too much.

Adelaide slouched, but her gaze wouldn't leave Marguerite. "There's a Totresian law that allows him to annul our marriage if I fail to produce an heir after three years. Were you aware of it?"

Under her scrutiny, Marguerite couldn't lie; she acquiesced, turning to the rain-washed windows. Edouard had educated her on every single law and clause—and any secret ones, too.

"Would he dare invoke it? You know him best. All your life you lived with him." The queen's frightened facade melted as she angled farther forward. Her head cushion slunk to the floor, but no one made a move to pick it up. "Would he annul our union?"

Marguerite's fists clenched at her sides, but she hid them in the folds of her dress.

All these theatrics—they were to get information on Antoine?

Her heart was breaking all over again. Having to dig deep into her recollections, to remember the man who used to be her best friend, her confidante, her soul-mate, tore her insides to shreds.

"I'm sorry, but this is too difficult for me. You must realize this." Pressing her nails into her palms, Marguerite forced down the bile swirling up her throat.

"I beseech you," said the queen, pouting. "Would you think about it? Or better yet, would you talk to him? He would tell you the truth."

Marguerite wanted to shake her head, but it spun so much, she worried she'd lose consciousness.

She watched the person before her, once an eighteen-year-old debutante she served Clémentine with. A beautiful lady who claimed she wanted nothing to do with Totresian royalty. A foreigner whose French accent caused trouble among the nobles.

Now she was the woman who'd stolen Marguerite's place, her lover's heart, and her destiny in one fell swoop.

"Please, Majesty, you can't ask me to do this."

A service door nestled between the empty buffet tables whooshed open.

Marguerite and the queen both whipped to it—and froze.

"I agree, Majesty," said the surprise arrival, in her habitually disdainful tone. "You can't do that."

Dowager Clémentine swept over to them, green satin enveloping her like exotic jungle vines squeezing the breaths from her. Her walnut tresses tugged at her temples so hard they turned her eyes to serpent slits.

Marguerite gripped the edge of the table with trembling fingers to balance herself.

The queen crossed her arms. "Please, do join us, Your Grace."

The dowager dipped into the tiniest curtsy, then switched her gaze to Marguerite. "You may leave. Make yourself useful and stay away from my son."

Marguerite wouldn't be told twice. She sprang from her seat, curtsied, and scuffled out as quickly as her quaking legs would allow.

The guards closed the doors behind her, and she hunched against the wall, blowing out unsteady breaths, her hands pressed to her chest to stabilize her heartbeat.

Clémentine's threats didn't surprise her, but for her to scold the queen like that in such a public place? Adelaide was right— something *was* up.

Marguerite had wondered if Clémentine and Adelaide were allies, but such an intrusion brought her doubts. Then again—how did Clémentine know they were meeting? How did she hear their conversation from the storage room?

Adelaide's pleas, how she divulged private information. The dowager bursting in at the opportune time, waiting to see Marguerite's reaction to such a request; the situation felt rehearsed, but *who* had rehearsed it?

Marguerite peeled herself from the wall and swerved down the hallway, headed to her quarters. Adelaide was correct: the castle wasn't safe.

Marguerite fell onto her sofa. "Johanna, would you bring me coffee, please?" A sour taste lingered on her tongue. "I abhor their tea. I abhor *all* tea!"

Without a word, Johanna took off, only to leave place in the threshold for Céleste to arrive.

"Marguerite?" She hesitated.

"Come in, Céleste." Marguerite pinched the bridge of her nose. "Perhaps you'll bear with me a moment as I formulate some theories."

"Theories?" Céleste took one step inside; Marguerite kept her gaze trained on the floor, but she felt the frown in Céleste's words. "Are you all right?"

Marguerite raked her hands through her hair. "No, I'm not." She turned to Céleste—her eyes were bloodshot, tears stained down her cheeks. "Oh, my. What happened to *you?* Are *you* all right?"

"Oh," the girl wiped her face hurriedly, "I'm fine. Fell back asleep after checking on the girls." She sealed the door behind her and leaned against it, yawning.

Marguerite squinted at her. "Did you stay up all night reading?"

"Yes," Céleste wrinkled her nose, "I did. I shouldn't have, and I'm sorry."

"Your reading habits are the least of my problems. Sit." Marguerite motioned at a chair.

Céleste sat, but remained stiff-backed and flighty. "I'm sure we have a pile of them at the moment."

"A pile?" Marguerite molded into the sofa cushions. "I don't know what you refer to, but for now, *I* have bigger issues."

Céleste's brows inched upward. "What's happening?"

Marguerite kicked off her shoes. "I had breakfast with the queen today."

Céleste shoved her hands under her thighs. "The queen. Your nemesis, yes? Why?"

"Nemesis." Marguerite snickered. "A fitting word. And why? Because our dear queen seems to love testing my boundaries, whether she does it on purpose or not. Today's test? She revealed to me that she can't conceive an heir!"

Céleste tipped forward so fast she almost fell onto her nose. "Why would she say something so private?"

Marguerite's arms shot up. "Because she thinks we're still friends, after all this!" Her arms dropped back to her sides. "But she might have said it on purpose, to gauge my reaction, upset me. Who knows? And then the dowager was lurking nearby, eavesdropping, I think. She intervened, dismissing me. I'm unsure what happened next."

"The dowager?" Céleste scratched at her cheek. "She seemed friendly with the queen when I met them—well, friendly enough, I suppose. Why eavesdrop?"

"The dowager's motives are murky." Marguerite wasn't sure how far to go, how deeply to let Céleste in. It was a risk to bring her into the fold, and put her in danger, too.

But Marguerite needed someone else's input. She needed insight, an outsider's opinion. Someone who wasn't as biased about the dowager's cruelty, about all the ways she'd tormented Marguerite in her youth.

Someone who hadn't been subjected to the secrets and lies spread around court. And that someone had to be Céleste.

"But I think there's more to the reason why the queen wanted to meet with me, and why the dowager spied. I'd thought perhaps they were allied, but... the queen's disposition makes no sense, if that were the case." Marguerite checked the door. "Adelaide mentioned she feared for her safety."

Céleste scoffed. "She's the queen! Why wouldn't she be safe?"

"Because she has produced no heir. There's a law that states that if a royal marriage doesn't yield a child in the first three years, the union can be annulled."

"By whom?" Céleste's breaths visibly quickened. "I've never read of such a law, and none of my professors at the academy ever discussed it."

Marguerite let her head hang, a curtain of golden hair concealing her expression. "It's an ancient law, only known by advisors and royals. Anyone in the royal family can enact it, or any who sit on Antoine's council. They can ask for a vote."

"A vote? Do you think…" Céleste placed her palm at the base of her neck. "Could the king enact it because he wants to separate from the queen?"

Marguerite's eyes burned with her own questions. "Antoine is an honorable man, and if he forsook all we had and chose her… no. Not after all he endured to get to this point." She fanned herself. "Someone else will do it."

Silence lingered for a moment as Céleste wrung her hands, opening her mouth every few seconds to speak. Eventually, words formed. "The dowager?" She gulped. "You often mention how sly she is. So is it her? You think she will request the annulment? How would that benefit her?"

"That is a question I have no answer to, and it's the reason I'm so worked up." Marguerite shrugged. "You should have seen the queen when the dowager came in. She barely held her composure. Any other noble might have been fooled, but not me. I know her."

Céleste tapped a finger to her mouth. "So you say the dowager will interfere in her son's marriage?"

"Yes," said Marguerite, without an ounce of hesitation. "She ruined our engagement, and though she may have been behind *this* union, her desires always shift. She never liked Adelaide. Adelaide was to serve one purpose: conceive heirs. If she's not doing that, she's of no use to the dowager."

"No use? So she'll dispose of the queen, just like that? Would the dowager do such a thing to her own son?"

A chortle broke free from Marguerite's mouth. "You don't know her as I do." She stood and stared at the door. "She's manipulated Antoine for years, and he's too blinded to care."

Céleste planted her feet as if to stand, too, but remained seated, fists clenched. "He's the king! He wouldn't allow this to happen, would he? You know his mother, but so does he—"

"Not as well as I do. He's too distracted by his duties to see the truth. He never saw it in our youth, when she bullied me, though he claimed he did." She spun away, fists on her hips, and paced to the hearth. "Deep down, he's aware he needs to banish her from court, and she is too." Ideas blossomed in her head, things so preposterous that they may be true. Things she should have thought of before. "She'll distract him by plotting to remarry him to another lady of her choice. Or… by doing something far more drastic, like taking him off the throne altogether."

"But," Céleste got up, teetering side-to-side, "what would happen to the queen?"

Marguerite snarled at the flames in the fireplace. "She has too much knowledge, so they can't send her home to her father. Is that why she keeps trying to befriend me? To help her against the dowager's schemes? Help her stay married to my ex-fiancé?"

The clock chimed.

"One, already?" Céleste stretched her arms.

Marguerite glowered at the clock. "Where is my coffee?"

"Is there anything I can do? Anything else you'd like to, uh," Céleste winced, gently approaching from the side, "tell me? I can keep your secrets, Marguerite. I already have."

Marguerite cocked her head, studying the girl's colorless face, her eyes still red. *Was* it fatigue, or was she hiding something from her chaperone?

The bedroom door swung open, and Johanna came in to

deposit a tray of drinks and delicacies.

"Your coffee, Miss," she curtsied, "and a few snacks." She returned the way she came, quiet as a mouse, sealing the door behind her.

Marguerite hurried to the tea-table and snatched her mug. She took three swigs, exhaled in relief, then turned to Céleste. "I trust you, Céleste, I do." Another sip. "But these heavy burdens I carry… I can't share them with you, not yet." She glanced into her cup. "The dowager always has several things in motion; only one of those things involves me. As for Adelaide… I'm not sure, but this hunch I have? It's legitimate. My hunches about that woman have never been wrong before."

Céleste nodded. "I understand, but…"

"No," said Marguerite, putting her cup down. "I'm sorry, Céleste. Not today."

"I must ask, because it may involve me, at some point." Céleste shifted her weight. "What of the princes? Can they vote on such a matter? Would they operate for their mother?" She returned to the tea-table and plucked a biscuit from the platter. "Would they go against their brother?"

Marguerite flinched. "Sébastien would have a say, as he's on the council, but… no. He respects Antoine too much. Jules is also on the council, and owes Antoine a lot. But if Clémentine issued the right threat, she might persuade them to obey her. She's their mother, and no matter how they claim she can't control them, she always does. Always has."

Céleste sank her teeth into the biscuit and her eyelids fluttered in delight as she fell onto a chair. She chewed and swallowed. "And you're sure it all has nothing to do with you? That you're here for another reason?"

Marguerite dropped onto the couch. "Indeed."

Céleste puffed out a heavy breath. "So, to resume, the queen can't bear children. The dowager will use that excuse to ruin the royal marriage. The princes may be puppets at their mother's behest—have I forgotten anything?"

"Puppets, yes, perfect word." Marguerite reached for a croissant, zeroing in on the girl's peaked expression, the constant drooping of her shoulders. "Now, time is ticking. Do tell me what has made you so distraught?"

Céleste's mouth fell open. "How… how did you…?"

Marguerite sniffed at the croissant. "You said we had piles of problems. And you stayed up all night, but I'm quite positive you weren't reading. So what is it?"

"I *was* reading," Céleste said through gritted teeth, "but this morning, the girls put me in a bad mood. Esther and Harriet grumbled about Charlotte, who was going on about receiving an invitation from Jules. And Sébastien… invited Cristina."

Marguerite swallowed her bite. "Jules and Charlotte? I suppose he would like her bluntness, though I found him with someone else the other night. And Cristina? Odd, I thought Séb's type was more… Oh." She put the rest of her pastry on the tray, grimacing. "Oh, I understand now. This must be difficult for you. But he must meet with presented ladies, too. I assume his mother got wind of his admiration of you, and she forced his hand. I'm so sorry."

Céleste fiddled with her fingers, sending biscuit crumbs into her lap. "I didn't have much hope, anyway. I mean, a prince? With me?" She sniffled. "Impossible."

Marguerite patted Céleste's leg. "I admire you for putting on a strong front, but nothing is impossible." Her lips curved into a sympathetic smile. "I'm sure he likes you. You're worthy of him. But he must maintain a certain image, as a prince. He can't follow his heart, and especially not if his mother lurks, looking over his shoulder. This is for the best."

Though the girl acknowledged Marguerite's words, Marguerite knew she was only half-convinced, and would surely return to her room to cry for the rest of the day.

While Johanna supervised the luncheon between Charlotte and Jules, Marguerite introduced Cristina to Prince Sébastien.

Her mind wouldn't settle—Clémentine's threats, the mystery betrothal, Adelaide's requests, Antoine's insecurities. It all linked somehow, but Marguerite wasn't sure how to investigate without getting deeper into their mess.

Cristina was enthralled by the prince, her manners poised. She'd worn a dress Marguerite didn't approve of—too bright and too low-cut—but it didn't seem to bother Sébastien.

In fact, nothing bothered Sébastien. Marguerite knew him well and could tell—he wasn't enjoying the meeting. He was polite, but he stifled yawns and feigned smiles. He definitely wasn't there by choice.

Had someone pressured him? Forbade him from courting a seventeen-year-old lady-in-waiting? Someone like… his mother?

Sébastien grimaced when he excused himself. Cristina caught the look and squirmed. *Unrequited love,* thought Marguerite.

As Marguerite took Cristina up to her room, she bit her tongue to not warn the girl to lower her expectations.

Once in her chambers to prepare for the ball, Marguerite was joined by Johanna, who detailed Charlotte and Prince Jules' experience.

"They chatted, they flirted. He liked her," said the handmaiden, fighting a groan as she fastened Marguerite's stays. "I didn't believe it possible, but she might have a chance at wooing him."

Marguerite tried to find humor in the situation. Still, she worried. Why would Jules lean towards a girl like Charlotte? Especially after Marguerite had caught him flirting with Frances. Charlotte was well-bred and her father high-placed, but Jules preferred the light-hearted girls that frolicked in taverns, not the semi-proper ones like Miss Geitz.

Johanna enveloped her in a vermilion gown and straightened out the petticoat. "This concerns you," she said, tugging on Marguerite's medium-length sleeves and fanning out their ruffled edges.

"Everything in this place does." Marguerite tucked jewels and flowers into her hair as Johanna scooped it into a high bun. She powdered her face, rouged her cheeks, dabbed a light pomade onto her lips. "Tonight I'll pay close attention to everyone."

Later, she met the five contenders and Céleste in the main landing. "Best behaviors tonight," she ordered, as she took note of their outfits.

Harriet's open-back bodice was a bit daring. Cristina's

plunging neckline made her hiccup. Charlotte was over-the-top, Julia demure, Esther fluffed up in frills; nothing too out of the ordinary.

Downstairs, they swerved past nobles in radiant silks and mountains of jewels. A faint piano melody reached Marguerite's ears. From what she could tell from the clusters of aristocrats out in the East Wing, the royals hadn't arrived.

"Go on in," she said to the girls. "The herald will announce you, and you may wait close to the dais." The five hurried inside, but when Céleste tried to follow, Marguerite snatched her wrist. "No, you stay with me."

Céleste squinted at her. "Aren't we going in?"

"Tonight will be hard for you." She took in Céleste's pastel pink gown; the rosewood bows trailing down its bodice gave her an air of innocence. She appeared so put-together, but Marguerite knew better. "You have a lot on your mind, and your heart must be heavy."

A visible lump formed at the top of Céleste's exposed throat. "I'll be all right."

"You will." Marguerite squeezed her shoulder. "I don't know what will happen, but don't get your hopes up."

Céleste puckered her lips and nodded. "I won't."

Marguerite released her. "When your turn comes, you will meet a wonderful man who won't be in such a hurry to marry. Sébastien is a prince with a deadline. He can't follow his heart, but when it's right, I hope *you* can."

She ached as she spoke—she knew Céleste's pain better than most.

"Thank you, my lady."

Marguerite guided her through the crowd clogging before the entrance. Seas of colorful nobles stood on either side of the crimson carpet, chatting, fanning their faces while surveying the arrivals. The royal orchestra filled the room with gentle hymns to pass the time while waiting for the royals.

The herald cleared his throat. "Céleste Richel, daughter of the Marquess of Valeville, student of the Totresian Royal Academy for Noble Girls. And her chaperone, Lady M—" The herald paused, squinted at Marguerite, and sighed. "Lady Marjorie."

Heads turned, whispers erupted from painted mouths. Marguerite hadn't been announced at the presentation, so she'd managed to enter unnoticed; tonight, all eyes were on her.

Onlookers ogled as she and Céleste strode down the carpet. Marguerite's chin weighed more than several tons of marble, but she kept her shoulders straight, sucking all her anticipation into her gut.

Who is Lady Marjorie? they'd all wonder. And why was a chaperone being announced when entering the ballroom?

She and Céleste settled behind the eight contenders, near the platform.

The herald's thrumming staff prompted the last-minute courtiers to pour into the area. The orchestra halted its melodies, and everyone swiveled to the doors.

"Their Majesties, King Antoine and Queen Adelaide of Totresia!"

Marguerite spun to watch them. Antoine wore a shockingly vibrant red coat—a color he abhorred—and the rest of his ensemble was white. On his arm, his stunning queen sported a white dress trimmed with gold, sprinkled with red roses.

He appeared on edge, stressed. She smiled wide, happy as ever.

Attendees lowered into bows and curtsies.

"Their Highnesses, Prince Sébastien and Prince Jules of Totresia!" They walked side by side, Sébastien in aubergine velvet, his hair tied back, his expression somber; Jules in light brown, his amused gaze fixed on the attendees. As he climbed atop the platform, he winked at the contenders below.

One person remained to enter, the one Marguerite didn't want to curtsy for.

"Dowager Queen Clémentine of Totresia," said the herald, voice shaky. "And for the first time, Princess Cordelia of Totresia!"

Gasps and low mumbles broke out from the guests.

Cordelia was sixteen; the Masquerade aside, one rarely attended balls until eighteen. Céleste was the exception, as Marguerite's assistant.

But it was no mistake. The princess traipsed in on her mother's arm, swathed in gray and peach, each step taken with purpose and pride. The dowager was draped in ruby-red and black lace, looking every inch the sorceress part she played in Marguerite's nightmares.

Once they were all atop the podium, Antoine gave a short—and forgettable—commencement speech. At its end, he shifted his weight and huffed. "To start the events, my brothers will choose their first dance partners," he finished, his tone devoid of emotion.

This moment would determine the front-runners for the princes' hearts. It was one of the most important instances of the night; of the entire season.

The two royal men descended, approached the contenders,

and Marguerite held her breath.

Jules extended his arm to Frances—unsurprising—and she accepted. Charlotte scoffed, but Marguerite kicked her in the shin. In response, the blonde lifted her nose in the air.

Guests parted to allow Jules and Frances to take their places on the dance-floor.

Sébastien, after scouring the ladies prostrated at his feet, offered his palm to Cristina. She flushed as he accompanied her to where Jules and Frances stood.

Céleste shuddered.

Marguerite pressed closer to her, hoping to give her courage.

After a few beats, other eligible men sought dance partners. Emeric requested Esther's company, and without hesitation she bounced across the carpet with him. Husbands invited wives, timid boys approached lavish ladies they fancied. The room came alive.

By the time the tune reached its middle, only Harriet and Julia remained. Even Harriet's father had snagged one of the contenders from another academy. He'd combed his unruly beard and almost appeared charming, but he wouldn't fool Marguerite.

Cordelia's sweeping dress caught Marguerite's eye as she sailed across the dance-floor.

She was dancing, too? Surprising considering her age and standing at court.

Her mother was on the dais, in conversation with one of her ladies, caring little for her daughter waltzing about in someone's arms—someone Marguerite realized she didn't know.

She hadn't sighted him in the crowd when entering the ballroom. He stood out now, among the dancers; tall, a muscular build, a confident posture. Unbound, dirty-blond locks of hair framed his pallid face and stopped at his shoulders. Even from afar, Marguerite saw his onyx eyes: cold, so impenetrable they froze her to her spot.

He spun Cordelia with ease, an eerily disturbing smile on his thin lips. His inky-colored attire smeared through the ocean of bright colors worn by other guests.

Something about him caused ripples of shivers to crash down Marguerite's spine. She stared for so long the music changed. Partners thanked each other, and men located someone new to dance with.

Cordelia and her mystery friend meandered towards the platform.

"Céleste, do you—" Marguerite's speech was cut off as someone slipped in front of her, blocking her view. Her breath caught in her throat when she realized who it was. "Oh, Highness," she curtsied, "forgive me."

Sébastien chuckled. "You're forgiven." He extended his palm to her. "Join me for a dance? Please?"

Still fighting to breathe, she pressed a hand to her breastbone. "Shouldn't you invite a contender? This might give the wrong idea."

Céleste mumbled an excuse about being hungry before dashing to the buffet.

Sébastien examined Marguerite with a wince. "It won't. For old time's sake? I beg you."

A few loitering nearby sent questioning glances at them.

"You break tradition, Highness," said Marguerite through clenched teeth. "And draw unwanted attention."

"*You* draw attention by declining." He seized her forearm and hauled her away from the crowds, ignoring her protests.

She fought to keep her jaw in place. Her gaze found Antoine atop the dais. He glared at them and shook his head.

"I'm not sure what game you play, Séb." She curtsied, and reluctantly allowed him to escort her onto the dance-floor.

Sébastien bowed, then placed his hand on the small of Marguerite's back. "It's not a game. I wish to discuss Céleste."

He'd never been so serious, yet *no one* took him seriously. Antoine hardly had when they spoke earlier that day. His mother had called him an imbecile. Now Marguerite questioned his request to dance with her to discuss things?

"What about her?" Marguerite bristled as they took off, following the upbeat rhythm. "You gave her false hope. I assume your mother interfered? What more is there to say?"

"I know." He twirled her so fast it made him dizzy. He hadn't danced like that in years, not that he ever *liked* to partake in such activities.

"And?" Marguerite asked, as the rhythm slowed suddenly.

"I've made up my mind," he said, his words so soft he was sure she battled to hear them as the tunes accelerated again.

"You what?"

"I've made up my mind, Maggie. I don't care about appearances or threats." He gripped her waist, his lips near her ear. "I will fix this."

His mother's warnings ran wild inside his head, but he ignored them. No one would stop him from courting Céleste. He'd vowed as much after their first meeting, and solidified those feelings after their night spent in the Winter Garden. He hadn't been able to quit thinking of her—she'd been showing up in his dreams.

No, it wasn't love, not so soon. Even he wasn't such a fool to succumb so easily. But he'd read enough to recognize the signs, the potential.

Céleste Richel was everything he'd ever wished for. She could hold a conversation, she loved reading, and her sense of adventure matched his. And she was *spectacular*. Those eyes, like a dove's feathers. Her nervousness—so charming.

He refused to let anyone stand in his way. Not even his dangerous, power-hungry mother.

Marguerite's mouth dropped open, but before she could formulate a reply, Cordelia brushed by them.

The spark in Sébastien's heart turned to ice. It was ill-viewed to dance with the same gentleman twice, and even a novice such as Cordelia knew that. Less so twice in a row, and with such a scoundrel of a man.

Sébastien ground his teeth and it took much focus to not stumble on the dance's steps.

Marguerite squeezed his arm. "Who's that dancing with your sister?"

He became rigid, loosening his grasp on Marguerite's waist.

As they swirled, they both had a perfect view on the man in question—he said something to Cordelia that made her giggle.

Sébastien's jaw clenched as he held in a growl. "Cornelius Schwartz."

Marguerite let go of Sébastien's hand to clutch her stomach. "Him? He… he's—"

"The Duke of Terter." Sébastien's lip curled. "A Giromian. I know, I've considered removing her from his reach myself, decency and etiquette be damned."

Her cheeks drained of color as she missed a step. "A Giromian at Torrinni court? What's happening?"

The long-lasting hatred between Totresia and Giroma had started eons ago, or so Sébastien felt. Their passive-aggressive relations were always on the verge of becoming *actively* aggressive, and neither side cared to take steps to rectify their disagreements. Edouard had mentioned wanting peace, at some point, but Sébastien wasn't sure why it never happened.

All he knew was that Giromians weren't welcome in Totresia, and Totresians weren't welcome in Giroma. Not unless there were special circumstances—official envoys, merchants of important goods, royal decrees.

Or princes who were hiding from their true identities—like Sébastien had.

Sébastien helped Marguerite recover from her imbalance. "Mother neglected to remind Antoine of some treaty we have with Terter, allowing their eldest son to join us, to choose a wife."

His mouth filled with acid, recalling how their mother admitted she'd kept such integral secrets from them. *From Antoine.* He was the king! How was he not aware of these treaties?

It had taken a lot to calm him down, and Sébastien didn't want to be reminded of it again—how he'd nearly laid a hand on his own mother. *Him,* the calmer, more mature of the brothers.

Marguerite almost stepped on his foot. "A treaty? With Giroma?"

Again, he ensured her misstep went unnoticed. "With Terter, specifically. I don't know anything more."

The musical notes crescendoed and sweat beaded on Marguerite's forehead. "Heavens."

Heat crawled up Sébastien's neck. He didn't want to blow up here, in front of everyone. It'd only fuel more rumors that he'd have to fight. "Mother dropped this on us out of nowhere. He was already en route. So we have another competitor, and not a friendly one." He spotted Céleste at the buffet, and the weight on his heart lifted. "But it matters not."

Marguerite scowled at him. "Have you lost your wits? A Giromian at court on your mother's orders? You must be—"

"Indifferent." He spun Marguerite towards the crowd near the buffet. "I mean, I'm livid about it all, I am. He shouldn't be here, I agree. But he's not my competition, and he's Antoine's problem, in any case. *I* have set my heart on someone he wouldn't dare to approach. Her." He jutted his chin straight at the blushing blond in pastel pinks, standing in front of the pastries, doing her hardest to look anywhere but at him.

Marguerite's nails dug into his suit sleeves. "Don't toy with her. Not if you can't guarantee your mother won't punish you both for it."

A different melody began, and nobles dashed about, seeking new companions.

Sébastien continued to admire Céleste, remembering all the conditions his mother had given, all the hoops to jump through to *get* the girl—they wouldn't deter him. He had no doubt such conditions would be fulfilled, especially if he put his mind to them.

When Sébastien truly fought for something—like when he'd begged to leave court—he always succeeded.

And he'd fight for Céleste.

"I don't toy." He placed a quick kiss on Marguerite's knuckles. "I've never been more serious." He then sauntered to the platform, leaving Marguerite to be engulfed by the couples starting a new dance.

Part Three

Céleste scrutinized the prince and the duchess as they danced. They were close, like family; she had no reason to be jealous. Still, every time they swirled or spoke or seemed too friendly, she cringed.

When they'd peered at her, she'd frozen. Sébastien smiled at her.

Smiled? Why? He'd played with her, hadn't he? That was nothing to smile about.

She sucked in a great breath, looking at Cristina, who was parked off to the side, in discussion with a decadently dressed noblewoman. *Her* dance with the prince had made Céleste's stomach churn. She'd been the first choice of the night, giving her the status of front-runner.

The status Céleste had been led to think she'd obtain.

Harriet stood nearby in her daring gown. Even she, as the daughter of the most disgraced noble of Totresia, held herself with poise. Céleste wondered how no one had invited her to dance.

Goosebumps pricked her skin. She had no right to compare herself to these ladies; they were presented, educated, here to find husbands. She wasn't.

She peered into the dense crowd, scanning through the throng of dancers. Who would Sébastien invite next? The thought of his dimpled cheeks and soft hands woke butterflies in her gut—the same that had unleashed when they'd chatted in the Winter Garden.

The same she'd sworn to kill.

Tucking her chin to her neck, she fought to shove down the reminiscence of the flicker of passion that once ignited in his eyes, the laughter that brought fresh air to her lungs. He'd reserve such things for Cristina, now, no doubt.

Céleste inhaled the stuffy ballroom air and closed her eyes, envisioning herself outside, lying amidst flowers. Or in a library, plunging into a fairytale.

When she wrenched her eyelids apart, she swerved backward as Charlotte swished by, locked in Jules' arms—in a steamy dance.

Charlotte had bickered about Jules choosing Frances first, yet there she was, in her second round of twirling about the dance-floor, beaming as if she'd always known he'd invite her.

Céleste peered down at her demure neckline, at the girly bows decorating her bodice, at the embroidery lining the hem of her dress. Maybe she hadn't been daring enough. Maybe if she'd put in an effort, Prince Sébastien wouldn't have opted for Cristina.

Charlotte's high-pitched giggle broke her concentration. She was now fawning over Prince Jules like he was a puff pastry filled with delectable fruit.

The instant Charlotte moved from in front of her, she saw Sébastien leaning against the bottom of the dais as he chatted with some aristocrat she didn't recognize. He caught her looking and grinned, nodding at her.

Her cheeks infused with a boiling heat, driving her to turn around and almost bump into Julia, who'd been lurking behind her.

"Pardon me, Miss Espinar." She tried to move around her, but Julia propped her fists on her hips, glaring between Céleste and Sébastien.

"Did I imagine that, or did the prince smile at you?" Redness spiraled from Julia's jaw to her temples. "What's going on?"

Céleste's tongue twisted in her mouth as she gawked at the floor.

"How inappropriate." Julia's voice laced with vice. "Why would he pay attention to *you*? An underage, barely passable student?"

"I don't know what you refer to." Céleste couldn't meet Julia's fiery eyes, worried the truth would spill out if she did.

"Liar." Julia whisked away, mumbling complaints under her breath.

Céleste clasped her hands behind her back and scoured the room for Marguerite. "Help," she whispered, yearning for a reason to run out of the ballroom and hide. "Marguerite, where are you?"

When at last she spotted the duchess near one of the windows, whispering something in Harriet's ear, she prepared to dash up to her. But upon seeing Harriet's scrunched brows and down-turned lips, she resisted, giving them space.

The two women gaped at someone by the platform, so she followed their gazes.

A man garbed in ink-colored silks was perched below where King Antoine stood on the podium. This unknown man was in conversation with the princess, who was absorbed in whatever he said. He was several heads taller than her, with lengthy waves of dark blond hair. He made a face, and with a flick of his wrist, he prompted the princess to giggle.

The king snarled down at them, not in the least discreet. His wife, though, drank in the mystery man's features. The dowager, in the distance, observed in silence, her expression neutral.

When Céleste looked at Harriet again, Marguerite had disappeared. *She needs to stop moving!*

Julia stormed back over, clutching a drink. "Oh, you seek Lady Marjorie? No, *I* will find her first, you shameful mouse."

Céleste had had enough of the girl's snide comments. "Leave me alone! It's none of your business if men notice me!"

Julia's face turned the shade of a ripe tomato, and she looked ready to stomp in fury. "The nerve of you, you little—"

"Apologies, ladies," said a honeyed voice, breaking through the orchestra's melody and whatever Julia had been about to insult Céleste with.

Céleste and Julia twisted to the new arrival—and both became still as statues.

The mystery noble—Céleste hadn't noticed him detach from the princess and come up to them. He was taller, more imposing up close. Her heart couldn't seem to beat properly as she studied his expression—veiled and eerie. Handsome, but… off-putting.

Julia batted her lashes and splayed a palm over her chest. "Hello?"

He laughed; a deep, enchanting sound that rattled inside

Céleste's abdomen. "Forgive me, I shouldn't walk up and frighten ladies. How rude of me."

A woodsy musk wafted from his coat as he adjusted his lapels. His eyes were like wells with no bottoms, no shine or glisten, no emotion. A cerulean badge shone on the right side of his broad chest; a pattern Céleste thought to be familiar but couldn't place.

He was quite dashing, but something about him bothered her. His tight jaw? His hollow cheeks? Or his overly suave timbre as he ogled them with parted lips? She couldn't figure it out.

"I seek to meet all the contenders this evening. I'm Cornelius Schwartz, the Duke of Terter. And you are?" He gestured to Julia and requested her hand to kiss it.

Julia accepted, her arm shaking, but not without sending a petrified peek at Céleste, first.

Céleste felt that same petrification. She remembered her geography lessons: Terter was a Giromian province. If her father had taught her anything, it was to steer clear of Giromians.

And yet here was one, at Torrinni Court.

38.
Marguerite

"The Duke of Terter is here."

Few folk at court would accept this intrusion. A lesser few would actually welcome it.

None knew the rumors Marguerite had had access to while at the academy, thanks to Johanna. She'd reported about Eugene Thatcher and his supposed dealings with Giroma, specifically with Terter. She'd overheard conversations whenever the foul man visited his daughter, Harriet—a rarity—and never hesitated to tell Marguerite.

When Marguerite had told Harriet of the duke's presence, the young woman's face had turned so pale, she was nearly transparent. She rushed to haul her father outside, likely to interrogate him, as Marguerite had asked her to.

Marguerite scouted the area in search of Céleste—to warn her, protect her, enlist her to round up the girls and keep them safe from the foreign man's slimy hands.

Cornelius Schwartz had a reputation that preceded him. She didn't want him anywhere near the contenders, even more so if he'd come searching for a wife.

Her intestines tied into knots when she realized she was too late—for there he was, kissing Julia's knuckles, requesting a dance that the young woman unfortunately accepted.

Céleste watched them glide off, her jaw about to hit the ground when she spotted Marguerite. She was panting as she approached. "My lady—"

"I saw." She gripped Céleste's forearm and towed her towards the lavish display of pastries.

Céleste's blue-gray eyes were cloudy. "He... and I wasn't able to..."

"I know." Marguerite fixed a curly strand of the girl's hair behind her ears and squeezed her shoulder. "You must recompose yourself. You look like a stampede of horses ran you over. Don't show any inkling of fear. Not here."

Céleste sniffled as Marguerite shoved a flaky pastry under her nose. "But I—"

"Eat." Marguerite pulled her out of the way as Prince Jules and Charlotte marched by.

They stopped, and Jules kissed Charlotte's hand, sending flares of redness up to the girl's temples. He lingered, his gaze on her face, then her décolleté, before excusing himself.

The moment he brisked off, Charlotte hastened over to Marguerite. "Oh, isn't he dreamy?" Her eyes sparkled under her batting lashes.

"Charlotte, would you find a way to, uh—" Marguerite

glimpsed Julia twirling in the middle of the dance-floor, oblivious to the scandal she'd caused. "Would you snatch up your friend?"

Charlotte's lips spread wide as she fanned herself. "What friend? Julia?" She spun on her heels. "Where is she? We have so much to talk about."

As Céleste munched on her delicacy—and grabbed another—Marguerite turned Charlotte towards the dancers. "Over there."

"Oh! Who's that with her?" Charlotte cupped a hand over her forehead. "I don't know him."

Marguerite's spine tensed. "The Duke of Terter."

"The Duke of..." Charlotte's jaw tightened. "Terter? In Giroma? Heavens, this is bad."

"Fetch her, now." Marguerite pointed Charlotte towards Julia and the duke. "Hurry."

Charlotte took off, though she seemed hesitant to interrupt. She tiptoed nearer to get a better view.

Marguerite flipped to Céleste, who'd scarfed down several biscuits by that point. "Where are the others?" She hadn't seen Cristina since her dance with Sébastien had ended.

Céleste swallowed her bite and motioned at a spot behind the buffet. "Esther is with Emeric."

Marguerite caught the two seated on a burgundy sofa, sharing a platter of macarons. "She's safe. Schwartz won't go near your brother. Harriet is interrogating her father, last I checked."

Her pulse quickened as she sighted Julia smiling at the man who spun her around.

Too many emotions streamed through Marguerite—anger, fear, confusion, sorrow. The wine fountain was a few feet away, but as she prepared to slide towards it, someone slithered in front of her.

Someone who'd draw attention.

Céleste gasped and dipped into a curtsy. Marguerite also curtsied, but dared a peek up, eyebrows scrunched. "Highness?"

Sébastien extended his hand to Céleste. "Hello again, Maggie." He focused on Céleste, waiting for her to accept.

Marguerite shot up, glaring at him, at Céleste, and at him again. "What are you doing?" She folded her arms to conceal her shivering.

He widened his smile as he neared the frightened Miss Richel. "Inviting her to dance."

The melody faded at the worst possible time. Nosy attendees in the vicinity ceased their conversations. Some lowered their fans, others sipped on their beverages while witnessing the scene.

Charlotte, naturally drawn to drama, emitted a sound close to a growl.

"Highness?" Marguerite noticed Sébastien's mischievous grin expanding. "Do you understand the chaos you're about to cause?"

"I told you, *you* cause chaos," Sébastien hissed through gritted teeth. "She won't rise if you don't permit it. I want to fix this. I must speak with her. Please."

Marguerite sank into a semi-curtsy. "Céleste." The girl side-squinted at her. "You need to accept his invitation."

"I can't," said Céleste, her voice so low Marguerite strained to hear it.

"You can, and you must." Marguerite's scalp throbbed in pain. If Céleste didn't dance with the prince, she'd embarrass them all—Sébastien included. He wouldn't forgive that, and his mother wouldn't tolerate it. "It's ill-viewed to refuse a royal, no matter your status or station." She grasped Céleste's wrist and tugged her up. "Go on. We'll discuss it later."

Whispers buzzed about them. A few of the dancers had slowed near them to figure out what was going on. Sébastien shooed them off.

Still, they kept their gazes on him and Céleste, and on Marguerite, too.

She nudged Céleste towards the prince. "Remember your manners."

Céleste hesitantly placed her hand in the prince's. "Apologies, Highness. I was under the impression I couldn't... wouldn't..." She silenced as he pressed his lips to her knuckles, then guided her to the dance-floor.

Gossip swarmed around her, and soon, Marguerite was unable to view the prince and her ward in the midst of such a scandal.

She shifted to the buffet. Her knees were weak, her feet in agony from running around the room. She reached for a goblet to fill it with wine, but Charlotte planted beside her.

"This isn't right! Is there nothing you can do?"

Before Marguerite had a chance to answer, Julia, done with her dance with Duke Schwartz, popped up on her other side. "What is that Richel girl doing? That's inappropriate! She's underage and not presented. I warned her!"

Marguerite slammed the goblet onto the table. Both girls leaned away as if she'd blown poison from her mouth. "You're correct. It's not right, and it's not appropriate. But there's nothing I can do. The prince will do what he wants, and it's Céleste he yearns to dance with. You," she flipped to Charlotte, "didn't you dance with a prince this evening? Why must you continue to bicker?"

Charlotte's eyes bulged. "I'm not—"

Marguerite rounded on Julia. "And you! Do you have any clue who you just danced with? Any clue what you've done?"

The raven-haired girl chewed on her lip and lowered her head. "I… he asked… I couldn't refuse—"

"You could have. You hadn't yet danced this evening, so you had every right to decline. Yes, you're to entertain all suitors, but he's not one of them! He's a Giromian, Julia! Do you understand how your father will react to this?"

Julia attempted to speak, but a shadow crawled across her face and she immobilized, eyes rounding at something behind Marguerite.

Marguerite swung around, sick of the interruptions. "And what do you—"

Her mouth clamped shut, because before her stood none other than the man she'd criticized, the man she'd threatened Julia about.

Duke Schwartz scrunched his nose in fake offense. "A Giromian? Why yes, that's what I am." He splayed a palm over his broad chest as he bowed, never disconnecting his onyx gaze from Marguerite. His dirty-blond locks fell down either side of his face as he smirked. "And this Giromian wishes to dance with you, my lady."

"Me?" When his smile widened, she wanted to gag. His charming high cheek-bones, his muscular build—any woman would have wanted him, would have squeaked, legs shaking in pleasure, turning to mush.

But Marguerite wasn't any woman. This man was a vile

businessman buried under a beautiful disguise.

"Yes, my lady. Shouldn't I converse with the person who chaperones most of the contenders at court?" His hand inched close to Marguerite's.

She'd danced earlier—she couldn't refuse.

She took his hand. A glacial sensation vibrated up her arms at their touch, and, fighting a grimace, she let him lead her to the heart of the room.

"It's unfortunate that I've never met you officially, my lady," he said as they arrived on the dance-floor. "I would remember a beauty such as you." His suave voice made her bite her tongue.

Women would swoon over him and beg for his attention were he anywhere else—but not in Totresia, where everyone knew his name, his reputation. Rumors spread fast in the ballroom.

"Save your flatteries, Your Grace." She drew a thin-lipped smile. "I'm not a contender, you need not impress me."

Cornelius chuckled, a deep, guttural sound that sent chills down her spine. He was much taller than her, forcing her to crack her neck to peep up at him. "But you're their chaperone. The key to their hearts. I disagree—you're essential."

Giroma wasn't so far north, yet everything about him, every inch of his skin, oozed ice. Like he'd escaped a snowstorm, icicles dangling from his knees, elbows, jaw-line. An air of crude confidence radiated around him, and she hated to admit he was a fine dancer.

"I'm here to find a bride, since Giroma had nothing to offer me." He twirled her, never loosening his grasp. "As per the accords between my family and the Totresian royals, I have a right to visit. I'm not here to steal anyone."

He rotated her again, catching her in his powerful embrace. She couldn't breathe, suffocated by his pine musk. His breath smelled of a sweet liquor that prompted her to wrinkle her nostrils.

It all reeked of Clémentine.

She kept her wits about her as fear tangled up in her gut. Was the Duke of Terter her betrothed? The man Clémentine had made accords with?

Marguerite's pulse sped out of control. The dowager *wouldn't*, would she? Giroma was an enemy territory. Passive-aggressive currently, but still… she wouldn't dare.

She couldn't.

Marguerite ignored her pounding heart-beat. Antoine never would have let such accords go on. It shocked her that Edouard had allowed them in the first place. For how long? Totresia traded certain goods with Giroma out of necessity, but agreements like these couldn't be legal. And a betrothal? Less so.

"And," the duke crushed his hand hard against her back, pulling her too close, "I'm testing the waters for King Romain. He also tires of Westten court, you see. I made a good case for him, so he will arrive soon. In a matter of days, in fact."

"King Romain? Here?"

This was wrong. Impossible. It couldn't be.

Her saliva felt like knives slashing down her throat.

Was King Romain her betrothed?

The music approached its last notes, the song so loud it muffled the voices screaming in her head.

She tried to make eye contact with Antoine, atop the dais. He was with his mother; a heated conversation. His spine was rigid, shoulders squared, fists tightened at his sides.

Cornelius pirouetted her from the view. "Yes, King Romain. He had plans to come sooner, but a royal Season is the opportune moment, no? All the nobles are here, the ladies are available, and King Antoine and Queen Adelaide were open to the possibility. Especially the latter—quite a convincing woman, she is."

Adelaide, convincing? Of what?

The instant the melody ceased, Marguerite wrenched out of his arms and dipped into a half-hearted curtsy. "Thank you, Your Grace. Such a pleasure. Welcome to Totresia."

She didn't wait for him to reply and darted towards the ballroom doors. She found who she sought within seconds—a royal page, isolated from prying ears, near the doors.

He straightened up as she stormed to him, saying, "Take note of my words and deliver them to the king at once. Discreetly."

The boy nodded and plucked a quill and paper from a nearby table.

Marguerite dictated the contents of her request in his ear. "Meet me downstairs after the ball. We must talk." She pulled away. "Sign it with the letter M. Thank you."

The page took off towards the dais, and Marguerite recomposed herself enough to return to the main event.

Not one, but two Giromians at court. And of all Giromians, the vile duke and Antoine's biggest rival, King Romain?

When she exhaled, she was certain smoke emerged from her nostrils instead of air.

Céleste fumbled with her steps, almost stomping on Sébastien's foot. So dizzy from the stops and spins, she struggled to recall proper dancing postures.

Was she dreaming?

When his hand pressed into her back, she came to. Nearby nobles devoured them with their scowls, servants carried on their duties, and guards were fixated on the prince's every move.

Were they all critiquing her—the underage, non-presented girl who had no right to dance with the prince? Or was this all happening in her head?

Halfway through their dance, the prince cleared his throat, further proving to her that this was no dream. "Forgive my silence, but you look stunning, Miss Richel. Céleste, I mean. May I still call you that?" He squeezed her hand, warmth radiating through his touch.

She couldn't meet his eyes, lest she lost her sanity. "Thank you, Highness. And yes, you may." On the inside, her heart swelled. Whenever he pronounced her name another butterfly came to life in her belly.

He guided her along, each move graceful. "Sébastien," he said, his voice drizzling with honey, prompting her to look up. "Please, call me Sébastien."

She forgot how to breathe. Her knees buckled as she drowned in his gooey gaze. It took all her might to not shrink to the ground and cry. Or laugh. Perhaps both at the same time.

"Céleste?" He slowed his pace slightly, as if ready to stop the dance. "Are you all right?"

"I beg your pardon, High—Sébastien. I'm fine." She let out a shaky breath, knowing she may regret her next words. "But I'm confused."

"Confused?" He twirled her. "I told you I would save you a dance."

"Yes, but..." The thumping inside her rib-cage increased. "You said... and then Cristina... and I thought, we thought..."

As he spun her again, she noticed Marguerite dancing—and when she saw with whom, she feared she'd cough up her lungs.

The Duke of Terter.

The duchess danced with the enemy?

Sébastien drew Céleste closer, dragging her from the sight. His enchanting features soothed away the image of her chaperone locked in an embrace with the vile duke.

"It's difficult to speak here." He glanced left and right. "Come."

He pulled her from the dance-floor, interrupting their dance before its end. He glided by dancers, their skirts whipping at his calves, past half-drunken aristocrats who begged for a moment with him. Women fawned as he slunk by, men waved, but he ignored them, tugging Céleste far from them all.

Once they reached the windows, a pale light filtered through the glass and basked his peach-smooth skin in a heavenly glow. In the reflection, she spotted him smiling.

She wanted to swallow, but her mouth had become too dry. Her heart raced so fast she couldn't think straight, couldn't see. All she knew was him—so near, and wanting to speak to her.

What did it mean?

"Highness—"

"Sébastien." He leaned against the window-pane, facing her, but so close she could have sworn she heard his heartbeats.

Her body went limp. If she'd been alone, she'd have fallen down.

"Sébastien, yes. I'm grateful for this special courtesy of dancing, as promised, but…" Her guts twisted into knots, but she wouldn't let her courage falter, not now. "You didn't need to. Sending a note of dismissal, or something of the sort, would have been appropriate. I'm not a contender, you owe me nothing."

Sébastien's bushy black brows bunched. "I fear I've misled you. I have no plans to stop courting you. This wasn't a goodbye dance." His fingers swept over his jawline, and Céleste wished he'd touch her that way. Soft, simple, calming. Like the dazzling men from her books did to the women they sought to marry. "You haven't left my mind since that night in the Winter Garden. I pray I haven't left yours?"

Her cheeks heated so much she saw them burning in her reflection. "Of course you've been in my thoughts, how could you not?" Her imagination, her dreams, threatened to spill out. How was it possible that this incredible man *wasn't* turning her down? "You're a prince! A handsome royal man who shouldn't court me, and I've doubted your intentions—"

"Then stop." He slid his index finger over her lips, hushing her. "No more doubting. Get used to me courting you, because I plan to present you to the king and queen. Soon."

She hiccuped. "King and queen? You… you can do that? But… and Cristina? What about her?"

He withdrew his fingertip, grazing it along his own mouth. "I will handle Cristina. She was a cover-up. I hoped I could erase the way I felt about you and follow my duties, but it was impossible. I will officialize you. Like you said, I'm a prince! I will do everything in my power to make that happen."

Céleste fanned herself. "So you don't want to court her?" Her legs wobbled and the lower layers of her dress stuck to her stockings.

His hand found hers. "No. I want you, Céleste Richel. You haunt my dreams, not her." He lifted her hand and hovered it near his mouth. His hot breath coated her skin in sweat. "Antoine will allow this. He wants me to be happy." His lips brushed her knuckles. "*You* make me happy."

"Oh." Overwhelmed by the butterflies fluttering in her belly, she twisted to the ballroom. Nobles clustered in groups; all looking at her. "Are you sure?"

He sidled in front of her, blocking her view of the nosy intruders. "I am."

"And Marguerite?" She flinched; her chaperone hadn't seemed too pleased with all this.

"I will handle her, too. Please, trust me. It's you I wish to spend time with, no one else."

His chest moved up and down, steady and serene. The seriousness of his expression, and the twinkling of his eyes. Yes, this *was* real.

He stiffened as he peeked at the podium. "Ah." He bowed and kissed her knuckles one last time. "Excuse me, my lady—my king needs me. We'll talk again soon." He didn't wait for her reply and sauntered to the platform.

She watched as he lunged between courtiers, navigating by those who still sought to waste his time.

Breaking from her dream-like state, she searched for Marguerite. When she located her near the buffet, between Charlotte and Julia, her soul shattered.

Marguerite's arms looked heavy, her shoulders drooping, her complexion paler than ever. She didn't look alive; as if she'd clawed out of her own grave and fought to breathe.

Céleste dashed up to her, pushing the girls aside. "Marg—" She caught her near mistake just in time. "Lady Marjorie, what is it?"

"That despicable... that disgusting..." Marguerite heaved, and Céleste hauled her away from the sniveling vipers. She thought of going outside for some air, but there were too many obstacles— angry and envious ladies—in the way.

Céleste settled for a spot between the orchestra and a service door. "The duke?" Marguerite nodded. "You danced with him."

"I had no choice," Marguerite said with a groan. "Etiquette dictated that I had to."

Céleste grabbed a napkin from a passing servant girl's tray

and whipped it at Marguerite's face, like a fan. "What happened?"

Marguerite's cheeks regained some color, but her eyes narrowed, dark like stormy skies. "The King of Giroma. He's coming here. *Here.*"

Céleste had recollections of heated conversations in Marquess Richel's office—screams about foul Giromian men like the Duke of Terter and King Romain. "Royal pains in the arse" and "scum" were the words she'd overheard most often.

"The king? You're certain?"

"Positive." Marguerite jutted her chin at the other end of the room, and Céleste whirled around to see she was motioning at the duke, loitering by the dais. "They invade our court, take the ladies. They plot."

Céleste rubbed the woman's arms in what she hoped to be soothing motions. "God, this is bad."

Marguerite was about to answer when Julia skidded between them, her fiery glower plastered on Céleste.

"What did you do? What did you say?" She gestured at the dais. "They're leaving!"

Céleste swiveled to the platform again—King Antoine and Prince Sébastien hurried down the steps, their expressions somber.

Céleste frowned. "I did nothing, I assure you!"

"Liar! You made him go, you little—"

Céleste shooed Julia out of the way and nudged Marguerite. "That's odd, no?" The king and prince scurried out the secret side exit. "Why would the king allow this? I thought he abhorred King Romain."

"He does. I'm as puzzled as you. Something is amiss." Marguerite's voice was low, cryptic. "There's more, but I can't say it here."

Julia's grunts broke their bubble of concern; she planted before Céleste again. "Why did you dance with the prince?" She snapped to Marguerite, her tiny frame quaking with fury. "And why did you dance with the duke? You were so irritated with me for it, and then you did the same? Such a hypocrite!"

All of Céleste's lessons of politeness and poise melted as she stomped her foot and thrust herself against Julia, squishing their noses together. "Listen, Espinar. I couldn't refuse a prince, and our chaperone already danced tonight, meaning she had to accept the duke. Aren't you up to date on your etiquette?" Julia scoffed, but Céleste wouldn't let her interject. "You owe Lady Marjorie respect, no matter your station! You humiliate her, and in such a public place, no less!"

Julia opened her mouth, but Marguerite ripped Céleste from her before either could start a fight they'd regret. "Enough, both of you." She shoved Céleste behind her. "She's right—you won't raise your tone at me like that again, understood? Now go," she pointed to Charlotte, in the distance, "relate all this to that dreadful friend of yours. And learn to mind your own business."

Julia strutted to Charlotte, and the two turned their backs to Marguerite and Céleste.

Blowing out a weighted breath, Marguerite wheeled to Céleste. "Thank you."

"You're most welcome." Céleste chewed the insides of her cheeks. "But you said there's more. What do we do? What does this mean?"

Marguerite's focus rested on the floor. "I don't know. But I will figure it out. I always do."

"Eat," said Céleste, echoing Marguerite's earlier orders.

Marguerite struggled to contain her bubbling rage; food wouldn't settle in her stomach if she forced it down. "No."

The girl stuck a plate of buttery croissants under her nose—pastries she'd enjoy were it not for the pangs of pain in her gut.

Still, she accepted the platter, taking a few bites to appease Céleste. The savory taste erupted in her mouth and transported her, if only for a moment.

Céleste glared into the crowd. "None of them seem to care. Why?"

Marguerite deposited the platter on the buffet. "I don't know."

Edouard's stern voice played on repeat in her mind. *"Keep Giromians at a distance. Ensure Antoine does the same."*

Why was Clémentine disobeying her beloved husband? Why

did Antoine let her?

Marguerite fingered her flower-shaped pendant as courtiers whipped towards the royal platform. Some whispered, some lifted to their tip-toes, all trying to see what was happening.

From their vantage point, Marguerite viewed it all without issue. Adelaide teetered at the edge of the podium, guzzling down the liquid in her crystal goblet. She swayed, flinging her cup at one of her ladies, then shook out her petticoats and froze upon noticing all eyes on her.

"Oh," she said with a hiccup—or perhaps a giggle, Marguerite couldn't tell. She attempted to descend the steps, and one of her girls ensured she didn't trip. "Thank you for attending such a lovely soirée. I'm off to bed!" Her slurred speech prompted more mumbles in the sea of attendees.

They curtsied and bowed as she tumbled by, her great train and ladies-in-waiting trailing behind her.

The dowager wasn't far on her heels, clutching the princess by the elbow with a tad more force than necessary. Cordelia turned a few shades of pink before Clémentine yanked her out. Her crew and Cordelia's followed, heads lowered.

When the doors closed, the crowds resumed their conversations and the music picked up where it had left off. Several individuals still gawked at the exit in shock; the rumor-mill would begin shortly.

"What on earth was that?" Céleste's eyes were round like saucers as she pivoted from the scene.

Marguerite was about to fetch a glass of wine, but caught someone else sneaking out—Duke Schwartz, his men encircling him like a fortress. He looked at the ground, as if hoping to escape with no one noticing. To his luck, no one had—except for Marguerite.

"That's odder," said Marguerite, jutting her chin at him.

Céleste's jaw looked ready to drop. "Is he following them?"

Marguerite wasn't sure how to reply. Was Cornelius Schwartz headed to his quarters for the night? Did he even have quarters at the castle?

Or was he creeping out to meet with Clémentine, to continue plotting? To fight with Antoine? To express more compliments to the queen—that he'd mentioned was a quite convincing woman?

She shivered. "There's more to this."

"Where is everyone else?" Céleste scanned the crowd. "I don't see the king, or Séb—I mean, the elder prince."

"They haven't returned from wherever they snuck off to." Marguerite frowned.

Near the patio doors, Jules was the only remaining royal. He wasn't alone; Frances was with him, her décolleté dropping low, one hand pressed to her abdomen as she giggled. Her cheeks were flushed.

The prince glanced left and right—meeting Marguerite's gaze and winking—then hauled Frances outside.

As Marguerite captured a goblet of wine, she witnessed Charlotte, clearly intent on storming up to the patio doors—to follow the prince and Frances.

Marguerite threw her arm out and stopped her. "Miss Geitz, where are you going?"

Charlotte's head snapped to her. "Outside. Am I not allowed?"

"Oh, I don't think so." Marguerite chugged her beverage and

set the glass down. "We're leaving."

"But the prince—"

"Didn't request your company, so leave him be."

Charlotte bared her teeth, but Marguerite ignored her, fluttering about the ballroom to gather up the girls. By the time she'd recovered them all, she was exhausted.

"The queen left, and the king hasn't come back, so we should make our exit." She ushered them into the hall.

Charlotte and Julia bickered under their breaths. After them came Esther, a dreamy grin glued to her face, and Harriet, whispering a thanks.

Cristina squinted at Marguerite through bloodshot eyes. And when she spotted Céleste, she scowled. "You." She said nothing else and darted into the East Wing.

"Care to explain?" Marguerite took hold of Céleste's arm as they marched to the King's Corridor.

Céleste chewed on her lip. "Later?"

As they swerved through the entryway, the Long Corridor clock chimed. Marguerite counted eleven rings; they needed to hurry if she wanted to make it back downstairs in time.

The troop marched up the stairs in silence. Cristina made it to the top before everyone else; she stormed straight to her room and slammed the door.

In the middle of the first-floor landing, Marguerite cleared her throat. "Wait, please." She craned her neck toward Cristina's room. "Will one of you relay this to Miss Condello?"

Esther nodded; the others shrugged.

Marguerite's lungs tightened, each breath harder to expel. "Come close, please. I can't say this out loud." Though Charlotte and Julia cringed, all the ladies huddled around Marguerite. "We have a problem."

"We do!" Julia snickered. "Thank you for bringing it up! This is preposterous!"

"You can't allow this." Charlotte scrunched her nose. "Is it not your job to chaperone us? This has gotten out of control. The prince approaching Céleste?"

Marguerite wagged her finger. "Enough, the two of you!"

Julia's lips sewed shut and Charlotte scoffed. Esther and Harriet glimpsed Céleste, but without the scorn of the other two— they had no idea what had happened.

"You're here to find husbands, not to bring each other down! True ladies don't do that. Whoever the princes choose to dance and spend time with is none of your concern. It's not forbidden for them to consider Miss Richel." Marguerite let her arms settle at her sides. "If I hear one more complaint, you may see your invitation to court revoked. I don't care if you were a favorite. Am I clear?"

Julia grumbled a faint "yes, Miss," and the others muttered in agreement.

Charlotte folded her arms. "Fine," she said, barely parting her lips to speak. "You're the headmaster's little spy, after all."

"That I am," said Marguerite, trying not to slap the lady for her insolence. "What I wish to speak to you about is something else: a Giromian visits our court. Duke Cornelius Schwartz of Terter." Esther gasped; she was the only one who didn't yet know. "He's not alone. Soon, the King of Giroma will join him."

Julia's chin dipped and Céleste squeezed Marguerite's upper arm. Charlotte yawned.

"Don't let your guards down. You will remember from your

lessons that Giroma isn't an ally. We trade essentials with them, but that's all. We don't seek marriages with them." She arched an eyebrow at Julia. "Understood?"

Seeing their slouched postures and blanching expressions, she sent them to their quarters and took Céleste towards theirs.

Céleste's feet dragged. "Marguerite… about Cristina…"

"She behaves like that because Sébastien danced with you? She's jealous. Threatened."

They entered Marguerite's chambers, and Céleste latched the door.

Marguerite issued a sympathetic smile. "I never expected them to attack you for it. A dance? You weren't even his first choice, Cristina was. They had no reason to explode like that." She sat at her vanity, dabbing a few touches of powder under her lash-line and retouching her lip-stain.

Céleste zipped up to her chair. "It was more than a dance."

"Ah?" Marguerite recalled Sébastien's claims: *"I will fix this."*

The tiniest of smiles drew across Céleste's lips. "He has no plans to stop courting me. We talked. He doesn't want to be with Cristina, he… wants me." Wisps of hair covered her eyes, but there was no mistaking the swirls of pink soaking her skin. She twirled the fabric of her dress around her fingers.

Marguerite pinched the bridge of her nose. "I warned him. If he aims to pursue you publicly, backlash will ensue. And not only from the ladies you attend school with."

"He plans to officialize me." Céleste shuffled her feet. "To present me to the king and queen."

Marguerite set a hand to her heart. "Oh."

That was what Sébastien had meant—he'd make it so that Céleste was an official contender, and no one would pester him with details.

Marguerite sighted her clock above the hearth and jumped—she had little time to make it to the rendez-vous point. "We must resume this at another time." She shoved Céleste to their adjoining door, feigning a yawn. "It's late, and I'm beyond fatigued, so off to bed!"

Céleste resisted her push, heels scraping against the hardwood floors. "But you were powdering yourself a second ago—"

"Out of habit! I saw blemishes, I fixed them." She narrowed her gaze. "I don't need to explain myself. Go!"

Though obviously unconvinced, Céleste huffed and slipped into her room.

Marguerite locked the adjoining door and seized a candle from her nightstand. She blew out all other sources of light, tiptoed to the exit, and slid into the hallway. After sealing her door as gently as possible, she hustled to the service stairs and raced down as fast as her heeled shoes would permit.

Only when she reached the basement landing did she slow her rhythm.

The lower level greeted her with nothing but a flicker of a dying torch near the kitchen door. She used her own candle to reanimate it.

Clanging noises came from the other side; curses from the cooks and maids as they finished their nightly tasks. A citrus smell whooshed under the threshold, reminding her of late-night escapades in her youth.

Those recollections no longer made her smile. They only

reminded her of Antoine, how he'd loved her, how he'd hurt her. How she wasn't supposed to run away, how he should have stopped her.

Now it was likely too late to stop anything. If Clémentine had plans set in motion, plans that involved Giromians…

This went far above Antoine's abilities.

Despite her pain, her confusion, her rage, Marguerite refused to see him destroy his kingdom. She'd promised Edouard to stand by him, and ensure he avoided Giromians.

"That duke won't infiltrate our court," she said softly, fixating on the door. "Nor will the king. Not under my watch."

Snuggled in her warm bed, a fire roaring in the hearth to her left, Céleste relaxed. She omitted the bad parts of the evening to focus on the positive. Despite her curiosity about Marguerite's evasiveness, she hugged one of her pillows, knowing she stood on the verge of a tall cliff leading to bigger things.

Could Sébastien make it happen? Her, an official, presented lady?

She had no notion how, nor if the king would allow it, yet her lungs filled with hope.

Her arms covered in goosebumps as she pictured Sébastien for the thousandth time—his silky black mane of hair, his chiseled jawline. Eyes so sparkling she'd swallow them up and become drunk on the taste. His dashing smirk, that spark of mischief lurking behind his demure facade. Sturdy shoulders, strong arms—but the grace of a swan when he danced.

How hadn't she been enamored the moment she saw him during her tour of the castle? She tried to remember him then, what he wore, how he held himself.

Her thoughts raced back to tonight. They'd danced, in front of everyone. If that wasn't proof of how serious he was, then she must have hallucinated.

Had there ever been an underage presented lady before?

Outside her room, a floorboard creaked, prompting her to sit up straight. She glared at her door, and another floorboard groaned, then another; each sound closer than the one before it. Releasing her pillow, she tilted forward to scan through the obscurity. Shadows fluttered under her threshold—someone was creeping by her door.

She willed whoever they were to keep walking down the hall, but the shadows lingered. Hushed voices slithered beneath the door-frame.

She clutched the covers to her chest. Who would sneak about at this hour? Had some drunken nobles made their way upstairs, in search of somewhere to sleep?

Something slipped beneath the door, and she gasped. She curled up, waiting to see if whoever this was would pry the door open, but the footsteps hurried off.

Céleste tiptoed over to investigate what had been slithered beneath her door—a letter, poorly folded, handwriting scribbled in blots of wet ink, a scent of vanilla dousing the parchment.

She rushed over to the hearth, using its flames to better see the words.

Consider this a warning. Next will be a threat. Your attitude displeases us.

We're favorites at this court. We have connections, and will destroy you if you don't listen.

Céleste suppressed a shiver. Threatening letters?

You have no authority to raise your voice at us. Next time you convince a lesser noble such as Lady Marjorie to interfere on your behalf, you'll regret it. This, we swear.

She squeezed her eyes shut, imagining the two vipers as they wrote this—because it came from them, Charlotte and Julia; Céleste had no doubt. Only they would stoop this low—she'd witnessed them doing such cruelties towards Harriet at the academy.

Stay away from Prince Sébastien. It's in your best interest. And steer clear of Prince Jules, too. We don't want your dirty paws on either of them. What you did to poor Cristina is inexcusable.

Céleste scoffed. "Ha! Don't pretend you care about her. You're only looking out for yourselves." Her hands shook, but she had to finish reading.

You don't deserve royal attention, no matter how noble your family name and bloodline are. Remember, you're seventeen. Unknown, unofficial, unimportant. No one. It's not your moment to shine, so stop trying to impose yourself. Don't test us again. We won't give you a second chance.

She felt the poison drizzling from Charlotte's tongue; this was her handiwork. Julia was only a pawn, nodding in agreement at whatever the vile blonde claimed.

Had they no courage to say such things to her face? It wasn't signed, but Céleste didn't need confirmation.

Thick sweat coated her forehead as she stood before the fire, bracing to toss the awful note into the flames. Thankfully, she stopped herself; she might have to keep it, to share with their chaperone.

They wanted to intimidate her into giving up the man of her dreams?

"Never." She re-folded the paper and put it on her vanity. "You soul-sucking leeches!" Her words came out raspy, low-pitched. "You will *not* take me down."

She was about to lie back down, sleep off her anger, but was it best to wake Marguerite and tell her now, before those girls fell asleep and pretended like nothing had happened?

"I hope they dishonor their families and go home without husbands," she said as she knocked on the adjoining door. "Marguerite?"

No answer.

"Marguerite, wake up! We must talk!" She pounded her fists on the wood before grabbing the latch and twisting—but it was stuck.

She pulled again and again, her hands aching. "Why lock it if you're sleeping?" With a huff, she gave up. "She would understand if I used the main door, right? It's an emergency."

After a few minutes of coaching herself against intruding on her mistress's privacy, she padded into the corridor and glided to Marguerite's bedroom door. To her luck, it wasn't locked, so she pushed it open.

A weak fire illuminated the sitting area, but all sconces had been extinguished. Even in the darkness, Céleste had no trouble noticing the bed was empty—and it was made, as if no one had been in it all night.

She rubbed her eyes. "Marguerite, are you there?" She squinted at the clock—after midnight. *She went to meet someone in secret again! To talk of the Giromians? Or to see the king? She's too cryptic, this duchess!*

After stomping back to her room, she flew to her window and pushed aside the draperies, peeping out onto the moonlit gardens. She said a prayer, hoping Marguerite knew what she was doing, wandering the hallways with so many plots afoot, so many people spying or sneaking about to issue empty threats.

Would Céleste ever have a decent night's sleep at Torrinni Castle?

The yellows and oranges from the torchlight by the kitchen door danced. Marguerite rubbed her arms as a chill cruised through the landing.

She'd been standing there for fifteen minutes, yet it felt like hours had passed. Had Antoine chosen to ignore her? Or had Clémentine intercepted the note?

But Antoine needed to be warned. Despite the pain he'd caused her, Marguerite owed him respect, for Edouard's sake.

As she refocused on the candlelight, the service stairs creaked. Vicious visions of Clémentine filled her mind.

Her heart pounded with such intensity she was sure whoever descended would hear it. But as she pivoted to the staircase, her shoulders relaxed.

Antoine emerged, holding a lantern. His chestnut and brassy brown hair cramped beneath his tricorn hat, and the edges of his wool travel cloak flapped against his bright red breeches. So attractive and mysterious—and she hated him for it.

"Maggie?" He slowed as he reached the last step.

"Majesty." She lowered into a curtsy. "Thank you for coming."

Uncertainty lingered in his expression. "You realize the risks?" He blew out his lantern and deposited it on the steps, next to Marguerite's extinguished candle. He took a handful of strides in her direction, but maintained his distance. "At this hour? And here? Mother has ears everywhere. She informed me she warned you yesterday."

His spicy musk wafted into her nostrils. "I had to." She stepped backward to escape his scent; before it enticed her into doing something she'd regret, like touch him. Kiss him. She *couldn't* kiss him. "Why is Schwartz here? Why does his king plan to arrive soon?"

He let out a snorting chuckle and it lacked the charm his laughter usually carried. "Right to business, eh? That's what this was about."

"What did you think it would be?" She scoffed. "My feelings regarding you haven't changed, but this takes precedence. What's happening?"

He released a weighted breath. "Romain will be here in a matter of days. We discovered this last night and finalized the decision this morning."

"Who else knew?"

He averted his gaze. "Mother, of course. She orchestrated it."

"And Adelaide?" Marguerite shuddered.

He glowered. "Why would that matter?"

"Because the duke may have mentioned her complicity in all

this. Word has it your wife had no trouble allowing the Giromians into the castle." She folded her arms. "Neither did you, it appears. What's wrong with you?"

He had every right, as the king, to scold her for her defiance, yet he spun and growled at the wall.

"I had no choice! It was an ambush. The duke was in the area for trading purposes, and King Romain was already on the way. Cornelius," he spat, "told Romain to come before I had the option to disagree. Which I would have." He kept his back turned, tensing. "You know I would have."

His discomfort made her want to console him, but her terror kept her rooted to the spot. "Since when do we let Giromians into the country for extended periods of time? Yes, we trade with them via messengers, and have met with them occasionally in France for exchanges of goods, but this?"

His fingers twitched. "Maggie—"

"This goes against your father's wishes."

He swirled around, fire in his hazel eyes. "Father isn't here. We have agreements with Terter which exempt Cornelius from the usual rules. Father told none of us about it, except for Mother."

She massaged her temples. "I don't understand how. Permitting that wretched man to steal into your court with such ease, to pluck a spouse among your brother's contenders? And Romain?" She refrained from adding her other fears—one of the Giromians as her potential betrothed, courtesy of Clémentine's schemes.

Antoine pressed his fist to his chin. "He was supposed to scout for a bride for Romain. But during the day he admired all the lovely ladies at court and activated the treaty for himself. Instead of coming to me, the King of Totresia, he spoke with Mother." He lowered his fist; his knuckles had turned white and his veins glowed blue. "He was apparently more comfortable discussing this with her."

"Why would she make secret deals?" She squinted at him, unsure if he was still the man she'd grown up with. "I told you to be on your guard, yet you enable her by permitting her to live here."

Smoke seemed to swirl past his sealed lips. "She's my mother!" His chest heaved up and down, and for a moment she regretted her quip, riling him up like so. "It would have happened anyway. Romain planned this. He wants to confront me. Years of passive-aggressive hatred have led us here, and that nasty duke is entwined in it all."

Her legs quivered beneath her skirts. "You're the king. Can't you overrule it all, including the treaty? What stops you from revoking it?"

His breath was hot, heavy with fury and liquor. "Father wished for peace, though he never spoke of it. Overruling, denying entry… it would anger Romain and Cornelius. Don't you recall what they're capable of? Romain's tantrums, his spoiled nature… if he doesn't get what he wants, Totresia will pay for it." He cracked his neck. "Which is what Mother pointed out when she informed me of her secret pacts."

"You do realize she has more things like this up her sleeve?" Her voice came out smaller than she'd hoped, but her words did the trick.

"What do you mean?"

"She controls this kingdom. This agreement is only the start. She won't stop—"

"She wants peace, like Father did! Her methods are horrible, I'll admit, but in the long run, she wants the bloodshed and the fighting to end." He paced, his powerful legs never wavering.

She peeked at her own legs and found them jittering. "Don't you worry about her plots? You said… you implied…" She hugged herself and angled away from his furious energy. "You fretted about her potential involvement with Adelaide, didn't you? And now you shrug it all off without a care?"

"I *do* care." His paces sped up, his boots shaking the ground. "But this was Mother's big scheme: Giromians at court. That was what she planned. Did Adelaide play a part in it? I don't doubt it. But most days, Mother operates alone and with her family's interests in mind. I still have no clue how you fit into it all, but…"

He didn't see it, didn't make the link between the Giromians arriving and Marguerite's reason for being at court.

"She means well," he added, his voice perking up. "She fiddles with Father's orders in ways that benefit her and her family."

"She should have no role in any of your father's commands. Nor yours. She's a dowager queen. She shouldn't be in your shadow, changing everything King Edouard did for this kingdom." She shifted back to face him, her heels screeching on the bruised hardwood floors. "I know *she* interfered to make you marry Adelaide, and not Edouard."

He betrayed no emotion, remaining stoic. *Too* stoic. "She did. On Father's behalf, since he was indisposed. She urged me to wed Ade."

Marguerite squeezed her arms tighter to her breastbone. Clearly, Clémentine had left out the parts about Marguerite being the daughter of an enemy, and Edouard orchestrating her father's death. Which worked in Marguerite's favor—she preferred Antoine to remain in the dark, if indeed his mother hadn't told him.

"Father decided he wanted a French alliance."

Marguerite's mouth dried up. "So that's what she claimed?"

"Among other things."

"Edouard wanted us to marry." She paused, a sour taste developing on her tongue.

Somedays, she still wished it had happened. She still wondered how things would have been if Antoine had kept his word, instead of heeding his mother's awful commands.

But it was never meant to be, was it?

She fought off the images of them together, as if they were blissfully happy, as if no obstacles had gotten in their way. "Do you truly think he switched his decade-long decision for a flimsy French alliance with a fickle lord like Adelaide's father? He was dying, and your mother—"

"Did what she thought was right."

Marguerite's fingers curled into fists. "Oh, and this is right? These treaties... these foreign men invading Torrinni to steal wives? Edouard never would have let it happen."

"You can't say that with certainty," he said, jaw clenching.

"I can, and you'd do well to remember your father wanted me as your advisor, too. I know you both well."

She flinched. Antoine, she knew, truly. But Edouard? Though she never let Clémentine's lies about what he did cloud her judgment, she wasn't sure King Edouard had always been honest with everyone around him.

Antoine planted before her, his chin lowered to connect their eyes. His woodsy musk enveloped her, sinking into her lungs. "Maggie…"

Her cheeks flushed as she drew away from him. "Why do you insist on making me look like an overreacting fool?"

He gawked, so reminiscent of a younger Antoine. Flashes of their youth fogged her vision, images she'd long since sworn to forget.

He exhaled, dragging a palm down his reddening face. "I'm not disagreeing with you, Maggie. You're no fool, and I trust your instincts. But Mother's games were revealed—she wanted Giroma at court. And that treaty? Mother said it wasn't Father's. It was created before he took power. I'm respecting the wishes of the monarchs who came before me."

They had differing recollections of Edouard, that was certain. The king she'd known wouldn't have continued such foul traditions. He abhorred Giroma and preferred its inhabitants nowhere near his family.

Clémentine, a partial foreigner herself, had other motives.

"If I'd stayed, this wouldn't have happened," Marguerite whispered, conflict warring inside her. She yearned to embrace Antoine, apologize for deserting him. But his foolishness created an urge to slap him. To curse at him for letting his mother blind him to the reality of the situation.

The man before her wasn't who she'd hoped he'd become.

Unable to put her thoughts into words, she closed her eyes, searched for her voice, her courage. Nothing came.

Her quiet prompted him to creep closer. "She was horrible to you."

The sentence surprised her, forcing her eyes open. "*Was?* She still is, Antoine. She signed a marriage deal for me with someone I don't know, and who might be on their way here right now to disrupt your court!"

"She was jealous." His eyebrows lowered. "Likely still is, if that's what she's up to. She saw you as a threat, because I loved you. So she and Father decided it was best if I listened to my brain, not my heart."

Her shock turned into frustration. She held in the impulse to pound her fists on his chest in protest. "I must be a large threat, for her to stop at nothing to get me out of the way. She held me prisoner for three years, Antoine. Three years, she played schemes under your nose, culminating in this: Giromians, coming to Totresia. For the first time in…well…as long as we've been alive, if not longer."

"Yes, but—"

"Antoine, *please,* would you wake up?" She sensed a bubbling volcano brewing up deadly lava in her belly. "She has been manipulating you for years, and you continue to let her! Just like she manipulated your father."

His features twisted, as if she'd abruptly ripped off his skin. "She may have manipulated Father, but not me. She had her reasons! Father instructed me to heed her every command. This clause… to marry Adelaide… occurred hours before the Masquerade."

"You didn't have to agree—"

His hands snaked around her forearm so fast, she couldn't stop him. And she didn't want to, because a part of her wanted this, no matter how deep beneath her fury. A part of her *craved* this touch, this proximity.

He yanked her so close their noses touched. "I *did*. You don't understand what was at stake, Maggie. What might have happened if I'd…" A trace of weakness flashed in his expression before he stiffened. "Defy my dying father? Whether or not Mother forced his hand, he ordered this. I didn't want to. I wanted to send you a note to alert you, but I had no time."

His fingertips woke goosebumps wherever they touched. She begged her tears to stay put, but they battered below her lash-line like tidal waves desperate to gush out and drown him.

She needed to get out of his grip, far from his burning touch, but… she couldn't move. It'd been enough to reanimate sensations in her belly that she'd thought to have laid to rest a long time ago.

Fading light poured over his features as he removed his hat. His curls fell over his forehead, a few brushing down his temples, one or two strands tickling against the bridge of his nose. Every breath he expelled weakened her, shattered every barrier she'd built to protect herself.

His lips opened, and as they came close, closer, *too close* to hers, a creak on the stairs broke them apart.

They pirouetted with muffled gasp, like two students caught cheating on a test.

Antoine slid in front of her, immediately shielding her. "Who's there?"

Daggers lined Marguerite's throat as she swallowed. She tipped to the side, too curious for her own good, and sighted the cause of their surprise.

"You had best split this up," said Princess Cordelia, her evening gown sprouting about her figure like spring flower petals. Her lips formed a straight line, her shoulders taut. "It's well past midnight, and Mother is prowling."

When Marguerite moved out from behind Antoine, she curtsied. "Highness."

"Prowling?" Antoine didn't budge. "At this hour?"

As her heels met the basement floor, Cordelia shook out her skirts. "I don't ask questions. But I spotted *her*," she pointed at Marguerite, "hastening down here earlier, so I kept watch. Then you also crept downstairs, and I know Mother. I arrived as fast as I could, but she will be here any minute."

Marguerite dared a peep at the princess as she straightened up. "Thank you, Highness."

"I did it for the king," the princess snapped, not looking at Marguerite. "I suggest you take these stairs, Antoine. Hurry."

"Fine." He fastened his hat and exchanged a glance with Marguerite before swinging by his sister. "Make sure Maggie gets to her quarters safe, would you? Please." He grabbed his unlit lantern and disappeared.

"You," said Cordelia, drawing Marguerite's attention from Antoine's distancing form. "Go through the kitchens. I will distract Mother, but you won't have long."

Marguerite craved to tug the girl into a bone-crushing hug, but her stern expression, so reminiscent of Clémentine's coldness, melted her bravery.

"Many thanks, Highness."

As Marguerite pushed the door open, Cordelia cleared her throat. "Meet me tomorrow. Late morning, in the reading room."

Marguerite whipped around to reply, but Cordelia had already started up the service staircase.

Upon waking, Céleste immediately remembered everything from the night before.

She grumbled as she stood up, stretched, and snatched the teacup on her breakfast tray. She sipped as she wandered to her door, and nearly choked on a gulp as she found a folded letter on the floor.

Worried about another threat, she bent to pick it up, fingers grazing the gold, silk-like stamp on the crisp paper—the royal insignia.

The words were scribbled in tight, slanted handwriting.

Céleste,

Would you please join me at the stables before noon? I wish to take you riding, so dress accordingly.

See you soon,

Sébastien

The hand holding the mug shook. She held the message with her other, swooning as she heard his suave voice resonate in her mind.

At least *that* had been a good part of the evening.

She got dressed, but before she could hasten off to meet with the man of her dreams, she needed to warn Marguerite.

She tried the adjoining door, happy to detect it was unlocked. "Marguerite, guess what—"

Her heart sank to find the room deserted, like the night before. The clock showed ten; was Marguerite out checking on the girls? The bed was untouched, the drapes pulled aside, and an empty cup sat on the nightstand—Marguerite's signature coffee scent filled the area.

"I'll go to the girls, then." Céleste cringed at the notion of confronting the ladies after the events of the evening.

Esther answered at once, a powder poof in one hand, a brush in the other. "What is it? I'm in a hurry. Meeting with your brother." Her cheeks flushed.

"Is Lady Marjorie chaperoning you?" Céleste's riding boots were tighter than she remembered, and she tried not to scrunch her nose at the pain.

Esther dabbed at her cheek-bones with the poof. "No. When I saw her earlier she said we would use a royal chaperone."

Céleste refrained from attacking the girl with her inquiries. "Where is she?"

"You're her little assistant, not me." Esther shrugged. "Check with Harriet or Cristina."

Harriet's room was Harriet-less. And when Céleste glanced towards Cristina's chambers near the royal stairs, she grew wary of disturbing her.

Her only other options were Charlotte and Julia.

With little choice—and unwilling to run about the hallways to figure out where the duchess had disappeared—she dragged her feet toward Cristina's room.

As she racked her brain for how to approach the scorned girl, the bedroom door opened. Cristina stood in the threshold, holding a note to her chest. She didn't see Céleste at first, but as Céleste stopped walking and opened her mouth to speak, Cristina's chin whipped up.

"Céleste?" She lowered the paper she held. "What are you doing?"

Céleste sucked in a deep breath. "I'm looking for Lady Marjorie, have you seen her?"

Cristina crossed her arms. "Why would I have seen her? Aren't you her assistant?"

"Indeed." Céleste was about to leave when Cristina trudged up to her.

"Wait!" Her expression was relaxed, a far cry from her frown the night before. "I wanted to apologize. I was upset that the prince chose you over me."

Céleste's pulse sped up. "You have nothing to be sorry for. *He* should apologize."

Cristina sighed. "He did. He sent me a note. And I received another." She bit her lip, stopping her smirk from widening.

"Who?" Céleste's eyes were set on the paper Cristina carried.

Cristina cupped a palm around her mouth. "Axel Espinar. Julia's brother."

Céleste didn't even remember seeing Axel the night prior. She knew him from the few times he'd visited the academy. As a friend of her brother's, he was always polite to her.

"Can you imagine how peeved Julia will be when she finds out?" Cristina swayed dreamily. "He's beneath my station, but Father will accept him. His family is well-respected. Anyway," she became serious, "I don't resent you. When I glared at you like I did, I hadn't yet accepted the situation. It was immature of me. I wish the two of you happiness, but," she flinched, "be careful. Entering a courtship with a royal is no laughing matter."

"I'm not laughing," Céleste later muttered as she prayed Sébastien would have a chaperone for them—because Marguerite had, yet again, evaporated.

***

A narrow-framed, aging lady waited by the entry doors as Céleste descended a few minutes later.

"Miss Richel?" Her tight, graying bun of hair shook as she waved Céleste to her, then tugged her outside. "I'm to chaperone your meeting with the prince." She hobbled through the courtyard, taking a small, pebbled walkway towards the far left of the property. "I expect you to be on your best behavior."

Céleste acquiesced. The lady sported the charcoal uniform of a servant, but she spoke eloquently, like a noblewoman.

The stables were a set of two extensive buildings linked by a tall entryway, bordering the left side of the castle ramparts. With its flattened, weathered coppery roof, it looked old and abandoned. Once they got closer, Céleste sensed a lively energy seeping from under the rusted doors. She smelled hay and horse droppings as she and the chaperone entered.

Dimmed candelabras decked the faded walls, and between them alternated nets and saddles dangling from old metallic hooks. A modest office sat in the back, its door open, showing a battered desk covered in paperwork.

Horses neighed from a corridor of stables to the left. To the right she noticed empty dog kennels.

"Some would say today is a good day for a hunt," said a voice arriving from the horse's side.

Céleste twisted in his direction, unable to stop the grin pulling at the corners of her mouth.

Sébastien held the reins of two beautiful horses—one black as his hair, nibbling at some hay stuck to his coat; the other golden with a mane as white as a cloud.

The chaperone curtsied and took the golden mare. "I will ride with Miss Richel, if it pleases you, Highness."

He nodded at her as he released the dark-haired horse and marched to Céleste. She dipped into a curtsy, but he plucked her up the instant he was within reach.

"Céleste." He took her hand and planted a chaste kiss atop it. "I'm delighted you accepted to join me."

"How could I refuse?" Her heart fluttered as she drank in the curves of his body beneath his beige riding coat. He wore a faded hat and matching boots over black trousers; looking every bit a dashing prince.

"I worried you might have changed your mind overnight," he

said, guiding her to the horse. "I couldn't locate Marguerite to confirm this with her." He helped her up, then the chaperone behind her.

Céleste fixed her skirts. "I also couldn't find her."

He hopped atop his black steed and settled into the saddle. "Such a mystery, our dear Marguerite." He directed his horse through the main doors, and Céleste followed. She'd ridden a lot at home, and enjoyed the view from higher up.

They crossed the main driveway and continued towards the forest. A gentle breeze whooshed through her tresses. She'd forgotten to bring a hat, but liked the freshness caressing her cheeks.

The castle's yellow walls paled in the overcast light, and as they trotted past, she admired the dreamy balustrades, the impressive stone, the magnificent windows. She imagined one of said windows was Charlotte's or Julia's and fought to not guffaw at the idea of them peeking out to catch her with the prince they'd threatened her not to frequent.

"What's so funny?" Sébastien brought his steed closer.

Céleste blushed. "I was appreciating how gorgeous your home is."

He gazed up to the dazzling roof with a cheeky smile. "I missed it while abroad." He slowed his pace as they rode near the forest line. "It's actually smaller than most European structures, yet I prefer it to the castles I encountered in my travels."

"How marvelous it must have been." Céleste peered ahead at the orchards, and at the further parts of the gardens in the distance. "To travel."

He shrugged half-heartedly. "It was at first, but not all places were as marvelous as you would expect."

She sensed the restraint in his tone, but couldn't help but push to know more. "Which places did you not enjoy?"

"The French weren't always welcoming, I'll admit. The British…pleasant enough, I suppose. But the worst…" He winced as he shifted to her. "Must I say it? You're the daughter of a prominent noble, you must know which country I despise the most."

A few breaths lodged in her throat. "Giroma," she said, keeping her voice low. "You went there?"

"I did." He tugged on the reins, slowing their trot to a brisker pace as he wheeled his stallion closer to the woods. "In fact, I stayed there the longest, since I knew my family wouldn't breach the country limits to fetch me."

As she urged her mare after his, she glimpsed the dense foliage concealing the forests' mysteries. "But they let you stay? The Giromians, I mean. Don't they hate us as much as we hate them?"

This time he halted completely, rotating to face the woods. He inhaled the wintry air. "I was in disguise, in the beginning. I stayed with friends. We have allies in Giroma, believe it or not." He glanced at the chaperone, then jumped off his horse, landing without difficulty on the grass. He offered his palm to help Céleste down, and she accepted.

They stood side-by-side before the forest entrance. Sébastien took her hands in his and she felt his warmth radiating through her.

"Giromians are aggressive. I'm positive your father and brother know this. I imagine Marguerite warned you of the one currently at court?" His eyes, usually sparked with a mix of joy and playful mischief, turned dark.

"I met him. He danced with Julia, and he informed Marguerite that King Romain would join us soon?" Heat fluttered to her neck and cheeks.

"Yes, Antoine told me. Father," he groaned, "would have died before letting this happen. I'm certain yours will hesitate to keep you at court once he discovers. Which is why I wished to spend a few moments with you, in case he…" He brought her hands to his mouth as he closed his eyes.

Lost in the moment, her lips parted, her jaw going slack. Once she'd swallowed his words—his desire to spend time with her— she came to. "It won't please him, but Emeric is here. He wouldn't remove Emeric from court during a royal Season. So long as my brother is with me, I'm safe. Father won't summon me home."

Sébastien's eyes crinkled once he opened them again. "You're safe with me, too. I care for you, Miss Richel, and wouldn't let any harm come to you. I promise."

Butterflies woke in her belly—he *cared* for her? He'd keep her safe? He was the shining knight, the dreamy prince; she was the damsel to be rescued from her mundane life.

But a bitter taste remained in her mouth because of the Giromians. She lowered her chin. "You worry because of that duke?"

When he tipped her chin back up, his mouth was so close to hers, she wondered if he'd kiss her. A gesture that would sweep her off her feet, further anchor her affections for him—but she wasn't ready for such physical demonstrations, much as she imagined them. His fresh breath was enticing and his lips inviting—

He pulled back a few inches. "The duke isn't a good man, no

matter how many ladies already fawn over him. And Antoine abhors his king, yet lets him into our kingdom? Yes, I worry. My mother… ah, I shouldn't be telling you this, but you can inform Marguerite. She was in a panic last night and we didn't get a chance to speak again."

"What about your mother?" Céleste bit her tongue to not spill out all she already knew, thanks to Marguerite's venting session.

His eyes bore into hers. "She's deep into all this Giromian business. I assume Maggie figured that much out, but make her aware to tread lightly, will you? The same goes for you. More so once you… well, once Mother understands I intend to court you."

Céleste gulped. "She doesn't yet know?"

He placed his hand on her shoulder. "I mentioned it to her, but I've not confirmed anything. I bet she has someone trailing us as we speak—so she knows. She always does."

"Is that bad?"

He spun her towards their horses. The chaperone eyed them, one brow raised at their proximity. Sébastien didn't seem to notice as he aided Céleste back onto her saddle.

"I suppose we'll see. You'll meet her officially, soon enough."

Céleste hoped soon enough wasn't *too* soon.

44.
Marguerite

Marguerite tossed and turned so much overnight, her entire body ached. Her mind drowned in waves of lustful images she was ashamed to remember. But was also buried in angry thoughts towards Antoine—how he'd succumbed to his mother's pressure, how he'd kept such facts to himself for so long. How he still let her sway him into conducting her odd agendas, and how he'd endangered his kingdom by allowing Giromians in. And he did nothing. *Nothing*.

Could he have overruled Clémentine three years ago? He was only a crown prince, but he should have fought. He'd remained passive, heeding his mother's command over listening to his gut.

Once in her comfortable, simple day-dress, Marguerite tugged her hair up, slipped on heeled slippers, and checked on the girls.

Cristina received a note from Axel Espinar, requesting to meet her. Marguerite assigned Johanna to chaperone, pleased that Miss Condello had moved on from Sébastien. The other girls required no particular help, and Céleste would keep herself occupied—Marguerite had a meeting to attend.

With Cordelia.

Standing before the reading room door, she hesitated to enter. Cordelia was on the other side, and she had no inkling what awaited her.

She swallowed, perked up, and knocked.

The door opened to reveal a frowning girl who started to curtsy, but Cordelia, speaking from a chaise to the left, stopped her midway. "She's not royal." She didn't remove her sight from the teacup she held up to her lips. "Lady Marjorie, come in, please."

The girl settled on a chair near the door and looked into her lap.

"Ladies-in-waiting." Cordelia rolled her eyes as she motioned to a cushioned seat beside her. "They either obey too much or have no notion of what they're doing."

She sounded like her mother. The same spice in her tone, the same sharpness when reprimanding her staff. Yet in her bundles of cerulean silk and her loose up-do, she almost seemed serene.

A thick-bound book rested in her lap, and a doily laden tray lay on a stand between her chaise and another. Soft light pooled in from behind the thin curtains covering the floor-to-ceiling window.

"Sit." Cordelia waved at the girl by the door as she deposited her mug. "Leave us, please. Have Clarisse meet me here in thirty minutes. You may attend to whatever else you wish."

After a trembling curtsy, the girl departed.

Once the door closed, Cordelia deflated in her chair. Her glacial facade melted like an ice-cube in summer, and she blew out her cheeks in a most non-royal fashion. "Thank the Heavens. I can't stand that one." As Marguerite lowered into her spot, the princess gestured at one of the teacups on the tray. "That's coffee, by the way. You still drink it?"

Marguerite's eyes widened. "You remembered."

Cordelia let her book slide to the floor as she reached for a biscuit. "How could I not? Something Mother would find despicable and unladylike? Surely I would encourage that." She nibbled on her treat, her once somber gaze softening. "Well? Didn't you want it?"

Marguerite scrambled to pick up the cup and blew off the steam. The refined but bitter smell wafted up her nostrils and as she took a sip, tension poured from her muscles. "Oh, that's good."

"From my personal collection. I figured it would put you more at ease." Cordelia fiddled with her hands. "I must apologize to you for my behavior. Chilly stares, icy demeanor, mimicking Mother. I expect it confuses you?"

Marguerite remained calm, but felt jittery on the inside. "It goes beyond confusion, Highness." She took another sip and set her cup down. "What's going on? When I left you were a girl desperate to escape into her books and follow her brothers on adventures."

Cordelia sent her a sneering glance worthy of her mother, but then winced and turned away. "*You* left. That's what happened. I was angry, still am. You ruined your future, angered Mother. Now she wants to destroy more than your future: she wants your life."

"Princess." Marguerite crossed, then uncrossed her legs. "She's wanted my ruin since the moment you were born, maybe even before that. Bringing me here is a new tactic that unsettles me."

Cordelia fixated on the door. "Agreed. The only way to

discover more is for Mother to think I despise you too." She snapped to Marguerite. "To do that, I must play the part. I've been posing as her ideal daughter for years, but as of recently I've also ensured the staff fears me as they do her. I complain a lot. It's horrific." She sighed. "The instant I heard you were still alive and coming here, I knew she had plots, and I knew I had to save you from them, no matter my feelings. So forgive me, but I must keep up appearances."

"Except for now?"

"We have until Clarisse arrives. Mother is occupied."

Marguerite chugged more coffee to ease her nerves. "You're forced to act this way because of me. I'm *so* sorry. You needed me, and I…"

Cordelia took another delicacy from the platter. "What's done is done. I forgive you, Maggie."

Marguerite's insides warmed when the princess used her nickname. She reached over to take Cordelia's free hand in hers. The princess didn't cringe at the contact, didn't pull away.

She chewed her bite and swallowed. "So, prisoner in the basement of the Royal Academy for Totresian Noble Girls?"

Marguerite released her and took a biscuit. "For three years."

Cordelia snorted, and a few crumbs tumbled onto her gown, then dropped to the floor. Her lips curled. "Quite bold of Mother to treat you like so."

Marguerite nearly choked. "You… um… you know your mother was behind that?"

Cordelia grinned, though there was nothing pleasant about the sight. "I know everything, Maggie."

"Everything?" Marguerite's hands shook.

"Everything." The princess drew one leg over the other, revealing her shiny silver shoes.

Marguerite recognized them—Clémentine used to wear them in her solar. *Uncomfortable bastards,* she called them.

Cordelia caught her glancing and lifted her skirts. "Mother's." She pointed at the pearls in her hair. "Mother's." At the ruby pendant dangling from her neck. "Mother's. Everything belongs to her. *I* belong to her. And therefore, I know everything *about* her."

She once bickered about hating her mother's pass-me-downs and whined about not attending balls. Complained about tutors and detested soup and wrote poetry about the places she wanted to visit.

But Cordelia wasn't thirteen anymore. She was sixteen: a true princess, a perfect daughter, and a spy.

"She loves you. Always has. It makes sense she would want you to *be* her." Marguerite's spit turned to acid at the thought of a second Clémentine roaming the halls and terrorizing anyone in her passage.

Cordelia groaned. "I may look like her, but that's all. Never will I be as foul as she is—not for real, at least."

"Do any of your personal staff know the actual you? I mean, are they included in your ruse?"

Cordelia shot up, almost knocking over her teacup. "Never. Mother employs them. You're the only one I trust with the truth."

This was Marguerite's opportunity to pry deeper; to dig up answers about Clémentine's plots, and maybe Adelaide's. To potentially find out who her betrothed was—if Cordelia knew so much, she'd have those answers. "Princess—"

"Stop calling me that." Cordelia sank into her seat.

"Cordelia," Marguerite flinched, "what's with your mother's

latest coup? Giromians? Last night Antoine mentioned obligations, things your father established?"

The princess glared at Marguerite. "Don't meet with him anymore. She'll know. And the Giromians… I have no inkling what their presence means, but it's not well received. Séb told me no one is happy about it, and they're all certain Mother ordered it, and Antoine bent and allowed it."

Marguerite bit the insides of her cheeks. The nobles at court could tell Clémentine used Antoine as a puppet?

"We, her children, try to protect her reputation, but Mother does what Mother wants." Cordelia's lips twitched. "And Mother is up to something."

"She always is," said Marguerite.

"No, this is different. These are worse schemes than you can imagine." She blinked rapidly. "She's been corresponding with Dowager Pauline of Giroma."

Had she been standing, Marguerite would have crumbled, her legs giving out. Thank God she wasn't clutching her mug, as it would have shattered at her feet. "King Romain's mother?"

Pauline of Giroma had been the Giromian regent until her son turned fifteen and snatched his reign from her. It made no sense for the Giromian dowager to be on speaking terms with Clémentine— their husbands hated each other.

Cordelia's eyes narrowed. "The very same."

"I'd ask how you know, but you've already made that clear." Marguerite's fingertips brushed down her jaw and landed on the table. She gripped the edges and squeezed out all the tension developing in her arms.

"I assure you it's true."

Marguerite's thoughts swirled like tornadoes, blowing away any other suspicions she'd had since she arrived in Torrinni. Why would Clémentine need Giromian alliances via a snide duke and a temper-throwing king? Why would she communicate with a woman she'd always despised?

Marguerite's insides churned. "I'm wary of these folk."

"We all should be," said Cordelia, rising to shake out any lingering crumbs from her skirts. "That duke sought to seduce me at the ball. I played along, naturally, for information, but I got nothing." She snickered, cheeks flashing bright red. "How disgusting."

The teenager in Cordelia showed; the one who tried her hardest not to care what men thought of her, but who lit up when one had eyes on her. Even a vile one like Cornelius Schwartz.

"You're the Princess of Totresia—a key to whatever his plots are. Because I presume he has plenty without your mother's aid." Marguerite finished her biscuit and dabbed at the corners of her mouth with a napkin. "Beware of him and his fancy words. I hear Schwartz is tricky, as is his family. It shocks me that your mother let him parade you about last night. I thought she loathed Giromians."

Cordelia prepared to reply, but a knock on the door interrupted her. She set her tightened fists on her hips and swirled around. "Yes?"

In the threshold was a page boy, and Cordelia welcomed him inside. He bowed, but his gaze was on Marguerite. "Lady Marjorie, someone summons you to the stables."

She gaped at Cordelia. "Me?"

Cordelia waved at the page boy impatiently. "Who?"

The page shifted from foot to foot. "I… well… Lady Marjorie is the recipient, so—"

Marguerite rose so fast she became dizzy. "You may tell me in front of Her Highness."

He lowered his voice. "The king summons you, my lady."

"To the stables?" Marguerite rubbed the back of her neck. "He wishes to ride?"

Cordelia's eyebrows raised. "Remember what I said—don't meet with him."

Marguerite tried to flatten a few loose hairs slipping from her up-do. "He summoned me. He's the king. I'm furious with him, but what choice do I have?"

Cordelia stood there a moment, her eyes like black pits, mouths of monsters wanting to devour Marguerite whole.

"Fine," she said at last, falling back into her chaise. "Don't say I didn't warn you. I will make sure Mother's spies are occupied. You!" She snapped at the boy. "Fetch my ladies and tell them to monopolize as many staff members as possible. I'm feeling faint." She slapped a hand to her forehead and slouched into her seat.

The page hustled out—believing her ruse.

Cordelia jutted her chin at the door. "Go."

Marguerite obeyed, reluctance weighing in her gut like piles of sharp-edged rocks.

45.
Antoine

"Y"ou can't keep wavering! You must be firm. Unlike three years ago."

Marguerite's voice buried deep inside Antoine, transporting him out of the stables, out of Torrinni.

Out of his mind.

He'd been in such a state since last night—drunk with worry, overwhelmed with concern—that it had taken him time to comprehend all the things Marguerite had told him.

He'd needed to hear them all again, and she'd certainly complied, but he rather regretted summoning her in person, considering what her presence did to him. How it drew him back to the years before he'd made the wrong choice, the days where he could touch her, hold her, kiss her without scruple. Without fear of rejection.

Being so near her brought back urges he hadn't had in years, a physical burning he'd forgotten existed. A passion that took him by surprise because he *never* felt that towards Adelaide.

"What would you have me do?" He struggled to keep focused on her without caving to the desire growing in him. Even angry— *especially* angry—Marguerite was a wonder to behold.

But she was closed off to him. She'd made that clear enough in the other times they'd met in secret; this one would be no different. If anything, she might touch him—by slapping him.

"I have no proof that she's conspiring against me." He tried to keep his voice curt but knew it was lacing with spiraling anger. "Is she plotting? Yes! She most likely is! But until we have a way to solidify this, I can't send her away!"

"I told you last night—you have your proof. The Giromians!" Marguerite smacked the back of one hand into the other. "That's the proof! She went behind your back and enacted treaties you had no inkling of! Isn't that enough?"

"That's not why I summoned you here." He groaned, stuffing his hands in the pockets of his cloak before he did something regrettable with them like grab her arm again, as he had before, which was far too intimate for her preference. "I wanted to make sure you were okay, after our discussion."

He wasn't okay, not after everything he'd found out about his mother and her ties to Duke Cornelius, and apparently, King Romain. And not after getting so close to Marguerite last night, sensing that bubbling in his gut, that yearning he'd suppressed for so long.

Marguerite snorted; even that sound was charming, coming from her. "You dare pretend to care? Your mother unleashed enemies into your castle and your wife is suspicious and my betrothed wanders the halls of your home unbeknownst to all of us.

And you wonder if I'm all right? That reaction is three years too late."

"You think our predicament pleases me?" He slumped against the facade. "What Mother did wasn't illegal. Uncalled for, yes. But she had every right to allow Schwartz in."

"And the king? Your biggest foe?" She folded her arms, keeping them tight against herself; protective.

"I can do nothing until Romain gets here." He nearly slammed the back of his head against the wall. "We'll chat. Rectify this. It would shock me if coming here was his idea of a good time."

Marguerite guffawed. "You, chat with Romain? Your sworn nemesis?"

"We're both monarchs now. Things are different. We can be civil." He licked his lips. "And you will do the same. Be on your best behavior and leave the questioning to me, do you understand? Don't snoop. This is perilous business, and I wouldn't have you involved."

Another snort from Marguerite. "Too late for that."

Her defiance should have made him writhe, want to lock her up for insubordination. Instead, all it did was fascinate him. Her stubborn nature had always made her appealing to him, and now more than ever.

But also now more than ever, he had to resist the urge. It'd been years since they'd touched, kissed. He couldn't let his imagination run wild, not anymore.

"I was with your sister when you called for me, did you know?" She turned away from him. "She advised me that your mother is communicating with Pauline."

"Pauline?" He jerked away from where he'd been slouched

against the facade. "You mean… no, you can't possibly mean—"

"Yes, *that* Pauline—the Dowager of Giroma." She swiveled to him, her triumphant expression unsettling his stomach. "Isn't that proof? Isn't that a reason?"

"That… is big news." He swallowed, his throat dry. He scratched at the base of his neck. If this was true, that meant his mother *was* up to something involving more Giromians than expected. "But how would Cordelia know that?"

Marguerite studied her nails, turned sideways, only allowing him a view of her profile. "Your sister is the closest person to your mother. Don't you trust her?"

"I do, but why would she tell you and not me?"

"Because you wouldn't listen! She knows you as I do." A hint of sorrow broke through her composure. "She worries too. We didn't speak of it, but I wouldn't doubt that she sees your mother playing against you, like me."

Antoine rolled his eyes. "Yes, back to your assumption Mother wants to take the throne from me, as you've mentioned three times in the past twenty minutes."

"But wouldn't she make deals with our enemies and dethrone you to have someone easier to manipulate in your place?" It was a genuine question; Marguerite wanted his opinion.

He huffed. "She never favored me. I was Father's favorite, and she despised it. Is that enough to unseat me? Would she betray me? Well…" The answer came to him with such intensity that it nearly struck him down. "Yes, yes she might."

If surprised by this, Marguerite didn't show it. "With the law."

"What are you talking about?" He shuddered with realization. "*That* law?"

"Your wife told me she can't conceive, and it frightens her." She faced him once more, her expression far more serious than he'd ever seen it. "And it should frighten you, too. Your mother overheard us discussing that."

"Right, because Mother lurks—"

"A king suspected of being unable to produce heirs… if that were to get out—you see where it leads, no? How that anchors my beliefs that your mother doesn't act in the benefit of you and your kingdom?" She arched one eyebrow.

He expelled a disheartened chuckle. "Adelaide and her mouth, of course. Yes, Mother might use that law to her advantage. And bringing you here for some supposed betrothal without my knowledge, and giving access to the Giromians… Indeed, why not? She's scheming something, naturally, but how would I know what?"

"You're the king," she said, her voice darkening. "You have plenty of resources."

"Fine." He stomped a foot and glared at her. He hated curiosity, but Marguerite had instilled it in him with all her theories. "You've awakened doubt in me. Happy?"

She didn't falter; she maintained his glare. In fact, she glared back. Such boldness made him quiver with desire.

"Will that rouse you to do something?" Her snippy voice turned off his desire at once.

His old brown travel cloak flapped against his legs as he trod back and forth on the hay-covered ground. He squished his tricorn hat in one hand, his other bunching and unbunching at his side. "The Giromian involvement is all Mother's doing, but I'm uncertain that's proof enough to send her off. The law part… I'm afraid we must wait and see if she has a role in invoking it. That would be concrete proof."

Marguerite scoffed. "So you would wait until she pulls another stunt? Until she threatens your God-given position? You would allow things to get that far?"

"What choice do I have?" Marguerite was right, damn her, but he couldn't admit that out loud. Not when he still had so much left to figure out. "I must give her the benefit of the doubt. Accusing her outright of wanting to interfere in my life, remove me from my throne, set someone else in my place? It's audacious to state this without absolute proof, no matter how convinced you are."

He caught her staring at him, but she quickly shook herself, rubbing the back of her neck. "Your love for her blinds you. She has a history of making deals behind your back. She coerced you into believing your father's wishes were for you to marry Adelaide, not me. She locks me up, promises me in marriage to someone we don't know the name of. Then she allows Giromians in without your explicit consent? Do you not consider her capable of plotting to take what's yours, so that she may retain some authority?"

He threw his hat to the ground. It bounced off a pile of fodder and landed between where he paced and where Marguerite stood. "She's complained about me being heir-less for years, but…"

"She wants to secure her legacy." Marguerite squinted at him, as if seeking to enter his mind, reorganize it to her liking. "To ensure her bloodline continues. It's essential."

"There are too many coincidences." He wished he hadn't thrown his hat; he'd have liked to tear it to shreds to calm his nerves. These realizations were too abrupt, the things he'd dismissed so obvious now, he hated himself for missing them. His cheeks heated in utter embarrassment. His mother had been more involved than he'd ever anticipated. "I should have known."

Marguerite nodded slowly. "Far be it from me to pity you, but… this wasn't all on you. She's sly. She's fooled everyone. You needed a knowledgeable advisor, someone who would see through her plots, but you have none. She took advantage of that."

"I have advisors, good ones." He growled. "No one detected Mother's intention to continue using her influence for what she saw fit. She wants someone on the throne she can manipulate. She wants… who?"

Marguerite bit her lip. "That, I don't know."

"A noble of her choosing? Oh!" He punched one hand into the palm of the other. "One of my brothers?"

She let out a heavy breath; one he could have sworn sounded relieved. "It could be anyone. And what of Giroma?"

He picked up his hat, brushed it off, and clutched it to his chest. "It pains me to think Mother would deal with them, betraying her own flesh and blood. But that part of her scheme requires more investigation." She opened her mouth, but he raised his hand, shaking his head. "You'll leave that to me. I don't want you wrapped up in their ways. The duke… the king… they might have a game of their own, and I won't risk your hide for answers that I can obtain myself."

"And your sister? She poses as a perfect daughter, and that foul duke hovered around her last night."

"Mother wouldn't permit anyone to harm a hair on Cordelia's head, and you know this." He scratched the stubble along his jaw-line. "She's safe. So we must outsmart Mother. If you skip steps, it will endanger you, especially. We don't know who she plans to marry you off to." Pain flared up at his temples as unbidden images of Duke Schwartz appeared, his grubby hands all over Marguerite. "Don't think I'm not worried with those Giromians coincidentally showing up at the same time as your return to court. I wish to protect you. Please, heed my orders."

She nodded, but he knew she wouldn't obey. She'd do things her own way—the way Edouard had trained her to.

Had she not run from court, Antoine might have solved the issue of his mother far sooner. He'd have noticed her temptation for power and cut it off before it blossomed into this—Marguerite would have been there, as his advisor, whispering in his ear.

How marvelous would she have been, had she been allowed to marry him? Granted more power than the dowager, the ability to help him preserve his kingdom from all threats.

But which threat was worse—Giroma, or his mother?

Antoine didn't realize he'd started walking towards Marguerite until she recoiled from his approach.

He paused, relaxing his taut jaw. "I will seek a solution, I promise. Thank you for waking me up. For what she's conspired, she will pay; if we can prove it. And if we do, I'll sever her ties to court. No more spies. No more conspiracies. Father may not have advised it, but *I* am king, not him."

She gawked at him, her big, beautiful green eyes so hypnotic, he couldn't look away. They lulled him closer, desperate to hold her; to pretend like he hadn't smashed her heart with his political decisions.

Decisions orchestrated by his mother.

"And what of your," she cleared her throat, breaking her gaze from his, "wife? Don't neglect her possible involvement in all this.

Is she trustworthy? Innocent? A puppet, like you?"

He spat. "Puppet? How demeaning." He took another stride forward, and Marguerite shuddered. Her arms were rigid, ready to shove him away, but he continued to advance towards her. Not to invade her space, but simply to see her closer, capture her perfect features to memory.

Just in case.

"Antoine," she cautioned, though her body language was anything but cautious. She was flushed, leaning forward, stroking her throat.

"Adelaide is not innocent." One step closer. "Trustworthy? Debatable." Another step. "As for being a puppet... why not? She was all too keen to take your place and only started moaning about her fears of infertility since you arrived. She never mentioned them before. It's too coincidental."

Marguerite's forehead scrunched. "I spent a lot of time with her in those days, and she didn't want to be queen, not of Totresia, at least. She despised your mother. What drove her to change?"

"If ever a day came where I comprehended how that woman's mind works... Money? Bribery? Her father might have played a part, too. Don't forget his supposed alliances with people like Napoléon, folk who hunger for Totresia."

"She does enjoy her luxuries." She wrung her hands. "I will be more wary. Since my return she's invited me to tea and breakfast. I should find some way to decline her next summons."

Antoine made a final rush forward, lessening the space between them. The edge of his boots met the hem of her dress, her powdery scent taking over his senses.

She didn't pull away, but trembled at his proximity. "Antoine, we can't—"

"Refuse to meet with her, if possible." His chin was inches from her forehead, his lips bracing to place a kiss on her delicate skin. Maybe on her cheeks. Maybe her lips—

But *no,* he couldn't possibly go that far. No matter how much he'd always loved her, no matter how irritated Adelaide made him, he'd *never* do that. Not like this.

"If Mother controls Adelaide, she will ensure she warps your mind, pushes you to do something stupid. Make you think you're still friends when you're not. I can't fathom how she knew so much, but let's assume it's part of Mother's games. Assume Adelaide *is* a pawn on Mother's chessboard. Mother wanted you here for an engagement she never told me about, and which Adelaide might be aware of. That's more dangerous than I anticipated."

"Antoine, no." Her fingers twitched as she steered herself out of his reach.

He winced, trying not to show disappointment at her rejection, though it was much smarter for her to refuse him than to allow him to hold her, to steer this into the wrong direction. "If you have no choice and are stuck with her, share nothing of your knowledge. Play her game."

She placed a palm over her heart. "But Antoine—"

"Promise me, Maggie. No matter our history, I'm your king. Please, do as I ask."

She lowered her head. "As you wish, Majesty."

"I must go." He put his hat back on. "Be on alert at all times. Trust only Cordelia, no one else. Aside from me, of course."

She tugged at her cloak's sleeves. "Understood."

He hesitated, stretching his fingers towards her. "Would you let me say goodbye the way we used to? The polite way?"

She flinched, but cautiously drew her arm up, her fist towards him. "I suppose. Only because you asked first."

He kept some distance as he brought her knuckles to his lips, placing a soft kiss over them. It took every fiber of his being to not tug her close and place a kiss over her mouth, instead.

"I never wanted this," he said, letting go against his deepest wishes. "I should have been more assertive, more aware of Mother's attitude. More aware of how she may hurt you."

"You're three years too late," she whispered. "And nearly twenty too late for your mother's behavior."

"Still, I regret every single second of tears you might have shed on my behalf." He searched the depths of her soul for an ounce of forgiveness. "If I'd fought harder, disputed Mother's orders… it would have been against Father's dying wishes, but I should have known. I was a fool."

When she said nothing more, he crept to the stable door, opened it, and exited into the faded gray light.

Céleste *wanted* to remember how her heart had filled with admiration after spending time with Sébastien. Or even how paralyzed and nervous she'd been upon finding out she'd be officially meeting Dowager Clémentine soon.

But she didn't want to feel *this*—confusion, doubt. Sheer fear at all the conspiracies, the distrust amidst the royals and advisors.

After returning her horse to the stables, she stumbled upon two people arguing in the entrance—two people she was quite sure weren't supposed to be seen together in public.

Marguerite and King Antoine.

She eavesdropped long enough to know he was the one who'd summoned her there, to check on her after their argument the night before. Which meant he was the one Marguerite met with when Céleste had come to tell her about the threatening letter from Charlotte and Julia.

She overheard them debating—Marguerite yelling and King Antoine denying all her claims—about Dowager Clémentine's role in the Giromian arrival, how she needed to be shipped out of court, how Queen Adelaide acted suspiciously, and something about that special law that might annul the king's marriage.

And also something about *dethroning* him? Céleste had hurried off after that, heart racing, unsure if she wanted to listen to anything else that might make her nerves worse before meeting with the dowager.

She needed to lie down and clear her mind; their speculations were heavy. Her temples flared with pain, and her gut was uneasy.

In her quarters, she sank to the ground, propped up against her door. Something on the floor caught her eye, and she picked it up—another letter decorated with the royal emblem.

"Sébastien?" She stood up, her earlier delight returning in the form of butterflies in her abdomen. "Another outing?"

Miss Céleste Richel,

You're invited to a queenly dinner this evening, with all contenders in the royal Season.

Please present yourself in formal wear at the dining room, with your invitation, at seven o'clock sharp.

Peace Above All

The note slipped from her grasp as she tugged at her hair.

"A queenly dinner." Her knees buckled. "But... I'm not eligible, not yet presented! How? Why?" Her hands were clammy, her muscles limp, her eyes rolling to the back of her head—

Then she remembered. *You'll meet her soon.*

"Oh." She glared at the note at her feet. "He knew how soon. Likely after this dinner? Or will she be there?"

She couldn't decline the invitation, but to accept meant to let everyone see that he pursued her, officially. That last night's dance wasn't a mistake. Cristina had moved past it—but what would the others say? Charlotte, Julia, those she hadn't met; she'd be vulnerable to their scrutiny, exposed to their attacks.

Her thoughts swirled around violently as she fell onto her bed, after setting the invitation on Marguerite's vanity, for her to see.

Why hadn't Sébastien explicitly warned her about this? He'd been so vague—charming, yes, but *vague*.

She wasn't quite sure how much time had passed when the adjoining door burst open, drawing her out of her reverie.

Marguerite perched in the doorway, clutching a letter—the invitation. "They invited you to the dinner?" She stepped inside, her dust-ridden dress hem brushing over the floorboards. "You received this today?"

Céleste nodded.

"Have you seen Sébastien? Is he aware?" Marguerite sat on Céleste's vanity chair, brandishing the letter up like a dagger.

"He's aware. At least, I think so." Céleste slumped onto her bed. "We went riding today, and he might have warned me about this… in code. I wanted you to accompany us, but I couldn't find you, and neither could he, so we used a royal chaperone."

"So he *is* serious, if he got you on the list of those invited to this." She waved the note.

Céleste groaned. "But I'm not presented! Now he throws me

in the mix with those… those gossiping vipers?"

"They're not all vipers. They're nervous, like you." Marguerite slouched in the cushioned seat. "More so after receiving this, I assume."

"But who would approve this? The queen knows I'm not a contender, so why allow it?"

Marguerite stood up, leaving the note on the vanity as she stretched. Her eyes were red-rimmed. "Sébastien wants to present you, and they can't postpone this supper while they wait—it's a scheduled event. So they're including you, because you *will* be an official contender soon. If he has his way."

Céleste kicked her heels hard on the mattress. "I wish he would have warned me, so I'd have time to prepare, to secure appropriate attire, or… to find a way out of this."

Marguerite lowered onto the bed beside Céleste. "Sit up." She seized Céleste's wrist to lift her into a seated position. "There's no way out. You wanted this, Sébastien wanted this, so now you must both face the consequences. You will accept this invitation. Fret not, I'll guide you."

Céleste scrunched her nose. "Fine."

"I imagine the girls are wary, too. There's little time. Fetch them for me, would you? Tell them to meet in my room at once. You will attend this meeting too, but I will let them discover your new situation at the dinner, where they will have no choice but to react tactfully."

Without waiting for a reply, Marguerite snuck into her quarters and closed the door.

***

Céleste led the contenders to Marguerite's suite. Most had never been inside, so they awed and oohed as they took their places in the sitting area.

Céleste settled on Marguerite's bed, hands clasped in her lap, avoiding pointed glares and sneaky sneers.

Marguerite sealed the door and leaned against it. "I expect you all received the note for a queenly dinner?"

Harriet grunted near the door. Esther flushed. Cristina acquiesced. Charlotte and Julia, huddled on the sofa, mumbled a bored *"Yes, my lady."*

"The queenly dinner is a custom at Torrinni court, and it's quite the affair. Usually the queen hosts it, but our dowager may take part in it too, as she oversees most of the Season's activities. No men are allowed."

Céleste's reluctance grew. She'd met both women in the Winter Garden with erroneous addresses, embarrassing herself. Now she was a secret, non-presented, last-minute future contender.

She expected nothing less than a catastrophe to unfold.

"Be on your guard. Refrain from gossip," Marguerite squinted at Charlotte, "and hold yourselves like proper courtiers. Wear formal attire, but nothing scandalous." This time she eyed Cristina, who turned red as a beet. "Nothing considered day-wear. You will be shunned for under-dressing. The queen will mock you without scruple."

Marguerite speaking with such ease about season proceedings and knowledge of the queens was suspicious. It shocked Céleste that none of the girls spoke up about it, but then again Marguerite *was* a chaperone, so perhaps it made more sense to them.

"Consider it an interview. Even if the princes don't yet favor you, and another fancies you, the queens are testing the option of placing you at court, evaluating your chances of being one of their ladies-in-waiting which, if you recall your history lessons, is a big deal."

Esther squealed, Harriet stiffened, Cristina pulled up her plunging collar. Charlotte and Julia whispered.

"Should you need extra help to prepare, there are ladies-in-waiting at your disposition." Marguerite opened the door. "I wish you all luck—this is an important step in your new lives as ladies of the Torrinni court. Now hurry and get ready—you must be at the dining room at the right time, or else they will deny you access."

Charlotte and Julia whisked out first. Cristina hurried after them, still yanking at her collar. Harriet and Esther followed, Esther's excited tone reverberating down the hall on her way to her chamber.

The instant they'd all disappeared, Marguerite hastened to Céleste's room. "Now, we must find you a gown."

***

Céleste tugged on her golden gloves. "Are you sure?"

"You look delightful. As if going to a ball." Marguerite weaved a golden ribbon around Céleste's hair, like a headband.

Unlike Sébastien, the queens liked extravagance. Marguerite insisted Queen Adelaide loved exuberance and over-the-top patterns that screamed *look at me!* But Céleste cringed at her reflection, her paler-than-usual skin, her bright pink lips, the rosy dots on her cheeks.

"Did you endure *this*," she twirled to motion at her pale blue gown with gold trimming and threading along the bodice, "when you were a contender?"

It was one of her most elaborate outfits, and she'd hoped to keep it for a more elaborate party, but Marguerite promised it would serve better here.

"Of course." Marguerite fixed the creases in the petticoat. "But I grew up in this castle, was raised in these customs, so I was used to the laws and traditions. We can't compare our experiences."

Thinking of Marguerite's days in Torrinni brought the king to mind; thinking of the king reminded Céleste of the secret stable meeting earlier. "Where were you all day?"

Marguerite flinched. "I told you, it's all right that you rode with Sébastien without me. He was smart enough to have another chaperone."

"This isn't about that." Céleste's eyes narrowed, and in her reflection she saw them turning their irritated shade of gray. "I wanted to share with you that I received a threatening letter last night."

"Threatening letter?" Marguerite paused in the middle of fastening a silver pendant around Céleste's neck. "After the ball? From who?"

"The sniveling sissies who bugged me all evening!" She swiveled to face Marguerite, fists on her hips. "But you weren't there for me to warn you, since you spent the entire afternoon elsewhere!"

"Watch your tongue. You may have a prince courting you, but I'm your chaperone, representing your headmaster." Marguerite adjusted the necklace. "I wasn't gone all afternoon—only for a few hours, attending to business that doesn't concern you."

"Are we in danger?" Céleste grimaced as Marguerite pivoted her to the mirror again. "I'm about to enter a room filled with snakes, with a target on my back. I'm attending an event hosted by the queen who stole the man you love, with the potential presence of the queen of conspiracies."

Marguerite parked in front of Céleste and gripped her shoulders. "*You* will be fine." Her smile was far from genuine.

"You're not convincing."

Marguerite dragged her feet to a couch and sank into it. "Giromians are here, allowed in by the dowager. The king fights for his birthright. The queen is a fickle fiend, and the princes and princess are oblivious to the truth. But *you*," she attempted another smile, this one more heartfelt, "aren't in danger. Only if you mess this up, but I doubt you will." Her jaw tightened, but Céleste perceived honesty in her tone.

Céleste fanned herself. "All right, I trust you."

"Good. Now make haste and get there before they slam the doors. Don't forget your invitation!"

Pulling out the crumpled parchment from her bodice, Céleste dashed out, unprepared for the dreary ditch she was about to fall into.

Marguerite descended to the library to relax in front of the fireplace—to clear her thoughts after her complicated encounter with Antoine.

That final look he'd given her remained imprinted on her brain. It wasn't enough to persuade her to forgive him, but it did persuade her that he never truly meant to hurt her. He never knew how deeply involved his mother was in his life.

Alone but for the librarian, she gazed into the fire, installing herself comfortably on the library's cushioned chairs. It had taken her a while to compose herself and reenter the castle, and by then it was too late—Antoine had re-embedded into her heart.

But she'd be damned if she let him see it.

When her eyes started to hurt from the entwining yellows and oranges popping in the hearth, she plucked a few books from the dusty shelves, intent on reading about current nobles, to figure out who Clémentine might have chosen for her to marry.

She ended up reading *Laws of Totresia* and *The Mysteries of Giromian Rule* instead. They piqued her interest due to the current state of affairs, and she settled at a table to further analyze their contents.

The first tome unveiled nothing she didn't already know; Edouard had coerced her into reading similar books throughout her youth. The second was about King Romain and his reign.

She tapped her chin in rhythm to a ballroom tune as she turned each page.

"Dowager Pauline oversaw affairs for most of the young king's life, but he demanded that she step aside on his fifteenth birthday, against his advisors' wishes."

She'd never met Romain, but Antoine had during trips with his father. He'd spoken of the Giromian monarch as spoiled, prone to fits if he didn't get what he wanted. As an adult—he was of an age with Antoine and Marguerite—he might have matured into a more stable man. He might be handsome and attract attention in Torrinni.

That bothered Marguerite more than she wished to admit— what if *he* was the one Clémentine had arranged a marriage with? Though she wondered what this would serve for Clémentine. She'd have to acknowledge Marguerite as duchess for it to have any real political power.

How would Marguerite fare married to the Giromian king she was taught to hate?

The next page revealed a drawing of Dowager Pauline.

Her hair was pale, but she had the same stony gaze as the

Totresian dowager; a similar stiff posture and thin, curling lips. One might think they were related, with how the artist had portrayed their features in such similar fashions. *With all Clémentine hides, who knows?*

After another page flip, she encountered a map of Giroma. Though it was a smaller country, Giroma had a military force to be reckoned with. Terter, the fortress-style city where Duke Cornelius Schwartz hailed from, was a training center for soldiers, according to the text.

If she were to marry him, she'd end up living there as *his* duchess.

She cringed. In the next section, she found information on him and his family. He had a reputation—how much of it had made it into a history book in the Torrinni Castle library?

His father and the former King of Giroma had many alliances and disagreements throughout their lives. Terter often sought its independence from the country.

The library doors creaked open, prompting her to leap up and slam the book shut before shoving it aside. She peeked toward the source of the noise, her heart pounding.

Two individuals entered, their heads lowered. Both were men—one in a beige and forest green ensemble, a mop of brown hair shaking atop his head as he laughed. The other wore navy, a white scarf wrapped around his neck, black tresses tugged into a ponytail.

When they lifted their chins, Marguerite let out a sigh of relief.

"What brings you two to a place like this?" she said, hands on her hips as she wandered from the table.

Their faces lit up. "Maggie." Sébastien grinned as he approached.

Jules scooped her into a hug. "So lovely to bump into you!" A boyish smirk played over his lips.

She smacked Jules' chest. "Let me go, you rascal."

He released her, and she fixed her skirts. She should have curtsied in salutation, but with the librarian half-asleep at his desk, and the rest of the room empty, she omitted the formalities.

Sébastien placed a kiss on her cheek. "Hiding out in the library? That's more my style."

"Shouldn't you be upstairs waiting for the girls?" Jules guided her to her chaise in front of the fireplace. He plopped on one to her left as Sébastien sank into the one on her right. "I expect they're halfway through the first appetizer course by now?"

Sometimes, she forgot he was seventeen and about to choose a wife. But he was still the rebellious teenager eager to escape the confines of his prison—the castle.

Sébastien stretched his legs. "We were going to venture out into the city, but Antoine forbade Jules from leaving court. Some novels about faraway places will have to do the trick. We need to pass the time while our contenders dine with our sister-in-law."

Jules snorted, kicking at the air. "*Your* sister-in-law. Mine will always be Maggie. I can't stand that two-faced devil."

"Jules!" Marguerite gawked at the doors. "Her staff might be lurking, you must watch your language!"

Sébastien crossed one leg over the other. "I doubt it. They'll loiter by the dining room, desperate for juicy gossip."

Jules straightened up and turned to Marguerite, his tawny eyes aflame with mischief. "Adelaide doesn't scare us."

"What about your mother? Is she at the supper? What if *she* lurks about?"

Despite their hair of unique shades and their eyes of different hues, their skin and jaw-lines and eyebrows were so identical, they might have been twins. They even had the same build: sturdy shoulders, broad chests, long legs. Like their elder brother; like their father.

"How many times must I tell you? Mother doesn't frighten me," said Jules, though Marguerite caught one of his eyelids twitching.

Sébastien scoffed. "She disturbs me. But as I also told you, she can't control us." For a flash she saw him as a teenager; unlike Jules, he was no rebel. He tagged along on adventures, but most days preferred to snuggle in a corner and read a book on sword-fighting tactics.

"I've missed you both," she said, trying to hold in the tears rushing to her lash-line. Antoine's actions had dug a dreary trench between them, but they'd never left her mind.

"Our brother is an idiot." Jules leaned over to eye Sébastien. "This one would have made a fine queen."

As she prepared to scold him—or thank him, she wasn't sure—Sébastien grumbled. "Mother is to blame. If she hadn't interfered, things would be different."

Heat sprawled up Marguerite's cheeks. "Speaking of your mother." Antoine had warned her to be careful—but they were the princes. She could trust them. "What's she up to? Yanking your brother's strings in any direction she pleases, summoning Giromians to court, summoning me... What *is* she doing?"

They used to tell her everything. Marguerite knew first-hand when Sébastien had taken up secret weapons training. Jules had told her before anyone else when he realized he found women *and* men attractive. Would they still confide their woes in her, all these years later?

Jules tensed as he set an elbow on the arm-rest. Sébastien slid his slender fingers through the frayed ends of his ponytail. They peered at one another, as if waiting to see which would cough up details first.

Marguerite scowled. "Would you deprive your beloved brother's ex-fiancé of important plots that might involve her?"

Jules cleared his throat, and though Sébastien shook his head, the youngest prince ignored him. "We think she conspires to remove Antoine from his throne."

Marguerite rolled her eyes. "I'm ahead of you on that, but who will she choose as the new king?"

"Maggie," Sébastien stammered, about to rise from the chair—she seized his wrist and stopped him. "Maggie, please."

"Don't hide things from me." Her voice came out fiercer than she'd intended, but it did the trick. "Tell me what you know."

Jules squeezed her shoulder. "We *don't* know."

Sébastien stood. "This doesn't concern you, as much as I love you." He folded his arms. "We're looking into this, and it's best if you stay out of it."

Jules gripped the corners of the arm-rests, his nails like claws about to shred through the material. "She's family. And if Mother plans to invoke the law—"

"*The* law?" She pressed her lips together. "Your brother and I discussed this today. Adelaide mentioned it to me at breakfast recently. I think your brother is finally… figuring some things out."

Jules released the arm-rests and got up. "Good. He must fight Mother on this. Not that I want him to stay with that hag—"

"Jules," cautioned Sébastien, gaping towards the doors.

"Have either of you spoken to him about all this?"

Sébastien scratched his chin. "Not really. We've not found an appropriate moment to bring it up."

"Maggie," Jules' voice grew insistent, "he listens to you. Somewhat."

Marguerite gulped. "Hardly. Today was the first time I managed to get through to him."

"Right, well, Antoine needs to gather more nobles to his side, in case someone invokes the law and asks for a vote." Jules patted Sébastien's back. "Maggie can tell him this, yes?"

Sébastien swiveled to the flames. "I don't think it's wise to bring her into this."

Marguerite got to her feet. "How did you both find out about this?"

"We have our ways," grumbled Sébastien, still focused on the fire.

Jules tutted. "What I don't understand is why punish Antoine if Adelaide is the one who can't conceive? Totresian royal men are fertile, capable of producing many heirs. Look at us! Father had three sons and a daughter—but sources say Mother would blame Antoine for her lack of grandchildren?"

"Sources?" Marguerite's gaze narrowed.

"That witch cowers in Mother's skirts, praying to not lose her crown. We," Jules motioned at himself and Sébastien, "agree the marriage should be annulled. We should send that wretched red-head back to her real home, and replace *her*, not Antoine."

Marguerite grunted. "If only things were so simple."

Jules pulled out a silver flask from his jacket pocket. Sébastien and Marguerite frowned at him, but still he swigged some of the liquor. He winced, then smacked his lips. "I think Mother is holding back now that you're here. Yes, she summoned you—I still wonder about that—but your presence makes things… complicated."

"It always does," said Marguerite with a heavy breath.

Sébastien finally pulled his gaze from the flames, pinching the bridge of his nose. "We're thrilled to have you here, but before you arrived… we believed we were on to something." He waved at Jules to hand him the vial of liquor. He took a tiny gulp, coughed, and fell into a seat. "That's foul."

Jules laughed, then offered the flask to Marguerite, but she refused. "On to what? Reasons why she'd unseat her own son? Why she'd want Adelaide gone years after replacing me with her?"

"Potentially," said Sébastien, shrugging. "Not that last part, though. That we're unsure of."

"Your parents abhorred the Lord of Avignon and argued often over Adelaide's presence at court. Yet they chose, at the last minute, to force her into Antoine's arms? I still don't know why Antoine bent so easily."

"Some sordid accords, no doubt," said Sébastien, massaging his temples.

A dangerous lump formed in Marguerite's throat. Something came to life in her gut—a glob of fear, a wad of questions, a ball of confusion.

She pointed at Jules' flask. "Give me that." He smirked as he threw it at her; she caught it with ease. "Being here has given me a migraine." She tipped the liquid into her mouth and hissed as it blazed down her throat, leaving a malt and spicy cinnamon taste on her tongue. "Séb was correct—this is horrid!"

Jules chuckled as she fired the flask back at him.

She should have told them she knew why she was there—that a man in the castle, or on his way to it, was to be her husband, at their mother's behest.

How to tell them they'd never get her as a sister-in-law? That they may be doomed to Adelaide forever, or worse, another queen *and* king, if Clémentine had her way?

When lining up at the dining room entrance, the contenders had spotted Céleste and snickered. They'd asked her why she was there and what she wanted, snorted at her formalwear, commented on the eccentricity of her outfit.

When she'd raised her invitation, they'd laughed. Scowled. Only Esther and Harriet verified the note she held and smiled weakly in acknowledgment. Cristina nodded with little kindness; the remaining ladies curled their lips, scrutinizing Céleste as they all entered the dining room.

As she swept inside, crimson walls enclosed her, littered with royal portraits and landscapes. Chandeliers hung above the long mahogany table. So intimidated by the grandeur, Céleste thought of retreating to her chambers—but Esther and Harriet nudged her towards where the queen stood waiting for them.

An array of ladies in vibrant gowns fanned out around the

elaborately dressed woman. "Welcome," she said, as the contenders and Céleste lowered into curtsies.

She wore a white gown that covered her perfect figure like regal flower petals. Her ruby crown glistened atop her fiery hair, which was piled up in a giant bun of glittering curls.

She explained seat assignments; those closest to her were *early favorites*. She motioned at who sat where, and why.

Céleste expected to be at the end of the table, but as Queen Adelaide rattled off names, she worried she might have been forgotten. Everyone else had been given their spot, yet there she stood, cheeks uncomfortably warm.

The queen wandered to the end of the table, stopping beside her radiant dinner throne. She pointed to the seat to her right—one of the closest seats at the table.

"You'll sit here, Miss Richel," she said, loud enough for all guests to hear. "At my side."

"Oh," Céleste whispered, hurrying to take her chair.

She hadn't prepared for sitting beside the queen. She hadn't prepared to be exposed as Sébastien's front-runner yet.

Cristina was given the chair to her left, which seemed to delight her—she smiled.

Directly across from Céleste sat Frances, her lapis eyes swirling with distaste. Céleste remembered her: daughter of the Marquess of Mara, disliked by Marguerite, Prince Jules' *plaything* at the inaugural ball.

Charlotte perched beside Frances, but Frances was closest to the queen—meaning Charlotte was a second-choice, not a first.

By her was Harriet, face reflecting permanent surprise at being invited to anything important. She peered at Esther, sitting across from her. Julia frowned as she settled to Esther's left.

Céleste didn't have time to ponder the other contenders or question their seat placements—ladies-in-waiting delivered champagne and servant girls arrived with trays of food.

The queen cleared her throat. "Ladies, it's a feat to have made it this far, and I applaud you. A privilege for you, but also for *me*. It pleases me to meet you before some of you join my family. So, to start, a toast!" She raised her glass. "To Totresia! Peace Above All! And to you, contenders—may you all find your husbands at court!"

The sparkling taste lingered on Céleste's tongue, turning bitter. And it remained, even after bowls of creamy potage and leafy greens coated in heavy dressing and chunks of buttery potatoes and tender meats drenched in a delectable wine sauce.

She spent most of the evening focused on the table linen and its intricate floral patterns. She strained to ignore the whispers floating around her, and to cease worrying about why the queen hadn't said a word to her since she'd assigned her seat.

As she broke open a biscuit, the queen accorded her a glance, at last.

"Céleste Richel. Our newcomer," she said, her tone bathed in honey but laced with a sourness Céleste wanted to cringe at. "I apologize for not conversing with you sooner."

Céleste's chin quivered. "It's quite all right, Majesty. I'm honored to be here."

"As you should be." The queen lifted the rim of her cup to her candy-apple lips—her second refill of the night. "You're Prince Sébastien's front-runner. Your father is a well-trusted and valued member of my husband's council. Though he remains in Valeville, far from the action."

Most conversations in the surroundings died down as everyone tuned in to the queen and Céleste. Someone muttered, "*she's here for Sébastien?*" and another called her "*a presumptuous social-ladder climber.*"

Her face burned. "Court is too active for him, Majesty. He prefers to advise from afar, while maintaining the security of our borders."

It was a rehearsed reply her father had begged her to give, if anyone asked why he never traveled to Torrinni. In truth, he hated the castle and its drama—he'd beseeched her to never reveal that.

Frances studied Céleste, but said nothing, showed nothing.

Charlotte pouted after each bite she charged into her mouth. Who she was most angry at—Frances, for earning Jules' spot of honor, or Céleste for simply being there—Céleste couldn't tell.

"Of course," said the queen, her voice oily, overly slick. "We're most thankful for his service." Her chest puffed out, her breasts about to spill from her décolleté. "That reminds me— ladies!" She clinked a utensil to her glass. "Now that we've gotten to know one another, I must warn you that the dowager will select a few of you for tea tomorrow!"

Céleste could have sworn her breaths were the loudest sounds in the area.

"Oh, don't look so frightened! The princes will confirm to her their favorites this evening. It will be a quiet affair, I promise." She guzzled down the rest of her drink and lifted her goblet for another refill. A butler poured, but she yanked the cup away before he could finish and drank from it again. "If you're not a prince's front-runner, fret not. You may join me in the solar for delicacies and knitting. But if you *are* a favorite, you'll receive your invitation first thing in the morning."

Céleste's forehead was covered in sweat, but at the same time, glacial chills spiraled down her spine, causing her to shake.

Would she receive a letter from the dowager in the morning?

She was grateful her sleeves were long enough to hide the goosebumps popping up on her arms.

"It's intimidating—I would know." The queen leaned towards Céleste, keeping her tone at a normal volume. She smiled. "You know, I started as you did. The unknown contender. The one everyone underestimated. But I won. I'm the Queen of Totresia, and will stay as such. Don't be fearful. I wasn't, and look at where it got me."

Céleste struggled to focus on anything else. *'I will stay as such.'* What did that mean?

Hadn't the queen mentioned her woes to Marguerite? Was she no longer afraid of losing her spot?

She tightly grasped her silver pendant, indenting its patterns into her thumb and forefinger. "I appreciate your advice, Majesty."

The queen took a lazy bite of her biscuit. "The dowager is scary. Oh dear, do I know that well! But I learned she only gets aggressive if you show weakness."

Céleste stiffened. "Aggressive?"

"Oh!" The queen's giggle sent a few crumbs flying to the tablecloth. "Not *physically,* of course. I meant that our dowager seeks strong, confident ladies for her boys." She dabbed her napkin to the corners of her mouth. "She wants women who can carry a royal title and handle an immense amount of stress without batting a lash. Never appearing flustered or frustrated or worried."

Céleste plucked her water cup from the table. With each swallow, another drizzle of sweat poured from her temples.

She nearly spilled when the queen's gloved hand wrapped over hers. "Everything is a test here. Meeting the dowager will be your biggest one yet. Especially… well, considering your status… she will judge you with more harshness than others."

"My status?" Céleste's nostrils wrinkled. Her father was a marquess, her brother an esteemed member of court; what about that would displease the dowager?

The queen lowered her voice. "Underage and non-presented. It matters not how well-placed your father is. Until we confirm your contender position, she will reserve the toughest of verdicts for you." She winced. "This title—*princess*—is heavier than you think. Be ready, Miss Richel."

With that, Adelaide mumbled something at Frances, prompting her to giggle politely. Charlotte squeezed closer, yearning to fit in, her high-pitched laughter ringing in Céleste's ears.

Céleste picked at her bread, rehashing the queen's comments, praying to unearth the hidden meanings in what she said. Was that a warning, or a threat?

The roaring fire's warmth sent tides of happiness to crash over Jules' body. He'd forgotten how to relax, how to simply spend time with his loved ones.

Mainly because those loved ones were either gone or never available to meet with him.

"Three years, hm?" He clasped his hands behind his head, fingers digging into his messy curls.

Sébastien was the only one Jules saw often, but they were so different, their appetites in stark contrast; Jules loved to roam at night, but Sébastien preferred sparring or reading during the daytime.

Though Sébastien was far too busy thinking about the Richel girl, whom he'd bumped into at night in the Winter Garden. He'd told Jules all about it, and Jules had warned him to beware. The Richels weren't a family to play around with—if he was serious about the girl, he'd better make it clear as soon as possible.

"Come January, yes," said Marguerite, looking the most comfortable Jules had seen her in years. "It's hard to believe."

"Oh, the things you've missed." Jules yawned. "I haven't been a proper gentleman at all times."

For a young man of seventeen, Jules had had many adventures, and as a result had just as many secrets. Well, *mostly* secrets; Antoine had an ongoing list of his misdoings, and his mother was on to him. Though why she'd let him get away with his antics so far, he wasn't sure. Perhaps Antoine protected him from her; or perhaps she was holding on to the evidence to use against him later.

Manipulation was, after all, his mother's love language.

Sébastien snorted. "That's an understatement."

Marguerite's brows lifted though an amused grin spread across her lips. "Is that why Antoine refuses to allow you to leave the castle at night?"

Jules flushed. "Perhaps?"

To admit to anything within earshot—even in the mostly abandoned library—was too dangerous. Yes, his brother and mother had much knowledge of his comings and goings, but there were more detrimental secrets they'd yet to uncover, and he wished them to remain that way.

Even Marguerite, unaware as she was, could be used against him.

"And you?" She pivoted to Sébastien. "Your travels! I imagine you've seen more than most eighteen-year-olds can boast."

Jules refrained from guffawing. Poor Marguerite had no idea what Sébastien had been up to in recent years. Some of those memories would shock her, as they were more along the lines of things Jules would do.

"Indeed," said Sébastien, the light flush over his cheeks confirming Jules' thoughts. "I wish I had more time to detail them for you."

Marguerite patted his wrist. "We will find a moment. I'm not sure how long I'll be here for, but—"

The library entrance blasted open, prompting all three to whip their necks towards the doors. A few bookshelves blocked their view, but there was no mistaking that screeching voice.

"Where are they?"

The air changed—Jules felt it, that unpleasantness that manifested in the form of toxic fumes and swishes of skirts and grunts of displeasure.

His mother had found them.

She wouldn't be wandering around this area at this time of the evening for no reason. Especially not after proclaiming to all that she'd adhere to her regular schedule while Adelaide entertained the contenders.

No, Clémentine was *spying*. She was doing what she normally sent her lap-dog Mary to do.

But who, exactly, was she spying on?

Marguerite stiffened, any inkling of comfort draining from her.

Jules shot up from his chair. "Mother?"

Marguerite scrambled up too, but backed away, toward the fireplace.

As always, Sébastien remained calm, but he shuddered, nonetheless. He, like Jules, refused to heed his mother's requests, but that didn't mean her surprise visits were welcome.

The dowager slowed her storming pace as she located them. Her scowl deepened upon noticing Marguerite. Her fists clenched as she pressed them to her hooped hips.

"What's the meaning of this?" Her obscure gaze scanned them all, but lingered on Marguerite.

Marguerite lowered into a curtsy, quaking.

Jules set his hands on his hips, in perfect imitation of the dowager, as Sébastien sidled in front of Marguerite to shield her.

They were like children again, running through the hallways, being reprimanded.

"What do you want, Mother?" Sébastien's tone was glacial, and he straightened up, not a lick of fear in his posture—or so, he surely hoped. But Jules recognized it without effort.

Dowager Clémentine sniffed out fear, used it to sway everyone around her.

One of Clémentine's sculpted eyebrows arched. "What do *I* want?" Her ladies, sprawled out about her like feathers in a bird's tail, hid behind their fluffy fans.

She had known they were with Marguerite, of course. But Jules knew *her*—she was putting on a show to spread more fear. Her uncaring attitude proved she had leverage—and Jules doubted it was against Marguerite or Sébastien.

She'd come to make a point, to remind Jules who his obedience served.

"Get on with it," he said, his voice wavering, making it difficult to contain his true thoughts. If he played along too fast, everyone would know how Clémentine held his leash, kept his secrets for a price. They *couldn't* know, not until he found a way to escape her games. "We were enjoying a nice moment with

Marguerite, so if you don't mind—"

"I *do* mind." Venom dripped from her burgundy lips. "You were to turn over your lists of choices, and instead I find you here with her?"

Sébastien groaned, and Jules understood why.

Clémentine had set this task upon them earlier that day. But she knew who Sébastien's favorite was, since he'd had to beg her to consider Céleste, and then he'd had to barter with Antoine, too.

"So you might invite them to tea tomorrow and torture them?" The afternoon tea with the favorites was a tradition. Sébastien seeking to deny it would only anger the dowager further. "I made it clear I had no desire to do that."

The gentle wrinkles at the edges of Clémentine's eyes pinched. "*She* kept you distracted. Perhaps she trifled with your common sense, too? We talked about this. We will honor this tradition, Sébastien." She snaked closer, the hem of her dress akin to the arms of an octopus. She stopped inches from Jules. "So I ask again—where are your lists?"

Jules, panic brewing within at the secrets his mother would expose if he didn't obey, fished inside his emerald-colored jacket.

Sébastien could argue all he wanted, but Jules' hands were tied. He'd wanted to draw this out, but the longer Clémentine was near him, the closer he was to crumbling.

No one could see him crumble.

"Marguerite didn't distract us. She's within her right to be in the library." He pulled out a crumpled parchment, and handed it to Clémentine, who gave a curt nod in thanks.

In agreement—he did his part by obeying her, and she'd keep her mouth shut a little longer. At least, until another opportunity to use him came around.

With an irritated huff, Sébastien smacked a crisp parchment into her grasp. "My choice hasn't changed. Why do you need it in writing?"

"That doesn't concern you." The dowager's lips spread into what would have been a smile, but Jules knew better. "I will consider these choices and decide if I agree with them. We have little time, after all."

She'd *already* considered. Already made her choice. That was what this was all about—reminding everyone of their place, of her authority over Torrinni court. Over her children.

Marguerite scoffed, breaking the silence.

Jules grimaced, lowering his head to rub at his temples. She should have stayed silent, let the dowager flitter out, and then they could discuss the situation more freely. A scoff, however, would irk the dowager into a fit.

Clémentine had been about to walk away without reprimand, Jules knew, but instead, she stilled. "Excuse me?" Almost in slow-motion, her gaze narrowed on Marguerite. "Do you have something to add, Marguerite?" She pushed past her sons, still clutching their notes in one hand. "Some snide comment you wish to utter regarding what I said?"

Sébastien gave Marguerite a rapid shake of his head, and Jules did the same, as discreetly as possible. She wanted to say yes, to protest such hasty decisions. She'd want to remind the dowager of her place, that her sons were princes, deserving of respect.

But this wasn't the time or place for her to choose to no longer be intimidated. Clémentine was on a war-path—a path that the brothers had yet to uncover.

He'd rather not see Marguerite obliterated.

Marguerite's conscience must have prevailed; her chin drew downward, defeated. "No, Your Grace. I had something stuck in my throat. I beg your forgiveness."

Clémentine seized her chin and jerked it up, forcing Marguerite to face the flames reflecting in her muddy eyes. "Right. Because you know your place. My sons should remember it, too, but they prefer to dwell on past feelings." She released her, her nostrils widening as if to emit fiery fumes.

Marguerite rubbed her chin but averted her gaze.

"Know this, sons of mine—your marriages aren't about feelings. They're about who I see fit as princesses, potential queens, ladies qualified to join the Totresian royal lineage. As the senior member of said lineage, my decision matters most."

Jules' insides flipped upside-down. He'd known this was coming, and still, it jolted through him like lightning.

Clémentine had chosen their brides long ago. Sébastien would probably get away with courting and marrying the Richel girl, but Jules…

The dowager indeed had intelligence on him, but it was more than he'd anticipated. It was something big enough to *force* him into whatever schemes she was orchestrating. She hated Frances— had said as much many times—and she'd already urged him, seriously, to consider Charlotte Geitz as his main option.

He hadn't put Charlotte on his list. Heat coursed up and down his limbs as he realized his mistake.

It didn't matter who *he'd* chosen, because Clémentine would make him do as she pleased, and if he didn't… well, she'd prove just how many of his secrets she'd been privy to all along.

Though words of retaliation burned inside his mouth, he said nothing. Sébastien shifted his weight.

How would she do it? Blackmail, as was her preferred method? Ambush? Surprise? Clémentine had many skills in her tool-kit, and though he was her favorite son, she'd still use all her wits against him to get what she wanted.

He feared that what she wanted would involve him far more than simply being next in line to the throne.

Clémentine clicked her tongue. "Also in my power as senior representative of the royal family, I would ask that you refrain from seeking company with *her*. She's not here as a friend, but as a noblewoman come to meet her betrothed, then leave with him. She's not the appointed aristocrat your father adored. That," she thrust a bony, ringed finger at Marguerite, "isn't the duchess you grew up with."

Sébastien froze, mouth halfway open to retort.

Jules had heard it too—*To meet her betrothed.*

Marguerite was summoned to court… to marry someone?

So Marguerite *was* involved. Clearly, Jules' mother had drawn her here with awful promises of marriage, great means to get her out of the way so she could proceed with her sordid plans. Sending Marguerite off so she wouldn't be around to thwart any plans. Were he not so furious, Jules would be impressed.

Clever, Mother. Forcing him to marry the woman of her choice, for the alliance of her choice, by holding his secrets in the palm of her hands. But Belnau? There was nothing of worth there.

Sébastien remained silent. He knew, like Jules, that interrupting his mother's rant now would only worsen the situation.

"Return upstairs to await your students, Marguerite."

Clémentine pirouetted towards the door. "Someone will be watching to ensure you don't dawdle once I'm gone. Rest assured—I always know where you are."

She and her fan-wielding ladies exited.

The instant the doors closed, Marguerite's legs gave out and she tumbled onto the rug before the fireplace. Jules slumped beside her and pulled her close, one arm around her shoulder; Sébastien kneeled in front of her.

"She doesn't command you," whispered Jules, gripping her tight. The words were as much for Marguerite as they were for him, though they were a lie.

"A betrothal? To whom? Since when?" Sébastien snickered. "I will inform Antoine of this behavior."

She attempted to stand, but she wobbled. Sébastien caught her, and Jules helped her straighten herself.

"No," she said, her voice strained. "Antoine already knows, I told him."

"And you didn't tell *us*?" Sébastien caressed a few tears from her cheeks, frowning.

"I'm sorry, I… I couldn't. The more people I admit it to, the realer it becomes."

"And Antoine?" Jules squeezed her hand.

"He will do nothing. He never does." She tugged herself out of Jules' grasp. "I will heed her warnings and retire. Thank you both for a lovely moment reflecting on the past."

Sébastien moved forward to block her. "Let one of us accompany you to your chambers. You're distraught—"

She gently pushed him away. "No." She smiled, but it was more of a wince. "I will be all right."

Clémentine had struck again, spewing poison everywhere she roamed. It took all of Jules' strength of mind to not dash after his mother and berate her, once and for all. To do what Antoine still hadn't done—demote her.

But if he did that, he'd destroy his own future, too.

"I won't permit her to harm you anymore," Sébastien said, as Marguerite took a few shaky steps to the doors. "She won't demean you like that in my presence ever again. You will always be our Maggie. Betrothed or not."

Through gritted teeth, Jules added, "Agreed."

A downpour of tears gushed from her lash-line just as she turned away. "Th-thank you. Good evening." She covered her face with her hands and left.

Sébastien twisted to his younger brother. "Did you know?"

Jules dragged a hand down his face. "You act like Antoine trusts me with that kind of information."

Surprisingly, he *didn't* know. But even if he had, he wouldn't have told anyone. Showing his hand like that, taking a side, would put him in more danger. Betraying the woman who harbored all his secrets, waiting for the opportune moment to release them? Out of the question.

He prayed he wouldn't have to go up against the one person who'd always defended him, saved him. His kingly brother.

"I must cut our evening short," Sébastien said, patting Jules' back. "I must have a little tête-a-tête with our beloved brother king."

And Jules let him go, because he had his own investigating to do, before his mother found more ways to impose her will on him.

She'd never run upstairs so fast, never sensed so much wetness on her face. She hadn't cried like that in years and was grateful no one saw it—except for the princes.

"I'll discover your plots and set them aflame," she whispered, jaw clenched as she entered her room, gathering her emotions.

The instant she fell onto her bed, her adjoining door burst open. After a rustle of fabric and a squeak, Céleste propped herself atop the mattress.

"What happened to *you?*"

Marguerite wiped her face with her sleeve. "Nothing." She wasn't ready to unload all the feelings brimming at the surface. "How did it go?"

Céleste kicked off her shoes and let out a dramatic sigh. "It was awful."

"Was the queen unpleasant?" Marguerite imagined that

Adelaide was mild in comparison to the dowager and her scorching mood.

"Not outright, no." Céleste hunched over. "She said I was a newcomer and implied I would encounter more difficulties soon. And that I would face the dowager tomorrow."

"Ah, yes." Marguerite straightened up, sniffling, doing her best to not flinch at the word *dowager*. "The afternoon tea. It's tradition to meet with the mother of the main catches of the season. As you're a favorite of Sébastien's, I expected this."

"But," Céleste took a large swallow of air, "there's more to report. About the queen."

Marguerite moved to the edge of the bed, dangling her legs beside Céleste's. "Tell me everything." She'd take anything over thinking about her encounter in the library.

Céleste gulped. "She implied that she would remain Queen of Totresia. As though she no longer feared for her position, as she told you."

"Ah." Marguerite folded her arms. A few laces of her bodice came undone, allowing her lungs to expand. "Well, I spoke with the princes while you were at supper. They confirmed something is up, and they've been investigating. They worry about that lack of heir law, too, and that their mother is interfering where she shouldn't. Clémentine is pushing them to find brides too fast. I know they're princes, and finding the right woman to continue the legacy is important, but it's a lot of pressure. Why do they need wives so soon if not to... well..."

"For one of them to take the king's throne?" Céleste narrowed her gaze on Marguerite. "But where does that put the queen? She must not be in the loop about this."

Marguerite fiddled with the folds of her gown. "The queen's role in all this is blurry. She may well have no clue of the dowager's intentions, or the dowager promised her something else in return. But what would equal or surpass being Queen of Totresia?"

Céleste's voice hopped up a notch. "Perhaps she's to become queen of a *different* place?"

"Oh?" Marguerite's eyes widened. "*Oh.* Céleste!" She lept from the bed. "*That's* why Adelaide isn't afraid. She will remain queen but not of Totresia!"

"But back to the princes," said Céleste, barreling to the sitting area, snatching a treat from an abandoned tray of delicacies. "If I'm Sébastien's favorite, and if the dowager covets the throne for *him* to replace Antoine..."

"No." Marguerite considered a delicacy herself, but her stomach was too upset. "*If* her plan is to use the princes—and that's a big *if*—it's Jules she'd want. He's her favorite, and he's next in line, anyway. But we must put all this aside, for now. Tomorrow, you will meet Clémentine. She's tricky."

Céleste fumbled with a macaron. "She will hate me. I'm unofficial, underage, and not presented."

"But you're Sébastien's only choice. If you care for him, all will be well." Marguerite watched as Céleste slowly chewed her bite, her gaze vacant. "You *do* care for him, yes?"

Surely he gave her the same feelings as Antoine once gave Marguerite—pulse quickening, butterflies in the belly. Warmth spreading through her being, an uncontrollable urge to smile all the time. All the sensations a young woman would experience when meeting the man of her dreams.

All the sensations Marguerite had thought she'd always love.

"Of course I do," Céleste swallowed, "how could I not?"

"Good." Marguerite gestured at the adjoining door. "Then I will see you in the morning. Wake me when you receive your letter."

***

Marguerite slept little, if at all. When she woke, the gray skies had dissipated and a pale blue, cloudless canvas soared overhead.

As she finished dressing she heard a squeal in Céleste's room, followed by Céleste barging in, brandishing a letter.

Without a word, Marguerite read it.

Miss Céleste Richel,

I formally invite you to afternoon tea.
Please present yourself at the music room at one o'clock.

Regards,
Dowager Queen Clémentine of Totresia

"One o'clock in the music room." Marguerite set the letter down. "Usual spot, usual time."

Céleste wiped sweat from above her brow. "Please tell me she doesn't plan on making us play something?"

With a sour chuckle, Marguerite guided the girl behind her changing panel. "I doubt it. Those are later tests." She ignored Céleste's dropping jaw as she fished through the girl's armoire for appropriate attire. "You bathed yesterday, yes?"

"After riding?" Céleste scoffed. "Certainly."

"Here. This will serve." Marguerite threw a cream-colored gown with black patterns at her.

She then combed Céleste's messy mane into a high bun and stuck a few bows atop the pins.

After adding rouge and pomade, she nodded. "Clémentine will like this." Marguerite headed to her room. "I will call Johanna for breakfast and check on the girls—don't move."

An hour later, Johanna brought their morning meal. Marguerite told them both how Charlotte had received a letter but Julia had, as well.

"Strange. She's not a favorite. Unless Prince Jules made a drastic change last night?"

Marguerite bit into her bread. "Who knows? Nothing is set in stone. It may be some other ploy we've yet to unearth."

At a quarter past noon, Marguerite inspected the creases in Céleste's clothing and fixed a few drifting strands of her hair.

Once satisfied, she pushed Céleste into the corridor. "Go. She appreciates early arrivals." She flashed her a weak but genuine grin. "Good luck. Be yourself. Sébastien cares for you, and he will fight for you."

The farther Céleste walked, the more confidence poured out of her like a leaking vase. By the time she reached the music room, her abdomen was clenched in pain.

In a daze, she knocked, and the door promptly opened.

An elderly man in Totresian burgundy eyed her, then moved out of the way, saying, "Miss Richel, daughter of the Marquess of Valeville."

The piano in the middle grabbed her attention before anything else. She blinked from the light pooling through the windows, waiting for her vision to adjust.

When she spotted the guests seated to the left, she hesitated at the threshold.

"Don't just stand there, Miss Richel. Come in." The snake-like timbre sent chills down her already trembling legs.

The dowager, garbed in pale canary and periwinkle, waved

her in with her free hand. Her other clutched an ornate cup. She perched on an elaborate chaise near the piano, her curls looser than usual, but that didn't change her scornful glare.

On the coffee table were untouched trays of delicacies and a few more steaming mugs.

As Céleste curtsied, the dowager motioned at a chair to her left. Her lacy sleeves swept over her knees as she beckoned Céleste to the designated spot.

The sofa was occupied by Charlotte and Frances. Julia, closest to the door, had parked in another chaise at the opposite end of Clémentine's.

Céleste hurried to her seat as Charlotte's mouth forced into a polite smile. Frances kept a safe distance from her, cramped close to the left arm-rest. Julia looked up, spotted Céleste, then glowered into the lap of her wheat-colored dress, still as a statue.

Her presence made little sense—Jules lusted after Frances, and occasionally Charlotte, but no one had noticed Julia. Had Sébastien added her to appease his mother?

Tension coated the vermilion walls. Julia shrank into her seat, avoiding looking at anyone. Charlotte tilted her head towards the dowager, her nose in the air. Frances was the only one who appeared indifferent, if not bored.

"I do hope your presence will break the unease in here," said the dowager, after a slow sip of her drink. "Miss Espinar's addition to the roster has displeased Miss Geitz, from what I gathered."

Charlotte shifted in her spot. "Your Grace, I—"

"No need to comment, Miss Geitz." The words, so cold, created an uncomfortable silence, more dreadful than before. "But I digress. Please, Miss Richel, help yourself to tea. Fruit and flower blends. The lavender one is my favorite."

"Many thanks, Your Grace." Céleste chose a mug and sniffed at it. "I look forward to trying it."

The dowager gave Céleste a moment to take a few sips before setting her cup onto a saucer. "Now that you're all here, I wish to clarify a few things. Miss Richel is Sébastien's only choice. He was adamant on that." She contemplated Céleste's garb from head to toe, pinching her lips. She then switched to Charlotte and Frances. "You two are here for Jules, of course."

Frances blushed. Charlotte winced and recovered with a too-radiant smile.

Clémentine glanced at Julia, still shriveling in her corner. "You." Her tone changed; harsher than nails scraping on marble, a hint of fire in each word. "You're not here for my sons."

Everyone gasped, except for Julia, who seemed to have forgotten how to breathe.

"The person who wishes to meet you isn't here yet, nor is his mother available to inspect you. But *I* am. And since he's royal, I thought it best to include you today."

Sudden understanding engulfed Céleste like tidal waves.

She and Marguerite had been sorely mistaken with their theories the night before.

Charlotte hiccuped, and Frances craned her neck to Julia, eyebrows arched.

"Cornelius Schwartz, Duke of Terter, joined our court recently on behalf of his monarch. After scouring the many options, he chose *you*." Clémentine looked ready to gag. "Miss Espinar, you will be formally introduced to King Romain when he arrives at court."

Frances' jaw sank, Charlotte scoffed, and Céleste's teacup nearly spilled into her lap.

Julia's chin whipped up. "The King of Giroma? Me?"

"Yes." Clémentine plucked her cup from the table. "Though he's also eligible, the duke was to decide on options for his king first. After careful observation, he thought you would be most interesting to his monarch."

Charlotte gritted her teeth. Frances resumed her uncaring demeanor as she nibbled on a macaron.

The lavender blend didn't sit well on Céleste's tongue, and the new situation added a layer of acidity she hadn't prepared for.

Once past the discomforting news, Clémentine asked about their upbringing, their favorite activities, what they excelled at. She remained polite, but mumbled quips under her breath—Céleste heard them all, seated so close. She accorded little attention to Frances, was stern when talking to Julia, and snarled when addressing Charlotte.

Julia was the most uncomfortable, and no one made her experience any easier with their negative attitudes.

Céleste felt a pinch of sympathy for her; it wasn't her fault. She hadn't wanted to attract Giromian attention, surely? But she'd danced with the duke when she shouldn't have, and thus prompted him to offer her to his king.

By two-thirty, with all topics covered and most cups empty, Clémentine stood up. "Thank you for your company, ladies."

When Julia curtsied, the dowager barely batted an eyelash at her. When Frances thanked her, the woman fought a yawn. And when Charlotte stretched her lips into her prettiest pout, the dowager fiddled with a loose strand of her sleeve and ignored her.

Céleste realized it was her turn to leave, and her stomach tied into millions of knots. "Thank you for your invitation, Your Grace. I was most honored to have tea with you."

When she rose from her impeccable curtsy, Clémentine stared at her, then nodded once before sitting back down.

Céleste's heart stopped beating.

A nod? She'd never learned the meaning of such a gesture from a member of the royal family. Miss Bertillon, her etiquette teacher, had never mentioned it. Ignorance and yawns were one thing, and evidence of displeasure—but a *nod?*

She sealed her mouth to not say anything idiotic, and ran to her room.

52.
Marguerite

After Céleste scampered off to tea, Marguerite received an invitation of her own.

Lady Marjorie,

In honor of King Romain of Giroma's imminent arrival, we're holding a special ball tomorrow night. We request you and the graduates of your academy to join us in welcoming him to Totresia.

We <u>highly encourage</u> your presence at this event, at eight o'clock, in the ballroom.

Regards,
Their Majesties

She crunched the paper in her clammy palms. "The nerve!"

Antoine hadn't written the note, but neither had Adelaide. "This reeks of Clémentine!"

The words were identical to letters she'd read from the former queen, and that vague, inky underline meant obligatory presence, no exceptions.

Mandatory attendance to a ball in a Giromian's honor? Antoine would never do such a thing, and neither would Edouard. Marguerite stomped to her bed and fell atop its lavish blankets. Her temples throbbed, jolting pain down her cheek-bones, her jaw, her neck.

She massaged her forehead as her door burst open, prompting her to shoot up from her lying position. She relaxed upon seeing Johanna, slinking in with a cup of what she hoped was coffee. "Miss? Is everything all right?"

"Oh, thank God." Marguerite padded over to her. "After the foul news I just received, this is most welcome."

"The ball?" Johanna's gray eyes laced with concern—of course she was aware. Most servants at Torrinni Castle received intelligence on special events before anyone else. "I listened to a few whispers—the staff has had little time to prepare for such a grand arrival."

"That despicable woman!" Marguerite snatched the cup from Johanna and downed half its contents, uncaring for how scalding the liquid was. "She did this! All this plotting, but to what end? Giromians at court, welcomed by grand parties? Why? What do they have to do with any of her schemes?"

Johanna tilted her head to the side. "What have you uncovered?"

Marguerite related the recent discoveries to Johanna, pacing as she sipped.

"Well," said Johanna, her usually proper posture shrinking as she lowered onto the couch, "to steal her eldest's son's throne and give it to her favorite so she might better manipulate him into doing her bidding… It's elaborate."

"But do you believe it?" Marguerite sat by her. "Is it plausible?"

Tugging at her braided raven hair, Johanna looked into her lap. "I'm unsure why she would be so opposed to whatever King Edouard ordained. Why would she want to control the throne? Didn't she have enough power for the eighteen or so years she was queen?"

Marguerite had asked herself the same questions, but never came up with the right answers. "She's greedy."

Johanna's gaze flickered with worry. "You've known her longer than me, so I trust you to better understand her motives. As someone she also often manipulated, I'm unsurprised. But these accusations are fuzzy. She may have admitted to the Giromian alliances, but the rest… the rearranging of the royal bloodline… she will cough nothing up easily."

Marguerite sighed as she pressed into the sofa cushions. "This wouldn't be her first offense. She forced Antoine's hand against me. And when I ran, she locked me in an academy and feigned my death to keep everyone off my trail. I would have no issue telling this to nobles in the council, if necessary."

"But," Johanna rose and tapped her chin with a fingertip, "that still doesn't explain the Giromians. Or why the dowager still hasn't told you who your betrothed is. She said he's here, no? Where is he? Why have you not met him yet?" She ambled to a painting on the wall that had tipped sideways and fixed it. "Those treaties between Terter and Totresia make no sense. The dowager abhors Giroma. Why would she celebrate these foreigners? Why not push her son to destroy them?"

"For all we know, *that* is the plan: invite them here to destroy them face-to-face, away from a battle-field." Marguerite's hands shook with tension. "But it's too easy, and surely someone like Romain would anticipate that. So why would she let them in? Giromians will ruin her family, and her family is all that matters to her. Yet she has forsaken those she loves to plot her way into power." She flinched. "Unless… it's all a ruse to get rid of *me.*"

Johanna leaned against the wall. "Get rid of you?"

Marguerite swallowed. "What if the duke is my betrothed? Or someone in King Romain's entourage, on his way here now?"

Johanna's sigh was deep and trembling. "Then she lied to you. She said your betrothed was at court. I wish I had your answers. But in the meantime, this ball is happening. We can't prevent it. Shall I warn the girls? Or would you prefer to do it yourself?"

"The girls."

Marguerite removed herself from the sofa. Her undergarments clung to her flesh as she hastened to unlatch the window. A gust of fresh air blasted onto her face and she breathed it in, a slither of relief pouring into her.

"Yes, if you please. And also," she jolted around as Johanna grasped the doorknob, "keep your eyes and ears open. Anything off… report it to me at once."

After a quick acquiescence, Johanna disappeared.

How long had Clémentine been planning this ball? How long had she known of Romain's arrival?

Antoine was Marguerite's best bet to find out more, short of intercepting the dowager and forcing the truth out of her. The princes had given her all they could the night before; armed with their knowledge, she had to confront Antoine. Again.

A knock on the adjoining door lugged her from her troubled thoughts.

"Yes?" Something clogged her throat, turning her voice raspy. "Is that you, Céleste?"

The door creaked open and in came the Richel girl, eyes like marble saucers. She hurried to the sofa where she sank and huddled into a ball.

"What's the matter?" Marguerite approached her and squeezed her forearm. "Did things not go well with the dowager?"

A visible lump throbbed at the top of her throat. "She dislikes Charlotte." She inhaled, her chest caving inward with the motion. "And Frances… she sneered at her a lot."

Marguerite cocked a brow. Frances and Jules spent more time together than appropriate; or so she assumed, having caught them sneaking about a few nights prior. The dowager might have been aware of such frolicking, but wouldn't that press her to favor Charlotte, instead?

"And Julia?"

Céleste chewed her lip so hard she left teeth marks in her skin. "She was there for…" Her cheeks drained of color. "For the king. The *Giromian* king. That duke picked her for him, and the dowager invited her because… *royalty*…" She plunged her head between her knees.

The throbbing in Marguerite's skull was like hammers on stone. "What?" She'd prepared for many eventualities, but Romain stealing one of her girls hadn't been one of them.

And that dismissed the discussion from the night before—King Romain *wasn't* coming for Adelaide?

"That monster!" She shot up, hands clenching with such vigor her nails dug deep into her palms.

Céleste sniffled. "I agree, he's vile, that duke—"

"No, the damned dowager!" She winced. "I mean, the duke *is* vile, but the dowager…"

"The situation peeved *her,* too. The way she looked at Julia…" As Céleste sat up straight, her heels hit the floor with a gentle click. "Charlotte was furious at Julia, too, or so the dowager said. When I came in it appeared she had stopped her from clawing at Julia's neck."

"What?" Marguerite was at Céleste's side again. "Charlotte and Julia fighting? In the presence of the dowager?"

Céleste lifted her shoulders. "I don't know if they fought, but the dowager implied they caused much unease in the room. Then she interrogated us, and the tea was this disgusting lavender blend and when I left, she nodded at me."

Marguerite's insides stopped tumbling to and fro as she seized Céleste's hand. "She *nodded* at you? Only you?"

"Yes! I ran from there so fast I got lost and might have frightened a horde of squires and servant girls," said Céleste, leaning forward, breaths heavy.

To Marguerite's knowledge, Clémentine had never nodded at any contenders in all her years of hosting afternoon teas for mothers of bachelors.

"A nod is a secret sign of royal acceptance." She hauled Céleste into a bone-crushing hug.

Céleste flushed again. "So it's good?"

"Yes." Marguerite wandered to her vanity, where she fixed her hair and shook out the wrinkles in her gown. "But pretending to be angry at Romain's interest in Julia is conflicting. I will figure it out in due time. The foreign king will be here soon, and they're throwing a ball in his honor."

"A ball? For him? There's no honor in having him at court!"

Marguerite waved her into her room. "Do you see now why nothing makes sense, but everything links to Clémentine? She weaves her web of lies, thinking no one will notice. But *we* do. The sooner I convince Antoine to send her off, the sooner we might breathe."

"Is that where you're headed?" Céleste shifted her weight, kicking at a clump of dust nestled in a crack of the threshold. "To speak with the king?"

"No." Marguerite tried not to suffocate from all the information taking up space inside. "I have two girls to chat with about their behaviors in front of royals. Julia got the attention of a king, and Charlotte is the second choice of a prince. She's jealous."

"I would pay to see Julia and this king together, and Charlotte snickering in the background. Not that I want her to marry a Giromian, but… oh, the shame. The scandal!" The smirk smearing across Céleste's face was priceless, but Marguerite couldn't dawdle about to admire it.

"Agreed, but first I must make sure they don't plot each other's murders out of spite. It may be dangerous if they become rivals."

Jealous contenders, foreign kings, plots to unseat monarchs—never had Céleste imagined such drama would unfold at Torrinni Castle.

She'd been so eager to unravel her own mystery—the identity of the Duchess of Torrinni—and now she was *part* of a mystery. How things had changed for her… some for the better, some for the worst.

She received another letter, this one unfolded, as if slipped under her door in haste by someone who wished to remain anonymous.

Her attention fell on the royal seal at the bottom. She swallowed; her throat was drier than a desert.

The signature was Sébastien's.

My dearest Céleste,

By now I suspect you're aware of the ball in "honor" of King Romain's arrival. Though it displeases me, it's the perfect occasion to present you to the king and queen!

With it being on such short notice, I'm afraid we have no time to summon your father to court as your escort. I have dispatched a messenger to make him aware of my intentions, and to reassure him you will have someone to accompany you: your brother! I've not spoken with him yet, but I assume you will do so?

Also, Mother told me about your afternoon tea, and I have rarely seen her so impressed with any lady at court! Congratulations!

Sincerely,
Sébastien

Céleste studied each word, imagining him saying them in his elegant and musical voice, his perfect lips parting into a sweet smile, a few locks of his hair brushing against her cheeks. Shivers scrambled down her spine.

"But what will I wear? I have nothing that will do for such a formal occasion!" Massaging her temples to ease the throbbing in her scalp, she blew out a few unsteady breaths.

She'd have time to ponder her attire options later, with Marguerite's expertise—first, she needed to chat with Emeric.

Would he manage to put aside their arguments for such an important matter? They hadn't spoken since he'd stormed out of her room the night of her arrival.

Heart pounding in her throat, she pulled out a blank piece of parchment.

Emeric,

I have significant news! Meet me in the Winter Garden as soon as you're able.

Love,
Céleste

She folded the note and stole out into the hallway. As she debated between taking the service stairs or continuing to the main landing, a page boy bumped into her.

"*Oh!*" they said at the same time, toppling against opposing walls.

The boy came to, adjusting his maroon coat as he inclined his head. "Apologies, Miss."

He proceeded to the left, but Céleste shoved her letter into his hand. "Would you please deliver this to Mr. Richel? It's urgent."

The boy hesitated to accept the paper. "Yes, but I was…"

"It can't wait," she said, straining to convey her impatience. Emeric would have dropped a few coins into the boy's pocket for conducting business on his behalf, but she didn't keep money in her skirts. "Mr. Richel will see you rewarded for delivering this with haste."

That sparked interest in the boy, and he took flight with the letter at once, headed in the opposite direction.

Céleste descended the service stairs, smiling in disbelief. Courted by a prince, tutored by the former Duchess of Torrinni, accepted by the dowager—her life had taken a turn towards the unexpected.

In the Winter Garden, the rich rose and tempting tulip scents filled her with pleasure. She twirled on her heels, basking in the sunlight dripping in from the glass ceiling.

Her feet carried her to the same spot where she and Sébastien had spent an entire night confiding in one another—a night she'd never mentioned to Marguerite. Its memory often chased away her nightmares.

The simple thought of the prince warmed her insides as she sank onto the stone bench. Tiny butterflies came to life in her gut and her extremities tingled with trepidation. She'd never once imagined, not even after reading torrid novels about forbidden romances, that this would happen to her.

So caught up in projections of her innermost desires, Céleste's mind wandered.

At the sound of approaching footsteps, her fog dissipated, and she saw Emeric, garbed in gray, coming up to her. Esther was at his arm, in layers of ravishing rosewood and raisin. A chaperone loitered behind them.

"Sister?" He took in her slumped form against the tree, brows furrowing.

The corners of Esther's mouth twitched. "Miss Richel. Pleasure to see you so… relaxed? Unlike last night."

"Last night?" Emeric's head swung to his companion. "What happened last night?"

"Oh, weren't you aware?" Esther batted her lashes at him.

Fixing her scrunched-up face, Céleste rose and smoothed out her gown. "The queen invited me to dinner."

"She *what?*" Emeric's voice was so high-pitched with shock that Céleste didn't know how to interpret it. But then he grinned so wide Céleste wondered why she'd doubted he'd be anything but content. "You dined with the contenders?"

Esther patted his forearm. "She made a swell impression. They say the queen liked her."

"But why were you invited?" Emeric's face was flushed with joy before it sagged in confusion. "You're not a contender. Not presented. Not of age."

"Haven't you heard?" Esther tugged her arm from under his. "Your sister is a favorite of Prince Sébastien!"

His eyes shifted to a vibrant sky blue, rounding like croquet balls. "The prince? You caught his attention? How?"

Esther launched into the beginnings of an explanation, but Céleste cut her off. "It matters not how, but it's true. The prince and I have met occasionally, and we quite enjoy one another."

"Enjoy?" Emeric dragged a hand down his face. "This… Father will be… does Father know?"

"Sébastien told me he sent someone to inform him, so he will soon."

"You call him by his *God-given* name?" He seized her upper arms and drew her close, as if about to hug her, but changing his mind halfway into the gesture. "How… what… *how*? Why wasn't I aware? If a prince had settled on someone, I should have known. Why didn't I know?"

Céleste recalled how Sébastien had shooed curious onlookers away before their first dance. How he'd appeared to want no one to disturb them. Perhaps he'd made sure no one mumbled about his courtships, either.

Emeric stiffly adjusted his lapels. "Well, if *that* was your big news, I'm happy to hear it. Thrilled. It's a bit soon, and I'm not positive you're mature enough for it, but I suppose you remember how old Mother was when she met Father?"

Céleste nodded. "I do, but there's more."

"More?"

"More." She chewed on her lip. "He asked that you lead me to the dais at the ball tomorrow night, to present me to the king and queen. To make me official."

The delight in his features evaporated. "The ball." Every inch of him seemed to recoil, to shrink into a shell like a shy tortoise. "Tomorrow night? The one honoring that horrid Giromian?"

Esther clapped her hands, oblivious to Emeric's developing anger. "A ball? Oh, I must have missed my invitation. Was it planned?"

"No," said Emeric, clenching his fists at his sides. "A last-minute addition to the season events, to welcome the King of Giroma to our court."

"The King of—" Esther gasped and covered her mouth. "Oh. Oh, well, that's different."

"Indeed, it is. It's a party I don't wish to attend, since it shines a light on someone I detest." Emeric's expression flashed with hostility, and his shoulders tensed as he further tightened his fists.

"But," Céleste took a tentative step towards him, "I need you there, as my escort. If not, there will be no presentation. The prince… it will disappoint him."

Emeric grunted. "I'm sorry, but it's Father that I don't wish to disappoint. Attending such a joke of a festivity in his name would dishonor him. Your prince knows how opposed we Richels are to anything Giromian. So if he wishes to court you in an official manner, he will delay this and find another ball for me to escort you to."

Esther pressed her palm to her breastbone. "Do you mean to say you won't attend? It will be such a lavish affair, surely you might accompany your sister, then blend in the crowd and pretend like you're not there? Or better yet—leave once she's dancing with the prince! You wouldn't need to—"

His snarl silenced her. "I encourage you to enjoy the frivolities without me. I won't hold your attendance against you. As a season contender, they expect you there. But *I* can't go. And in truth, neither should you," he said, zoning in on Céleste. "It will infuriate Father to discover you participated in such nonsense. I refuse to walk you up to a dais where that foreign idiot will stand alongside our beloved King Antoine. Never."

Céleste's earlier butterflies flew out her mouth and soared up to the ceiling, smashing into the glass. "You wouldn't make an exception? Swallow your pride for once in your damned life?"

She knew she'd gone too far when Emeric towered before her, his jaw clenched, his hot breath crashing over her like lava. "Do *not* speak to me like that again." He stepped backwards, fixing the cuffs of his sleeves. "If His Highness cares for you as you claim, he'll be patient. It's his season; there will be plenty of balls to announce you at. But not this one."

Without another word—or waiting for Esther—he stormed off to the door straight ahead and squeezed out.

Esther shrieked about being abandoned, and Céleste's eyes

blurred with tears.

Charlotte whined about how Julia was undeserving of such major majestic attention. She complained on and on about Julia being unintelligent, unimportant. How she had no talent for being a lady and succeeded in her studies thanks to others.

But Marguerite reminded her of the biggest detail: Julia had attracted *Giromian* attention.

"We don't want that," Marguerite had said, as the braying blonde lounged on her pastel pink bed. "It will displease her father, and she knows it. Don't be jealous, but don't be joyful for her demise, either. She's your friend."

Charlotte spat out all sorts of profanities, so Marguerite left.

She found Julia huddled in a corner of her chamber, panicked. *That* meeting took a little longer.

Far from the bickering, Marguerite reapplied powder to her face, to bury the redness that had settled on her cheeks, the dark circles curving below her eyes.

She had to make good on her word; she had to talk to *him*.

"It's his fault! Planting discord among my girls—how dare he?" She slammed a fist onto her vanity, knocking over a few of her beauty supplies. "Choosing before his king's arrival; why? How would he know? Why not pick… *ha!* Frances! That would put *her* father in a pickle."

Despite her rising anger, she snatched a parchment and scribbled.

Your Grace,

I wish to discuss your decision to submit one of our esteemed students as a prospective bride to your king, without having met her first.

If you would please meet me anywhere that's convenient for you, I would be most grateful.

Regards,
Lady Marjorie

She hastened into the hallway and chased down the first page boy she encountered, begging that he deliver her note to the Duke of Terter.

She checked on the other girls. Only Harriet was in her dwellings; Esther had gone on a walk with Emeric, and Cristina had a chaperoned date with Axel Espinar.

By the time Marguerite was done with her rounds, the page reappeared, his face flushed.

"He… the duke… my lady… he was otherwise occupied. He won't meet with you." He hunched over to catch his breath.

Marguerite frowned. "What was he doing that was more important than discussing the love-life of his king?"

The boy hiccuped. "I can't tell you, my lady. He said—"

"Whatever he said is void." She seethed, and the boy looked at his feet. She jerked his chin up. "He's Giromian. I'm Totresian. Would you heed his commands over mine? He may currently outrank me, but I doubt our king would take kindly to his staff taking sides. Wrong sides."

The page's cheeks were scarlet, so she released him, but she didn't soften her glare.

He rubbed the base of his neck. "No, my lady, I wouldn't."

"So," she stepped backwards, "tell me where he is."

"The art gallery," he said, before scampering off in the opposite direction.

She knew her temper had flared through her usual composure, but she didn't care. She hurried downstairs. The entryway was quiet, the Long Corridor easy to navigate, the West Wing deserted—as if fate wanted her to reach the duke unencumbered.

She arrived at the art gallery in record time and stopped at its threshold. There he was—with his troop of miscreants that he called friends. He stooped in front of a half-naked statue, zeroing in on the private parts. He chuckled at something one of his companions said.

As the duke straightened up, his skin glowed nearly white in the sconce light. "Such art wouldn't be so obvious at home," he

said, his voice dry as he dusted off his velvet maroon ensemble—
as if the statue had soiled it.

He swung in Marguerite's direction—without noticing her—
and she witnessed once more how broad-chested he was. How
defined his arms were, how confidently he carried himself. How
his eyes were emotionless pits of onyx.

When he smiled, she had to hold the wall to halt her shivers
from toppling her over. Everything about him screamed *doom*.
Handsome, enticing, and delicious—but dangerous.

She gathered her courage and swooped into the space,
clearing her throat. "Your Grace?"

When he took note of her, a sly smile pried his thin lips apart.
He raked a hand through his luscious dirty-blond locks. "I should
have expected this."

"I know this castle well, Your Grace. And its staff." She
fought a smile of her own; one of triumph over his petty tricks.

He grumbled a curse in his Giromian dialect, then to his men,
he said, "Would you all excuse us? It seems the academy chaperone
and I have much to chat about."

The men—nobles and squires—swerved by her, scowling.

"Pardon their rudeness," the duke said, once the last
gentleman had left. "They were the reason I wouldn't see you." He
laughed, a sensual sound Marguerite hated to let affect her.

"Save your pleasantries." She sucked in a breath, and his
pungent musk forced its way into her nostrils, making her choke.
"I want to understand what sort of game you presume to play."

"Game?" He arched a bushy eyebrow. "You think I jest? You
doubt my intentions? My king's intentions?"

She held in a snort. "Of course I do. Our dear dowager may

have permitted you to take up temporary residence here, but you're not welcome. Nor is your king. What gave you the right to pluck a bride for him among my girls?"

As a seductive smirk swept over his mouth, the duke ambled closer, hands in his pockets. "*Your* king, my lady. He wants to speed up the process. The sooner I choose someone for myself and my king, the sooner we will leave, since we're not welcome."

The closer he got, the darker his eyes became. Marguerite feared falling into them and spiraling into a doomed ditch of death.

She was dizzy, but had nothing to steady herself as all that surrounded her were fragile sculptures and priceless works of art. "My king asked you to pick one of *my* girls?"

Cornelius was so close now that she smelled his liquor and tobacco scented breath. He was of a height with Antoine, chiseled and charming, but his tone was tinted with poison. "Technicalities. He implied I should hurry, so I did. Miss Espinar is a fine choice, no? Would her father not delight in seeing her engaged to a king?"

She snarled. "Not a Giromian one."

His smile faltered. "I appreciate how you look out for your graduates, my lady, but I must ask that you step aside. They're available ladies of the court. Their chaperone can't interfere when someone offers marriage." His elegance became ferocity, his teeth like fangs dripping with toxins, his fingers like swords yearning to tear into her flesh. His presence was heavy, coating her limbs with sweat as he circled her, every ounce of his earlier allure melting. "It's not your place to interrogate *me*, a duke."

Unprepared for such spite, Marguerite tiptoed backward. She stretched her arms behind her, worried she might bump into a statue. "Like you said, I'm their chaperone. Meaning—"

"That gives you no authority to question me." He stopped walking and stroked his chin. "My lady… no," he narrowed his gaze on her, "*Your Grace*. Marguerite, yes? Once a duchess, if I'm correct? Surely you understand my position." He rubbed his lips with his fingertips. "I'm still a duke. You lost your title long ago, and if you seek to retrieve it, you will leave me to my orders."

She covered her mouth—to prevent a gasp, a hiccup, or her breakfast from spewing out, she wasn't sure. "How would you—"

"If that's all, I'll be on my way, *my lady*." He snickered. "I thank you in advance for keeping your lovely little nose out of affairs that don't concern you yet. But it was a pleasure, as always." His shoulders were high and proud as he continued out of the art gallery.

Her knees buckled. He knew who she was? And what was that about retrieving her title?

Her abdomen tightened so much that even breathing in and out and closing her eyes wouldn't lessen her agony.

She'd yet to tell anyone at court who she really was, aside from Céleste. The royals all knew, naturally, as did Johanna. Some of the nobles, but they'd all been bribed by Clémentine to not speak of it.

Who had told the duke?

Antoine wouldn't dare share such knowledge with a foul fiend like Cornelius Schwartz. Neither would Johanna. Céleste had never spoken to him, and the princes and princess steered clear from the man, as far as Marguerite was aware.

So that meant Clémentine had loosened her tongue. Or Adelaide. But why?

She tried to swallow, but her throat was too scratchy.

Pacing between statues and vases, she begged her pulse to stop throbbing. If Clémentine had told the duke, did that mean the duke was Marguerite's betrothed?

She'd tried to dismiss the idea after talking to Johanna; Clémentine had claimed her fiancé was already there. Cornelius, as far as she knew, had only just arrived…

There was more to this. It was too obvious, and too confusing all at once. Why promise Marguerite to a Giromian duke that everyone hated? Was it Clémentine's idea of punishment? Her way of fully demonstrating her hatred towards the duchess?

"I need to get upstairs." Marguerite wobbled down the halls like a sleep-walker, caught up in past comments that swirled in her brain like a witch's brewing potion.

On the main landing, she swiveled on her heels and squinted at the passage up to the royal floor. She chewed her lip, clenched her fists, blew out her cheeks—and approached the carpet-covered staircase.

Three steps up she halted, squeezing the banister as if her life depended on it. But she couldn't turn back. "He has to know. I have to warn him."

At the top, the two guards flanking the entry to the royal floor gaped at her; one in suspicion, about to block her.

The other tilted his head in recognition. "Duchess Marguerite?"

"*Former* duchess." She winced. "I know, I shouldn't be up here, but I have pressing matters."

The guards exchanged a glance, and the first shrugged. "You were always so kind." He let her through.

"But make it quick," said the second.

She thanked them as she emerged into the royal landing. The immensity of the place warped her senses—the ornate statues and sparkling marble pillars lining the designed walls; the painted portraits and lush landscapes; the swaying chandeliers, some unlit, casting areas in dancing shadows.

Guards were parked at every corner. Servants rushed about, but none paid her any heed, as if she still belonged there.

Her instinct drove her towards the hall that would lead to her old room, but as she marched in that direction, a familiar, sultry tone echoed across the landing, coming from the opposite side— the king and queen's hallway.

"Maggie?"

Marguerite was at once aware she'd made the wrong decision. "Majesty." She tipped into a hasty curtsy.

Adelaide's flamboyant locks flowed freely, and her burgundy satin gown grazed the carpeted floors as she approached. "I thought that was you."

"Forgive me, I—"

"They let you up here?" Adelaide studied her. Her three ladies garbed in shiny silks hovered a few feet back, watching with intrigue when the queen motioned for Marguerite to rise. "Not that it doesn't delight me to see you."

Fighting the shaking of her limbs, Marguerite clasped her hands at navel-level. "I needed to speak to… your husband."

The queen's perfect pout twitched. "Why? Are you—" Her brilliant blue eyes widened. "Are you referring to what we spoke of the other day?"

It was Marguerite's only means to cover up the truth. "Yes. Among other things. I need to report some behavioral issues I've noticed." Every muscle turned rigid as she fought to keep her teeth from clattering, to sustain a semi-smile that would convince the queen.

Adelaide set her hands on her hips, her ruby and garnet rings glistening in the candlelight. "I will see that he receives your message, then. I imagine he will be in touch soon."

"Thank you, Majesty," said Marguerite, curtsying again, grasping the edges of her gown with such force she might have torn the fabric.

"No." Adelaide leaned in as she passed, her crimson lips brushing against Marguerite's ear. "Thank *you* for upholding our friendship despite all I've done to you."

She paraded to the stairs, her eager ladies at her heels.

Relief washed over Marguerite, but it was brief. Antoine's warnings resonated in her head—his reminders to not trust Adelaide, to avoid her at all costs, to assume she played a bigger part in all the schemes.

Against his wishes, Marguerite had wandered into the queen's potentially deadly trap.

Too fidgety to return to her empty room, Marguerite went to the library and settled in her favorite chair near the fireplace. A perfect place to ponder, prepare, reflect.

She couldn't sit still. Three names circled over and over in her mind.

Clémentine. Cornelius. Adelaide.

She wasn't yet positive that the third one was complicit. But the more she thought of it, the more she worried just about anyone could be involved.

Clémentine hated Giromians, and the duke wasn't reputed for

being a kind soul. What would push them to work together? Had they struck a bigger bargain than him picking a wife among the Totresian contenders? King Romain's arrival was part of it, yes, but was there more?

Cornelius hadn't chosen someone yet. Or had he?

Was Marguerite his intended?

Had the dowager made some sordid bargain with Giroma, promised the king he'd have his pick of a Totresian wife, and offered up Marguerite to the duke—Marguerite, a prized and beloved ward of the late King Edouard?

Why would a foe of Giroma strike deals with its king and highest ranking noble? Did Clémentine seek the peace alliance all Totresian monarchs had prayed for, to end the centuries of passive-aggressive fighting?

Thoughts flurried in and out of Marguerite, draining her energy. She sank into the comforting cushions, yet their softness did nothing to assuage her fears. It was too much. Too intense. Too unreal.

Did Clémentine not see how she would weaken Totresia by removing Antoine from power? Out of her three sons, he was the strongest. The better-versed in royal politics. The one with the real claim. Jules was a child; a reckless, drunken, loose-lipped fool that she adored, but who wasn't ready to be king.

"Unless he lets her control the kingdom while he goes on with his frolicking…"

She couldn't wait for Adelaide to deliver her message to Antoine—if she even intended to. Marguerite needed to find him first, before Clémentine and Cornelius had any chance to set things in motion.

If Antoine wasn't upstairs, where would he be? There were few nobles out and about that day, and no lines of lesser men and paupers in the entryway, meaning he wasn't holding court. Would he be in the meeting room? His office?

As she traveled down the Long Corridor, she heard a viperous voice that halted her heart-beats and squeezed her insides.

The sound came from ahead, around the corner, in the King's Corridor—where she needed to go.

"…of course he's not here when I need to make arrangements. Have you seen our monarch today?"

The dowager was in Marguerite's path.

Marguerite pressed herself against the edge of the Long Corridor wall; the footsteps stopped feet away.

"He mentioned needing a walk," said another individual Marguerite recognized—Princess Cordelia. She had less spite than her mother, but had trained her tone to be almost as sharp. "He was in a mood."

"As usual." The dowager's footsteps took off down the King's Corridor again. "I will oversee operations, but would you find the queen? Tell her I request her approval of certain fabrics."

"Of course, Mother." Cordelia zoomed past, going in the other direction, towards the vestibule; luckily, without seeing Marguerite.

If Antoine needed a walk, like Cordelia claimed, then Marguerite knew where he was—the same location she used to meet him when they required space from Clémentine's hovering, a break from the pressures of royalty.

55.
Céleste

Too many emotions filled Céleste at once. Fury, fear, despair—if not a mix of all three.

The tears she'd tried so hard to hold in spilled down her cheeks.

She had no idea how much time had passed since Emeric had stormed out, but she sat against the tree trunk, her knees pulled up to her chest, shielding her as she sobbed. Beside her, Harriet—when had *she* showed up?—sat, heels tapping to the ground.

Esther paced before them in a puff of silk and taffeta. "This won't do. It's one thing to speak down to his sister, perhaps, but to me? The woman he courts?"

"Calm down," said Harriet, her tone a breeze of fresh air compared to Esther's strained squeaks. "It sounds to me he had his reasons."

"Reasons?" Esther glared at her friend. "I care naught for his reasons! A gentleman doesn't speak like that in the presence of a lady!" She cleared her throat. "Two ladies. Forgive me, Céleste."

Harriet spun to Céleste. "Yes, our contender for Prince Sébastien, asked to present herself in front of the king and queen during a party for a Giromian." She crossed one leg over the other, her foot jiggling. "Would you say he disrespected you? Or Esther? Was he out of line by refusing this?"

Céleste winced as she swallowed. "He used tones, but he wasn't out of line. He has a temper, and it gets out of hand if he's triggered. Esther and I—we triggered him."

Esther dug her fingers into her auburn curls. "By asking him to attend a ball with us? To present you to the king and queen?"

"No." Harriet pressed a fingertip to her lips. "By pushing him to attend a ball where a Giromian is the guest of honor. I know your family, Céleste. My father does, at least. The Richels would rather choke than be in a room with a Giromian. More so one of a feeble reputation such as the Duke of Terter. We have dealt with him and he's unpleasant. I expect your brother was furious about that, and livid with a second Giromian arriving. The *king*."

"There must be a way to change his mind." Actual fumes seemed to whoosh up from the top of Esther's head. "He wants me to go by myself? How will that make me look? Courted by him one second, deserted the next? Rejected by the princes, now by the son of a marquess? I will end up with a squire! Or a page boy! Ahhh!"

Céleste would have laughed were she not so distraught herself. Esther was quite the sight in her bundles of bouffant skirts that were about to eat her whole, her hair unwinding like loose balls of yarn.

Harriet got up and grabbed Esther by the shoulders. "He's stubborn." She side-glanced at Céleste. "From what I've learned, all Richels are."

Céleste wiped her nose and lowered her feet. "He won't go to the ball."

He would shame her before tarnishing their father's reputation. Any tiny twinges of hope she'd held on to fizzled into nothingness, and the pit in her belly grew larger.

"Then I can't either! I can't show myself! If I'm to marry into the Richel family, I must follow their rules. If he boycotts the foreign king's arrival, then so will I!" Esther stomped up to a bush and ripped out a few of its roses.

"I doubt Lady Marjorie will allow that." Harriet pried the poor flowers from her hands before she tore them to shreds. "Besides, you're not engaged to him yet. You may do as you please. I have no one to go with. We can be there together."

"But you don't understand—"

"I do, more than you can imagine. I have no prospects, and never will. So I'm asking you to accompany *me*." Harriet attempted to drag her back to the bench. "We will discuss the specifics later. Shouldn't we help Céleste? She's one of us now, we owe her."

Esther grumbled. "Axel Espinar might accept to escort her. He has to be there, since Julia gained favor from the Giromians."

"And he's courting Cristina, whose father would murder her if she didn't go."

Céleste rose from her seat. "Ladies, I appreciate your help, but I wish to retire to… think things over."

Harriet's shoulders sagged. "Are you sure?"

Esther plucked another rose and ripped it before Harriet could take it from her. And as Harriet swiveled to her friend, Céleste snuck out.

Her fingers ached from the constant clenching of her fists. Her calves were so tight she wondered how she walked—but she continued. Head held high as if nothing were amiss, as if she hadn't lost the opportunity of a lifetime because of her selfish brother.

Each step to her bedroom brought more rage to bubble in her gut. Each breath she took made it harder and harder to not cry. But she had to wait until she was alone, until no one would see her.

Once in the dark desolation of her chambers, she slid down the back of the door, her teeth shredding into her lower lip to not let her sobs explode out like gunshots.

Prince Sébastien wouldn't wait for a better time. Marguerite was quite clear: the princes were in a hurry. To thwart their mother's plots—or to play into them, no one knew—they had to announce their favorites and put wedding plans in motion.

By postponing her presentation, Céleste would dampen those plans. Sébastien wouldn't have the right to delay the proceedings if he wanted to be with her; his mother wouldn't allow it.

She remembered what Marguerite had warned her about only days prior.

"He can't follow his heart."

"Then perhaps it wasn't meant to be," Céleste said to herself, as a surge of tears unleashed from her eyes. Numb with sadness and disappointment, she stood up, her vision so clogged she couldn't quite see straight. "I need to lie down," she whispered, crawling to her bed, falling atop the sheets, letting their softness cradle her away from her sorrows.

Soon, her cheeks were sticky with tears, and her eyes burned.

Faint light slithered in through her window. A knot tightened in her stomach as she slid into a seated position, groaning. Thank the Heavens she had no social events until the next night—she was in no shape to be seen in public.

"Social events…" More tears threatened her eyes, but she threw her pillow across the room and kicked her covers off. "I'm done crying for today."

What was she to do? Show herself in front of everyone after losing her courtship with Sébastien? She had enough shame as it was, un-presented and underage; now she was a rejected contender who couldn't even convince her own brother to escort her to her presentation. She had no right to attend frivolous parties, no right to carry the Richel name.

She forced herself up and stretched, her limbs stiff from her curled up position. Her throat was dry and scratchy, and her steps uneasy as she wandered to her wash basin. She splashed her face with tepid water, and winced as she spotted her reflection in her vanity mirror.

Her eyes were bloodshot, swollen, as if someone had punched them repeatedly. Her locks were messy threads dangling over her shoulders like worn-down ropes.

She dried her face and slipped on her night-wear, then sat at her vanity to brush through her tangles. Each bristle pricked her skin and scarred her scalp.

Would Sébastien forgive her, forgive her brother?

She pulled her brush harder through her strands.

There she was, at court, exploring royal life, getting to dance in the royal ballroom. She'd discovered romances like those she read about in books, and she'd gotten the opportunity to *live* one—

But her brother had destroyed it. She'd found a man accepting of her, but fate decided she wouldn't go down that path. His offer came with a price: *limited time*. There'd be no way to bargain for more. The king had made too many exceptions already; a ward of his once beloved duchess or not, he wouldn't make any more for Céleste.

Sébastien would forget about her in minutes. He was a man she'd met a week ago and found dashing, but that she knew better to hope for.

She recalled when she'd first seen him in the ballroom, so mysterious. Then the night in the Winter Garden, how his eyes had glittered, so warm. His broad shoulders, like a blockade against harm; his soft hands like the comfort she'd never known she needed. His dazzling yet discrete smile, so charming.

Word would soon break out that she wouldn't be presenting herself to the king and queen the next day. Rumors would glaze the walls and linger on viperous tongues. Céleste Richel, the unloved. Céleste Richel, the reject.

She'd have to be confined to her room until some other rumor came about and the stories about her were yesterday's news.

Her fire had extinguished.

As Marguerite had said—someday, Céleste would discover the right man for her. One she might not love, who might not be handsome, who might not be a gallant prince or a mysterious knight, but who'd put the pieces of her soul back together. She didn't need Sébastien, and he didn't need her.

As she dragged herself to bed, she found her *Golden Girl* book on her nightstand.

"I solved the mystery I came to solve. That was my goal—not finding a husband, like the other contenders. I'm not a contender."

She cradled the book under her chin, snug under her blankets.

Soon, the drama would subside. The princes would find fiancées, and she'd return to the academy, to get back to her routine. No more fantasies of royalty and luxury. Not for her.

"What do you mean, you're the one she chose?" Antoine's fists clenched. "What kind of cryptic language is that?"

Jules, hands stuffed into his pockets, grimaced. "I've been… quiet. Trying not to choose sides—"

"*Sides?* Jules." Antoine scrubbed his face with one hand, his other remaining clenched. "What are you talking about?"

"Mother… she's up to things, and she *knows* things about me, and I… I don't know if I can hold her off much longer, Antoine. I can't say much else, but as your brother, I wanted to warn you. You have to do something about her, and fast. Before she puts it all into motion!"

Antoine had come out to the secluded forest clearing surrounded by holly bushes and covered in dry brown needles—for a reprieve. To escape the Giromians crawling into his home, the schemes his mother continued to operate behind his back. To run from Marguerite, knowing full well she'd come looking for him soon.

She haunted him wherever he went, even though she'd made herself scarce.

Jules had told him about how he and Sébastien met with her the night before. The questions she'd asked, the doubts she'd expressed—doubts shared by both siblings, which was why Jules had come to him in his seclusion.

But Jules only made things worse. He made no sense, was evidently panicked, and slightly angry—though it was unclear towards whom, exactly.

"Did *you* share things with Mother?" Jules tensed up, glowering at Antoine as if he'd slapped him. "You know everything about… well, *everything* I've done, so perhaps you…"

"Jules." Antoine felt like *he'd* been slapped, not his brother. "Come now, you know me. I was only trying to keep you in line when I threatened to tell Mother, and I thought it worked. But I'd *never*. Never."

To think his own brother would accuse him of conspiring with their plotting Mother—a sour taste developed in Antoine's mouth.

Jules had started this, anyway. Showing up to disturb Antoine's quiet-time, yelling and gesticulating all sorts of theories, and telling him their mother likely plotted to dethrone him. And replace him—*with Jules.*

If anyone was conspiring, it was *him.*

"Why are you only informing me of this now?" Antoine glowered at his brother's bright, lime-green suit. Why did he always need to draw attention? Was his reputation not boisterous enough?

Jules removed one hand from his pocket and swept it down his face. "I… wasn't yet certain."

"Oh, and now you are?" He held in the urge to grab his brother by the throat. Jules was always sneaky, secretive, but if he worked with Clémentine, it'd be betrayal.

"Not out of choice," Jules said, scoffing as he turned away. "And no, still not certain, but I truly believe it."

"Why should I trust you?" Antoine sensed heat flaring up his neck. "Séb at least left Torrinni because of her drama. But you stepped right into it?"

"Antoine—"

He sliced the air with his hand. "You're inept to be king, even she knows that. Your gambling habits? Frivolities in that damned tavern? She knows about those, and she's chosen not to care? This makes no sense."

He hadn't wanted to believe it when Marguerite suggested it—the annulment of his marriage, then the forced vote to make him abdicate his throne in favor of someone easier to manipulate. But Jules wouldn't have come to warn him if it wasn't real.

He was about to say more, but stopped, hearing twigs snapping nearby.

A sliver of late-afternoon sunlight peered in through the branches overhead. He saw someone—*Marguerite*. She'd stooped near a tree, seemingly trying to be sneaky, but failing.

She let out a loud gasp at being caught by Antoine's stare, and lifted her arms in surrender. "Sorry to interrupt, but," she breached into the clearing, "actually, it does make sense."

Jules' jaw dropped. "Maggie?"

Antoine's eyes narrowed on her. "What are you doing here?"

"I need to talk to you. Jules and Séb spoke to me of all this." She sidled up to Jules, exchanging a knowing glance. "So it's you she aims to replace Antoine with?"

Jules shifted his weight nervously, doing all he could to not look at Marguerite. "I'm not positive, but... Sébastien would decline. And I think she's still angry with him for renouncing his place in line for the throne. She'd want no one outside of the bloodline on the throne, so... it would have to be me."

"This is absurd." A vein pulsed at Antoine's temple. "Does she want to throw me off my throne via some secret law only a few of us know about? Perhaps. But replace me with *him*? Why cause such discord between brothers?"

"That's another matter altogether," said Marguerite, taking a tentative stride towards him.

"Jules." Antoine's mouth pinched into a thin line. "Leave us. We will finish this later, with Séb. I don't care what you say, I want his opinion. He's our voice of reason."

Without another word, Jules disappeared through the bushes, fuming.

Once he was out of earshot, Marguerite seemed hesitant to get too close. "What's the matter with you?"

"Conspiracies." Antoine groaned as he massaged his tense jaw. "All of you come to me with your theories about Mother doing this, and Mother doing that, but no one has the proof I need to eject her." He stormed towards his hat, which he'd thrown to the ground in rage at Jules' claims.

"The fact that everyone comes to you with these conspiracies should be your proof. I have more to add, so—"

"Naturally." His lip curled as he picked up his hat, dusted it off, and scowled at it. "Since you've returned to court, all the plots have reanimated. Why do you provoke Mother so? Why does she hate you?"

Marguerite crossed and uncrossed her arms. "Would that I could figure that out. But speaking of hatred—I believe she's definitely in league with the Duke of Terter."

Antoine put his hat on. "Is she now?"

"I tried to confront him, and he called me Marguerite, *former duchess*. No one else at court has said a word about me, aside from you and your siblings, and your wife. I've never met him before today, so he would have no way to recognize me. I doubt you spoke with him about this?"

Antoine pushed the rim of his hat from his eyes. "Me? Speak with the likes of him? Never. The boys wouldn't either, or Cordelia. Adelaide… I'm not sure. You think Mother informed him of your identity? Why?"

"Who knows why she would spill such secrets about me?" She combed her fingers through her hair, for a moment distracting Antoine, making him yearn to weave through her curls, smell their flowery scent once more. He inhaled deeply, erasing the image before it consumed him. "Yet another mystery I have to solve," she added.

Duke Schwartz's arrival was no mystery; Antoine had put two and two together the instant Marguerite mentioned her supposed betrothal. "You're lying." He ripped his hat off, smashing it against his chest. "You think he's here for you, don't you?"

Marguerite's jaw fell, her mouth opening—but Antoine wouldn't let her speak.

"Well, *I* think he's here for my wife." He snorted. "She's been drooling all over his elaborate Giromian threads since he got here. She thinks I didn't hear her blabbering with her birds at the ball, but when she imbibes so much liquor she loses herself. She's obsessed with him."

"Adelaide fawned over Cornelius in plain sight?" Marguerite's head flinched back slightly.

"When he showed up, she changed. More secretive, distant. That's why I warned you against her. I'm betting Mother's arrangement with the duke is regarding *her,* not you. She'll rob me of my throne, and instead of sending Adelaide back home to Avignon, she'll pack her up to return to Terter with Schwartz. Giving Adelaide away was part of a negotiation, I presume. And that negotiation would establish a sort of alliance between us and Giroma." He clutched his hat hard, as if it would somehow protect his heart from the storms to come.

"Adelaide... marry the duke?" Marguerite gulped loudly. Antoine's eyes glued to her throat before he shook himself, reminded of the time and place—wrong. "But is that not a downgrade? I would have expected her to marry... someone higher up."

"Like I said, she's obsessed with that two-timing, fickle fraud of a Giromian duke. He hasn't chosen a bride, despite claiming that was what he came here for. I'm aware of Romain's choice: Miss Espinar. To be frank, I don't have any inkling why *he's* coming here at all."

Marguerite chewed on her lower lip. "Adelaide and Cornelius."

He blew out his cheeks. "That's my theory. You thought she'd leave with Romain?"

"Trust me, she wouldn't settle for a duke after being married to a king."

Antoine glared at the darkening sky. "But Romain won't take her. A king marrying another king's ex-wife? It's unheard of in our history."

"And this," Marguerite stomped her foot, "isn't proof enough for you? Your mother is unapologetically weaved into this plot, no matter what it is, and it's not sufficient to incriminate her?"

He jerked his chin back in place, his gaze burning into Marguerite. "I've yet to see her pulling the strings, Maggie. I'm going off rumors; off your instincts, Jules'. I believe you, all of you, I do. But no, it's not enough."

Marguerite's shoulders sagged. "Then this is worse than we feared."

"She can't dethrone me without a unanimous vote. I'm uncertain what the nobles will do, or if she has already started overturning them, but my brothers are on the council. Neither will agree to this."

"She'll resort to blackmail?"

"And King Romain is a visiting royal—he'd be allowed to request to sit in on that vote, and I'm sure he and his duke will offer words of wisdom that'll persuade everyone against me."

"You still have devoted followers. Those who swore to your father. And your brothers won't allow this, like you said. And I—" She flinched. "Well, I don't count anymore, but I won't let it happen either. But your mother..."

"Mother organizes balls for the nobles, to cover the fact that she consorts with enemies and betrays us. Who knows what else she has up her sleeve." He sighed, his breath tipping his hat sideways. "I can't ship her off until I find out."

The woods darkened, and each sound startled Antoine. Whether the noises were critters or wolves or spies, he wasn't sure, but didn't wish to find out.

He readjusted his hat as he marched to his horse. "It would be best if you returned to the castle." He seized the reins and gestured at Marguerite. "You'll take my horse; I'll walk. With all we know, you and I should remain apart. No more meetings in basements or forest clearings."

She agreed, but as he helped her onto the saddle, she grimaced. "I think Adelaide is looking for you, by the way. I asked her to deliver a message to you—"

If she hadn't already settled atop the horse, Antoine would have dropped her. "Why? When?"

She averted her gaze, getting settled. "Before I arrived here, I searched for you on the royal floor."

"They let you up?"

"The guards recognized me." She glanced at him, those turquoise eyes awash with shame, sorrow. Desperate for forgiveness.

If he stared into them too long, he'd forget all his own troubles and focus on fixing hers. "Marguerite," he cautioned.

She shuddered. "I'm sorry, I wasn't thinking."

"Indeed." With his free hand, he patted the horse's backside, prompting it to take off. "I will handle this. Get inside before it gets too cold."

When she'd left to find Antoine, the sun had commenced its slow descent, casting shadows in the faded grass.

She kept checking behind her, worried someone had followed; now, she prayed no one had.

She inhaled the crisp evening air as the horse hopped over roots and piles of leaves. They passed through a wetter section of the woods, full of echoing howls and muffled chirps and muddy odors that made her nose itch.

When she broke through the last branches, the castle's canary side facade glowed gold under the torches. As soon as she rounded the corner, she found nobles climbing into carriages. Others seemed to be arriving, but she couldn't see the insignia on their vehicles.

Only once all carriages were gone, she hastened to a squire who lingered at the foot of the steps, and bade him get the horse back to the stables.

The main doors were open; warmth and voices seeped out. An ominous sensation thrummed to life in her belly—something unfamiliar that unsettled her, but she couldn't explain why. As if a new presence had appeared at Torrinni Castle, and its stench dribbled out into the courtyard, wrapping around her like a deadly snake.

As she passed the threshold, she saw guards in cerulean and silver, helms with black feathers erupting from the top. Nearby were a few dark-dressed dames on the arms of similarly garbed men, rubies dangling from their necks and decorating their sashes.

Such exuberant extravagance?

The Giromians had arrived.

These were the middle-class aristocrats King Romain always traveled with. But where was *he,* this other monarch that Antoine had hated all his life?

Someone snatched her wrist and dragged her up a few steps of the main staircase.

"What in the world—" They didn't release her until they were halfway up, and her wrist throbbed. She whirled around, preparing choice curses to bellow in their face, but froze upon meeting a pair of chocolate eyes curtained by disorderly black locks. "Séb?"

"Quiet." His voice was a rough rasp. "Where have you been?"

She squinted at him. "Why do you ask?"

He extracted a note from within his jacket and shoved it into her palm. "Read this."

If Sébastien requested anything of her, she'd never hesitate. She unfolded the parchment.

It was unfamiliar handwriting, ink dug deep into the parchment; whoever had written wrote in haste, angrily. And it was signed by Emeric Richel—Céleste's brother.

Marguerite read over the words at Sébastien's insistence. "You want to present her at the Giromian welcome ball?"

"And *he* won't escort her." His eyes turned wild. "I spoke to him after he sent me this. He still declined. *Declined.* Denied me, a Totresian prince!"

As the son of Barnabé Richel, a man so stubborn he'd moved far from court, this didn't completely surprise Marguerite. Emeric would have learned at a young age to have firm beliefs against Giromians, so attending a ball honoring one of them would be against his morals.

"What did you do to him?"

Sébastien scoffed. "Nothing. I'm not Mother."

The earlier lump that had taken residence in her throat cleared up. "What would you have me do? If her sibling won't accompany her, then who can? Her father is many miles away. Can you postpone it?"

His messy mane swished over his face, concealing his expression. "No. Antoine would have, but Mother insisted if this girl was who I wanted, it was now or never. If I postpone… she'll get further involved."

Marguerite snarled. "Giromians at court. Naturally, the Richels will steer clear of that, as should Céleste." She tried to push past Sébastien, whose large shoulders blocked the way up. "She must be devastated. I should check on her."

"Wait." He grabbed her upper arm, bringing her far more close than appropriate.

She gasped, worried everyone downstairs would notice them and have questions—but one quick side-glance revealed that all the foreign guests had moved out of the foyer.

"I want Céleste, do you understand? She's my salvation from—" he waved a hand around them, "—all this nonsense. My escape from the weight Mother leaves on my shoulders." He gritted his teeth and his fists clamped shut—a genuine copy of his older brother's temper flares.

Marguerite's heart skipped a beat. "What do you want *me* to do about it? I can't magically summon her father to us, nor can I persuade Emeric to change his mind."

"With your title, you can escort her." A glimmer of hope lifted the corners of his mouth and sprayed across his face like a flicker of moonlight.

"My title?" As a duchess, she'd have a high enough status to fill in for Marquess Richel. But she'd been stripped of everything after Clémentine locked her up. "I don't have a title, Sébastien."

"You do." An air of triumph prompted him to fix his posture. "You're still the duchess of Torrinni."

"But your mother—"

"It doesn't matter that she locked you up. Or that she spun tales about you being dead or never existing. Nothing was ever signed to remove your title from you. Antoine never decreed anything. As far as Totresian law is aware, you... disappeared."

"Disappeared." She blinked. "So I'm... still a duchess?"

"Sort of, yes. Enough of one that you could act as Céleste's guardian, escort her, and present her to court." He cleared his throat and Marguerite caught his nose twitching. "With prior permission from the king, that is."

"Ah." She crossed her arms. "So there's the catch."

He clasped his hands in a pleading prayer. "Mother is foul to you, but if you ever loved me, if you still do, and if you care for Céleste, would you do me this honor?"

Marguerite still had plots to unearth and evil to stop; the country was crumbling to pieces, and she had to save it. Save herself, before she was shipped off, likely to Giroma.

Antoine and his throne would have to be patient. Uncovering the identity of her future husband would also have to wait.

"Have you spoken to Antoine about this yet?" She didn't want to reveal she'd been with him, in case the walls had ears. "I overheard that he's in a mood today."

Sébastien flicked his wrist. "Mood or not, he always vouches for my happiness. This would make me the happiest man on earth, so he wouldn't dare refuse."

Saying no now would shatter him and ruin Céleste. Knowing her, she lay crying in bed at that very moment, dreading her existence.

"Fine. But *you* will talk to him, not me. Once you have his blessing, send me the details. I need to go check on her."

He pulled her into a bone-crushing hug. "Thank you. I owe you more than you know."

A slight smile formed despite her doubts. "Oh, that you do."

She rushed to Céleste's quarters, knocking once, twice, thrice—but if the girl was within, she said nothing.

Marguerite snuck in anyway and a frigid air swept up her skirts. Obscurity accompanied it, and silence. No fire flecked to life in the hearth, and the curtains were wide open, displaying the early evening sky.

The moon's glow showed Céleste curled up in her blankets, one arm squeezing her pillow, her other embracing a book.

The book.

Though tempted to take it, Marguerite didn't want to wake her.

She pulled the drapes shut and reignited the hearth's flames. A tiny gleam glossed over the wood, and a gentle warmth spread up her arms.

She returned to her room, where Johanna awaited to disrobe her.

"Everything well, Miss?"

"No, but it will be." She removed her cloak and lowered into the vanity seat cushions as Johanna brushed through her tangled curls. "There's been much development, but I'm too exhausted to speak of it now. I need you to wake me early tomorrow. Have the main seamstress meet me in Céleste's room as soon as she's able— I have a mission for her."

"A mission?"

"We need to pick a dress for her, and have it scaled up to the dowager's requirements. Tomorrow, at that dreaded ball… Céleste will be presented to their Majesties. It's her presentation ceremony."

To be Céleste's escort was a bold move that would risk revealing Marguerite's true identity to all—but Sébastien was her family, and she'd vowed to look after Céleste.

***

Céleste woke as Marguerite rummaged through her closet.

Morning sun blasted in, causing the girl to cover her eyes, then rub them. "What's happening?" She sat up, blinking. "What are you doing?"

Marguerite threw a dress atop the growing pile on the floor. "Inspecting your outfits."

"For what?" Céleste threw her covers off, sending the book she'd been nuzzling all night falling to the floor.

"You need a white dress. I was certain I saw one when the royal staff unpacked your things." Marguerite returned to the armoire, frowning at its contents.

"A white dress?" Céleste set her feet on the floor. "For what?"

Marguerite gestured at her to join her. "For an important occasion."

Céleste clumsily ambled up to the duchess. "What occasion?"

Marguerite scoffed. "Do you need coffee? Or did you hit your head while you slept? For your presentation, tonight!"

Céleste winced and stumbled backwards. "My presentation? But I can't…" She pressed her hand against her chest. "My brother declined to accompany me, I assumed you would have heard by now?"

"I did." Without looking at her, Marguerite pulled out of the wardrobe while wrinkling her nose. "I found a loophole in that situation. Well," she spun around, "Sébastien did, and enlisted my help. So here I am! The issue is rectified."

"How?" Céleste shuffled her feet.

Marguerite flinched as she studied a patterned, pale blue dress—not pale enough to pass as white. "I'm the Duchess of Torrinni, since apparently, I never lost my title. I outrank your brother. While we're at court, I'm your chaperone and guardian. Since your true legal guardian—your father—is too far to attend, and your brother won't be present, it falls on me to escort you, if the king approves. And he did."

"The king? And Sébastien… and you will…" Céleste's legs quavered so much she had to hold her vanity chair to not collapse.

"You *will* get your official debut tonight." Marguerite dove into the closet again. "Do you have anything suitable for a royal presentation?"

Céleste stuck out her lower lip. "Well, there's—"

"Aha!" Marguerite tugged out a white number with short sleeves, ruffles down the front, bunched at the bottom.

"That was the one I was about to mention." Céleste took a few strides up to the garment as Marguerite held it up. She caressed the silky fabric. "But it was for the Masquerade."

Marguerite laid it out on the bed. "We can use it for both. For tonight, it will require a few minor alterations, and tomorrow we will leave it to the seamstress to make it Masquerade-approved. We will need to lengthen the sleeves and un-bunch the bottom." She paused, fingertips drumming on her chin. "Any minute now. Johanna—"

A knock interrupted, followed by a soft voice in the hallway. "Miss Richel? My lady? May I come in?"

Marguerite clapped. "There she is!"

A short, middle-aged brunette wearing a light gray garb and a navy apron entered the area, peering at Céleste from head to toe. She didn't smile, but her eyes weren't unkind. "Come closer, child."

Céleste obeyed.

Marguerite closed the door and leaned against it. "This is the head royal seamstress. She altered my dresses while I lived here."

Céleste jumped—from Marguerite's revelation or the woman

suddenly poking her with pins, Marguerite wasn't certain. "So *she* knows who you are?"

Marguerite placed her index finger over her lips. "Less talking and more obeying what she asks you to do, yes?"

The seamstress bade Céleste to hop onto a stool and dropped her box of utensils and materials with a loud sigh. "Stand still." She circled Céleste. "And the dress?" Marguerite picked up the precious garb, handing it to her. "Hmm… exquisite fabric. Shouldn't be too difficult. I have identical silks downstairs." She snapped. "Put it on, then! Quickly!"

Céleste hastened to her changing panel and dropped out of her nightgown. Marguerite handed her undergarments and stays, then helped her tighten the laces in the bodice.

"It's like wearing a cloud," the girl said minutes later, showing herself.

"It's spectacular." Marguerite brushed the back of her hand over the waist and down the petticoat. It draped over Céleste's figure so perfectly, she wondered if it'd been tailored to her. It was her understanding most of the girl's dresses had been her mother's; this one might have been crafted for Céleste alone. "Fit for a contender to a prince."

The seamstress' impatient timbre broke their moment. "Yes, yes, a dress fit for a princess, etcetera, etcetera… get over here so I can perfect it!"

The woman made Céleste put her arms out. She pivoted around her, studying every inch, every crease, every curve. She wrapped measuring tape around Céleste's shoulders, forearms, wrists, and waist, then scribbled her results in a notebook.

Céleste closed her eyes, lost in her thoughts—smiling.

"You may relax. But don't take that off yet," ordered the seamstress, sinking into the vanity chair to review her notes.

"It's not tight-fitting like most dresses," Céleste said, cautiously twirling. "It's like I'm soaring. Soaking in a milk-bath."

Marguerite couldn't look at her any longer, not without heaps of memories washing over her. The situation was so eerily similar to the day she'd tried on her first Masquerade dress; when she'd found out she *would* attend, after Clémentine had initially revoked that right from her. The joy, the relief—it was so short-lived. So ephemeral.

She wished she'd known that day how everything she'd loved would be snatched away in one night.

Céleste beamed at her. "It's perfect, isn't it? Oh, the nightmares I had last night—but this, this trumps all of them." Marguerite held in her tears, but her emotions must have shown, for the girl's smile faded. "Are you all right?"

Marguerite nodded, biting her lip. Opening her mouth was a bad idea; she had no control over what would spew out.

"Are you sure?" Céleste patted her arm.

She straightened up, sniffling. "I'm fine. Lots to organize, little sleep last night. Nothing I can't handle."

Céleste's shoulders drooped. "Why don't I believe you?"

With a weakened sigh, Marguerite crossed her arms. "I'm worried. Whenever things go well in this place, they tend to reverse their course and implode. I'm cursed, and I pray you don't suffer my fate." A loose curl fell over her cheek and she blew it off as she meandered to the window.

Céleste cocked her head. "What fate?"

"That of becoming a runaway duchess turned prisoner in

punishment for her crimes." She fought to conceal the tremble in her voice.

"Crimes?" Taking care to not step on the hem of her gown, Céleste joined Marguerite. "You have committed no crimes."

"I have." Marguerite's grin was grim. "The crime of loving a crown prince."

"Sébastien isn't him."

"I know." Marguerite hoisted herself onto the bed. "But you remind me of myself. So enraptured by the beauty of court and the mystery of royal men. You see nothing of the snakes hiding in bushes, the monsters in the shadows. This place is foul, and I fear Sébastien may not be able to protect you from it. Like Antoine couldn't protect me."

Céleste moved to sit beside Marguerite, but the seamstress moaned. "Don't sit! You will ruin the gown!"

"Fine. The crown prince had obligations, choices made for him." Céleste parked before Marguerite, hands on her hips. "Sébastien isn't even next in line! With how he has vouched for me already, would he let anyone harm me? Would he pick someone else over me, at the last minute?"

Marguerite lowered her chin, fearing another wave of tears; ones she might not be able to prevent. "I don't want you to fall into Clémentine's evil grasp, to succumb to her traps and schemes until she forces you into running like she did to me."

Céleste squeaked, her gaze wavering back and forth between Marguerite and the seamstress. "Oh! My lady, is she—?"

Marguerite waved at the latter. "She's not one of the dowager's servants. She belongs to Cordelia."

The woman clapped her notebook shut. "I must go if I want

to finish in time. Disrobe, please. Hurry!"

Céleste returned behind her panel and removed the elegant layers, holding them out for the seamstress.

"I will bring this up when done—hopefully before dark." The seamstress leaned near Marguerite. "Fret not, Your Grace. Your secrets will go with me to the grave."

Once Marguerite composed herself, she threw a pistachio green outfit over the panel for Céleste to change into. "Put this on. We have details to go over while you eat your breakfast."

Marguerite wanted to have faith in Sébastien, to trust he'd shield Céleste from the atrocities of Torrinni court and the backstabbing natures of his family members. But his mother would be a problem. Would she block his desires, overstep his plans, halt their courtship?

Céleste's name carried weight. Richels always supported the current monarch, and the dowager wouldn't dare forget that. She'd do nothing to anger her late husband's most fervent advisor, Marquess Barnabé Richel. She wouldn't lay her filthy claws on Céleste, lest Marquess Richel and Emeric changed their allegiance.

Marguerite could only pray that would never happen.

58.
Marguerite

Marguerite's mind piled up with doubts and concerns.

After the ceremony, Céleste would be a full-fledged contender. She'd have to learn to fend for herself and prepare for insults. Underage privileged girl, sneak, cheater—the list of insults would be endless.

Seated at her vanity, Marguerite twirled her tresses into a large bun and decorated them with pearls and jewels. Rarely did she wear off-the-shoulder gowns, but they were a trend in Totresia, thanks to Adelaide. To escort the daughter of a revered noble to meet the royals, she needed to blend in with the crowd.

The deep navy shade Marguerite chose was her idea of honoring the Giromians. They were known to love bright ceruleans and pretty peacocks; this color was more ominous, reflecting how she felt about their invasion.

A feeling that would put her front and center for all to see, because she was alive—not disappeared or dead.

She inhaled, exhaled, and joined the girls near the stairs.

Charlotte showed up first, in light peach and black lace. Julia wore pale gray and blue, as Marguerite had requested. Esther sported extravagant bundles of brilliant pink, distraught at being without her courtier for the night. Harriet regaled in peach-pink and white, the fabric smoothing her silhouette in suggestive ways—a bold choice. Cristina arrived last, her demure burnt-orange outfit less revealing than most outfits she wore.

"Are we ready?" Charlotte tapped her foot, glaring at the carpeted staircase.

"We await one more person." Marguerite saw her final contender coming over with timid steps. "Here she is!"

The girls and Marguerite pivoted to Céleste, her brilliant white dress outshining theirs. She twinkled like a star, hypnotized like a diamond. The seamstress' adjustments were impeccable; Céleste was a princess in all but the official title.

"Is this okay?" she whispered to Marguerite. "Johanna promised me I looked fine, but…"

"You look lovely." Marguerite gestured to the staircase, and patted Céleste's hand. "Onward, ladies!"

Céleste's strides were uneven. "It's too much."

"I'm with you and will guide you through this."

Most of the attendees had already entered the ballroom, eager to view the elusive and temperamental Giromian king.

At the doors, the guards took note of their arrival. "The Giromian monarch hasn't yet arrived, but we urge you to make haste, ladies," said one of them.

Marguerite shooed the girls inside. "Pick your places before the dais. Céleste and I need a moment."

The five contenders scurried in, and the guards closed the doors behind them.

Marguerite listened as the herald announced each of them, and panic swelled inside at the notion that she'd be next.

All gazes would be on her.

How would Dowager Clémentine react?

Céleste shuddered. "Are you sure this isn't too extreme?"

Marguerite noticed the flecks of gray in Céleste's big blue eyes, like dove wings flapping to take flight. "It's a ball, a special one at that. Would they want the Giromian monarch to outshine one of their own? No. Sparkles and shimmers are acceptable. Encouraged."

Céleste wriggled about. "It feels excessive."

"They will accept you." Marguerite bit her tongue to not speak her thoughts out loud—her fear that *she* wouldn't be accepted, because she was supposed to be dead. "Antoine isn't like his mother; he would never play such games. And Adelaide knows better than to deny a Richel."

"Right." Céleste gulped. "I'm a Richel."

"The daughter of a prominent marquess that Antoine values, that his father valued before him. Your name guarantees acceptance. Now, stand tall, control your shaking; you're about to be announced to the King and Queen of Totresia!"

As Céleste fanned out her skirts, a few sudden, swift claps from afar prompted her to gasp.

"Bravo!" The condescending, sinister tone came from farther down the hall, an area cloaked in shadows.

Marguerite's heart stopped as she swiveled towards the

source of the noise. "Hello? Who's there?"

She regretted asking when a set of steady footsteps announced a person approaching. Something lodged in her throat—that same ominous feeling she'd had the day before, upon sensing the Giromians.

A tall figure emerged from the darkness.

"Wait by the herald," she mumbled to Céleste, shoving her to the doors without removing her focus from the nearing individual. "I will handle this."

The doors opened and closed, and Marguerite was alone.

"Who's there?" she repeated, squinting at a young man who walked with the poise and confidence of someone important. He had a smug look about him, with blond, medium length hair, high cheekbones. He wore a waistcoat of silky brown with matching breeches.

"Nice speech," he said, his eyes like glowing green orbs in a dark forest. They narrowed on her, and she froze.

As he got closer, she spotted the silver and gold sapphire-encrusted crown atop his head. Then the cerulean sash across his torso, littered in badges and intricate insignia.

She refrained from cursing, but was powerless to stop her widening pupils. Her knees bent, and she sank into a curtsy. "Your Majesty." She couldn't take her eyes off his clean-shaven face, his lips pressing together as he assessed her. "Thank you."

He stopped a few feet from her; a rosy aroma emanated from his clothes. "Oh, I mean it. So encouraging. It made *me* confident. Not that I need to be."

She hesitated to rise. He hadn't indicated she could, and she didn't know much of the Giromian customs. "It's an honor to meet you, Majesty. Before everyone else, too. Welcome to Totresia."

King Romain chuckled as he pulled her up. At his touch, a shock-wave rippled up her arms and tensed her shoulders.

He was half a head taller than her. Not too broad-chested, but still intimidatingly dashing; one might say *flashy.* But the icy feeling of his palms made her want to recoil.

She kept her wits about her as his eyes scanned hers. He sneered, though it almost came off as a smile. "And you are?" His breezy voice sent shudders racing down her back.

"Lady Marjorie, chaperone of the contenders from our Royal Academy for Noble Girls."

"Ah, Lady Marjorie, yes." He brought her hand to his lips, grazing her knuckles. "Also known as the great Marguerite?"

"How… why would you say that?" She wished she could wrench from his grip and hurry inside the ballroom to escape him and his powerful presence. She'd rather be ogled by the crowds than stuck here, under the scrutiny of this stranger.

"You're famous. My men mentioned you to me. A lady at a royal court, concealing her true noble identity? Intriguing. I promise, I won't tell a soul." He winked.

That large-mouthed duke had outed her, without a doubt.

"Famous, me?" She struggled to keep her voice level and her legs balanced.

"Much more beautiful than the tales portrayed you." He released her, his sultry stare taking the breath from her lungs. "But lovely as you are, I'm here for someone else. Brunettes are more my type."

A tiny part of her shrank in relief; not that she wanted him to find her attractive, but to discover he wouldn't chance at seducing her filled her with glee. He wasn't here for her. He wasn't her mystery betrothed.

After all, why would Clémentine give her away to a king?

"Good to know." She motioned at the doors. "I believe they're expecting you. Where is your entourage?"

He stuffed his hands in his pockets as he passed her. "Already inside. I like to wander the halls when they're empty. Oh, the things one can discover when all the aristocrats are out of the way."

He didn't give her time to analyze his cryptic comments as the guards ushered him in. Light blasted out into the corridor, but she was rooted to the spot, unable to follow. Unable to comprehend his words, and unsure if she wanted to.

Part Four

It
All
Falls
Down

454

Was she dreaming? Was this really happening? The knots from the night before had untied. Céleste had quit grimacing as much, and the numbness in her heart was replaced by a flicker of hope.

She was being presented to the Torrinni Court.

She stood by the herald as commanded, but a few folks in the crowd noticed her. They examined her outfit choice, whispered about her hair-do, the accessories she wore.

All she could think of was the man who'd clapped at Marguerite's words. She'd sighted his blond hair as she shuffled into the ballroom, but had no time to observe anything else.

The doors burst open—the individual she'd seen in the corridor now towered in the threshold. Everyone turned to him; there was a certain flair about his posture, a flamboyant confidence and energy from how he carried himself.

He removed his hands from the pockets of his silky brown

suit, and the badges and insignia plastered on his sash glittered in the chandelier light. Atop his tresses was a gold and silver crown decked with sapphires.

His evergreen eyes skimmed the room as the attendees lowered into curtsies and bows, Céleste included.

The herald tapped his staff to the ground. "King Romain of Giroma, a revered guest of our royal court!"

He marched down the carpet as if it belonged to him. The nobles rose as he passed them, some silent, some muttering.

Céleste craved to witness the foreign king inclining before Antoine, his most fervent enemy.

She sidestepped, ignoring the herald's grunts about waiting for her escort. On the podium, Antoine wore silver and black, a crown of ruby jewels on his tamed mane. He glared at the Giromian King, but Adelaide, engulfed in crimson and gold, beamed. Sébastien and Jules peered down at the foreign monarch with obvious disdain.

King Antoine waved him up. "King Romain, we honor your presence in Torrinni." His voice was stiff.

Céleste tried to glimpse the dowager, who lingered in the background, but the ballroom doors creaked open again, and Marguerite emerged.

She snatched Céleste's arm. "Ready?" Her eyes were alert like a magical fire, and her lips looked like she'd dug her teeth into them.

"Are *you?*" Céleste's toes bunched in her shoes.

"We don't have a choice," Marguerite snapped, tugging her to the edge of the rug.

"Introducing Miss Céleste Richel, daughter of the Marquess

of Valeville. And her escort, by royal decree, Lady Marjorie!

They glided down the path at a brisk yet respectful pace. Marguerite kept her chin tucked, but Céleste's focus stayed on the foreign king, who studied them.

Something was off about him. He was comely, with strong shoulders and muscular arms and a sturdy gait, but his smile was too forced. And his eyes were too invasive—like he read through her, through Marguerite, and didn't like what he saw.

What had happened in the hallway?

Before Céleste knew it, they'd made it to the bottom of the platform. She gulped and lowered her head.

Marguerite curtsied hastily, then slid to the side, leaving Céleste alone.

Céleste also curtsied, feeling like her throat was closing up, blocking her airways, stopping the blood from rushing to her heart—

"Miss Céleste Richel," said King Antoine, his rigid tone making her shoulders tighten. "I welcome you to our Totresian court, no longer as a ward to your chaperone, but as a contender to my brother, Prince Sébastien of Totresia. Rise."

Céleste did as bid, stealing a glance at him to gauge his demeanor. His features had softened.

"You're ineligible for marriage until you have completed your studies. But you may be courted by any bachelor at court, though I daresay they would have to fight my brother for that." Chuckles came from the audience; even Céleste released a giggle.

Queen Adelaide grinned, and Clémentine, from afar, gave a swift nod. Jules mimicked a slow clap.

Before Céleste could peek at Sébastien, her gaze wandered to

King Romain, who was, to her astonishment, looking at Marguerite—with a raised brow and a smirk.

With interest. Too much interest.

She tore away from the sight only to spot Duke Cornelius perched by the right edge of the dais—*also* staring at Marguerite. If Romain's ogling had been disturbing, the duke's was worse. He wore a dark grin as he scanned the woman's silhouette.

Céleste held in the urge to regurgitate her lunch, and moved on to contemplate the only person who mattered.

Warmth spread up Sébastien's cheeks, his eyes bright and blissful. He took a step towards the king.

"Take your contender, Brother, and open the night, would you?" Joy erased Antoine's irritability, if only for a moment.

Sébastien descended and captured Céleste's hand to kiss it. "You look splendid," he whispered, lips lingering atop her knuckles.

She flushed, turning away to hide her redness. As she did so, she noticed Romain had leaned down to say something into Cornelius' ear.

Both gaped at Marguerite *again*.

Marguerite was oblivious, fixated on the windows.

"Well done," she said to Céleste, before disappearing towards the buffet, out of view from the interested Giromians.

As the prince led Céleste to the dance floor, she refocused on him. So dashing, so proud to display her on his arm. The crowds parted to let them settle in for their dance.

With his fingers wrapped around hers, he pulled her to stand before him. He tipped her chin up, forcing their eyes to meet—his were soft with sweetness, overflowing with admiration.

"Céleste."

Everything around her, every worry, every jeering, jealous woman, every intrigued man—all blended into a uniform blob. All noise faded, save for the beginning notes of a ballad. All the lights shimmered like stars in the night sky, sprinkling over Sébastien's face.

"Sébastien." She fought her lips wanting to part as he held her hand and slid his other to her lower back.

They took flight. Familiar butterflies woke in her gut, dancing with them. Their wings flapped with such fervor she was dizzy, detached from the world in some delirious daze.

"I meant it," he said, lips brushing against her earlobe, creating vibrations that spiraled down her spine. "You're a vision."

"And you," she gulped, "are the most handsome man in this room."

Sébastien spun her, and all the troubles burdening her melted at her feet.

"Thank you for *this*. For giving me a chance, though I didn't deserve it."

Sébastien pulled her closer. "You deserve everything and more. I'm sorry for making you confront your brother like that. I should have made the arrangements myself." As the music sped up, and other couples joined them on the dance-floor, he tightened his grip on her hand. "You need not worry about a thing. I'm ever so grateful your brother mentioned you, and more so that I got to you before anyone else."

Only the day before, she'd fashioned herself as a fraud, not belonging at court, too immature to have a chance at courting such a marvelous man. Yet now, each word he said, each compliment weakened her knees and animated the butterflies.

Céleste had begun the ascent toward royalty—an ascent she never expected she'd even come close to.

460

Forcing happiness took more energy than Marguerite expected. Concealing her worries beneath smiles and curtsies took more strength than she had.

Her mind raced too much to appreciate Céleste and Sébastien's first official dance, so she meandered to the wine fountain and dunked a goblet into the burgundy liquid.

King Romain's words pounded inside on repeat. *"Oh, the things one can discover when all the aristocrats are out of the way."*

Thank goodness Antoine had ordered her to be announced as Lady Marjorie, for now—had her true name been pronounced, she'd be dodging more stares and itching to hide.

Her heart sped up as her gaze drifted to the royal arrival from an enemy country. His defiant yet decadent self was parked beside her former fiancé. Though different in every way—Antoine was taller and stiffer, and Romain flaunted his wealth all over his badge-littered chest—they had the same contempt in their expressions, and similar heavy crowns atop their well-kempt manes of hair.

Lurking below them was the duke, garbed in dark colors that brought out his pallid skin.

He was staring at her again, through the flock of damsels, past the dancers and the giggly girls at the extremity of the dance-floor. The corners of his mouth twitched upward. A cold air loomed about him, his eyes so dark they were like two globs of infinite night sky without stars.

He and Romain looked alike—the same glacial aura about them, the same lengthy waves of hair, the same gruff demeanor, devoid of emotion.

As she glanced at the kings again, she found them watching a lonely girl across the dance-floor, her raven curls tucked and twirled at the nape of her neck—Julia.

Romain said something to Antoine, who flashed the most spite-filled smile Marguerite had ever seen, and motioned in Julia's direction.

She had to get to the girl before Romain did. She deposited her untouched cup on the table, and in a few leaps, she reached Julia and tapped on her shoulder, drawing her from her daze-like state.

Julia jumped. "Oh, Lady Marjorie, apologies, I…"

"Compose yourself, because King Antoine will arrive soon to introduce you to King Romain."

Julia's posture rigidified. "Right. Yes. The king. An opportunity of a lifetime, wanting to meet me… best behavior."

Marguerite took Julia's hand and squeezed it, wondering if Viscount Espinar, her father, was aware of the situation. "It's not an opportunity, but you must show caution. I don't trust this man, and neither should you."

Marguerite's frown deepened as, to her dismay, it was the Duke of Terter who accompanied King Romain to where she and Julia waited.

Julia's arm twitched, and Marguerite pushed her a few inches forward. "You'll be fine. I'm right here."

Once they managed through hordes of fawning ladies, King Romain and Cornelius Schwartz arrived. Marguerite and Julia sank into curtsies.

Cornelius cleared his throat. "Majesty, I present to you Miss Julia Espinar, daughter of the Viscount of Malaros, a prominent noble in southwestern Totresia." He leered at Marguerite as she rose. "And her chaperone… Lady Marjorie is what she apparently goes by."

Romain helped Julia up. "Enchanté, Miss Espinar." He brought her knuckles up to place a discrete kiss atop them. "I've heard much about you."

"Likewise, Majesty," said Julia, with a subtle tremble in her speech that she recovered from by batting her lashes. "It's an honor to meet you at last."

He tucked her arm under his and led her toward the floor-to-ceiling windows.

Marguerite sighed, only somewhat relieved. She gave a rapid incline of her head to the duke and began to turn around—but he seized her wrist.

"A dance?" Though his tone had warmed up and a sly seductiveness simmered in his eyes, everything about him drove her to recoil.

"Excuse me?" She tried to tug from his grasp, but he held on tighter.

"Come now," he slid close, "*Marguerite*. Can't we move past our spat?" He sounded amused; like he anticipated she'd defy him, and thrived off the thrill of her denial.

She cringed. "Spat? Is that what you call it?"

He swept his tongue over his teeth. "Why not?"

As disgust coiled in her stomach, she understood she had no choice. He had her cornered. To refuse would draw unwanted attention—and many already observed them, likely curious why they stood so near one another.

"Fine." She permitted him to guide her to the dance-floor, and from their spot she saw Romain and Julia in deep discussion. The girl's cheeks were flushed as she fanned herself, but Romain's gaze was trained on the dais.

Before Marguerite could figure out who'd caught his attention instead of the woman he'd traveled to Torrinni for, Cornelius jerked her into his arms.

Marguerite inhaled a sharp breath, praying for her nerves to steady. When he set his hand on her back, she did her best not to grimace—no warmth came from his fingers wrapping around hers.

He was an eloquent dancer, but nothing about him prompted her heart to flutter or her legs to shake. While others fretted about how chiseled and charming he was, she fought a headache worse than any she'd ever had whenever in his presence.

If this was her betrothed…

Acid bubbled up in her mouth.

When his prodding eyes showed a hint of playfulness, she gagged. When his daunting but dazzling smile should have threatened to weaken her knees, she didn't falter.

"I'm sorry for our recent interactions. All I do is for my king. I never meant to offend you."

She snickered at his overly melodious voice. "All I do is for *my* king. For my country. So you must understand my suspicions and wariness, yes?"

As they swirled, he glared at the platform, where Antoine was standing. "I assume *he* is who you wore such a daring dress for tonight? What with your history—"

Marguerite chewed the insides of her cheeks, resisting the urge to wrench herself free and slap him. "I must ask you to avoid bringing up such matters, Your Grace."

The cunning curl of his lips showed he had no intention of heeding her warnings, yet he chose not to taunt her again.

"Forgive me. I forget my sense of humor is often lost on Totresians. But I do apologize, nonetheless. It's beneath me to be so cruel and careless." His timbre was laced with sweetness—too much sweetness.

He peered at the dais over and over. Antoine's comments rumbled in her mind; those suspecting the duke and Adelaide were in cahoots. Was *that* who he looked at as he danced with another woman? Was the queen promised to him in return for some part in a sordid scheme organized by the dowager?

Or was Marguerite his intended all along?

When the music crescendoed and changed, he backed into a dramatic bow. "My thanks, Lady Marjorie."

To her relief, he scattered through the crowd and disappeared before she could react.

Courtiers glowered at her—envious, jealous, or mad that she'd danced with a Giromian again? What option did she have? If she wanted answers, she had to put herself in perilous predicaments.

She returned to her glass of wine, still full and untouched, and downed its contents in one large gulp. She didn't care to savor the taste; she wanted the liquid's effects to drown her woes.

Why did the duke bother to apologize? Why did he dance with her? They'd both endured their first time as a formality, but this felt different. He tried too hard, made her choke on his fancy phrases and his strong perfume. Was he putting on a show for his king? Or trying to keep her occupied while other plots formed?

She drained another cup of wine, enthralled by the woodsy, raspberry flavor. She peeped at the platform, at the man she'd once loved. The man who'd let all this happen under his nose and did nothing to stop it.

Even from afar, she saw iciness coating his hazel eyes. She had no idea who he reserved such frigidity for, because he wasn't looking at her.

At his side, Adelaide fanned her flushing face with a red-feathered fan, pouting in pleasure as someone spoke to her. Someone at the foot of the dais. Someone with a crown.

Romain was mesmerized, enraptured in her. Julia stood beside him, oblivious as she, too, chatted with the queen, but it was obvious to anyone else that Romain was only interested in Adelaide. He leaned towards her, his lustful body language indicating admiration, appeal, possibly arousal.

The queen seemed as engulfed, swaying back and forth in her spot, her gown's hem swishing over the edge of the podium, brushing against Romain's arm.

Had Antoine noticed this inappropriate exchange?

Sure enough, the Totresian king was sending his dagger-filled glares at Romain.

Adelaide was certainly promised to one of the Giromians, that much was clear, but which one? Both were in awe of her, and she shamelessly flirted with whichever one stood closest to her.

It made more sense for Romain to be interested in stealing her away from Antoine, but Cornelius had ogled the queen all night. He was nowhere to be found now.

"Were we mistaken?" Marguerite whispered to herself, covering her mouth with the rim of her cup that she quickly emptied.

Once her drink was replenished, she searched for Clémentine.

Was this part of her ploy? To trick everyone, to use Adelaide as a distraction as she sought to dethrone her son? Or was it *all* a distraction for something else?

Distraction for the real enemy among them—Marguerite's betrothed. Could he be *worse* than a Giromian like Cornelius, or a fussy king like Romain?

The dowager loitered in the background, studying the scene. She clasped her hands as a sly grin slipped across her darkened lips. She kept to the shadows of the thrones, but no matter the distance— Marguerite knew that look, that glimmer of pleasure in her eyes.

She approved of the flirting between the Queen of Totresia and the King of Giroma, didn't she?

Too many new factors came into play in too little time, and Marguerite had no inkling how to talk to Antoine about them.

Céleste's shoulders twitched. The new sleeves of her dress were itchy. But she plastered on a grin, reminding herself it was all worth it.

She was a presented lady, officially courted by the man of her dreams.

Sébastien handed her a glass of sparkling wine. "To your presentation," he said, taking her free hand to place a warm kiss on it. "And to our official time together."

A strand of his perfect curls pirouetted down his cheek, and she resisted the urge to brush her fingertips against his skin. Blushing, she looked down as she sipped her drink. Her mind raced a million miles a minute.

She noticed the peachy-pink hue of her lip-stain on the glass as he pulled her cup away.

"Hm?"

"You're overthinking, I see it."

"How would you know that?" She was spinning. Was it the wine? Or his perfumed presence weakening her resolve to contain her emotions?

"I noticed your eyes turn to a feathery gray when you're troubled." He passed his thumb over the spot where her lips had left traces on the goblet.

Butterflies flung themselves at her stomach linings with such intensity, she might have fainted.

And she never wanted them to stop.

She tried to pry her drink from Sébastien's clutches, a ravaging thirst drying her tongue. "Troubled?" She sensed her chin tipping downward again, but he lifted it once more.

"Yes. What troubles you?" Each word blew a breeze of his breath over her, wine and mint and a hint of cigar.

"I'm having difficulties accepting that this is real." She bit her lip.

He squeezed her chin a little tighter, each finger pad on her skin firing a flush of warmth up her cheeks and down her neck. "It seems the same things trouble us, then."

She wanted to scream, to cartwheel. How to behave like a proper lady when her ribcage was about to burst, and her feet wanted to leap across the dance floor to express her joy?

Charlotte swished past, locked in a steamy dance with Jules.

Sébastien chuckled at them. "Can you imagine if I'd ended up with *that*?" He seized Céleste's hand and held it tight, as if worried she'd fly away. "I'm lucky, because I found you instead. A level-headed, beautiful young woman who has no intention of chasing titles and crowns. Am I right?"

She peeked at Charlotte, tried not to gag, then pivoted back to

Sébastien. "Yes. I suppose you are."

Her mouth twitched into a grin as a passing noble saluted them, and Sébastien carried on a polite conversation with him. She didn't listen; she was in the clouds, lost in fairy-tale feelings.

When Sébastien touched her arm, she gasped, falling out of her reverie. "Oh, I'm sorry—"

"Come," said Sébastien, tugging her through the crowd of nobles. "Let's go outside for a moment."

He brought her over to the glass terrace doors, motioning for a guard to open them.

Once out into the wintry air, the cold filtered over Céleste. The freshness was a welcome reprieve from her overheating skin.

Sébastien muttered something to the guards before closing the doors.

She'd never been on the ballroom patio before. Its candles and torches lining the overhead and trailing down the pillars were accentuated with vibrant waves of cascading ivy. Flowery vines crawled up the surface all the way to the ceiling. A full moon sprinkled a nearly blue glow over the stone ground.

"This view is marvelous," she said with a contented sigh.

"It is," he said, coming up behind her.

"The moon—so bright. I don't think I've ever seen it so big." When she swirled to peer at him, he'd come so close to her she nearly bumped into him. "Oh!"

He caught her, steadied her. "I mean *you* are marvelous, not the view of the castle grounds."

Though frosty wind whipped at her exposed neck, she flushed like she'd been plunged fully clothed into a hot spring. "Should we not have a chaperone? I mean, for appearance's sake, at least."

"We won't stay out here too long," he said, voice deeper than usual. "I just wanted to be away from the noise, so we could hear each other better."

She nodded in agreement. "It *was* quite loud in there."

"Yes," he put his hands in his trouser pockets, "and I really wanted to speak with you about something important. It's only been days since I met you. But it's like I've known you much longer."

"Much longer?" The butterflies multiplied, her heartbeat like a horse taking off at a gallop.

"But I remember that day with such precision—you rose from your curtsy, so flustered at seeing my brother and me. It was charming."

Céleste scrunched her nose. "Childish, you mean."

"No." He smiled. "A normal reaction when one is surprised by a royal, I'd say. Though yours was more intense, and something about that intrigued me. And your name... I know it well. *Richel.* Such an honorable family."

She was bewildered by his tone tickled with honey, infusing warmth into her body despite the cold. "But *me?* So suddenly?" She inhaled a crisp breath of air. "I can't deny this connection, these emotions, but—"

"But what?" Moonlight spilled over his features, and she admired every detail. The freckles near his nose, the dimples by the corners of his lips, the scruff poking at his jawline. "As you said, we have a connection. Something woke in me the day your brother mentioned you, Céleste. A hunch, if you will."

The longer she stared into his eyes, the more she didn't care for propriety. She wanted to drown in him until he engulfed her whole. "A hunch?"

"Are you afraid?" A shred of fear flickered across his features.

"Of *you?*" She gulped. "Never. But I must admit, after all this, I'm… nervous."

"I am too, Céleste. It's all so unexpected. Never in my life had I imagined one of these frivolous festivities would provide me with the woman of my dreams."

"Woman… of your dreams?" If it was still cold outside, she couldn't feel it—she was enveloped by heat, as if she stood too close to a hearth.

She liked it; the sensation of burning, *yearning.* Something she'd only read in her books.

"I hate balls. Ladies prancing about to gain my affections, win my approval. But you, shy and sweet, utterly unaware of your beauty—*you* gained my attention. You won. *We* won."

"Won? We… Oh." Realization caught up to her—why he'd take her outside, away from everyone, to talk. Why he'd begged for her to be presented tonight, why he'd been adamant on Marguerite's help. "*Oh!* Do you mean… are you…?"

He pressed her hands to his lips and nose and breathed in their scent. His breath heated her up, and though muffled, his voice was determined and steady when he spoke again. "We have fifteen days to bathe in this connection we have. After that, I would like to announce you as my future bride at the Masquerade."

Her legs gave out as the butterflies multiplied in her belly, her heart overflowing with emotion.

Sébastien held her to stop her from falling to her knees.

"Oh dear." Blood rushed to her head so fast she could no longer see. All she wanted was to watch his expression, imprint it inside her mind forever. To remember this moment, this joyous occasion.

Had Prince Sébastien just *proposed* to her? Had she said yes? She hoped she'd said yes.

"Oh dear."

He fanned her with his hand. "I know, it's soon. But I've never been so sure of anything in my life. It might be foolish, or stupid, but I mean it. I'm serious."

Her words stuck in her throat, and she fought to keep her limbs from quaking. "Sit… I need to… *sit…*"

He guided her to a bench under the gleaming, hanging torches. He watched her, mouth down-turned. "Are you all right? Perhaps I shouldn't have sprung that on you so suddenly."

"I… it's…" She let out a heavy sigh, attempting to drown out the rush of feelings. "Me? You want *me?* Are you certain? Me, as a princess?"

"There's more to this than a title," he said, studying her face closely. "Wearing a crown is one thing, but I seek a lifelong companion. A partner."

He exuded such tenderness and fondness, she shrank in her seat, overwhelmed by his grace.

"So, what say you? We have a long time to get acquainted with one another, of course. We can't marry until after you graduate."

She shook, her nerves getting the best of her; not because she was reluctant, but because this was something straight out of her dreams. How had the prince read her mind, yet again?

"You're… asking me? Asking if I want this?"

His eyes creased. "Of course. It's your life too. Your heart."

Said heart swelled to proportions she'd never dare try to

describe. "It would honor me, Highness—I mean, Sébastien. It would… please me."

"Then it's decided." He grinned at her, the slightest blush blooming over his cheeks.

Whispers of wonderful tingles shot down her cheeks and jaw as he reopened his eyes and stood, offering his hand to help her up.

Still savoring their private encounter, they returned inside to the heat of the hearths and the cluster of bodies.

The music slowed. Guests swerved to them, intrigued. Bracing to spread rumors.

Regardless of the potential gossip, something akin to pride woke in Céleste's abdomen. These guests ogled her, envied her—because she was the one and only contender to Prince Sébastien's heart.

So filled with delight, she came to an abrupt halt when she gazed at the dais, and a set of ice-rimmed brown eyes gazed back.

The dowager was resplendent as ever; poison disguised as an elegant flower. A smile swept over her lips, and there it was again—*the nod.*

Where was Marguerite?

Clémentine. Cornelius. Adelaide. And apparently, Romain?

Clémentine pulled the strings. But why would she permit the Giromian king to steal her son's French bride, her kingdom's sole tie to France, the alliance she'd brokered years ago amidst widespread disagreement?

Marguerite was so absorbed in her woes that she'd lost Céleste and Sébastien in the sea of nobles. With such potential plots afoot, she worried for the girl. She'd be safe with Sébastien, but who knew what schemes his mother had in mind, without him knowing.

Desperate for a break, she brushed towards the ballroom doors. From there, she'd have a better vantage point to scan the room.

She parked between the herald and the watchful guards, sighting couples dancing drunkenly, men debating topics not-fit-for-the-public, spilling their drinks as fearful servants looked on. Groups of over-coifed women gossiped and pointed at other women who also gossiped.

It was a typical ball at the royal court. Its main event, fun and invigorating; its outlines full of whispers.

Antoine had disappeared. She couldn't find Cornelius and the swarm of Giromians who followed him. The queen rested on her throne, her attendants nearby. Romain danced with Julia, Jules flirted near the windows, and the dowager was staring at someone entering from the patio—

At Céleste, her arm hooked with Sébastien's.

The girl marched in with a radiant smile. But when her gaze turned to the dais, where it met Clémentine's, utter panic clawed into her expression. Though she maintained her posture, she looked all around as if worried someone might bite her.

Sébastien seemed unaware his contender appeared like she'd spotted a ghost.

He led Céleste to the buffet, then steered her off to meet friends, one of which was Axel Espinar, with Cristina at his side.

Where were Esther and Harriet?

Marguerite prepared to step through the crowd, but sensed a violent tug on her forearm, pulling her out of the ballroom. She had no chance to glimpse who'd grabbed her and was dragging her out into the East Wing.

The ballroom doors shut behind her, and her head spun from the sudden motion.

Her mysterious captor yanked her toward the door straight across from the ballroom—the Winter Garden.

"Don't ask questions." That voice—a brisk, feminine tone.

The sconces from a nearby wall illuminated Marguerite's captor—a young woman, her dark curls unkempt. She stepped closer to the glass door, cloaked in a gown of lavender and lace. Her eyes were so tenebrous they frightened Marguerite.

"Cordelia?" All her manners were gone as the princess opened the Winter Garden's door and threw Marguerite inside. "What is this?"

The door slammed behind them, sealing them in the fragrant garden.

Cordelia's cheeks were a deep red. "An order."

Marguerite flinched. Cordelia's disheveled state disturbed her. "What's wrong?"

Cordelia jutted her chin to an area to Marguerite's left. "I'm a messenger on a mission to deliver you here."

Marguerite pivoted to where the princess had indicated. Bushes and trees, flowers galore, a stone bench—and a shadowy figure looming behind shrubs.

She flipped to Cordelia and said, "A messenger for what? For whom?"

The princess silently took off through the exit to the Long Corridor.

Marguerite returned to the mystery silhouette. Who would request to speak in private in the middle of a ball? Who would have the princess in such a state?

None of Marguerite's panicked thoughts matched the silhouette's face as it erupted from the shadows.

"You?" She crossed her arms, shielding herself.

His crown was crooked, his jaw set. "Me." King Antoine's silver coat twinkled in the torchlight as he approached, his lips curled into a snarl. "Forgive the manner in which I brought you here. I had no other alternative and no time."

She knew that intonation, that flicker in his eyes—fear. Anger.

Her arms coated with goosebumps. "What is it?"

"You were right to have so many doubts." His voice was clipped. "About everything. Mother, the Giromians… everything aligns. I believed you. I even insisted Adelaide had a part, and that damned duke, too. But there was more, so much more."

She took a stride in his direction. "Is that why you asked me here? To tell me I was correct?"

He cut through the air with his hand. "To explain it all to you. That dreaded king posed as an admirer of Miss Espinar when in fact, he came for my wife."

She would have gasped, but she'd seen it too. "I'm not surprised, with how they ate each other up earlier. In public, too, in front of Julia? No shame." She pressed her hand to the base of her throat and swallowed.

"So you caught me watching them?" She nodded, and he grumbled. "King Romain came for a bride, yes. *My* bride."

She pushed her palm harder against her chest. "That's what I thought, remember?" Her heart thrummed so fast she feared it might jump out and scream. "But how are *you* certain?"

He unclenched his fists, but his fingers were bent, twitching. "You think I rested on my laurels and waited for information to come to me? I *dug,* Marguerite. I sought out people who I knew would talk if given the right sort of… incentive. I know who Mother's informants are, who works for her. Speaking of Mother," he scrunched his eyebrows, "I believe she wants to seize the throne from me, after all. If they annul my marriage, take my spouse, leave me on my own, it makes it easier for her to prompt the vote to force me off my seat. Easier for her to put someone else in my place." He seethed. "The games she plays, the ways she tortures others for her own designs? She ruins her own flesh and blood for power. It's humiliating. I regret not stopping her sooner. I'm so sorry, Maggie."

Marguerite ignored his sweet scent and the liquor on his breath, and grabbed his hand. "It was a hunch. You couldn't have known. And yes, you made mistakes, but she manipulated you all your life. You, your brothers, your sister, even your father."

He didn't shy away from her touch, but the pain in his expression didn't dissipate. "Maggie… the duke…"

"Yes, the duke." She let go of him and strode backwards. "He has a role. *He* ogled the queen, too, so what does that mean?"

His shoulders drooped, his fingers stopped twitching. The fury in his demeanor melted, replaced by something Marguerite wasn't sure she could identify. A heavy weight pushed him down, forcing him to appear tinier than he was.

"What?" She squinted. "What do you know?"

"He has no interest in Ade." He lowered his head. "That was… a ruse."

Marguerite's feet were restless. "So he's an actor. What is he here for? What's his purpose?"

Even before Antoine reached for her wrist and brought her close enough to sense his pulse out of control, she knew.

She'd always known. The moment the duke was revealed, the moment she'd met him, felt his eyes roving over her body in the most inappropriate ways.

Marguerite tried to pull away from Antoine, but he gripped her tight. "Antoine, please. Stop beating around the bush and say it."

He averted his gaze. "I don't want to tell you this. I don't want it to be real."

Fire licked the insides of her veins. "You must confirm what I already knew, deep down."

He dragged his free hand down his face. "The Romain and Adelaide situation isn't concrete yet, but this news... it's legitimate. Mother confirmed it. I coaxed it out of her, finally."

"How?" Marguerite gulped. "She wouldn't reveal something like that so easily, Antoine. What... did you do?"

"I agree, it might have been too easy." His fingers twitched, though still grasping her tightly. "But it's the truth. She had no reason to lie. And what did I do? I spoke of Father, of how he wouldn't stand for this behavior, and how I wouldn't anymore, either. I reminded her of her place, and that the more secrets she tried to withhold from me, the more she'd be hurting me. Us. Our family."

Something lurched in Marguerite's belly, something that had been dormant. Anticipating the worst. Praying against it, but knowing it was there. It was coming, and it'd sweep her away.

"You spoke of Mother choosing your betrothed, and indeed, she has. Cornelius Schwartz."

How she yearned to be shocked, to crumble and cry and protest this decision. But she'd figured it out. She'd known for years Clémentine planned to marry her off to someone of her choosing.

But *why* him?

"She said it's been in the works for a long time." Antoine cringed, bringing a closed fist to his mouth. "You, Duchess of Torrinni; him, Duke of Terter. An alliance between Totresia and Giroma."

A warm, tingling sensation spread through her body, leaving her numb, neutralized.

And though she'd been prepared for this, she still collapsed. Her hands smacked against the pebbled ground. Tiny rocks tore into her palms, her knees felt like they'd cracked. But if there was pain, she felt none of it.

While conversing with Axel Espinar, Sébastien kept Céleste close. She and Cristina exchanged pleasant smiles, but it was clear they both wanted to be anywhere but there, listening to hunting adventures.

Axel had such similar features to his sister, they might have been twins, but there was a sweeter, softer energy about him.

A young squire snuck up and whispered something to Sébastien.

"She *what?*" The prince gaped at the ballroom doors. "Cordelia isn't to be near the ball."

The squire mumbled again, and Céleste strained to listen—she heard the words *urgent* and *duchess*.

Sébastien waved the boy off. "I need to cut this conversation short." With a perplexed smile, he saluted Axel and Cristina, and drew Céleste to the food-spread.

She noticed the tension lining his forehead. "What is it?"

"Cordelia." He kissed her knuckles. "She dragged Marguerite out to meet someone in the Winter Garden."

Céleste's heart skipped a beat. "The Winter Garden?"

"I will handle this. Stay here. It's your night as much as it is that foreign king's."

Before she could retaliate, he slipped through the crowd, disappearing.

Alone in an ocean of unknown faces, Céleste kept near the platters of delicacies. The overwhelming perfumes made her nauseous and the music made her head spin. Everything and everyone around her became a blur.

From a platter she snatched a vanilla-flavored macaron, stuffing it into her mouth. The flavorful treat did the trick to steady her.

As she chewed, she focused on the dais where the queen and the dowager were in a deep discussion. The former's cheeks were spiked scarlet, and the latter spoke with pinched lips. They stood close, both tense. Were they arguing?

Whatever their discussion, it resulted in Adelaide drunkenly storming off to the patio doors and venturing outside.

The orchestra's melody picked up. Several dancers swayed by so fast they sent Céleste teetering against the buffet table. Colors swirled in her vision and her dizziness returned.

Perhaps she needed another pastry, something to keep her mind occupied. Or wine—a bit of alcohol might calm her down.

Once her cup was full, she frowned upon sighting Charlotte with Prince Jules. His hand was wrapped tight around her upper arm as he spoke into her ear.

There was a dangerous appeal about him as he leaned against

a wall, enraptured by Charlotte's much too low neckline.

Céleste guzzled down half her drink to not cough up the macaron she'd eaten.

Disgusted as she was, she couldn't pull away from their flirtatious moment. Charlotte chewed on her lip, a suggestive mannerism to her batting lashes. Jules made her giggle and fan herself. They'd had too much to drink; they kept bumping into each other and stumbling.

Hate Charlotte as she might, she admired her confidence, her effortless way with seduction. For someone who'd portrayed the very embodiment of chastity and virtue at the academy, she had quite a deck of cards in her hand now.

Céleste drained the rest of her beverage, the taste lingering in her mouth, blurring her senses. She was no stranger to alcohol; she'd snuck sips of sparkling wine at her father's domain, and cups of the cherry liqueur her manor's orchards were famous for. But she knew well how she became inebriated with two sips. She had embarrassed herself once at a younger age, but hadn't drank much since then.

The reminder of that embarrassment prompted her to fill her cup again.

Cristina twirled in Axel's arms on the dance-floor. Esther laughed with an elderly lady. Harriet conversed with her father.

All alone, Céleste studied the dowager atop her throne on the platform. She stared at all the same people Céleste did, without much care.

Céleste downed her drink, then filled it again. And again. And once more. The longer Marguerite and Sébastien remained out of sight, the more anxious and conflicted she felt. The alcohol numbed those feelings, but only slightly.

The colors that used to blind her blurred into globs of red and pink and green. The flickering candles were like hovering fireflies, buzzing at her. She laughed.

Where was Sébastien? Marguerite? The king?

Another bout of giggling came from nearby—Julia.

The more she drank, the more Céleste felt pulled underwater, liquid inundating her ribcage and stomach and inside her shoes. Everywhere she looked, she saw shadows. Outlines of ladies in bouffant dresses. Men with dark eyes, muttering in tones she didn't understand. Waves of curls, gleaming tiaras, rings adorning black-gloved fingers.

Everyone plotted while she drank herself into a coma.

Her abdomen tightened as a wave of nausea navigated up her throat.

Many others in the ballroom had fallen prey to the dangers of drinking, and it showed. They traipsed about like no one watched, dancing too close, stuffing themselves with food. If Céleste were sober, it would have disgusted her.

But she was one of them.

The crowd of nobles started to thin. They stumbled to the doors, bade drunken farewells to friends and foes alike. From the corner of her blurred vision, she caught the Giromian king departing with a group of party-goers.

Céleste's mind whirred so fast, she nearly burst—but two figures appeared before her, halting her sickness from spilling to the floor.

"Céleste?" The voice was too buoyant. *Esther*. "Are you all right? You look pallid."

Céleste sucked in a breath to steady her queasiness. "Uh… I… No, I'm not."

"Heavens," the second figure said, hair like twinkling tangerines, tone stern—*Harriet*. "She had too much to drink."

Céleste sulked against the buffet table.

"This won't do. We must get you upstairs before you bring shame to your name," whispered Esther, slipping one arm under Céleste's. Harriet grabbed her other.

"Shouldn't we wait?" Céleste fought hazy images of girls on the dance-floor, exchanging slobbery kisses with their dance partners.

Harriet peered about the area. "Where is Lady Marjorie?"

"Snuck out. She likely needed some reprieve from," Esther waved, "all this. Those Giromians… I should have taken Emeric's example and not attended."

"Wait!" Another individual joined their trio—Julia. "Are you leaving? I should go, too. The king retired."

Esther turned her nose up and dragged Céleste out of the way, but Harriet motioned to the exit where they were headed.

They scurried along, and Céleste struggled to not stumble over her own shoes, forcing Esther to slow her pace.

"Did you see Charlotte and the prince?" Julia scoffed. "Half her décolleté was spilling from her bodice. So disgraceful. Her father won't appreciate that."

"Isn't Charlotte your friend?" Harriet said, sliding out into the corridor.

Julia passed over the threshold next. "Not after… well, anyway, her attitude is atrocious. Shamelessly flirting in the public eye like that?"

Far from the hovering guests, Céleste's thoughts cleared a little.

They made it to the entryway, where a few nobles loomed by the guarded, giant doors.

One of the men detached from the group, halting in front of Harriet. In her state, it took Céleste a bit to recognize him. Towering, salt-and-pepper hair, a gruff voice that burned Céleste's ears—

Harriet's father.

His graying mustache twitched as he snatched Harriet's upper arm. "Leaving so soon?"

Harriet hung her head, trying to tug him away from the girls. "Not now, Father."

"Did you," he leaned in, his tobacco and wine scent wafting up Céleste's nostrils, "do as I asked?"

"Can we speak of this tomorrow, please?" Harriet's tone was prudent, but still she sought to lead him away.

Instead, he shoved her aside and parked before Julia. "Good evening, ladies," he said, his words honeyed.

Céleste's insides did back-flips, causing the veil over her eyes to lift. He wore a burgundy suit, his breeches too tight, the fabric of his coat stretching over his gut. His overwhelming presence incurred instant fear.

"I'm Eugene Thatcher, Vidame of Limesdale—and you are?" He extended his hand to Julia, ignoring Esther's squeak and Céleste fighting not to gag.

Julia began to give her hand to him. "Julia Espinar, of—"

Harriet nudged him away. "Tomorrow, Father. Please. We're tired and our feet hurt, and we wish to go to our rooms."

He snagged Harriet's chin, clutching it so tight, her skin turned red. "Watch your attitude, girl." He threw her off as he ogled Julia from head-to-toe, eyes predatory. "It was a pleasure to meet you, Miss Espinar, and I hope to see more of you." He issued a brief bow and returned to his associates.

Esther gave Céleste over to Julia, like a ruined package she wanted to discard. She then helped Harriet find her balance. "What was that about?"

Harriet nudged them all to the steps. "He seeks a bride, remember?" A subtle tremble hid in her otherwise composed voice. "Apparently he likes Julia."

The dark-haired girl's nose wrinkled in disgust.

Only when they reached Harriet's door did they pause.

Harriet took Julia by the hand. "I have to educate you on how to avoid Father's interest at all costs. I dislike you, Julia, but I don't wish his affections on anyone." She started down the opposing corridor, but turned to Céleste. "Tell Lady Marjorie about this. You will see her before I do. She needs to be aware of my father's prowling."

Esther accompanied Céleste down the other hall to her quarters. She made sure Céleste was lucid enough to get herself into bed, then left.

Once inside her room, Céleste massaged her temples. That man's disgusting demeanor would stay with her forever. How he stood so close to Julia, studied every curve of her breasts and hips, every inch of her face, licking his lips like one would at a five-tiered cake dripping in chocolate.

Why would a vidame seek to take King Romain's promised prize?

She leaned against the wall, heat from the nearby hearth blossoming over her ankles and legs. She removed her shoes, pulled out the pins in her hair.

Would she remember anything tomorrow?

He'd hated to say it aloud, hated to watch her crumble on the pebbled ground in agony. Every time he thought to help her up, he feared the simple touch would cause her deeper pain, or worse—it'd reignite the spark between them. A spark neither could afford to bring back to life.

Duke Cornelius Schwartz of Terter was Marguerite's intended.

A *Giromian.*

And Antoine was so livid he felt like fire raged in his chest, flames chewing at his heart.

He loathed himself for not reacting sooner, for continuously insisting he needed proof.

Of course he didn't need proof. Clémentine would always use Marguerite in her manipulations. And on top of it all, this time she'd made a deal which, if broken, could lead to a war Totresia had been avoiding for centuries.

That was what Cornelius had threatened, when Antoine confronted him, after wrangling the truth from Clémentine—if Antoine didn't let this union happen, he'd have Romain's wrath to deal with. Clémentine had also insisted, the same speech coming from her mouth. She'd denied, through and through, until Antoine brought up how disgusted his father would have been with her attitude. How humiliated he would have been were he still alive, discovering Clémentine's awful alliances. That had loosened her tongue—if only enough to discover *one* of her ruses. Antoine had no doubt she had more.

Marguerite sniffled, and that was enough to jolt him back into action. He wrapped his hand around her wrist and gently tugged her up. She allowed the physical contact, at first, until their eyes met, and something flashed in her gaze that prompted her to pull out of his grasp and wobble backwards.

He reached out to halt her from falling, fingertips outstretched. "Be careful—"

"No." She stabilized on her own and brushed off her gown. Dirt dropped from the fabric. "Don't touch me. Not now. Not *you*."

Antoine was about to speak, but the door to the King's Corridor exit creaked open.

A forest-green clad Sébastien stood in the threshold, fists on his hips. "What's going on here?" His gaze zoned in on Marguerite as he strode down the path to them. He then glared at Antoine, taking in his crooked crown, untucked shirt, scruffy coat. "What did you do?"

Antoine glared at his brother. If only it was that simple. If only that was all they'd done—snuck out for a private moment, to tend to the fires in their bellies, to address the attraction that still lingered between them.

"I know what this looks like, but we—"

The middle prince's expression swirled with fire. "You snuck out here? To do what?"

Marguerite shivered so hard she knocked a few leaves off a nearby bush. "He tells the truth. He was informing me of dire news. About me, and…"

Antoine understood her hesitation. Just as he hadn't wanted to say it, she didn't want it to be real, either. Why would she accept that she was marrying a conniving duke from a country that had always inspired her fear?

He cleared his throat. "Mother's newest plot. Her biggest, perhaps. Annul my marriage to Adelaide, gift her to Romain, push for the vote to remove me, put Jules in my place, and ship Maggie off to Giroma with that disgusting duke."

"She what?" Sébastien stormed up to Marguerite. "Is this true? Mother is marrying you off to… *him?*"

"It's all true," Antoine said through his teeth with forced restraint. "My staff caught wind of whispers about Adelaide and Romain, which *he* couldn't confirm or even speak of without turning beet-red. I confronted him myself, earlier. Mother had no trouble affirming the rest."

"Why?" Sébastien folded his quivering arms. He was usually the tempered brother. "Why toy with Maggie like that and basically *sell* her for an alliance? Because that's what it is. An alliance is what Father wanted." He rounded on Antoine. "And you'd permit Mother to take your wife, to carry our already fragile French accords to our enemy?"

Antoine ran his hands through his hair. His attendants had taken such care to tame his tangles, but their efforts had been in vain, what with all his pacing, grunting, shaking of the head. "I don't have all the answers yet. This is all new. Unforeseen."

"Mother taking your throne from you… it's real, then?" Sébastien blew out a weighty breath that billowed through his curls. "Jules and I had hunches, but…"

"Jules mentioned them to me. We *all* had suspicions." Antoine's arms shot up as he growled. "But what am I to do? All the key players are at court, everything is set in motion! If the nobles rally with her, if they heed her—"

"They won't." Sébastien glowered. "They can't. You're their king!"

"And Mother is their former queen, once married to the monarch they revered. I'm not Father." Antoine's arms lowered. "I'm a failure."

"No," said Sébastien. "I'm sure they think you're the best king they ever had."

"Not all nobles will listen to her," said Marguerite, sounding distant. "Many know of her scheming. She can't hope to convince them all."

Sébastien grabbed Antoine's upper arm. "We, your brothers, won't allow it. We're part of your council, we vote like everyone else."

Antoine's blood boiled as he twisted to his sibling. "My *brothers*, you say? Although Jules conspires with Mother to capture my throne?"

Sébastien shook his head. "If it is what she plans, I doubt Jules had a say in this. She must be holding on to some of his secrets."

Marguerite's skin took on a greenish tint. "But if it ends up being true, would he try to fight it? He's easily manipulated. Easy to influence."

Sébastien winced. "All his recklessness of late is unsurprising. He's always been defiant, dreading his responsibilities. Yet he's also complied with all the rules of our season. He's obeyed every order Mother gave him. It may be a ruse, but…"

"We can't be sure." Antoine kicked at a few pebbles as he marched to a rosebush. "I can't accuse him of giving in to her demands without proof, but… he *did* imply to me that he's deeply involved, and not necessarily of his own will. He could have come to me sooner, could have asked for help, and I would have…"

He couldn't acknowledge that Jules would agree to this, would let his mother sway him with such ease.

The version of Jules that Antoine had argued with in the forest—he didn't *want* to take Antoine's title, did he? He was rebellious in nature, but would he go so far as robbing his eldest brother of his birthright, all to preserve his secrets?

Who did that benefit? Who did it serve?

"It makes no sense," Marguerite said, clutching at her stomach. "He never wanted such a royal role, did he?"

"No." Sébastien grumbled as he crouched to play with a few rocks. "He wrote to me during my travels. He hated being second in line. Mother was horrible to him. Expected too much."

"So did she pressure him on this? Did she—" Marguerite gasped. "Did she threaten him? Does she have something she can use against him, to coerce him into doing whatever she asks?"

Jules had enough skeletons in his closet; the question was,

how many of them was Clémentine aware of?

"It wouldn't shock me," Antoine said, at last. "During the years you were gone, he was out of control. Drinking, gambling, gallivanting about town with that noble-bred wench who cares nothing for her upbringing."

"Frances?" Marguerite fiddled with loose threads of her sleeves.

"Among others," added Sébastien, rising to his full height. "He wasn't monogamous. He wrote to me about his adventures."

Antoine moaned as he dragged a palm down his face, his forehead and cheeks heating up with nervous sweat. "I sought to hide all his escapades, but… he accused me of telling Mother about them. I would never tell her, though I threatened to… which means she already knew, of course. And she must have used what she found out against him."

"Clémentine knows all." Marguerite held her hand to her chest, and it took all of Antoine's might not to rush over and take her in his arms, to beg her forgiveness for years of not seeing her suffering. Instead, he planted his feet and looked down. "I'm well-placed to be aware of that," she added.

"We can't make assumptions." Sébastien set his jaw. "If he came to you, Antoine, he may not be fully accepting of her plans. I can't trust that he would stoop so low. He's our brother. Our blood. Perhaps that was his way of asking for help."

Marguerite hugged herself, again tempting Antoine into coming close to her, taking her in his arms. He wouldn't, not unless she allowed it—and in her current state, swaying to and fro, a glassy look in her eyes, she'd likely slap him if he approached.

"Mother seems to believe otherwise," said Antoine, fists tight, fingernails biting into his palms. "This was all I needed. I must get her out of court, out of the castle. For good."

"And me?" Marguerite's chin sank. "What am I to do? I braced myself for marrying that horrid man. But… I can't. I can't do it. He's…"

"Traitorous. Dangerous." Antoine took her weakness as a call for help; when he attempted to take her hands in his, she didn't fight him. "We will fix this."

"Yes," said Sébastien, wrapping an arm around her shoulder. "To do that, we must block Mother. Once we deal with her, everything else will fall into place."

Antoine's fingertips lifted Marguerite's chin up. Her gaze was so vacant, yet with so much heaviness in its depths. Her body fought gravity, her arms trembling.

"I will save you," he said, swearing to himself that he'd never again see her harmed. Never again be responsible for her pain. "*We* will. I betrayed you before, but it won't happen again. You won't marry that duke. You won't go to Giroma."

Though she relaxed slightly at his words, he knew she still doubted him. *He* doubted himself.

Did he have enough power to win against his ever-scheming mother?

"**C**éleste?" Marguerite gently pushed the adjoining door open, unsure if the girl was asleep yet.

"Yes?" Her soft voice came from the bed. "Who's there?"

Marguerite tiptoed closer, showing herself in the firelight. "Who else would use my adjoining door?"

Céleste had been curled up on her duvet, clutching her belly. "Sorry, I'm… what time is it?" She heaved herself into a seated position and groaned. "What's going on?"

"Heavens." Marguerite caught a whiff of the girl's breath as she approached. "How much have you had to drink?"

Céleste set both hands on either side of her, slightly spinning. "I don't know."

If she was still under the influence of alcohol, she might not notice the tear-stains on Marguerite's cheeks, the smeared powder. She might not ask too many questions that would force Marguerite to rehash the evening in detail.

Marguerite had come to warn her, simple as that.

"There have been some… developments." She couldn't maintain Céleste's glossy gaze. "I need to speak with you now, before everything changes."

Marguerite's chest ached as she battled to differentiate reality and fiction.

Had she fled the Winter Garden in a dazed panic, abandoning her girls to the ruthless nobles in the ballroom?

We will fix this.

Antoine's voice vibrated in every confine of her brain, trying to reassure her, but it was too late for that. If Clémentine held the keys to her destiny, she was doomed.

She'd never been so eager to leave the castle and its schemes.

"What happened?" Céleste moved aside and patted the mattress as she winced up at Marguerite.

Marguerite sniffled as she lowered onto the bedspread, keeping her distance. "Antoine and I spoke tonight, in the Winter Garden."

"Ah." Céleste nodded quickly, then cringed. "I heard something about you disappearing."

Marguerite's fingers twitched. "We suspected his mother wanted to unseat him." Céleste nodded again, slower this time. "Now, we fear it's true. We're not sure in what order the events will unfold, but we think she plans to dethrone Antoine, give his wife to Romain, and put Jules on the throne in his stead since he's easier to manipulate."

Céleste flushed. "But what of Julia? And then… what of the duke?"

Marguerite snagged a pillow and clutched it tight. "Romain was never interested in Julia. He came to cooperate with Clémentine, to make her eldest son look weak, easier to remove from the throne." She did her best to suppress a shiver, but it was so intense she nearly fell off the bed.

"And you're sure?" There was a pinch of uncertainty in Céleste's voice, a subtle slur that made Marguerite wonder if this discussion would be better to have in the morning. Céleste had had far too much to drink.

"Antoine's spies insist. Sébastien agrees with it. We all assume Jules is locked in some deal with his mother. She has something to persuade him, force him."

Céleste hiccuped and grimaced as she held a hand to her stomach. Her curls tumbled down the sides of her face, wisping out of her up-do. "So Prince Jules works with the dowager?"

Marguerite took the girl's hand in hers. "I'm sorry for putting you through all this. For confusing you. Our theories, our assumptions—" she choked.

Céleste massaged her temples with her free hand. "You forgot one of my questions. The duke?"

"The duke is here for me." Marguerite's throat was scratchy, and she yearned for water.

"What?" Céleste's arms fell to her sides as she recoiled. "*What?*"

"We're to marry." The words were acid in Marguerite's mouth, melting through her gums. "He's the man Clémentine plans for me to wed. A plan several years in the making."

Céleste's mouth opened wide. "I… you mean… *marry* him? That's why she summoned you here?"

Marguerite smelled the girl's wine breath and a gentle flower aroma from where she'd spritzed perfume. The combination of both scents comforted her more than anything ever had. "Yes. I tried to give that foul woman the benefit of the doubt, but…"

"But she's a viper," Céleste snorted, "like you said. And I'm involved with her other son."

"It's all so senseless," Marguerite said, rearranging the pillows behind her, if anything to give her shaking hands something to do. "I can't put it past Clémentine to overthrow her own child for power, but plotting with Giroma? Giving up the French girl she set on the throne? And then," she gulped, "sending me out of her way, united to a Giromian? She's been evil all my life, but this is beyond. Edouard never would have done that."

The bed wasn't large, but big enough for the two to lay next to one another.

"You knew King Edouard well?" Céleste settled on her side, keeping her gaze on Marguerite. "My book claimed he loved you dearly." A sliver of moonlight peeped in, sending a slice of light from her forehead to her chin. Her eyes sparkled.

"He was nothing like his wicked wife. He would never approve of such plots, such alliances. He'd have hanged her for trifling with his eldest son's claim. His birthright. Edouard was about tradition and maintaining his ancestor's laws… This would outrage him."

Céleste sighed. "You're right. It's senseless." Her breaths were labored. Despite smelling like she'd bathed in liquor, she was no longer slurring. Perhaps the severity of the situation had sobered her. "I should have believed you immediately when you detected schemes. How can I help you? Shall I write to my father? Is there anything he can do?"

For the first time in hours, Marguerite wanted to laugh. "Your father? He wouldn't lift a finger in this situation. He never cared much for me."

Céleste shot halfway up to her elbows. "He wouldn't like the dowager disturbing the original order of things. He's a firm Edouard supporter. If he heard she plotted to overthrow his eldest son, he'd be furious. And Giromians at court? I'm sure my brother told him."

Marguerite glared at the ceiling, the moonlight zigzagging over the curved designs as if trying to form messages, to give her answers. "You may be correct." She patted the girl's hand. "But I will ponder further on that after some rest. And I'll find some means to communicate it to Antoine and Sébastien, so they can add it to their investigation."

"Investigation?" Céleste stifled a yawn.

"They're looking into things. Holding meetings, sending out letters. They'll dispatch envoys around Totresia, ensuring more nobles aren't bought by Clémentine or any of the Giromians."

"Bought, yes." Céleste combed her fingers through her hair as she lay back down. "To convince them to vote against the king."

Marguerite tugged on the covers, bringing them over her and Céleste. "We should make ourselves scarce. There are no scheduled balls in the next few days, and the girls can use other chaperones to meet with their suitors. Sébastien may call on you, and your brother, too, but decline anyone else. Even the graduates. Stick to our quarters."

Céleste yawned. "Of course… in the morning…"

"Sleep well."

For a moment there was silence; heavy, yet familiar. Marguerite melted into the mattress, but she couldn't doze off yet, no matter how tired. Falling asleep would bring on nightmares she wasn't ready to endure.

Céleste suddenly flipped onto her side and tapped Marguerite's upper arm. "Marguerite?"

"Yes?"

"I have *one* question."

"And what would that be?"

Céleste exhaled, and a whiff of alcohol hit Marguerite's nostrils. "May I call you Maggie?"

Marguerite's eyes wrenched open. "What?"

"May I call you Maggie? Your nickname? The king calls you that, Sébastien does too." She fought another yawn. "And I want to, as well. I'd like to think of myself as… well… your friend."

"You *are* my friend." Marguerite smiled.

Amid all the chaos, hiding in the fog of frightening despair, she had something positive to cling to. She had Céleste.

"So can I?" Céleste's tone muffled as she pulled the blanket over her mouth.

Though dreadful pictures danced in Marguerite's mind—Antoine bowing before Jules, Adelaide seated on a cerulean throne with a sapphire crown on her head, Cornelius smirking from inside a black velvet carriage—her grin widened. "Yes, Céleste. You may."

When she woke, a throbbing pain resided in Céleste's scalp, like someone had scraped it off with a blade. Her temples pounded like hammers breaking her bones.

She jumped when memories poured in—Marguerite, *Maggie,* sleeping in her bed, telling her of the dethroning, the queen's reassignment, and the shocking union to come with the duke.

Marguerite was still asleep, her golden locks spread over the pillows, parts of her navy gown protruding from beneath the covers. She looked so peaceful.

As another sharp pang stung in Céleste's temples, her bedroom door opened—Johanna slipped in with a tray laden with food. Her gray eyes widened, but otherwise, she seemed unsurprised as she tiptoed forward and deposited the tray on Céleste's vanity.

Two plates of eggs, ham, a slushy-looking porridge, and two

mugs—one with a floral fragrance, the other heavy with the scent of coffee.

Johanna inclined her head. "I don't know every detail, but… I'm aware of most of it," she whispered, chin jutting at Marguerite. "I'll be around, gathering information for her—she'll want me to, I know her."

Céleste wiped the sweat forming on her forehead. "Thank you, Johanna." She hadn't realized how essential Marguerite's handmaiden was, how knowledgeable and perceptive.

Marguerite was lucky to have her.

Before she scurried off, Johanna took Céleste's discarded dress to bring down to the seamstress, to re-alter it for the Masquerade. Though at that point, Céleste wasn't sure she wanted to go.

Once Johanna was gone, Céleste loosened her corset. She released a lengthy breath as the pounding in her skull lessened while her waist and chest relaxed. How had she slept in this?

She changed into daywear, then perched on the edge of the bed, beside Marguerite. So at ease, so tranquil—it pained Céleste to wake her.

She rubbed the duchess' shoulder, and almost at once, her bloodshot turquoise eyes wrenched open.

"What… what is…" Her gaze landed on Céleste. "Where am I?" Her voice was groggy as she licked her lips and swallowed.

"My room," said Céleste. "Do you remember? Last night?"

Marguerite hung her legs over the side of the bed and winced as she bent over and placed her head in her lap. "How could I forget?" She emitted something that sounded like a snort. "I'm surprised *you* remember. You were bathed in alcohol."

Céleste ignored the jape. "Johanna brought us breakfast." The egg scent wafted into her nose and her stomach grumbled.

Marguerite lifted her head enough to glance in the food's direction. "Coffee? That's all I want."

Céleste approached the tray and plucked the cup of dark, tar-like substance. She brought it to Marguerite, who snatched it with fervor.

The duchess breathed in the steam and took a sip, not once twitching at the scalding liquid. "The girls?" She sipped again. "Did Johanna check on them?"

"I didn't ask." Céleste's memory jolted. "Speaking of the girls… We have another problem I have to tell you about. I was too frazzled before, but…"

"Speak," said Marguerite, keeping the rim of the cup against her lips.

"The Vidame of Limesdale may have set his sights on Julia."

Marguerite's eyes narrowed then widened. "Excuse me?"

Céleste scrunched her nose. "Harriet held him off, but he introduced himself to Julia as we were retiring, and Harriet told me to warn you."

Marguerite's grip around the cup tightened. "He must be part of all this, since Romain will marry Adelaide and pass Julia on to someone else. But why the vidame?" Clutching the mug with one hand, she massaged the corners of her forehead with the other. "Harriet told you to warn me because she knows. *She knows*. Her father enlisted her in his schemes, but she wants no part in them, I'd wager."

"His schemes are tied to the dowager's? To the Giromians?" Céleste's mind whirled with too many questions.

"The dowager is tied to anyone with dangerous intentions." After a few steps to the adjoining door, Marguerite pivoted and frowned. "We will isolate ourselves for the next few days, like I said. Thatcher won't touch a hair on Julia's body, I swear it."

Céleste made a move to follow her, but Marguerite flicked her wrist in dismissal.

"No. Stay out of this, for now."

Most of the day, Céleste overheard Johanna coming and going, bringing items to Marguerite. Céleste couldn't decipher her whispered messages, even when gluing her ear to the adjacent door to listen.

Later in the afternoon, Céleste slipped in to see empty coffee cups piled up on Marguerite's nightstand, heaps of opened books on the tea-table, notes scrunched on the vanity. There were half-eaten meals on her bed, used handkerchiefs on the floor, and the curtains were closed. The air was so stuffy, Céleste coughed. It had been half a day since they'd started their seclusion, yet Marguerite's room looked like she'd sheltered herself for weeks.

Céleste had tea with Sébastien later that day. When she tried to ask questions or to brought up the situation, he shushed her, not deeming their location safe enough to discuss such things. Though he seemed glad she'd been made aware of everything.

That evening, she caught a piece of a conversation between Johanna and Marguerite. Something about *a storm coming, poison brewing*. Nobles from around the country were arriving—those on the council who didn't reside at court. They were pouring in, taking rooms upstairs, some staying in the city.

Marguerite claimed it meant a meeting would take place soon—a big one. *The vote.*

The next day, December nineteenth, Céleste coaxed some information out of Johanna. Julia only met with Romain if he summoned her, which he did, to maintain appearances. There'd been no sightings of the vidame trying to meet with her, and Johanna swore she was protected at all times.

The day after that, Marguerite breezed through the adjoining door, a light brown gown clinging to her figure, her hair unfastened and wavy.

"What is it?" Céleste nearly fell off her chair.

"Harriet is coming to talk with me." Marguerite dragged her into her chambers. "You must be there as a witness." She motioned to Céleste to sit at her vanity. "I've been trying to speak with her since we left the academy, but… I struggled to get a letter to her, worried that her father would intercept it. But with all of Totresia's finest now at court, he's occupied."

A knock signaled the vidame's daughter's arrival.

Harriet's shoulders were tight, nervous. She had no reaction to Céleste being there. Her strawberry curls were tangled down her back, swirling under the folds of her silky beige dress. The flames in the nearby hearth illuminated her distraught face.

"He's been far from discreet. He's watching me," Harriet said, her voice low and cryptic. "So is the dowager."

Céleste clapped her hands over her mouth to cover her squeal.

Marguerite lowered onto a couch and waved at Harriet to join her. "Clémentine is watching you?" Her nostrils flared. "I always figured you were tied into her schemes somehow. Lord Knowles said she was adamant on having you at court, but I presumed that was your father's doing."

Harriet peered into her lap. "Father and the dowager have

some sort of bargain. She warned me, seconds before Lord Knowles met with us at the academy. She told me I would go to court. I know little of whatever their agreements are, but the dowager, who has always despised my father, works *with* my father."

A sharp silence swept through the room.

Marguerite glared at the fireplace. "For how long?" she said, finally.

Harriet shrugged. "Unsure. I only had suspicions of it in my last semester at the academy."

"What do they scheme together?" Marguerite's words hissed through her clenched teeth.

Shivers ran down Céleste's spine.

"I don't know," said Harriet. "But the timing... the nobles arriving, the tension... Father mentioned something about a vote the dowager planned to initiate soon."

Marguerite shot up from the sofa, her gaze trained on Céleste. Céleste got up too, though lacking the same confidence, her legs unsteady.

"Is he involved in this vote?" asked Marguerite, her voice shaky. "Involved in controlling its outcome?"

Harriet pursed her lips. "He's met with many nobles in secret. So... maybe?"

"*Bribery*," Marguerite and Céleste said at the same time.

Harriet's chin perked up. "He did let slip something about a rebellious act. Is that..." Her eyes rounded. "A rebellious vote? My father is behind the scenes, changing the outcome of it all?"

Céleste's blood turned to frost, sending her into a fit of shudders.

Marguerite seethed, stomping back and forth by the sitting area. "Did you say anything to him?"

"You mean defy him?" Harriet snorted. "He's already ruined our family name and my future. Nothing I say would persuade him to stop."

"Is Marquess Richel here? Richel *Senior*?" A pinch of fear tugged at Céleste's innards. "Did he come for this vote?"

"No," said Harriet, rubbing her arms as she sat up straight. "Your brother is here in his stead. Same with Julia's father, with Axel."

"Your brother would never vote against Antoine." Marguerite's paces stopped. "Axel will follow him, I'm sure. And Sébastien. But those are the only three I'm certain will fight this rebellious act, though I assured Antoine otherwise. I can't even be positive about Jules. Who knows what Vidame Thatcher and the dowager and whoever else works with them might do to sway the reticent ones." She brought a fist to her mouth and bit down on it.

"This is my fault," said Harriet, taking her head in her hands. "I should have stopped him."

Marguerite came to the girl's side. "You're not responsible for his actions. I don't blame you."

"But what do we do, Marg—Lady Marjorie?" Céleste bit her tongue.

Harriet rolled her eyes. "It's fine, I know the truth. She's Duchess Marguerite. *The* duchess of Torrinni. It's a long story, but no need to use code names with me."

Marguerite nodded—she knew that Harriet knew. Had *she* told Harriet?

"Fine." Céleste crossed her arms. "But none of us can get into that meeting and warn them. If Harriet tries to delay her father…"

"He will harm her." Marguerite, recovered from Harriet's surprise knowledge, tapped her chin. "I must do something. Something I can't come back from. It's perilous. Some might say stupid." She sat on her bed. "Leave me, girls. I'm going to fix this, and I ask you both to forgive me in advance. This won't end well."

67.
Marguerite

It was a last resort and likely dangerous, but unavoidable. Her only course to save Antoine, though it put her at risk. It also put Clémentine at risk, which might be deadly for Marguerite. But what choice did she have?

Antoine promised her that he'd get her out of her betrothal to Cornelius. In the meantime, she had to save him from his mother's plans.

When Johanna popped in later with her fourth cup of coffee of the day, Marguerite bade her summon Dowager Clémentine.

Johanna's normally demure demeanor faded to show raised eyebrows and a slacking jaw.

"I need to speak to her." Marguerite took a few sips of the strong brew and sighed as the liquid warmed down her throat.

"Should I give her more information?" Johanna hesitated at the door. "Will she know what this is about?"

"She'll be too curious to pass up another opportunity to berate me." Marguerite gestured at the door. "Go, now. Before I change my mind."

Johanna left, and Marguerite drained half her cup.

An hour later, when Johanna returned, Marguerite leaned against her bed-frame, arms crossed.

Johanna plucked the discarded coffee mug as well as an empty platter from the tea-table. "Why are you *asking* to speak with her?"

Marguerite bit her lip. "Something to help save Antoine, his kingdom. It's foolish, and I will regret it, but it's for the best."

Johanna slouched. "You can't clarify more?"

Marguerite shook her head. "In case it backfires, which I have no doubt it will."

"My lady—"

"I'm sure you're aware she's marrying me off to Duke Schwartz."

Johanna bunched her lips. "I am."

Marguerite sighed, her body heavy, her heart in pain. "I know what the dowager's plans are, and I want her to know I'm aware. I want to look her in the eye as I tell her she won't succeed."

With an incline of her head, Johanna backed away. "I understand. I support you, my lady."

"Is she coming? Responding to my summons?"

Johanna's cheeks splotched with violet. "She said she was busy, but will stop by soon."

"Soon." Marguerite scoffed. "She'll let me stew for a few days, knowing her. Fine." She hurried to her vanity. "Then I have a few letters to write and other things to take care of before I confront her. Thank you, Johanna."

***

Soon ended up being the next day, the morning of December twenty-first.

As Marguerite slipped on her day dress and smoothed out its sleeves, someone knocked on her door. She opened it, preparing for the storm.

There she was, in all her sordid splendor—Clémentine, her chocolate eyes hardened, her gray and pink gown tight over her well-preserved figure.

Fighting a frown, Marguerite curtsied. "Your Grace."

Clémentine shoved inside. Once the door was closed, she halted in the middle and spun. "So you're *summoning* me now, are you?"

"I needed to gain your attention somehow."

"And coming to me never crossed your mind?" Her voice was sharp, its edges digging into Marguerite's gut. "You know my schedule by heart, do you not?"

"This is a delicate matter that I wanted to ensure we were *fully* alone to discuss." Marguerite did her best not to sneer. A single facial expression would give Clémentine ample room to critique, to wound.

Marguerite needed her wits about her for this.

"What do you want?" The dowager's gaze rested on the door, her foot tapping to the ground. "What's so important that you need me to sneak around like this?"

"My title." Marguerite cleared her throat, wishing she'd had more coffee—then remembering that the scent would trigger Clémentine further.

"Your title?" Clémentine arched an eyebrow. "What about it?"

"Is it..." Marguerite shifted her weight, keeping as much distance between them as she could. "Is it still mine?"

Clémentine's eyes narrowed on her. "Duchess of Torrinni, you mean?"

"The only title I've ever had, yes." Marguerite sensed her pulse racing.

"I assume so," said Clémentine, studying the bulky rings on her slender fingers. "I wouldn't have been able to arrange your marriage without it. Your betrothed isn't interested in pauper prisoners."

She held in the thought she had about her *betrothed*. "I assumed as well, but I must be sure. It's the only way I can put a stop to your bullying." She knew the taunt would sting Clémentine, but the dowager would have no trouble plunging her sword deeper into Marguerite's belly.

The dowager's lips curved upwards. "I have no idea what you refer to."

"You do." Holding in a snarl, Marguerite whipped past her, walking until the sofa loomed between them. "Your schemes haven't gone unnoticed, Your Grace. But might I remind you that you need unanimity for your plans?"

The dowager's flinch was so brief, Marguerite might have missed it had she not been eagerly awaiting it. "I still don't know what you mean."

"This foul meeting you've plotted." Marguerite's chest rose and fell so fast she was winded. She'd never used such blatant defiance towards Clémentine before.

"Foul meeting?" The woman's gaze lingered on her, cutting through her like a slice of pie.

"Stop it." Marguerite's hands clenched. "I *know*. I know all of it."

The dowager's demeanor shifted, as if she were a casket of wine being uncorked, her emotions pouring out like waves of red. "*That* foul meeting." She glided over to Marguerite like a panther pouncing on its prey. The couch remained between them, but that didn't seem to bar her. "Unanimity? Fret not—I have it where it matters most. Everyone has a weakness, and it turns out I have ways of figuring them out."

Dull blades lined Marguerite's throat as she tried to swallow. Her legs shook under her dress; she'd never been happier to have so many thick layers of fabric hanging from her hips. "The king can protect those who vouch for him. Those who never doubted him and remained loyal."

"He can." Clémentine's fingertips twitched as if about to grab Marguerite by the neck. "But you can't help him. You will no longer be around to threaten my family. I'm sure you know about *that*, too? Who your betrothed is and where he's taking you?"

There was no point pretending—Marguerite nodded. "I'm not fighting that. I'm fighting your awful plots towards your son."

With a snort, the dowager moved backwards, her extravagant lavender scent lingering in Marguerite's nostrils. "Stop meddling in affairs you can't comprehend. What did you think you could do? Go around bribing nobles by reminding them you, the Duchess of Torrinni, are alive and defending King Antoine's honor? Do you not see how weak that makes him look? You'd worsen the situation."

Marguerite hid her smirk; the dowager hadn't figured out what *her* plan was. "We'll see about that."

"This foul meeting you mentioned? You don't know when or where it is. You won't be present to stop what's meant to happen from happening." Clémentine slipped out of the room, the door closing in her wake.

"That's what you think," mumbled Marguerite. Angst wrapped around her intestines like snakes, but she wouldn't bow down yet.

In the days she'd isolated herself, Johanna had fed her information. Harriet provided insight on her father's comings and goings. Page boys and servants working for Antoine ran errands for her.

The dreaded council gathering to decide on Antoine's fate was in an hour. Thanks to Johanna's friends among the servant staff, Clémentine wouldn't attend it.

But Marguerite would.

"I will bring you and your evil conspiracies down, once and for all. You will frighten me no more, Clémentine."

All she needed was to ensure Antoine would allow her entry into the meeting, where she'd prove she was alive, and show her true allegiance to him.

Other nobles would follow suit at the sight of a resurrected duchess, a woman whose identity had been trifled with one time too many.

She hoped.

She was ready. Spine straight, worries tucked deep down, she regained her courage, her memories, her confidence.

The Duchess of Torrinni was back.

He'd known it was coming. Nobles ushered in on short notice from around the country; whispers of clandestine meetings in the stables, in the tower, sometimes near the ballroom doors; odd looks exchanged in corridors.

His mother had done it, somehow—she'd convinced his own councilors to enact *the* vote against him. And she'd set it up for that day, hardly giving him enough information to brace for what was to come.

Marguerite had been warning him. Sébastien had, as well. Even Jules, in his own way, had brought it to his attention.

But it took Antoine too long to comprehend how serious this was. A part of him wanted to believe his mother *wasn't* the evil snake everyone saw her as. He wanted to believe everyone exaggerated, that she truly meant well.

When he'd finally figured it out, it was too late.

She was going to take his throne away because he hadn't produced an heir, and his wife was more valuable elsewhere.

He knew some would have his back—Sébastien, for starters. He also thought he could count on Emeric Richel, Axel Espinar, perhaps some of their friends.

But everyone else would see his marriage annulled, his bride taken to Giroma, his status—his damned birthright—forfeited, most likely to his younger, more immature sibling. Yes, they needed unanimity to decide this, but his mother would stop at nothing to obtain that.

He leaned over the lengthy oak meeting room table, blinded by the emerald and gold chandelier dangling overhead.

"What do we do?" asked Sébastien—the third time he'd asked in the hour since they'd been informed of the impromptu meeting. He'd been just as shaken when Antoine broke into his rooms earlier that day, to tell him all their mother had been scheming.

Antoine glared at the portraits lining the pine walls—monarchs, generals, saviors of Europe throughout the ages. None would save him today. The intricate designs on the turquoise and red carpets underfoot reminded him of when his father had paced over them, debating treaties and laws.

"Father never would have—"

A door creaked open, and at first he thought it was his office, behind him; instead, it was the main door.

He snarled, preparing to dismiss whoever had showed up early, disrupting his preparations with Sébastien. "Who would—" He snapped his mouth shut at the sight of Marguerite standing in the threshold. "Maggie?"

Sébastien's head jerked up from the list of names he'd been

scribbling on. "Maggie?" he repeated, squinting at her as if she were a mirage.

Though she hesitated at first, she fully entered the room, waving her hands at them. "No time. I'm here to help you thwart her designs." The door sealed behind her, a whoosh of air whipping under her brown skirts.

She was a revelation, an angel come to rescue him. Or had she come to announce more dire news?

"Her designs?" Antoine's eyebrows shot up. "You mean Mother?"

Sébastien marched around Antoine's throne and sidled up to Marguerite. "You were to keep to yourself, remember? Away from her."

Marguerite flinched. "I did. I've been isolated for days. My handmaiden fed me information, some of my girls told me of comings and goings, and I… I had to do something."

"Yes, well, you were also to stay away from Mother, and she's to be at this meeting." Sébastien's tone was snippy, more anxious than Antoine's.

Marguerite flinched again. "She's… not coming. I've distracted her."

"You *what*?" said both brothers in tandem.

"You heard me—my handmaiden arranged for her to be distracted, held back. Too occupied to come." She threw her arms up and huffed. "This is it! Her trick to prompt the nobles to vote, to annul your marriage!"

Antoine continued to watch her as if she were about to explode; Sébastien set his fists on his hips. "Yes, and we were coming up with a plan—"

"*I* am your plan." There was fire in her eyes, a fire Antoine hadn't seen swirling in her in years.

She was serious. She wanted to prove she was alive, and show her true allegiance to him.

If he weren't so angry at her for disobeying, he'd kiss her right then and there.

He scrubbed his face. "What have you done? Why are you here?"

"To fulfill my destiny," she said, chewing on her lower lip. "If only one time before I'm shipped off to… before I'm…"

"Oh dear." Sébastien shuffled his feet. "You've come to—"

"To speak on your behalf," she said to Antoine. "To be your advisor, the Duchess of Torrinni, as your father intended."

Antoine winced, turning away to hide his face. He clutched a clenched fist to his chest and took two deep breaths before spinning back around. "We had it under control."

Sébastien's shoulders sloped down. "Can she do that? Be your advisor, I mean."

Antoine hunched over the table. His gaze met Marguerite's, and he shuddered at the intensity of her stare. "She can." He straightened up. "And she's right—this is what Father wanted."

If Marguerite re-claimed her title, it would disrupt everything he and Sébastien had been working on the past few days. But she might be the only one who could stop the vote from happening.

Sébastien scrunched his forehead. "But the title—"

"If Mother is diverted, as Maggie claims, then it's now or never, Séb." Antoine remained focused on Marguerite, who hadn't wavered, hadn't shown an inkling of concern since she'd marched in. "You're messing it all up, but you mean well. We must take advantage of that, and rectify the situation after the vote."

Sébastien's nostrils flared. "Then we had best brainstorm this before—"

The doors opened, and in poured the nobles, bowing, papers pressed to their chests.

Some gawked or glowered at Marguerite, the intruder among men. Only Clémentine attended official meetings.

Everyone took their places, pulling out their plush green chaises, waiting for the proceedings to begin.

Jules came in and approached Antoine, but when he noticed Marguerite, he paused and blinked. "Maggie? Why are you here? Where's Mother?"

"Jules." She curtsied quickly and twisted to Antoine. "Where should I sit?"

"You're not sitting." If she was to make a statement, she'd have to be loud and clear about it. "You will stand beside me."

Sébastien sat to his right, sulking; Jules took his spot on the left, still appearing bewildered by Marguerite's presence. "What's happening?"

"Another female attendee today?" The voice was snake-like, oily; King Romain had entered the room, as was his right as a visiting monarch.

With him was the vile duke Marguerite was betrothed to. A roar rumbled in Antoine's throat, but he didn't let it out.

"Of all visitors," said the duke, his eyes lighting up in excitement as his lips curled.

Antoine clapped. "Gentlemen, take your seats."

Romain and Cornelius scurried to the far edge of the table.

Though she'd paled considerably, Marguerite stuck to her

spot. The men all fixed on her as if she'd fired a gun down the middle of their table.

"Be seated," said Antoine, though he didn't sit with them.

Chairs scraped, grunts echoed.

"Who is this, Sire?" said one man from the far-right.

Another complained, a few seats from Sébastien. "Wasn't the dowager supposed to attend today?"

"She had something to run by us, to put to a vote?"

Marguerite muttered something under her breath, not loud enough for Antoine to hear.

"This," Antoine yanked her closer, his hand firm around her forearm, "is the Duchess of Torrinni."

Many men in the room—save Antoine, Sébastien, Jules, and the Giromians—gasped. A deafening silence followed. No movement, no rustle of fabrics, no crunching of documents or tapping of quills.

A chilling voice broke through the quiet. "But wasn't she dead?"

Sébastien shuffled a few papers. "One of my dear mother's ruses, for her own protection."

Jules' eyes turned red. Antoine had never seen him so frustrated, filled with the same shifty temper as their mother.

"But why is she here?" Another voice wrapped in spite.

Antoine rolled his shoulders. "Let's cease the interrogation for now, as she has something to say before we proceed."

The gentlemen glowered at her, ready to devour her the moment she started speaking.

Her fingers twitched as her gaze landed on the disgusting duke she was to marry, his lips puckered at her.

Antoine struggled to contain his rage, his jealousy. He had no right to such feelings, not after what his mother had roped him into. Still, he couldn't help the growing loathing in his gut for this man, and the immense urge to slit his throat.

Marguerite inhaled, exhaled, clasped her hands. "Before Dowager Clémentine took me as her personal prisoner," more gasps, "King Edouard of Totresia appointed me as King Antoine's closest advisor. So here I am, to thwart the rebellious vote about to take place."

A few jaws dropped, followed by another round of gasps. Several fists banged on the table.

"What's the meaning of this?"

"Rebellious vote?"

"Sire, what is she talking about?"

"Yes, *Sire*," said Jules, leaning back in his seat, lips in a straight line. His resemblance to their mother, in this moment, was so uncanny it prompted chills up Antoine's arms. "What is this?"

Antoine stomped his foot. "Let the duchess speak."

If disturbed by all the interruptions, Marguerite didn't show it. She was resolute, her voice thundering across the room. "A rebellious vote to annul the king's marriage to Queen Adelaide; to point out how he's heir-less, to imply he's infertile. To place someone else on the throne in his stead." Some moaned mockeries and curses. "Such a vote would require unanimity. But with me here, you will never have it. The vote will not take place today."

Antoine's arm brushed hers. He bit his tongue before whispering, "Thank you."

A warm pride seeped through him. If Edouard were there, he'd heft Marguerite into his arms and congratulate her bravery.

Antoine had never loved her more than he did now, as she swept in to secure his throne while throwing herself to the wolves.

A chair dragged backwards; Sébastien stood up. "I also oppose such treachery."

Two men farther down—Emeric Richel and Axel Espinar—whipped up from their seats. "Us as well," they said, bowing.

A handful of others mimicked them, mumbling their agreement.

If she'd spent time bribing some of these men, Clémentine had failed. Antoine bit back a grin.

Marguerite had rounded up his fiercest supporters, and they stood up for him, brought courage with their unity.

But she wasn't finished. "If we discover someone bribed you, we will hold you accountable. Know this, my lords: those involved in such plots will be arrested and charged if you don't respect King Antoine's birthright."

Jules got up, banging his fist to the table. "That's out of line. It's not supposed to be this way." He bared his teeth, specifically at Antoine. "You don't know what you've just done, how much worse you've made things. I warned you." With that, he rushed out, slamming the door behind him.

Antoine watched him leave with down-turned lips. The pride he'd felt moments ago vanished. "So she *did* have something on him."

Sébastien grimaced. "It seems so. I can't believe I..." He rubbed his forehead. "Antoine, move it along," he said.

The Giromians were huddled at the end of the table. Other men had risen, clamoring their support of Antoine; a handful refused to move.

"I have to be drastic," Marguerite suddenly said to Antoine, voice lowered.

"How so?" He didn't remove his gaze from his constituents, fearful they'd grow violent. Some had the reputation for it, and he wasn't sure they'd left their weapons at the door, as was the policy.

"I have the name of one man who, for certain, participated in the bribery against you." She tucked a stray hair behind her ear. "Among other crimes."

Sébastien gave a quick incline of his head. "Do it."

Antoine pinched his lips, but blew out a breath, deciding to trust her. "I should ask how you know, but... Do it."

She returned to the men, coughing for attention. "Eugene Thatcher, Vidame of Limesdale, do you care to speak for yourself?"

Antoine might have let out a squeak of surprise, but everyone knew how sneaky the vidame was. He'd been the subject of many meetings in the past few years—dealing illegal arms, trafficking stolen goods, and gambling debts were among some of his offenses.

The man in question froze; he sat near the murmuring Giromians. "I'm uncertain what you imply, Mademoiselle."

Sébastien growled. "*Your Grace*, Thatcher! She's a duchess!"

Marguerite sneered at the crude man. "You bribed nobles to overturn the king, to annul his marriage, send his queen elsewhere, and consent to putting the younger prince in his place. You requested the hand of one of the academy girls as payment. Julia Espinar!"

Axel turned to Thatcher with tightening fists. "What?"

Marguerite resumed. "We're all informed of your less-than-legal deals, but you've always been protected, somehow. No one has ever had the gall to reprimand you. Well, I do. I accuse you of treason."

Eugene's face turned beet-red. "You have no proof!" His burgundy coat came undone as he backed from the table and shook his fists. "No one does!"

King Romain snarled. "I'd say you're quite cornered, Vidame. Accused in the presence of a fully staffed council. *My* intended interests you, hm?"

Cornelius brushed his long locks from his forehead. "Embarrassing."

Axel Espinar almost crawled across the table to strangle the vidame, but Emeric captured his wrists like cuffs. "And it's my sister you sought to steal off with? You wretched scoundrel!"

The vidame shook so hard, he couldn't clasp his coat. "She's not committed to anyone."

Romain sent a side-glance at Cornelius before grabbing the vidame by his lapels. "I traveled all this way for her, you despicable mongrel!"

The vidame didn't fight the foreign king's grasp. "But... but you..."

"Enough!" Marguerite rapped her knuckles on the table. "I have proof, Lord Thatcher—your daughter will be more than happy to back these claims, along with a few servants, and my personal handmaiden."

"Harriet is a *child,*" he roared, as fingers pointed at him.

"She's a contender in the royal season," said Sébastien. "And who *wouldn't* believe the daughter of a criminal such as you? She's privy to all your secrets, is she not?"

More accusations blurted out. Papers flew, quills drowned in spilled ink, hats fell from heads.

Antoine had half a mind to leave now, to let these men fight it out.

"Gentlemen!" His raised tone was enough to settle them. "There will be an investigation into the duchess' claims. In the meantime, Eugene Thatcher, Vidame of Limesdale, I strip you of your title, if anything for all the other crimes you've committed and been spared from. It will go to your next of kin until she marries a suitable match. I'm throwing you in a prison cell until I decide what to do with you." He snapped at two of his guards. "Lock him up."

The uniformed men hurried to the vidame, who couldn't move due to Romain's grip. They dragged him off, and the foreign king fell into his chaise with a heavy sigh.

"I hope this serves you all as a lesson," said Antoine. "Another attempt to remove me, and you will see the consequences. Council dismissed."

The men exited amongst buzzes and roars and rumors of bribery and betrayal. None spoke to the king; only a few acknowledged him with nods or grunts.

Marguerite didn't move from Antoine's side, shivering like a leaf in the rain. And just as Antoine made to take her hand, guide her into his office, King Romain marched over.

"Interesting," he said, lips pursed. "I see you're not one to trifle with, Lady Marguerite."

Cornelius bowed to her in the most demeaning way: low, exaggerated. "What a display." He dripped with a sweetness that made Antoine nauseous. "My future wife, how impressive. You're more cunning than we anticipated."

When Antoine saw her skin shifting to a sickening shade of

green, he took hold of her arm and yanked her into his office, away from the Giromians who sought to make her ill.

These vicious monsters hoped to take her home with them. And after what she'd done today, it was far more likely they'd succeed.

Sébastien followed his furious brother, who'd hauled Marguerite—*Duchess* Marguerite—and slammed the door behind her.

A growl grew in Sébastien's throat.

The familiar smell of tobacco and firewood wafted up his nose. It didn't matter how many times he'd sat in here with Antoine as the king; Edouard's ghost still lingered in the earthy, smoky scent. His presence was felt in the warmth of the flames flickering in the large hearth. His voice still reverberated off the mahogany desk, flashes of his arms waving in front of the faded map of Europe as he complained about other monarchs. Sébastien could still taste the digestifs consumed in the adjoining cigar room, after strenuous private discussions in this very place.

Antoine sat in his office-throne with a sigh. "Séb, please."

Sébastien, habitually so level-headed, stamped his foot. His younger brother's betrayal still rang bitterly in his ears. His mother's foul alliances, however less surprising, stung as well. "Is it true? This Thatcher ordeal?"

"It is," said Marguerite, frozen near the door. "His daughter confirmed it, as did several servants. Your mother, if coerced, would throw his name into the fire too, I bet."

Antoine put his face in his hands. "Was it worth the sacrifice?" He parted his fingers to show his widening eyes. "That was a direct hit on Mother's legitimacy at court."

Sébastien hunched over the desk. "It got us one culprit but surely attracted more!"

Antoine leaned back in his seat and crossed one leg over the other, his foot jittering. "Well, it was likely unavoidable."

"Unavoidable?" Sébastien's voice took on a register so deep, he hardly recognized it. "*You* allowed all these foul affairs to happen and did nothing!"

Antoine's foot stopped moving and his gaze narrowed on Sébastien. "Nothing? Don't you understand the risks I've been taking? Mother controls the court! I'm her pawn! I've been investigating, seeking the ultimate proof to send her off, like we discussed the other night in the Winter Garden. I *had* a plan."

"The beginnings of a plan," Sébastien scoffed, "but Mother is still here and organizing votes behind your back! The Giromians still infest our hallways! Maggie is still engaged to that monster and you left her in the dark—now look what she's done!"

Marguerite marched over and moved Sébastien out of the way. A whiff of her floral perfume swept around him, soothing him—only slightly. His knuckles had turned white.

She stole Sébastien's spot before the desk. "I saved the throne, no? Wasn't that the intention?"

"Well…" Antoine rubbed his fingertips to his temples.

Sébastien rolled one shoulder, then the other, forcing his body to relax. "Your solution is temporary. Once the duke takes you, Mother will regain her position and favor. Your sacrifice was noble, but why didn't you warn us?"

Marguerite glanced at the thick-curtained window. "I had to do something. The only way out of this, for me, was to take back what I once was. What your father wanted me to be: the advisor. I had to reveal who I was—otherwise, no one would listen to a low-level school chaperone. A duchess raised from the dead?"

Sébastien sensed his temper flaring up again. "But—"

"She threatened you. She apparently has Jules eating out of her palm, and everyone's secrets stored in her brain. I couldn't let her harm anyone like she harmed me."

Antoine readjusted his posture. "She values family, yet she plots *against* family. She destroyed me to get Adelaide at my side instead of Maggie, and now that she's unhappy, she will destroy me again to access more power. To command us. She loves us, but only if we do what she wants."

Marguerite threw her arms up. "It only took you eighteen or so years to realize it."

He glared, a flicker of fury in his expression. But the longer Sébastien stared at him, the more he wondered if it *was* fury. There was a swirl of passion in his cheeks, hunger in his wet, half-parted lips, a hint of lust blooming in his eyes.

Antoine was still in love with her, and more so after how she'd barreled into the meeting and saved him.

"So you understand why I couldn't let her continue to manipulate everyone. She's no longer queen and never will be, and she needs to trust that you can rule the kingdom on your own." Marguerite lowered her gaze to the desk. "As your father would have."

"But…" Sébastien shifted side-to-side. "You should have told us."

"We already had a plan, though I admit I was delaying it, in the hopes of finding something else." Antoine stood. "And now—"

"We have to revise it." Sébastien slumped, the memory of hours of pouring over books in the library bringing on sudden fatigue to his limbs. "Your title? It was to go to Mother. You were to remain dead, or at least, your identity was."

"*My* title?" Marguerite's voice was a croak as she blanched. "To her?"

Antoine scratched his forehead. "By going along with her ruse—you, dead—it made you of lesser import to the duke. Schwartz wouldn't marry a *nobody,* regardless of years-long deals."

Sébastien saw her flinch, bring her hands to her face, cover her mouth. "Oh."

"And your title?" Antoine continued. "Giving it to her removes her aspirations of remaining at court, controlling me. As the Duchess of Torrinni, not a mourning former queen, she'd have to go to *her* home."

"We would have confined her to Torrinni Palace until further notice, so we could clean up her mess," said Sébastien, rubbing his forehead. "Which we've begun doing—we sent off most of her spies and allies, or locked them up. That may be why it was so easy for you to divert her and take her place in that meeting."

Marguerite dropped into a chair by the hearth. "Oh," she repeated, as dots of sweat formed above her brows.

"So," said Sébastien, kneeling before her, "temporary. The throne is safe while you're here. But until we identify a way to break this agreement Cornelius formed with Mother, you're still in the line of fire, and so is Antoine."

"Oh," she said for the third time, pressing a hand to her heart, another to the base of her neck. "I'd been prepared for an ugly result, but… not this. Not for it to backfire so dreadfully."

"I expect Schwartz will announce your official engagement at the Masquerade. He will make a scene. It's very much like him to do so." Antoine sank onto his cushions. "We have ten days to find a new solution. Ten days to thwart several plans: Mother's, the Giromians', and likely Adelaide's, too."

"And Jules'," added Sébastien, twisting to the fireplace, hands shaking. "We must sever his ties with Mother, discover what she has on him to turn him against us, his brothers."

"Oh, Jules," said Marguerite. Sébastien turned back around to see her propping her elbows on her thighs, her chin on her fists.

"After everything I did for him. All the times I covered up his debts, hid his adventures from Mother—she already knew. And whatever she is blackmailing him with is far more nefarious than I thought." Antoine left his desk to park behind where Marguerite sat. His eyebrows drew together as he gripped the back of her chair, his fingers millimeters from her shoulders. "I must use this time wisely. To think. Alone." He side-glanced at Sébastien. "I need to take another trip."

Whipping around in her seat, Marguerite gawked up at him. "*Another* trip?"

"Postpone meetings and watch over the court for me," he said to Sébastien. "You're the only person I trust." He cleared his throat. "Present company excluded, of course."

Marguerite's face turned red as their eyes met. Her lips parted, and she poked her chest out—likely unaware of how she sought his body, sought to be closer to him.

She still loved him, too. But Sébastien wasn't sure if she realized it yet.

Her chin dropped.

"Yes, Majesty," said Sébastien. "Count on us."

Antoine stepped to the door, and when Marguerite looked up, they exchanged another fleeting glance that brewed up a storm, even in Sébastien's gut. His brother's eyes revealed a tempest of tumultuous emotions; memories of days when they embraced, touched, kissing in what they assumed was secret. Sébastien had spied on them many a time.

In an instant, the connection was broken. Antoine departed, the doors sealing softly behind him.

"I'm an idiot," murmured Marguerite, melting into her seat.

"No." Sébastien fell next to her. "You did it for love." She narrowed her eyes at him. "You can't fool me—neither of you can. He will never stop caring for you, and you for him, despite all he did. But beware. If I see it, others will see it, too."

She focused on the fireplace. "I know."

"You will leave the organizing and planning to us." He placed his hand over hers. "Can you *please* lie low for the next ten days, without acting foolishly? Consult us whenever you get ideas?"

Her look was blank, her shoulders hunched. "I will try."

Sébastien stretched out his legs. "We must get Mother out of

Torrinni, and you un-engaged. Those are our motives." He felt her hand twitching beneath his, prompting him to pull away. "We will get through this, Maggie. We must."

Céleste grew stir crazy. Servants were far and few between, and Johanna had told her to stay in her rooms until Marguerite or Sébastien allowed her out. When Céleste peeped into the corridor, she found guards nearby, blocking her way.

Whatever was happening, it was serious.

Marguerite had disappeared after receiving a visit from the dowager—Céleste had pressed her ear to the adjoining door and overheard *that* voice. The seeping cold of her tone wrapped around Céleste's heart and suffocated her.

She worried about her brother. She hadn't spoken to him since his denial to escort her to Romain's ball, but he tended to hold on to grudges. Was he involved? Was his correspondence being watched? Was he still angry at her for being presented at a ball held in honor of a Giromian?

She tried to read one of the books she'd sneaked from

Marguerite's room, but her mind wouldn't rest. Instead, she glared into her fireplace, one foot tapping to the ground.

A loud knock broke the silence. "Yes?"

Esther burst in, at her arm a bewildered Harriet.

"Ladies?" Céleste let out the breath she'd been holding. Harriet's eyes were wet. "What's the matter?"

"My father… they escorted him from the meeting…" Harriet shivered uncontrollably, and Esther helped her sit in the vanity chair.

"The meeting? What meeting?" Céleste kneeled, taking hold of Harriet's quaking legs to stabilize her. "Escorted? What is going on?"

Harriet muffled a sob. "I was lurking. They set up that meeting, the vote… but it ended quicker than I'd expected. I saw… guards… dragging him out. Hands bound. Chains."

"She's been like this since I found her," said Esther. "One of the page boys fetched me, saying I was her best friend and should help her." She bit her lip. "She's inconsolable."

Céleste tipped Harriet's chin up. "The vote… *that* vote?" She rehashed Marguerite's earlier words. "Did it happen?"

Harriet sniffled. "I heard it was thwarted, but… that's not all that happened. Father… he was… denounced."

The door again blasted open, sending Céleste reeling. Harriet almost fell, and Esther squeaked.

Emeric flew inside, his gaze on Harriet. "There you are," he said, breathless. "The entire castle searches for you, Miss Thatcher!"

Harriet hyperventilated. "Oh dear… oh Heavens… I'm finished… jail cell… can't do it…"

Emeric approached her with caution. "You're not in trouble." He unfastened his coat and loosened his cravat. "Your father is. They took him to Torrinni Prison, on grounds of treason against the crown."

Esther hiccuped and Céleste found her balance. "Treason?" they said in unison.

"Apparently, he conspired with the dowager to dethrone the king and put someone else there."

"Will he die?" Harriet turned paler.

Emeric grimaced. "Unsure. The king advertised a potential trial, but over half the kingdom despises your father."

Harriet snorted. "You can say that again. But death?" She fanned herself, but no color returned to her cheeks. "What does that mean for me?"

"The king stripped him of his title and lands, which go to you, until you marry." One corner of Emeric's lips fluttered up. "Harriet Thatcher, you're the new Vidame of Limesdale."

"I'm a woman." Harriet slouched into the seat cushions.

"And the leader of your household. With your father out of the picture, you can rebuild, fix the reputation he tarnished. Become a respectable noblewoman. Eugene Thatcher was a corrupt man. Taking his place is an enormous responsibility, but you helped in his arrest. You're more than up to the task."

Céleste had never witnessed her brother so caring, especially toward a woman. And more so Harriet Thatcher, daughter of the disgraceful vidame.

He left Esther to murmur encouragements to Harriet and focused on Céleste. "This meeting was… different."

Céleste tucked her arms to her sides. "Was there a vote? To…

dethrone the king, take his wife?"

Emeric's eyes narrowed on her. "I'm not sure how you would know anything about that, but… no. The vote never took place. Your chaperone interfered." Before Céleste could gasp, Emeric drew her towards the window. "She saved more than one person today."

"My chaperone was there? Why?" She spread the curtains, and a bright beam of sun hit her face. "Who did she save?"

"Julia Espinar, as it happens, was being targeted by Eugene Thatcher." He sneered. "It seems King Romain was never interested in her, but that's yet to be proven."

Céleste felt slight relief. "So she's out of danger?"

"From the vidame, at least." Emeric sighed. "King Romain was offended at hearing Eugene wanted his supposed bride, so I expect he will continue to petition for her hand as an act to cover up whatever his true intentions are."

"And the dowager?" Céleste watched a bird soar up to the clouds. "She… met with my chaperone, earlier."

"She wasn't at the meeting, as was planned. She was delayed, or so the rumors say. Your chaperone claims the woman locked her up. *Locked her up?* I always respected King Edouard, but his queen… never liked her much. I believe it. She teams up with the likes of Thatcher and that miserable band of foreigners to spread discord at her own court? Deplorable." He leaned against the wall, watching Céleste as she did everything she could to avoid his gaze. "It was quite a gathering, the most dramatic I've been to since I arrived at court. Prince Jules stormed out, angrier than I've ever seen him."

"Oh." She pressed her palm to the window to keep herself

upright.

So the younger prince's involvement was deeper than Marguerite had thought? She couldn't imagine the sorrow King Antoine and Sébastien would feel at their brother's betrayal.

Emeric studied her. "She stood up to the vidame, you know. And scolded the nobles for not defending their king."

"My chaperone?" She envisioned Marguerite taking on a horde of angry noblemen and shuddered; why was she at that meeting?

"Your chaperone… the duchess." Emeric grasped her shoulder, his touch comforting. "She's the famed—and supposedly dead—Duchess of Torrinni. But you knew that, didn't you? You were adamant on finding her, and you did."

Céleste's heart stopped—*duchess?* "She used her title?"

"You should have seen her," he said, smiling, something akin to pride booming in his voice. "She all but arrested the vidame herself. Impressive woman." He rubbed his knuckles on his frock coat. "I don't know the details, but she was there as King Antoine's advisor, and took her role quite seriously."

If Marguerite revealed herself, that meant she'd made herself vulnerable. She showed everyone that they'd been lied to—by the dowager. And the dowager would seek revenge for such a slight.

The dowager, who'd been behind all this. Who'd had deals with Eugene Thatcher, deals with the Giromians. It was all connected—so where was Marguerite so she and Céleste could discuss it?

***

Hours passed. Céleste paced, dragged her nails down her cheeks so much she worried she'd peeled off her skin. Her head throbbed.

Johanna waited with her, also concerned for Marguerite's whereabouts.

No one had seen her since after the meeting had ended.

Once the sky swirled with velvety violets and sprinkled with glittering stars, the adjoining door burst open.

"Maggie!" Céleste dashed over to the woman in the threshold; disheveled, but not appearing to be in physical danger. "Where have you been?"

Johanna cracked her neck, surely stiff from how she'd been sitting. "Is everything all right, Your Grace?"

Marguerite stepped into the room. "Well…" Her wobbling caused Johanna to vacate the vanity chair and allow her to sit in it. She sank into the cushions and let out a lengthy breath, her voice frail when she finally spoke. "I was with Sébastien and Antoine. Brainstorming. I made a grave mistake—"

"You exposed your true self to save your king? We're aware." Céleste huffed. "Emeric told me."

"Why did you do it?" Johanna kept at a distance, angled against the armoire, fiddling with her messy braid.

Shadows danced across Marguerite's face. "I thought it was the only way. Thank you for delaying the dowager, by the way," she said to Johanna. "It was most helpful. But I only made things worse."

Céleste scoffed. "Yes, you did! Now the dowager will be *furious.*"

"That's not the only issue." Marguerite took a shaky breath.

"By revealing myself, my status, I made it possible for Clémentine to stay at court. Antoine was going to make *her* Duchess of Torrinni, which would pull her out of mourning and force her to the palace that was once mine."

Johanna bounded over and grabbed her hands. Any other servant girl would receive punishment for such a gesture, but Johanna was no ordinary staff member. "You acted for the greater good, Your Grace. You can't blame yourself."

Céleste struggled to envision the dowager anywhere but at court. "Are they brainstorming now?"

"Antoine left, needing to be alone." Marguerite stormed to the adjacent door, fists clenched. "But there's no other way. She'll prevail, and that disdainful duke will take me to Giroma after the Masquerade."

"Does he know that you know?" Céleste concentrated on the window, imagining the duke standing there, leaning forward—and she would push him out.

"He implied it." Marguerite pounded her fists on the adjoining door. Banging, banging, *banging* until she pressed her forehead to the wood. "Ten days—*ten days* to deliver myself from his wretched hands. How? *How?*" Thick tears traveled down her cheeks, landing on the collar of her dress. "Clémentine, Cornelius, Adelaide, Romain, and Jules. *Jules!* I practically raised that boy, and he turns on me like that?"

Céleste twisted to Johanna. "Would you bring us some supper? Tea for me—wine for her. An entire flagon, if you can. She needs rest."

Johanna took one gander at the shriveling Marguerite, plastered against the door, still fighting between fury and terror.

"Right away." She whirled out, running down the hall.

Once her footsteps receded, Céleste guided Marguerite to her bed. "Lay down," she ordered.

"But I—"

"Don't argue!" Céleste thrust her onto the mattress, where she curled up against the wall, knees to her chest. "You must have faith in your king, and in Sébastien. And in me. You made a mistake, but we won't allow that vulture to sweep you off to Giroma!"

"I told you, *she* will prevail. She always does."

"The dowager won't win." Céleste hopped onto the mattress, remembering something she'd read in her isolation. "The king still has to consent to such a match, no? She may have tried to trick him, but he will find a way around this."

Marguerite looked at Céleste, lower lip quivering. "Are you sure?"

Céleste brushed the tears from the woman's cheeks. "Trust the boy you used to love. The king, who, I think, still loves you."

She sniffled and chuckled at the same time. "Séb said that too."

Grabbing a handkerchief from the nightstand, Céleste rubbed below Marguerite's nose and dabbed at the liquid spilling from her lash-line. "Then it must be true."

Marguerite's breaths were choppy, but otherwise, she seemed to unwind. "Thank you, Céleste. I don't deserve you. I was hard on you at first, but you're a true friend. You and Johanna both."

"You *do* deserve us." She smiled, and Marguerite smiled back; not forced or faked, but a real, genuine smile.

***

Céleste didn't have nightmares that night. Despite the ominous tidings and the possibility of losing Marguerite, she slept without waking.

In all her time reading *The Golden Girl*, she never imagined she'd meet the Duchess of Torrinni and become her closest friend, her confidante, involved in all the schemes at court.

When her eyelids fluttered and she emerged from slumber, she stretched.

She tossed back the covers and set her feet onto the cold floor. The fire had gone out, and she rubbed her hands together for warmth. She snagged her night robe from the farthest bed-poster, and rushed to her window, prying the drapes aside. Day had barely risen, and clouds hovered in the sky, basking the grounds in a gloomy aura.

Unease woke in her gut. She couldn't explain it; maybe it was the gray glow outside, or the chill washing over her, but it prompted her to peep at the adjoining door. Waiting, listening, wondering what Marguerite was doing on the other side.

The sensation prodded harder as she took cautious strides to the door-latch. After a few breaths, she pulled.

Marguerite's room was as cold, if not colder, and the same hazy atmosphere as outside loomed within.

Once past the threshold, Céleste saw Johanna at the room's main door, blocking it—barring Marguerite from exiting.

"No, Your Grace," she said, a sternness to her voice Céleste didn't recognize.

"Let me pass, Johanna." Marguerite stood firm, two loaded bags over her shoulders.

"No." Johanna gritted her teeth, and upon spotting Céleste, she brightened. "Miss Richel, tell her—tell her not to run away again!"

As she spun to Céleste, standing agape in the adjoining doorway, Marguerite grimaced.

Her hood slid down her forehead, shielding her curls from view.

She'd have gotten away with it. She would have had no trouble getting out, mingling with a group of servants heading into town for their daily chores.

But Johanna knew her too well, and Céleste's instincts were beyond comparison.

Céleste's tentative voice caught on Marguerite's heartstrings. "Where are you going?"

She couldn't talk her way out of this. It was obvious—the essentials she'd gathered in haste were clear signs of an attempt to escape.

"She wants to leave," Johanna blubbered. "She wants to *run.*"

Céleste opened her mouth to speak, but Marguerite growled,

stopping her. "Can you blame me? What's left here for me except for my own doom? A doom that I caused?"

"*We* are left," said Johanna, her eyes cloudy.

"You don't need me," Marguerite whispered, worried if she spoke any louder, she'd erupt into tears.

It was the only way—disappearing. If she wasn't there, Dowager Clémentine could spread another rumor of her death. Everyone would once more forget about her, and Antoine and Sébastien could carry on with their plans.

The duke wouldn't be able to marry her because she'd be long gone. There'd be no war, because she'd no longer exist—Romain wouldn't launch an attack for that.

"You're sorely mistaken," said Johanna, not budging from where she barred the door. "Running away solves nothing, Your Grace, and you know that."

"But she—"

"*She* will find you again, and lock you up in a real prison." Johanna's fists tightened, her cheeks a bright red hue. "Running away solves nothing."

Marguerite disagreed—firstly, because *no one* would have found her this time. Clémentine's spies loitered no more, according to Antoine and Sébastien. They'd been rounded up, interrogated, some of them locked up, some given high fines for their crimes. A few had fled beyond the Totresian border into France—where they'd be more of a problem to the French.

The dowager's power was fading, at last. Marguerite wouldn't stick around to watch the consequences.

"If you run, you worsen your doom," said Céleste, regaining her ability to speak. "If you run, you abandon us all to the dowager's coups."

Though taken aback by Céleste's steady voice, Marguerite wouldn't falter. "If I run, she can no longer torment me. Antoine can relocate her, the Giromians can finally *leave*—"

"You really think they'll leave without you?" Céleste shook her head. "They came for Adelaide, and they came for you. Giromians aren't known to concede, are they? That's what my father told me."

The notion of Céleste's father being right made Marguerite gag.

The notion of *anyone* being right made her legs wobble, her resolve crumble.

She fell to her knees. "I don't know what else to do."

Céleste kneeled before her. "Nothing, like King Antoine asked you. Isolate yourself, rest, research if you must, but do *nothing* to mess with whatever he and his brother are working on. Otherwise you put all of us in jeopardy. Jules, as king? You said yourself how awful that would be."

Marguerite released her bags and lowered her face into her hands, allowing her suppressed sobs out.

***

Johanna prepared a hot bath for her. She claimed the steam would pull all the nonsense from within her bones. Marguerite didn't argue, too sore from clenching her jaw, fighting with those who didn't see reason.

The scalding water caused her to hiss, at first, but once she was settled and inundated, she relented to the heat. She relented to what her friends sought to do.

Save her.

She spent what felt like hours soaking in the tub, weighing the pros and cons. When she'd run from Antoine, all those years ago, she'd been young, prone to errors. This time, she was prepared. She had more knowledge, more courage; she'd have gotten away with it.

But where would she have gone? That had been her problem last time—not knowing where to hide. Clémentine's men had easily found her three years ago.

This time, it wouldn't be Clémentine's men coming after her. Antoine's, Sébastien's; Johanna and Céleste would lead the search.

"I'm sorry," she said to Johanna, who enveloped her with a soft robe as she exited the tub.

"You're not," said Johanna. "You're still deliberating, and I understand, but you're *not* sorry."

Marguerite pulled the robe tighter around herself. "You *don't* understand. I can't be here. There's no way to avoid my fate except for—"

"Cowering in the woods? Posing as a pauper for the rest of your life when you were meant for greater things? No." Johanna shoved her towards the armoire. "Everyone needs you here. Trust in the king. He doesn't want you married to a Giromian, and he'll prove it."

Johanna and Céleste took turns watching Marguerite, ensuring she didn't leave. They decided to spread the rumor that she was ill, that she needed rest and isolation.

While she would have preferred to leave, Marguerite appreciated the sudden solace from court life. Surely gossip had spread around the castle by now: Duchess Marguerite was alive, she'd assisted in Eugene Thatcher's arrest, and Dowager Clémentine was furious.

She'd rather not be seen.

She had a chance to think, to clear her head, to request books from the library to search for a solution.

Beyond her bedroom door, Cornelius lurked. He'd probably taunt her, licking his unpleasant lips whenever he sighted her. Romain would sneer and impose his dominance in every area he walked into. And Clémentine…

For years Marguerite had despised the dowager for all she'd done, but deep within herself, she'd hoped to one day understand why. To seek some way to forgive her, move past her cruelty. This—giving her hand to one of the worst Giromian nobles in existence, part of a family that deceived and destroyed? She wasn't sure she'd be able to rise above it.

To sit around and wait for that night—the Masquerade— sounded like torture.

A few days into her isolation, she fell onto her bed. "I can't go. I can't." She winced. "Maybe that's the only way; avoid the Masquerade, and he can't announce me as his bride, can he?"

Johanna was seated on a chaise, mending a ripped stocking. "Perhaps."

"Is Antoine back?" She sat up and glowered at Johanna, who kept her gaze trained on her work. "Have you told him about me trying to run?"

"No, and not last I checked." Johanna winced as she peered at the door. "Céleste is on a walk now, she may bring more news."

Céleste often went for walks, stating the waiting drove her

insane. She reported that many courtiers intercepted her with questions, like, "Where's the duchess?" or "Is she really still alive?" or "Why did Dowager Clémentine lie?"

The contenders also hounded Johanna with inquiries.

"Our chaperone is a duchess?"

"A woman, on the king's council?"

"Why was she at the academy?"

Word of Marguerite's exploits in the meeting room flooded the hallways of Torrinni Castle, but Céleste and Johanna kept mum.

Céleste had told Marguerite that lying didn't sit well with her. She felt Marguerite should confront everyone head-on. She'd assumed her role, she'd outed herself—she needed to live with it.

"He's not back," the girl said, entering the room a few minutes later. "Sébastien sent his regards and invited me to the Christmas Eve ball. Can I go?"

"You must," said Marguerite and Johanna at the same time. "And you must insist that I was too contagious to attend," Marguerite added. "Especially if you come across the dowager. She'll call your bluff—avoid her if you can."

Céleste padded to her room via the adjoining door, huffing. "All I do is avoid people, and I'm tired of it."

The Christmas Eve ball was a formal affair for contenders, upper-class nobles, royals, and whatever foreign guests resided in the castle. If the king remained gone, Queen Adelaide would host it.

Later that day, when it was Céleste's turn to monitor the duchess, she told of how she'd nearly bumped into Duke Cornelius. How Emeric had asked questions but prayed Marguerite recovered from her mysterious illness.

She'd pocketed a few macarons to snack on later, but Marguerite begged for them—her isolation had made her crave sugar.

She scarfed down three delicacies in a row and washed them down with coffee.

"Making up stories to protect you is exhausting," said Céleste, frowning at her dwindling stash of pastries. "You refuse to speak to anyone and only read the history books we bring you. Have you not considered that your answer is *out there?*"

In response, Marguerite snagged another macaron and plunged into the tome of royal titles she'd been studying.

For the Christmas Eve ball, Céleste wore a dark emerald gown. Johanna helped her prepare while Marguerite sulked, pretending to nap on her bed.

"Maintain the ruse," she heard Johanna say, before Céleste left. "If anyone gives you grief, tell them to take it up with your prince."

Inevitably, Marguerite fell asleep for real, and didn't awaken until Céleste bounced onto her bed, shaking her.

"What?" Marguerite's voice was groggy as she squinted, recognizing the girl in the faint firelight.

"Did you not want me to report happenings at the ball?" She crossed her arms, cocking her head. Marguerite waved at her to continue. "Queen Adelaide sends her well-wishes and offers her personal physician."

Marguerite snickered. "Swell." She yawned, wishing to get back to sleep. "Anything else?"

"Sébastien liked my dress," Céleste stuck out one finger, then another— "he's suspicious,"—another finger—"and the king is still not home."

Johanna, half-asleep on the sofa, shooed Céleste into her room and reanimated the fire in the hearth. "Sleep, Your Grace," she said, voice low and sleepy. "Tomorrow will be a new day."

That was all Johanna said—half-hearted encouragement to get Marguerite through each day of her self-inflicted confinement.

Of course Marguerite wanted out. Of course she suffocated, desperate for fresh air. But as long as Antoine was gone, she wasn't safe wandering the castle. It surprised her that Clémentine hadn't already come to force her out of her room and into a carriage with Duke Cornelius.

In the days leading to the Masquerade, she spent mornings studying scrolls of ancient Totresian laws. Afternoons sipping on coffee while perusing heavy books covered in dust. Evenings going over official letters with Edouard's seal. All while under heavy surveillance from Johanna and Céleste.

She'd given up on running away, but still, they watched her carefully; they didn't trust her. She didn't blame them.

"Nine days," she said, slamming yet another book shut. "Nine days of reading, research, isolation, and it was all for naught."

She'd found none of the answers she sought. No mentions of proper ways to break a treaty between a dowager and a duke without causing a war. No peaceful manners to rearrange a contract or change its wording. No means to ensure Clémentine hadn't gone behind Antoine's back and forged his signature to allow it all to unfold.

"Nine days of absolute isolation, and for what?" She sighed, sighting Johanna in the corner of her eye; she was perusing one of

Marguerite's discarded books, feigning disinterest in Marguerite's complaints.

Céleste barreled in through the adjoining door. "I've had enough of this!"

Johanna looked up, getting to her feet. "What happened?"

"Another near encounter with the duke. I believe he's seeking me out. Someone tells him where I am and he hurries over to confront me." Céleste glowered at Marguerite. "In place of confronting *her.*"

"I can't confront him," said Marguerite, gaze trained on the book she'd left open on her bed.

Céleste clutched at her yellow skirts. "No one else will!"

"I *can't* do it," Marguerite insisted. "You think he'll give up on me because I bat my lashes and pucker my lips? He works for the dowager. With her. Or she works for him. Who knows?"

"But the king—"

"The king is *still gone.*" Marguerite clenched her fists. "Until he's back, I can't leave this room." At first, it was because they wouldn't let her out; now, she didn't *want* out, not unless she was certain a solution had been found to her predicament.

"There's still time," said Johanna, voice soft. Her eyes were tired. She'd taken the brunt of Marguerite's complaints and doubts.

"There isn't. There's no alternative."

Céleste pressed her back to the adjoining door, closing it. "No alternative?"

Marguerite couldn't escape—not unless she physically, magically disappeared. "I must accept my fate."

Céleste crossed her arms, slowly approaching. "And what if I told you the king returned this morning? Sébastien had to cut our meeting short to go talk to him. Perhaps he figured it out? Perhaps he—"

"If he's not summoned me to talk, then he came to the same conclusion as me." Marguerite sucked in a breath, wondering why she hadn't yet heard from Antoine if he'd indeed returned. "I'm a hopeless case. You should have let me leave."

Céleste came close enough to seize Marguerite's hands. "To go where? I told you, Johanna told you—you wouldn't have gotten far."

"I would have tried." Marguerite wrinkled her nose. "It'd have been better than sitting here all day looking at books that have no solutions."

Céleste scoffed. "Then we take action. Let me speak to my brother, my father—"

Marguerite's disheartened chuckle cut her off. "If the King of Totresia and his prince of a brother have no options to keep me from the duke, I doubt your brother and father would."

Céleste lowered her chin. "It's worth a try."

"No." Marguerite stood. "It's too late."

As if to confirm her words, she received a stern missive soon after—not an invitation, but a *summons* to the Masquerade. Signed and sealed, from the dowager.

Be at the Masquerade, or else I will fetch you from the rooms where you feign your illness and send you off without even announcing it to the court. You'll be dead to them, yet again. Possibly <u>truly</u> dead if you push me too far. Surely you don't wish to further anger me, do you?

Marguerite chewed the insides of her cheeks.

The dowager got what she wanted.

Céleste, who'd come running at the sound of Marguerite's cries, shook out her skirts. "We can continue to feign your illness. One more day—we talk to the physicians, make them corroborate, assure the dowager you're contagious."

"She plotted this, from day one," Marguerite said, raking a hand through her tangled tresses. "I need to speak with Antoine, confer with him. But I have little hope he will have a solution. Especially if he only returned today. Nine days, and nothing."

Céleste huffed. "The ball is tomorrow. I imagine the king will communicate with you before then."

Marguerite headed to her closet. "You can brainstorm; I must pack. I predict that I'll be departing Torrinni after the Masquerade."

She hauled her trunk to the middle of the room and pulled its lid up. A cloud of dust made her cough.

Céleste hardly moved out of the way. "Can't the nobles vote against it?"

Marguerite fingered through her dresses. "It's a deal between the dowager, the duke, and the Giromian king. Antoine's signature was likely forged. Such a contract can't be nullified by a council vote. Only Antoine could block it, and he knows the risks if he does."

"What if…" Céleste tapped a finger to her chin. "If we send someone into the dowager's office… Johanna, maybe? To browse through her documents and retrieve this contract and burn it?"

Marguerite threw a handful of gowns into the crate. "Johanna will *not* sneak into the dowager's chambers. That's suicide." She plucked a few pairs of shoes from the rear of the closet. "Besides, I doubt the dowager would keep such a precious document in her office. She'll have it hidden. Or the duke has it. Or the king. Would you suggest breaking into *their* guarded quarters?"

Céleste blocked Marguerite from adding any other items to her trunk. "You must dispute this! It isn't right, not fair, and—"

"I'm powerless to stop it." Marguerite's nails dug into the silky fabric of the gown she held. "I chose this, remember? By putting Antoine's crown before my pride. I tried to run. But I will always end up right here."

Céleste's mouth opened, but no sound came out.

"She allied with a duke and a king, a man with views on Antoine's wife, another seeking to steal me from my home," Marguerite continued. "These treacherous deals will send troops to our doorstep if we falter. Haven't you learned of Giroma's frightful military in your studies?"

"Of course I have." Céleste's shoulders drooped.

Marguerite grabbed more silks and satins and cast them into the trunk. "If I try to confront her, I embarrass myself. If I run, she'll make me regret my actions. Clémentine knows everything, is ready for anything, and I should have remembered that."

Céleste said nothing, grouping Marguerite's beauty products in boxes and placing her jewels into leather pouches.

Johanna joined them with Marguerite's traveling bags and tidied the room. A glimmer of emotion showed in her eyes, but she, unlike Céleste, knew better than to push.

Johanna brought them a late lunch, and they ate in silence in the sitting area. Céleste pushed her vegetables around. Johanna slurped up her steaming broth and did all she could to avert her gaze. Marguerite pretended her stomach didn't churn with every bite of beef, every swallow of wine, every chunk of potato she squeezed down her throat.

Somewhere, buried beneath dread and despair, she did have hope that Antoine would save her. But he hadn't yet spoken to her, and Sébastien had said nothing to Céleste; nothing about Antoine's conclusions, if he'd made any.

She was doomed to be a Giromian duchess.

In the blink of an eye, the moment they'd all dreaded for ten days had arrived—December thirty-first.

The dread overshadowed what should have been an exciting event for Céleste. Her first Masquerade, and as the youngest official season contender in recent Totresian history.

She should have been smiling, celebrating; instead she frowned at her reflection. The gorgeous dress, the pearls around her neck, the diamonds dangling from her earlobes—none of it brought her joy, and it was visible. Marguerite watched her, sorry she lacked the power to render this night more enjoyable.

She inspected her handiwork—the silky dress fit Céleste somehow better than when she'd been presented. Her wig fit snugly over her curls, and Marguerite fastened more pins to secure everything.

Marguerite hurried to her own room to get dressed after telling Céleste to dab pomade over her lips.

"There has to be a loophole," said Céleste, her voice carrying through the open adjoining door.

"A loophole?" Marguerite cringed as Johanna tightened the laces of her blood-red gown.

"Something in some ancient book in the farthest section of the library. A bargain to strike, to find more time to thwart this deal?" Céleste grunted, her chair squeaking; she was standing up. "An addendum to the treaty that the king could create to protect you?"

Marguerite tugged on her sparkling white wig—a rarity, since she preferred not to wear wigs. The strands cascaded over her shoulders, and her long, lacy sleeves swayed as she stepped in front of her floor-to-ceiling mirror. Johanna fitted her lacy, ebony mask over her eyes; the golden designs around the slits momentarily blinded her.

"Don't you think?" Céleste swished into the room, her ivory and pearl mask settled over her face. "Oh!" She froze at the sight of Marguerite, who'd been twirling as Johanna verified every crease.

"I do think," said Marguerite, holding in a tear. Céleste looked every inch the royal wife she was destined to become. "But I also think it's too late."

"Maggie," Céleste's voice appeared to catch in her throat, "you look gorgeous!"

Marguerite waved her closer. "And *you* are the perfect portrait of a princess. This will please your father."

"Has he arrived?" Céleste bit her lip. "I thought he might seek me out to give instructions about how I should act tonight."

"Johanna mentioned his carriage rolled in late this afternoon," said Marguerite, sidling up to her.

Together, they stood before the mirror. What a pair they made; one in heavenly white, the other in hellish red. An angelic seventeen-year-old with a potential royal future ahead of her; a devilish damsel about to marry an evil duke.

Céleste scrunched her nose. "He'll be in a mood. He hates traveling. This won't do, he will find something wrong with it, he will—"

Marguerite seized her chin. "Stop it. You're dazzling, and he will love it. Sébastien will love it, too."

"But," Céleste's lower lip quivered, "tonight is… and I don't want—"

"Promise me something." Marguerite released her chin. "That you will allow nothing to ruin your evening. It's your first Masquerade, and it should be special."

Céleste hopped from foot to foot, whimpering. "How can you be so calm?"

"Well, I've attended a few Masquerades. And," Marguerite cocked her head, "I might as well enjoy the festivities while I can, no? Several of the girls may receive marriage proposals tonight, two of them from royalty. Isn't that something to celebrate?"

"But aren't you afraid?" Céleste set her hands on Marguerite's shoulders. "Don't you want to keep fighting? To *do* something to stop all this?"

A bead of sweat formed on Marguerite's forehead, just above her mask. "I can't stop anything. And it would be foolish to fear what's to come. All things happen for a reason. Never forget that. God has a plan for me, and I must trust that," she gulped, "He knows best."

"I don't want to go. Not if it means you'll leave with the duke tomorrow, and I'll have to stay and mingle with the likes of that dowager and the queen… and *Charlotte!*"

Marguerite pulled away. "I refuse to see you so down on such a glorious night. This is *my* issue. I appreciate your concern and your friendship. But I will be all right. I survived torture at the hands of the dowager; the duke can't be much worse." She flinched, but recovered with a bright, over-the-top smile.

Céleste moaned. "Fine, I won't sulk! At least not in the presence of others."

"Thank you." Marguerite guided her to the door. "Are you ready to make your brother and father proud? Show everyone how you are a beautiful, well-mannered contender?"

"You really won't ride off, hide?"

Marguerite scoffed. "Did you not just prevent me from doing so?"

"I did, but now..." Céleste lowered her chin. "Now, I'm scared."

Marguerite had surrendered and swallowed her pride to concede defeat to the woman who'd bullied her all her life. She wasn't scared; she was terrified. "Me, too, Céleste." She inhaled a deep breath of her room's lingering coffee and powder scent. "Me, too."

Antoine loitered at the junction of the King's Corridor and the West Wing, spying on guests as they arrived.

He'd spent nearly two weeks away, and hadn't missed the tense atmosphere. Nor had he missed the anxious knots in his stomach every time he came across a man with dirty-blond hair and a dark gaze.

And he certainly hadn't missed his mother's constant hovering.

She was far from pleased at her initial plot being thwarted—the vote to annul Antoine's marriage, then remove him from the throne. Her ally, Eugene, being locked up also caused issues—apparently she'd thrown quite the fit and secluded herself for several days to recover.

She'd be particularly unpleasant tonight, as both his brothers would be announcing their choices of brides.

But her main plot—getting rid of Marguerite—hadn't been thwarted, to Antoine's dismay.

He kept to the shadows of the secret corridor, the one mostly used by servants or by himself, when he sought to sneak out of the ballroom. From there, he witnessed many arriving garbed in their finest suits and most elaborate dresses, sparkling masks adorning their faces and intricate, wigged coiffures atop their heads.

Then he saw her—well, her troop of contenders, padding down the King's Corridor. Harriet Thatcher in burgundy, every bit the newly independent noble woman. Esther Bristol in pale blue, Cristina Condello in dandelion. Side-by-side were Julia Espinar in maroon and silver, her neck muscles taut, and Charlotte Geitz, in black and gold.

Black and gold—like Jules, whom he'd spotted earlier coming out of the Men's room, already tipsy on whatever foul liquor he kept in his flask. They'd exchanged a glance—Antoine refraining from pouncing on him—and Jules had disappeared down a different service corridor.

Céleste Richel marveled in white ruffles, and on her arm—Marguerite, in a bold blood-red number. She was a bewitching vision, or perhaps a mirage, the embodiment of all the desire she'd awoken in him.

She'd come to the Masquerade?

His fists balled at his sides.

"Mother," he grumbled, wishing he had a flask like his brother's, containing an even stronger liquor.

Marguerite's crew moved down the West Wing to the ballroom, but Marguerite hung back, keeping Julia with her. Antoine crept as close to the corner as he could, listening.

"If King Romain proposes to you tonight, come find me. If he doesn't, don't take offense. The Masquerade engagements are Totresian traditions, so he might only state his interest for you without yet offering you marriage."

Antoine couldn't show his face, but he heard the nerves in the girl's reply. "I understand."

The poor thing—she'd never asked for involvement in the Totresian-Giromian drama. She had no need to discover Romain's false intentions tonight, in presence of a large part of the Totresian population. Including her father.

He waited a breath, two, three, then made sure Marguerite was gone before drooping against the wall. He secured his black-feathered gold mask over his face, adjusted his ruby crown, tugged on the lapels of his creamy white suit.

As the biggest night of the year, the Masquerade drew the entire country to court. With so many attendees, it would take a while for everyone to settle inside the ballroom.

When he moved from his hiding spot, Adelaide was waltzing down the King's Corridor, her groupies rushing ahead to wait for her in the ballroom. In her fuchsia gown, she didn't match him, which was against tradition. For the first time, they hadn't consulted one another for their outfits.

Her bright gray wig was dusted with diamonds; twinkling lights flickered in her blue eyes. She quirked an eyebrow upon sighting him and offered him her arm. "There you are," she said, only mildly miffed. "I had hoped you'd wear something darker."

He chose to say nothing—too many ears were nearby. He'd already taken note of his mother in her baby blue gown, Cordelia at her hip in navy.

He took hold of Adelaide's arm, also visualizing King Romain in the distance, walking briskly to catch up. As a monarch, he'd walk with the Totresian royals, garbed in forest-green with a sharp-edged scarlet mask. He'd forgone his exuberant cerulean crown for a tiara of garnets—the tiniest show of respect. Shocking.

Feet away from the door, Antoine heard the herald announce, "Duchess Marguerite of Torrinni."

The room beyond was silent as the once-dead duchess made her way down the carpet.

The doors opened, blinding him.

Inside, wintry decals were on the walls and windows. Sprinkles of silvery powder smeared across the floors, and the buffet and dais' linens were like a fresh blanket of snow.

"And now, Their Majesties, King Antoine and Queen Adelaide of Totresia!"

"Brother," whispered Sébastien, lining up behind Antoine just as Adelaide tugged him past the threshold. "Anything?"

Antoine cocked his head quickly enough to see Sébastien in white, and a rigid-looking Jules at his side, his golden mask mostly concealing his sneer.

"Nothing," he said, before Adelaide hauled him halfway down the carpet.

The guests curtsied, gave compliments, sent well-wishes, but he didn't look at anyone, especially not *her*. And especially not the darkly-dressed duke looming at the bottom of the dais—the one he craved to strangle, to make disappear before he stole away the only woman Antoine had ever loved.

Once everyone was settled atop the platform, Antoine cleared his throat. "All rise. Before we continue, any rumors you may have heard about a shift of power are false."

He scanned the room. Jules stood stiffly to his left; Adelaide, to his right, chuckled. He couldn't see Clémentine, but he had no doubt she peered up at the ceiling, acting unaffected.

"I ask that you not spread such profanities at court, lest you feel my wrath. That being said," he took a step back and tapped on Jules' shoulder, "my youngest brother has something to share."

He felt flames in his eyes as he peered at his sibling, flames that engulfed him, traveling down every inch of his body, ready to combust.

He couldn't watch Jules pick a woman his mother had requested. It was too similar to Antoine's own season, his own life, when he, too, had his hand forced by his mother. "Good luck," he muttered, before hopping off the dais, brushing through the crowd.

They watched him, he knew. *She* watched him, too, surely wondering why he wouldn't stay and congratulate his brothers.

His throne was secure, for now. He had far more important issues to deal with—such as saving Marguerite.

He didn't go far, creeping out the secret exit. He kept the door open an inch in order to listen.

"After much debate," said Jules, voice loud but muffled by his mask, "I've chosen Miss Charlotte Geitz as my future bride."

Applause rang in the room as Antoine gritted his teeth. Charlotte Geitz—daughter of a prominent noble, graceful, obedient. Bold, from the gossip he'd heard. And malleable to whatever Dowager Clémentine's plans were.

Many might have expected Jules to veer towards Frances, but Antoine knew for a fact Frances had been shipped back to Mara just that morning—at Clémentine's behest.

"If she wishes to accept, it would honor me," said Jules, sounding stiff and unsure.

"Focus, *focus,*" said Antoine to himself, trying to tune out the noise from the ballroom. "How do I get her to safety?"

If only he'd known the conditions Clémentine had set—how had she forced Marguerite to attend? Had she seen Marguerite yet? What would happen if Marguerite were to… disappear?

The room silenced again; someone else must have made their intentions to speak known.

"If I may add something before the *soirée* commences," said Romain in his signature, oily tone. "I thank Totresia for being so welcoming. Though tonight I can't pronounce a betrothal, I wish to declare that I've found a favorite among the contenders." He paused, likely looking at the woman he'd been falsely courting. "Miss Espinar, it's my pleasure to prolong my sojourn at Torrinni court to become better acquainted with you."

Adelaide would be furious. She'd drooled over the foreign king, after all, surely expecting him to sweep her off her feet and take her far, far away, to Giroma.

Antoine still didn't understand this new game. Why would the foreign king *want* to stay in Torrinni?

"That's it," he clapped his hands once, "I actually *make* her disappear. She can't run off; Mother is watching. But if she's taken… that's a different story, isn't it?"

His office wasn't far—he hurried inside, scribbled a note, then lifted it closer to his eyes to better read in the semi-dark.

Maggie,

I came up with no solution to save you. That's why I avoided you.

Well... nothing aside from the option of smuggling you out of Totresia. He can't announce your betrothal if you're not there; he wouldn't dare.

Meet me outside of the ballroom as soon as you receive this.

-A.

It's risky, he thought, shaking his head. *But I'm out of options. She can't marry that monster.*

He snatched a page-boy loitering near the ballroom doors. "Deliver this to Duchess Marguerite, and no one else. Don't let her see you. Hurry."

It felt like hours had passed as he paced in front of the ballroom, waiting. The guards ignored him, used to his fits, his need to stretch and move his legs.

Had the note been intercepted? Or had Marguerite chosen to ignore him? Had she figured another means to save herself?

There *was* no other way; he'd checked. He'd scoured every book in his personal collection, at the royal library, at the quaint bookstores in Torrinni Town. His mother had double-crossed him, forging his approval before he'd had a chance to voice it. And to disagree with her after all the effort she'd put into this scheme... he'd look weak. Stupid.

He could *not* be perceived as a failure.

Perhaps Marguerite feared leaving the room. Dowager Clémentine was there, after all, and who knew what she'd threatened Marguerite with to make her attend.

At long last, the doors opened; a gap barely large enough to fit a person. *She* appeared, passing through said gap.

Marguerite held the crumpled note in her hands, her gaze landing on him. "Antoine?" She moved forward enough to allow the doors to close. The guards let her out without so much as a blink; they knew better than to question their king.

He extended his hand to her. "I don't know what I'm doing, but... I don't know what *else* to do."

At first she remained frozen, bewildered. "It's madness. There will be consequences. Your mother... she threatened."

"I'm sure she did, but... you showed yourself. Isn't that good enough?" He splayed his fingers wide, insistent, but unsure if she'd consent. If she'd trust him enough to save her.

As if some flash of lightning had struck her, she came to. She breathed in, hiked up her skirts. "Well... there are no other options."

She slid her hand in his; chills crawled up his arms. Were this in another setting, it would have been *the* touch to fuel them both, to push them over the edge they'd been looming at. He could feel it; all these weeks at the castle, all the secret meetings, the messages exchanged—they were still in love. They'd never stopped *being* in love.

Even when she rebuffed him, scowled at him, turned her back on him—Marguerite *still loved him.*

It was a good thing they were in a hurry and had to run, otherwise he'd kiss her. He'd hold her closer than he ever had, absorb her until they somehow escaped their tragic situation.

She squeezed his hand, bringing him back to the present.

"What are we waiting for? Save me, Antoine."

Perhaps it was the glistening fake snow covering the wooden floors of the ballroom. Or the crowd of aristocrats, staring at the dais. Or the bright-colored dresses, the over-decorated drapes, the fake flakes on the windows.

Or the fact that Marguerite had vanished into the crowd? Céleste couldn't put her finger on it, but something didn't feel right.

She intently watched her father and Sébastien conversing. Her cheeks flushed as they turned to her. Sébastien scrambled onto the podium and cleared his throat. Her father hurried to her and tucked her arm under his.

Marquess Barnabé Richel was an older version of Emeric, but with gray in his light hair and mustache, his eyes sharper, harsher; always wary, on alert. "It's time," he said, taking her closer to the platform.

She bit her lip to stop her smile from expanding. To calm her nerves, she looked around the room.

Duke Cornelius loitered, his stance menacing, his bulging arms crossed over his plain brown ensemble. He kept close to his king, who was flirting with Julia. Something was off about him, too. He was alone, searching, probing—for Marguerite?

Before Céleste could whip around to ensure Marguerite was safe from him, her father nudged her, which prompted her to peer up at the podium.

"Ladies and gentlemen, I beg your attention for a few more moments," said Prince Sébastien, silencing the room. He shuffled his feet. "Tonight, I will follow my brother's example and declare my betrothed."

Whispers broke out across the room.

"I'll break tradition by asking, in front of all, for her father's blessing to seek her hand in marriage." Sébastien motioned for Marquess Richel to step forward.

As her father let her go and marched over to the prince, Emeric took his spot at Céleste's side. He was radiant in his khaki suit, and he squeezed her upper arm. "You look splendid."

She beamed at him, and both returned their focus to Sébastien, and to Marquess Richel bowing before him.

"Barnabé Richel, Marquess of Valeville, esteemed councilor and friend to my father." Sébastien's tone was firm, though Céleste detected a hint of a tremble in it. "Will you grant me leave to marry your daughter, Miss Céleste Richel, when she comes of age?"

The world stopped spinning, but Céleste's head didn't. Her heartbeat raced a million miles a minute, and the butterflies flapped their wings faster in her gut, flinging themselves against her ribs.

"I will, Your Highness."

"Do you consent for her to reside at court to finish her

tutoring, so she may learn to become a princess?" Sébastien linked his gaze with Céleste's.

The winged creatures inside turned savage, so wild they hurt—and she smiled.

"I do, Your Highness." Marquess Richel adjusted his position and beckoned Céleste to him.

Her legs locked, and she couldn't move. Not in fear, but in awe—this was happening, *really* happening.

Emeric tapped her shoulder, breaking her astonishment. "Go!"

She issued a silent warning to the butterflies to *calm down*, and glided up to her father.

She sensed her mother's presence, wearing her signature lavender scent—like a subtle encouragement. She could hear her mother murmuring in her ear, congratulating her.

"You remind me of her on our wedding day," Marquess Richel mumbled as he set a hand on the small of Céleste's back. "She would be so proud of you. A proper lady, a future princess." The corners of his eyes crinkled. "Don't disappoint me."

The butterflies plopped to the pit of her stomach as if shot by poisoned arrows. Did he *have* to ruin the moment?

She refocused on the prince, who descended the steps. "And you, Miss Richel—do you consent?" He offered a nervous smile as he got to one knee in front of her, eyes sparkling. The crowd gasped at such a gesture; a prince kneeling for an underaged noble girl. "Will you be my wife?"

She almost screamed her innermost thoughts—*yes, yes, a thousand times yes!*—then remembered where she was, and who surrounded her. Propriety demanded that she remain calm, much as she wanted to explode with joy.

"Yes, Your Highness." She curtsied, ignoring her father's judgmental glare, and feasted her eyes on Sébastien rising to his full height, his smile no longer nervous—but brilliant. Her own smile widened so much her jaw hurt. "Nothing would please me more."

The instant Sébastien's hand wrapped around hers to heave her up from her curtsy, the butterflies reanimated.

His warmth traveled up her arms, and his citrus aroma enveloped her like a cloud of bliss. He brought her knuckles to his lips and placed a lingering kiss atop them. "You honor me by accepting."

As he twisted her to the crowd, the area filled with claps and cheers. They gawked, congratulated—

But the *one* person that she most needed to see wasn't there.

The prince appeared to have noticed too, as he led her towards the dance-floor. "Where's Maggie?"

"In my power as Queen of Totresia, I declare the Masquerade open!" yelled Adelaide in the background.

The music started.

"I don't know." Céleste peeked at the buffet, at the sofas, at the windows and patio door—no duchess.

"Odd. Antoine disappeared too. I had hoped he would be there…"

"…to congratulate us," Céleste finished. "I thought the same with Maggie."

As he twirled her, she continued her search, wondering if Marguerite was concealing herself from the duke. She scouted the secret exit, the main doors, the orchestra to the right—but nowhere did she uncover her chaperone.

She did notice Cornelius approach the podium and wave the queen to him. His face was beet-red, his fists clenched. The queen leaned forward as he lifted to his tip-toes, muttering into her ear. She grimaced as she pulled away, flicking her wrist at him. He stormed to the patio doors.

"I didn't know the king was gone," said Céleste, momentarily pressing her cheek to Sébastien's coat. The fabric was smooth and soothing.

"He mentioned before the ball that he was loath to listen to Jules' proposal. But I didn't expect him to leave the room completely. He must have snuck to his office, or to the cigar room for a digestif."

"Why does no one seem to care?" She tilted her head to better visualize her dance-partner, but his attention was elsewhere. "The queen makes announcements in his place, and no one reacts? Tonight and at the Christmas Eve ball."

"Antoine isn't the focus of these events. He may be the king, but I don't think anyone cares much if he goes outside or steps out of the ballroom for a while. It's not his season. If *I* had exited, or Jules, that would have caused a scandal." His cheeks blossomed with a touch of red. "We shouldn't worry. He'll come back once he's downed half a bottle of brandy and shouted a few choice words at his paperwork. It's how he unwinds."

"What about Marguerite?"

"Maybe she needed air? It's not an easy night for her." Sébastien slowed the pace, holding Céleste close. "We can't blame her for needing a moment to gather her thoughts."

Céleste stopped following the dance's steps and broke free

from his embrace. "Don't you see something amiss here? Don't you sense unease?"

"Should I?" He cocked his head, more amused than upset at her abrupt refusal to continue dancing. "I just became engaged to a wonderful young woman; why would I fret?"

"And I'm beyond joyful myself, but something is bothering me."

His smirk faded. "What?"

"Maggie, in danger of marrying a foe. The king, angry at said potential marriage. The king stomping out under the pretext of not listening to his youngest brother's speech. Maggie vanishing." She blew out her cheeks. "Don't you assume they might be together?"

He blinked. "Well, I…" He slid a finger under his mask to scratch at his lower lash-line. "I admit it's strange."

As more couples poured onto the dance-floor, she dragged him towards the buffet tables. "Did he have a plan?" She snatched a macaron and shoved it into her mouth.

Sébastien tucked a few wisps of hair behind his ears. "He was adamant that he had no solution to keep Marguerite in Torrinni. Or even in Totresia."

"And yet," she gagged as she realized the pastry was pistachio flavored, "they're both gone. Strange timing, no?"

"I suppose—" he whirled around at someone raising their voice behind him, near the veranda doors.

The music muffled most of the argument, but he and Céleste were close enough to pick up on it.

The duke.

"…you let *her* out! I must locate her. Now!" He shook a fist at one of the guards shielding the veranda doors.

"I didn't let anyone out, Your Grace. She must be inside." The soldier never flinched at the duke's grunts and groans.

"Let me out!"

The guard still had no reaction, not even looking at the duke. "By order of the king, no one is to leave until he permits it."

"Where is *he*? Gone from his own party? Doesn't that strike you as hypocritical?" Cornelius resembled a spoiled child throwing a tantrum about not getting the biggest piece of pie. "I demand to exit!"

"Not until the king allows it, Your Grace," chimed in the second guard, as unfazed as the first.

Cornelius charged to the other side of the room and sank into a couch behind the dais. A toxic veil of fury weaved around him.

Sébastien glanced at Céleste, brows shooting up. "What was *that* spectacle about?"

Céleste was dizzy. Lightheaded. Sick to her stomach, fearing the worst. "He senses a problem. He figured out Maggie was missing, and so is the king, and he's assuming—"

"That Antoine helped her escape?" Sébastien pried off his mask; lines from the seams had indented into his skin in swirling patterns. "That after nine days of research and discovering nothing, he had a stupid impulse to lure Maggie out to save her?"

Céleste covered her mouth with her hand. "What have they done?"

He crunched his mask in his palm. "If King Romain and Mother get wind of this, Antoine will lose his throne for sure. And Maggie?" He swallowed. "I'm afraid to think what might happen to her." He loosened his cravat. "We must intercept them before they do something rash. Something they might regret. Knowing them both… things can turn sour in seconds."

Céleste ripped off her mask. "Yes. Before it's too late."

74.
Marguerite

She sensed it. Tasted it. Sunlight—welcoming as it poured into her room, pulling her from slumber. Her fingertips twitched and she sucked in a deep breath. A painful pounding resounded in her head.

The sourness in her mouth got to her first—too much undiluted alcohol and too little food. She'd drank a lot the night before. Had it been enough to make her so stiff and groggy?

A shiver slid down her spine, and she became straight as a wooden plank beneath her blankets.

She'd escaped the Masquerade, after receiving Antoine's note. She'd met him in the East Wing. He'd sent word to all the guards, and they'd scurried to the gardens, then hurried down secret staircases and dim-lit corridors.

After that… it was all a blur. An obscure mess of foggy images and question marks. Voices, faces, fighting; there'd been grunts and punches, or what sounded like them.

The scent of a dying fire wafted into her nostrils as she pried her eyelids apart. Her sight was hazy. After several blinks—and a burning sensation in her eyes—she sighted the overhead canopy.

A deep indigo blue; not her usual forest-green.

She rubbed her eyelids once, twice, three times before concluding she wasn't imagining this. She tipped her chin down to view the sheets and blankets; not pale pink. These were charcoal-colored, silky. The thick fur-lined blanket atop them wasn't tinted green; it was navy.

This wasn't her bed. Not her room. The color scheme of indigo and woodsy browns and smoky slate reminded her of something, some*one*, but in her dazed state, she couldn't figure out what or who.

A metallic flavor coated her tongue. Her throat was scratchy.

To her right, she spotted a nightstand, two empty glasses resting on it. One had lip imprints on its rim. *Her* lips, no doubt.

Whose bed was this, and why didn't she remember climbing into it?

The pulsing in her brain worsened. She clapped a palm over her forehead, and her skin was scorching as she wiped off a few beads of sweat. Her stomach lurched, and as she lowered her palm to it, her heart stopped.

She was naked.

She *never* slept naked.

In a panic, she pinched her eyelids shut, praying for memories to return, something to explain her situation—but nothing came.

She stared at the cups, hoping they'd trigger her recollections. How did she go from racing down dark halls to here? Like this?

A sickening grumble in her gut urged her to set a hand over

her abdomen again.

Laughter echoed in the back of her head. Her saliva coated in an acrid flavor that made her gag. How much, exactly, did she drink?

Again she pictured the sets of stairs, the gloomy aisles, the ornate copper hallways with extinguished sconces—

A sharp flash pierced her like dull blades stabbing at her flesh.

Cerulean chaises. Brown stone hearth, roaring fire. Gray walls littered with mystifying paintings. Letters, spilled ink. Shoes coming off. Wigs thrown across the room. Dancing barefoot. Wine, lots of wine, lots of *spilled* wine. Laughs. Masks tossed onto tables.

Her scalp throbbed and she panted, praying for a reprieve.

The images wouldn't cease. Had someone poisoned her drink? Or had she had too much and fainted here, in this foreign yet strangely familiar place?

Her intestines knotted and a dizzy spell forced her eyes to half close, but she couldn't wait it out; she had to get up, locate her clothes, locate Antoine. He was the last person she remembered seeing.

Everyone must have been searching for her.

As she shifted her lower limbs, she felt a wetness under her buttocks. She slid her fingers over the spot—it was warm.

She shot up into a seated position and threw the covers off, to conduct a better analysis.

Bile coursed up her throat as she saw a dark stain, spreading out a few inches, reminiscent of when she was fourteen and found her first blood on her mattress cover. Clémentine and a chaperone explained the process, told her she'd become a woman—

"Oh, no."

It couldn't be that monthly discharge; she was never irregular.

She pulled her legs to her chest and fought the sickness trying to break through her sealed lips. She remembered the gossip that girls whispered in salons after hours—the only other reason a blood-stain would be on the sheets was if she had been intimate with a man for the first time.

She whipped her head to the left and located a human-shaped lump at the far edge of the large bed, behind a fort of cushions and blankets. A giant pillow concealed his features from view, but she knew that muscular back, those sturdy shoulders, the sound of his soft snores.

The morning glow shined over his short mane of messy dark waves.

A burst of agony raced to her temples as more abrupt pictures dashed into her mind. A casket overflowing with wine. Glasses clinking, cheers, singing. Laughter. Tears. Burgundy stains on white shirts, dress straps sliding down shoulders. Hands intertwining. Foggy faces, muffled tones.

Once the flashes subsided, she glared at the scar near his shoulder blade, the other by his spine; from falling from a tree.

Flash. Fabrics falling off, stockings slipping, buckles unfastening. Nails scratching through tangled tresses, digging into skin, dragging down lower backs. Glasses set on the nightstand. Moans. A breathy whisper. Moans. A tongue-twisting kiss. *More moans.*

"Oh, Heavens, no…"

She scooched up to his slumbering figure, her fingertips inches from the hairs sprouting over his arms. Goosebumps sprinkled across his skin.

Her lips had trailed kisses along those shoulders, those arms. She'd murmured into those ears, grabbed and pulled the untamed mix of chestnut and ash and amber curls.

They'd rocked, back and forth, back and forth—

Her heartrate took off so fast she worried she couldn't keep up. She gripped the sheets up to cover herself. He slept without a care in the world.

He needed to wake up.

She gently turned him towards her. He grunted, scratching at his bare, chiseled chest, smacking his lips, eyelids fluttering. Those eyes: heavenly hazel, swirls of pine, dots of baby blue outlined in earthy brown.

The puzzle pieces joined with one final recollection.

Last night, after escaping the Masquerade, they'd come here, to this chamber. Because she couldn't leave the castle yet; he hadn't planned that far. It would take time to hire a discreet driver, someone to accompany her out of town.

So instead, he'd offered liquor and reassurances. Shelter—no one would come looking for her in *his* chambers. He'd given promises she couldn't recall, protection she wasn't sure he could provide—with lips she hadn't kissed in a long time.

Lips. Kisses. She hardly remembered how it had started, but it happened. Weeks of holding back, of begging her body to *not* give in to him… and it was done. She'd been weak. *He'd* been weak.

It was inevitable.

And there he was, in all his early morning splendor. Mouth half-open as he breathed, the covers up to his hips, abdominal muscles exposed.

The dryness of her throat made her cough.

He opened his eyes. He seemed unsurprised by her presence. She clutched the sheets to her neck, fighting a wave of nausea.

He gave her a weak, weary smile. "Maggie?"

Her lungs squeezed, her hands shook. She was sore all over. "Antoine?"

He leaned up on his elbows, worry washing over his face. "What is it?"

She backed away, struggling to find words, to find her voice. "What have we done?"

A peek at the title of the third book in the series:

THE GOLDEN DUCHESS

GOLDEN BOOK THREE

ACKNOWLEDGMENTS

This was a LONG time in the making.

The Golden Girl is the longest story I've ever written. Originally, the first draft was well over 200,000 words. It was one of my most read books on Wattpad, its cliffhanger ending sparking all sorts of debates in the comments section. Some time passed, and I tried to trim the words—I got down to 170,000 and was satisfied.

But then, when I began the process of self-publishing the series, I knew for a fact that that many words *wouldn't* work. So I went through and trimmed again, and again, *and again,* and somehow got it down to this. I promise, this is the longest one.

This series is so incredibly important to me. The characters, the places, the story—so dear to my heart. So to anyone reading this—I thank you, sincerely, for supporting me and encouraging me and loving these characters and places and this story as much as I do.

To my beta readers: Adrielle, Lorraine, Rachal, Madison, Kayla, Alizae—I can't thank you enough for your invaluable feedback and friendship. Your enthusiasm for these books so far has made me feel all warm and fuzzy inside and I'm so glad to have such a wonderful team of talented writers and voracious readers on my side.

To my editor, Ashley—*thank you so, so, SO much* for taking this mountain of a project on, and guiding me through it with such grace and kindness. I've always loved your feedback during our NNAC meetings, and you just <u>get me</u>, you know? I look forward to working with you more in the future and truly value your friendship.

To NNAC—gosh, I'm so freaking happy to know you all. Emilee with your enthusiasm and guidance; Topher with your *Topher-isms* that make me laugh and your true skill for writing; Chanelle with your incredible vocabulary and warmth and positivity; Laura with your fantastic hugs and your thrilling excerpts. And Ashley—on top of being my editor, just being such a wonderful part of the group, and contributing a cozy space for us to meet. You're all real friends, and the feedback you've given me over the years has helped me get to this point.

To the co-workers who have to listen to me ramble on a daily basis and allowed me to bounce my ideas off them—you know who you are, and I thank you for your patience. And for yelling at me when I say I'll never reach my dreams—the way you believe in me is heart-warming. You tolerate my zoning out to live in a fantasy world, and it's appreciated.

To my soon-to-be husband, Matt, who supports me through absolutely everything, gives me time and space for my craft— which includes watching all sorts of historical dramas, from cute to raunchy, for inspiration (and sometimes watching them with me)—and is totally convinced that I'll be a best-seller and see my novels adapted to the big screen someday, I LOVE YOU. You have no idea how much you mean to me.

To my family—Mom, Danny, Nanny—for always supporting my work, sharing it, recommending it, buying it. My mom and grandma frame my books and prop them up in shadow boxes for everyone to see. Whenever I visit, I get a line of their friends asking me to sign *their* copies, and it's truly heartwarming. I love you all so much.

To the indie bookstores who carry this series (and my others) and lift me up, host book signings, and keep us indie authors wanting to write—you are doing the hardest, best work out there, and I can't express how much I appreciate you!

Speaking of indies—KEEP GOING. I see you out there struggling to make it—costly edits, book cover creation, and the endless, exhausting promotions and marketing we're tasked with. I'm telling you to never give up. We're all in this together.

And finally to Wattpad, for making me realize how much of a treasure this story was. For boosting it, recommending it, giving it the recognition it deserved.

Stephanie Rose is an author of paranormal ghost stories, of mythological thrillers, of quick-paced epic fantasy, and of romance—but one of her favorite genres to write is historical fiction.

The GOLDEN UNIVERSE is a series close to her heart, and she poured hours and hours of dedication into writing its characters and shaping its world, filling it with intrigue, drama, romance, and tension.

She lives in Nevada, and when not inundated with research for her books, or staying busy writing them, she can be found listening to music, reading, going on day adventures with her fiancé, Matt, or playing with her tuxedo cat, Crowley.

www.ingramcontent.com/pod-product-compliance
Lightning Source LLC
Chambersburg PA
CBHW031510010826
48973CB00012B/20